The Color of Warm

Jeff Henckel

Acknowledgments

Thanks to Randi and Ryan, who encouraged and helped me in this endeavor.

I also want to thank two people who I've never met.

Arnold Schwarzenegger, thank you for your speech on YouTube about success. Your comments kept me pursuing this novel when I could have quit. It also helped me get up at 3am every day to write. "You can sleep when you die."

Simon Baker, your speech when you received the AACTA Trailblazer award encouraged me to ask the question, "Why not?" Thank you.

This book is dedicated to my wife Kathy, and to Sabrina, Rebekah, and Brandon, my children. I hope I have modeled what it means to accomplish anything, no matter how big or small. You can do whatever you set out to do, so go for it.

The Color of Warm

Prologue

The man watched the prostitute drive her BMW out of the gated community. He started his pickup truck and pulled out from the curb to follow her, intentionally allowing a beat-up Honda Accord to get between them. Traffic wasn't too bad at 10:30am in Citrus Heights, and he knew where she was going. His wiper blades were on low, keeping the windshield clear. Then the rain picked up and sounded like a thousand little hands pounding on the top of his truck. He turned the wiper to high, though it barely kept up. Between the rain and the water kicked up from the surrounding cars, visibility was poor. She wouldn't be able to make out the Accord behind her, even less his truck further back.

At this time of day she almost always did one of two things. She either went directly to the gym or, on occasion, she left by foot and ran the trail along the American River. It had been raining hard and he knew that it was unlikely she would choose the trails. It was paved but with heavy rains it would have gotten washed over with mud and puddles. She would avoid that.

Satisfaction welled up in him when she pulled out in the car. He knew people. He prided himself on it. He smiled at the way he could lie, take advantage, and manipulate. That he was smarter than everyone else was one of his first epiphanies in life. Knowing where she was going before she even went only confirmed this fact. If it rained the day or night before she would run at the gym. If it was dry she would run the trail. Hell, he thought, he even knew which direction on the trail she would choose. She always ran towards Folsom lake away from Sacramento, away from the crowds.

When she pulled into Cal-Fit, a popular gym, he continued on by. No need to enter the parking lot. She would be at least an hour. He drove another mile and pulled into a Taco Bell drive-through. Thirty minutes later he was sitting in his truck off to the side of the Cal-Fit building. Anyone walking out wouldn't see him unless they turned around and looked back. To the casual observer, he was just a guy sitting in a truck eating a late breakfast or an early lunch.

He sat for another 45 minutes listening to someone explain how the country was going to collapse due to one political party's actions. It was true. This country was falling apart and it was, in large part, due to the idiots on the other side of the political aisle.

A few minutes later, she exited the fitness center and made her way quickly to the BMW. She was like everyone else, trying to avoid the rain with no time to stop and look around. Completely unobservant. She was wearing yoga pants and a lightweight sweatshirt that zipped up the front. He knew she was probably just wearing a sports bra underneath. Her figure was amazing. She worked out every day. She was in great shape, yet unlike many women who worked out hard and who were as thin as her, her breasts were big. Probably fake, he thought. He felt his body respond at the sight of her body. He watched her get in the car and he followed again at a distance until she pulled into a local grocery store.

Was she going shopping looking like that? She was going to walk around a grocery store wearing pants that looked like they were painted on? Worse, they had lace sides revealing her skin all the way up her legs.

She got out of the car and walked into the store. All he could think was slut!

Chapter 1

The stunning blonde-haired woman entered the bistro at exactly fifteen minutes to five. There were a few early groups of diners sitting at tables. Two men sat talking at the bar. There was no one waiting in the entryway. There were no single men in the place. As the woman expected, her target was still on his way. She knew that, like all the others, he would arrive five to ten minutes early. It was like clockwork. Too nervous to show up more than ten minutes early, too anxious to be late.

She wore an oversized white sweater that dropped down to her thighs, black leggings, and a pair of stylish boots that came to her knees. She was a 32C and wore a push up bra that filled out the sweater incredibly well. Her wavy blonde hair cascaded down over her shoulders. Her brown eyes were accentuated by dark eyeliner and thick lashes; her lips with bright red lipstick. Her makeup and her hair were done like a professional had attended to her for hours. In her case, she was the professional, and it had taken just over two hours. She would have described herself as above average, but never beautiful. The two men sitting at the bar would have disagreed. They'd noticed her the moment she walked in.

"Welcome to Back Bistro," the hostess had greeted her. "Will anyone be joining you?"

"Yes, one more." Then she added, "Can we sit outside please?"

"Sure." The hostess grabbed two menus then led the way past two open sliding doors to the patio. It was nearly empty of customers at this hour and, before the host could recommend a seat, Chelsea pointed at a corner table with the view she wanted.

"Can we sit there?"

"No problem."

She sat so she could look out from the patio to the intersection where anyone approaching the restaurant would most likely pass. The hostess placed two menus on the table.

"Jamie will be your waitress, she will be with you in just a moment."

And now the awkward moment that she hated. "If anyone comes in and asks for Chelsea..." she said as she looked at the hostess.

"Oh are you on a blind date?"

"Just let him know I'm sitting out here," Chelsea said, avoiding the question. She was irritated that the hostess had asked. It was one of the reasons she wore a wedding band on her finger. She was doubly annoyed that the ring had gone unnoticed.

"Oh, that's cool." The hostess was young and excited. She had probably been on a few blind dates, and assumed Chelsea was nervous so she tried to encourage her.

"If you told him what you're wearing and what you look like, he won't have trouble finding you. You look great."

"Thank you."

The hostess went back inside. Some song by a current female pop artist spilled out of the sliding doors to the patio. There were speakers on the patio, but the volume was nearly swallowed up by the sounds of the outdoors. If she had sat inside it would have been too loud. Then she thought, any song by a current female pop artist would be too loud. She wasn't sure who it was, Taylor Swift, Beyoncé, Katie Perry. She liked almost all genres of music but found those women annoying. She preferred throwbacks from the '70s and '80s or country. She looked around at the few patrons already at tables. Most of them were in their 50s and 60s. She never understood why restaurants played music that wasn't targeted to their audience. No doubt some host or waiter who was closer to 25 years old was choosing the music. It was a mistake, but the food was good, sitting outside was nice, and it was a convenient location.

Located in the Palladio, an upscale outdoor shopping area East of Sacramento in Folsom, California, Back Bistro was just the opposite of a chain restaurant. She liked the food but it was always changing as the cook no doubt fancied himself as too great or, at best, too creative to produce the same thing for any length of time. They also carried specialty beers, mixed drinks, and wine, the latter of which she preferred.

She had chosen the bistro because it was warm for early March, and the last few weeks had been cold and filled with clouds and rain. Sitting outside in the sunshine was nice. She had also chosen the bistro because at 5pm it wouldn't be crowded yet and she could see her mark coming. That's what he was, a mark. Someone to fleece.

She could always spot them when they approached, which was why she chose that particular table. Seeing a man in his 40s walking alone, she thought she spotted him, but realized it wasn't when he met up with a few other men. They were headed for the restaurant across the street which featured beer and barbecued meat. It was too early to be him anyway.

Her target would be like all the others in the past. Nervous, anxious, and cautious all at once. It wasn't the guy in his early 50s wearing the suit; he was none of those things. The man approached the intersection with confidence and was walking with a steady speed, not cautious at all. Not looking around, he passed through the intersection and out of sight, no doubt past the front entrance of the bistro. She felt a twinge of regret. That suit looked expensive.

She could rule out a number of men who were with wives or children. Whoever he was, he would be alone. She ruled out the guy in the shorts and T-shirt walking the dog. There weren't that many people perusing the shopping area at that time. Most were headed home to eat dinner, or if they worked and likely to eat at a restaurant, not off the job yet. This was a bedroom community, so most of the restaurants would likely not get really busy until 6:30 or 7.

The waitress approached with two glasses of water. "Hi, I'm Jamie and I'll be serving you tonight. Can I start you off with an appetizer or something to drink?"

"Just the water for now, thank you." It was stupid to drink wine or order anything before someone else was there to pay for it.

She continued watching the intersection. Whoever he was he would look around as he approached to make sure he knew no one in the area. He would likely stop on an opposite corner or across the street, and watch.

It could be the middle-aged dark-haired guy on a bench diagonally across the intersection. He looked to be about 35. He was just sitting and didn't appear to be watching the surrounding intersection. He occasionally looked down at his phone and fired off a text or two. Yes, it could be him. She wondered how much money he had. His looked like new blue jeans and he was wearing a short-sleeved pullover collared shirt you would see a guy wearing to golf. Golfers had money, she thought.

A moment later a woman in stretch pants and a red and black flannel shirt that didn't quite hide her backside approached him. Her boots came up to her knees. She was probably in her mid 20s, attractive and clearly in great shape. It was a look she could pull off well. She had a number of shopping bags and started talking as he stood. She hugged and kissed him. She showed him the bags, and though the conversation was inaudible at this distance the woman was clearly happy to share about the things she'd purchased.

The young woman's appearance made her jealous.

From her position in the bistro she could see one of the bags was from Soma and another was from Victoria's Secret. There were other bags. The young woman had spent some money for sure. The couple hugged and she kissed him again, then they headed away down the street and out of sight.

She wondered about them. Did the young woman work and use her money for the clothes? Probably not. She surmised that they could be married but it didn't matter. She assumed that he worked and paid for everything, and the young woman's hugs and kisses along with other affections was her way of paying him.

To her, every relationship was a series of transactions. The woman was young, pretty, and earning her keep. Part of the young woman's routine was, no doubt, working out every day. You couldn't wear those stretch pants and not be in great shape. She wondered how long he would be willing to sit on a bench, waiting for someone to spend his money. No doubt it was directly proportional to the young woman's ability to look good in those stretch pants.

Chelsea thought about what she was wearing. Similar stretch pants, but she let the oversized sweater cover more. At 37 years old she could still pull it off, but she had to spend more and more time at the gym making it work.

She glanced down at her watch. He still wouldn't be there for a few minutes. From her position on the patio she continued to watch the entire intersection as several more men passed. Not the old guy, he was walking hand in hand with someone who she could only assume was his wife. Old, stuck together, they must be unhappy, she thought. A young guy was walking quickly towards what he was after. He knew what he wanted and was going to get it. Hunting not shopping. Probably the sporting goods store or shoes.

She was so intent on watching the intersection that she didn't realize he was suddenly standing next to her table.

"Hello, are you Chelsea?" he asked. It was the confident guy in the suit. Not who she expected at all.

"Yes. Are you Simon?" She stood and as he said yes, she gave him a hug. She let the front of her body press up ever so lightly against his then backed away. He looked uncomfortable, almost embarrassed. She turned around and "adjusted" her chair, letting him see her from all sides, then she sat down.

Inside she was happy but surprised. Her immediate thought was, I'm going make a lot of money, but in the back of her mind she had a nagging question, how did she miss targeting him? She always saw them coming. No matter, time to start the transaction. Time to take his money.

He sat opposite her. "I'm glad you came."

She thought that an odd thing to say. He was paying her. They had agreed to meet.

"I'm very glad to meet you," she said and smiled. Her smile was infections but his was stifled. The wrinkles at the corners of his eyes and mouth were almost permanent and testified to the fact that he smiled a lot in life, yet it was as if only the corners of his mouth rose up ever so slightly. She thought maybe he was trying not to smile and wondered why.

He was a good-looking man, she thought. Tan with light brown hair, almost blond, he clearly spent time in the sun. His hair was a cross between curly and wavy and cut short. She couldn't tell if it was just the bleached-out color or if it was starting to grey in places due to age. He wasn't a large man, probably around 5'10, and looked to be in good shape. The suit was impeccable and she guessed it was tailored. He wore a wedding band, but that never bothered her. After all, she wore one too. People wore them for all kinds of reasons.

He started in, "I wasn't really sure how to do this, so I brought you a card." He pulled an envelope out of the inside of his suit coat and laid it on the side of the table between them. The envelope bore the name Hallmark.

"Thank you." She picked it up and placed it into her purse sitting at her feet. The thickness of the envelope told her that it contained more than just a Hallmark greeting card.

"Aren't you going to open it?"

"I can if you'd like, or I'll just wait till after dinner."

"No need. I just thought..." he didn't finish.

"You thought I'd want to make sure it was all there?" Now she laughed lightly and revealed, just for a moment, that she was playing with him.

"I didn't mean to offend."

She smiled again. "You didn't. But I think I'm a pretty good judge of character and I don't need to check it."

The waitress approached the table. "Welcome to Back Bistro, my name is Jamie and I'll be serving you tonight. Can I start you off with a drink?"

Normally Chelsea liked men to order first so she could follow suit, but before she could say anything, Simon nodded at the menu and said, "Please, anything."

She looked to find a wine that she liked, "I'll have a glass of the Pinot Grigio."

Simon looked at the menu a moment longer then looked at the waitress, "That looks good, Jamie, I'll have the same." Chelsea noticed his use of the waitress's name. He could be a person considerate of others regardless of station, but in this case he was putting on a show, she concluded. Most men tried to impress her, why would he be any different?

The key to fleecing them was making them feel important and special, and that meant getting them to brag. She picked up a menu and started looking at the dinner options. "So, Simon, tell me about yourself."

"I'd rather not." He remained quiet, looking at his menu for a moment. Then the edges of his mouth turned up ever so slightly. Even without smiling, his was a warm happy face. "But please, tell me about yourself." He paused a moment, contemplating. "It may sound strange but I'd just like to listen to you for now."

"What would you like to know?"

"Well, let's start with where are you from?"

"I was born and raised in L.A., but moved to UC Davis when I was 18 to go to college. After college I moved to Sacramento and have been here ever since." She paused. "What about you?"

"Again, I'd rather not," he said. This time the smile was gone. "But please go on. What did you study in college?"

So he wasn't a talker. She'd have to work that much harder. The more she knew about him the more she could manipulate and take advantage of him. For now, she'd use a few stories she'd made up about herself.

"Well, I studied accounting in college." Accounting was a safe college degree to lie about since no one wanted to talk about numbers on a spreadsheet. "After finishing my degree I realized it was not an area I wanted to work in. So I worked a number of jobs for a couple of years. Then I started working in a salon. I met so many great people and enjoyed the service industry, I stayed with that for close to three years. I worked as an esthetician and as a masseuse. After a few years doing that I branched out on my own, and here I am."

The waitress returned with two glasses of the white wine. "Have you decided what you'd like?"

Simon was staring at his menu so she took the opportunity, "Please, you first, I don't know what I want yet."

"Would you like me to come back in a few?" the waitress asked.

"No, I'll be quick," she replied then added, "Go ahead, Simon."

"Okay, well, I'll have the salmon and the house salad."

She always ordered a light dinner, but also tried to order something just under the cost of the men paying. Ordering more expensive items and drinks usually made the men feel like you were taking advantage. And of course, she was trying to take advantage, but on a much grander scale than just dinner.

"I'll have the Bistro Cobb Salad," Chelsea said as the waitress turned to her.

Simon stared across the table. His eyes weren't focused on her, but it was as if he was staring off in the distance right through her.

"Is everything all right?"

"Oh, I'm sorry, I was just thinking about something. Go on, you were telling me about yourself."

"Okay, well, I enjoy working out," which was true.

"I like to travel." Also true.

"I enjoy reading history and fiction and I love most musical genres." She continued telling him about the things she enjoyed. Usually men responded when they had a similar like or dislike as a way to connect, but Simon sat quietly. At times she couldn't even tell if he was listening which made her feel like she was just droning on.

The waitress arrived with their food and, seeing both their glasses of wine nearly empty, asked, "Can I get you more wine or something else to drink?"

"I'll have more of the same," Simon replied.

Chelsea nodded and said, "Yes, please. More wine would be nice."

Simon waited politely for her to start with her salad then took a bite of his salmon. Like all fish, salmon has a distinct smell and suddenly he was remembering the past....

ॐ

Pike Place in Seattle, Washington is well known and attracts both locals and tourists alike. Simon was a month into his freshman year at the University of Washington when he found himself walking the market. The men in one of the markets, famous for tossing salmon through the air to each other as they stocked their meat counters and sold the fish were doing just that, and Simon, like many others, stopped to watch. The fish were sometimes flung 15 feet through the air, from the back out to the front, where other workers caught them in the air and either placed them on ice in the displays or tossed them again to other workers who laid them in front of the butcher, who in turn was cutting them up for the customers' orders.

Not ordering anything but wanting to watch more, Simon stood back a bit from the counter. For a few moments he just enjoyed watching the fish fly thought the air, impressed as the men caught them each time.

A group of young ladies made their way in front of him to watch. He couldn't see their faces but assumed they were probably U of W students. A fish flung from the back came directly at the group of girls in front of him. Several of them let out a scream as they all turned away and ducked from the incoming fish. The guy at the counter deftly snagged the fish in the air as the girls all laughed aloud. Another fish was flung directly at them and even though they could see the fish would be caught they turned and ducked again. This time, however, the guy working at the counter had a rare failure and the fish slipped right through his hands. The momentum of the large salmon carried it right over the counter and directly into the back of the girl directly in front of Simon. It hit her hard enough to send her stumbling forward and into Simon whose arms instinctively wrapped around her to keep her from falling.

The girls were all laughing except the girl in his arms who would have gone to her knees but for Simon's help.

"Whoa." Simon looked down into her blue eyes. "Are you okay?"

The girl winced a bit as she caught herself against him. "Yeah, I'm all right. It scared me more than hurt. Thanks for catching me."

"No problem." His arms were still wrapped around her even though she was standing on her own.

"I'm Simon."

"Thanks again, Simon. I'm Allie."

Reddish brown hair fell down across her shoulders. Beneath those beautiful blue eyes, freckles splashed across her nose. Simon thought she had the most mesmerizing face he'd ever seen. He couldn't decide if she was beautiful, cute, or sexy, but decided it was all of the above. She was just a few inches shorter than him and his head spun as he realized he was still holding her.

Allie too was caught offguard. She was looking into a pair of blue eyes that she could best describe as kind. The young man could have been a model or a movie star. Tan, light brown wavy hair, smiling with a perfect smile that lit up his face, she thought he was perfect.

For a moment they were alone in the chaos of noise and voices. Just two people staring at each other, smiling.

Then the world interrupted.

"Oh my gosh, Allie, are you okay?" one of her friends asked.

Another girl slapped lightly at Simon, "Dude, let go of her. What are you? Some kind of perv?"

"Hey, I was just holding her up," was all he managed to say as he quickly dropped his arms from under hers and backed away.

"Well she's standing fine on her own, oh my gosh," one of the other girls countered.

The worker who'd missed the fish had come out from behind the counter, "Miss, I am so sorry, are you all right?"

Everyone was crowding around her so Simon turned to leave.

"It's okay. I'm all right," Allie said a bit loudly to everyone around her. Then, before Simon could leave, she shouted after him, "Hey, Simon, wait a minute." As she made her way toward him she turned to her friends.

"He was helping me," she scolded them aloud. Then she smiled, raised her eyebrows at them, and mouthed, "He's hot."

He waited as she made her way over to him.

"I'm sorry. That was ridiculous," she said, referring to her friends. Then, wanting to keep the conversation going, she started asking him questions.

"So what do you do, Simon?"

"I'm a student at U of Dub."

"And what are you studying?"

"Computer programming."

"And what do you want to do with that?"

"I want to start my own company someday."

"Hmm a big shot," she smiled in jest. "Kind of like Apple?"

He smiled at that. "I guess if I build a company like that I wouldn't complain."

There was an awkward pause. Simon wanted to know about this beautiful girl in front of him. "So what about you, Allie? I take it by this," he said, pointing at her University of Washington sweatshirt, "you are also a U of Dub student?"

"Yep."

"And what are you studying?"

"Right now my plan is to be a prosecuting attorney someday."

"Interesting," he said and smiled again.

Allie was completely taken by his smile and knew she didn't want the conversation to stop.

Turning to her friends, she said, "Hey, you guys go ahead without me. I'll catch up."

"Are you serious?" one of the girls said.

She turned her head away from Simon and smiled, ensuring her friend of her excitement at meeting him.

"Yeah, I'll meet you guys at Zig Zag," she said, referring to a cafe they were headed to a block away.

"Hey, she's serious!" one of the girls said.

"Have fun, you two." A few of the girls laughed as they looked at Allie and Simon.

"No problem, Allie," another said. "We'll catch up with you later."

She looked at Simon again. "Thank you, again. Sorry they were kind of rude at first."

"I don't blame them." He grinned and raised his eyebrows as if to say you never know. "They're just looking out for you. Protecting you from weirdos and pervs is a friend's job."

"Are you saying you're a perv?" she joked.

He felt lightheaded just looking at her. To him she truly seemed perfect. She was absolutely beautiful.

"Well a perv wouldn't admit it so there's no way of knowing."

"Oh, so you aren't denying it."

"No I'll deny it... not a perv... maybe weird but that's for you to decide."

"And how do I do that?"

"Tell you what, there is a Starbucks around the corner. Let's go get a cup of coffee. You can put your prosecuting attorney hat on and ask me as many questions as you'd like. Then you can judge for yourself."

"What's your last name, Simon?"

"Murray."

"I think I'd like to get that coffee with you, Simon Murray."

"And your last name?"

"Blakey. Allie Blakey."

The Starbucks was open all night and at 7am they were still sitting and talking. Allie looked at her watch. "Oh my gosh, my roommate is probably freaking out."

"Yeah, I wonder how long they waited for you at Zig Zag."

"I should be going," she said but made no move to get up. They both sipped coffee and said nothing. Simon was suddenly aware that the Van Morrison song "Crazy Love" was filling up the silence. The words seemed perfect for the moment and suddenly she laughed, "I'm glad that fish hit me."

"I am too," he replied, then added, "Wait, no. I'm sorry the fish hit you, glad I could catch you."

They sat silently as the Van Morrison song came to an end. She stood. "I really do have to go."

He stood too and they both took a few steps towards the door, the table no longer between them. Simon wanted to reach out and touch her, or kiss her, or anything. Don't be stupid, he thought to himself. She *will* think you are a perv. "Can I get your number?"

Allie laughed lightly as she had many times that night. "I wrote it on your napkin when you used the bathroom 30 minutes ago."

Simon thought her laughter was perfect. It was silvery, light, and birdlike. He kept thinking she was so beautiful. He reached over and picked up the napkin, her number clearly written on the bottom.

Even though it was morning, she didn't want the night to end. "Are you going to walk me to my dorm?"

"I think I better," Simon replied then joked, "Seattle may not be safe at 7am."

As he walked her back to her dorm, both were wishing the same thing, that they could continue. When they arrived, she stopped and turned to him.

"I need to go. I've got classes in two hours and I still have to finish some homework."

"Well, before you leave, have you decided?" he asked.

"Decided what?"

"I thought the whole purpose of our time at Starbucks was for you to decide if I was a creep or not."

"Oh that." She looked at him with a serious expression, then grinned. "Definitely not." Then she moved towards him quickly. She raised up on tiptoes, kissed him lightly, and moved away. She was only there for a fraction of a second. He had no time to respond at all. "Thank you." She turned, hurried to the door, and disappeared inside.

❧

"Simon?" The voice brought him out of his memory. He looked at her. Her eyes were brown not blue. Her hair was blonde not red. There were no freckles. He looked down at his meal. The salmon was gone. He'd eaten it as well as the salad. He looked down at his hands still holding the fork and knife and saw the wedding band on his finger. His hands started to shake ever so slightly.

Chelsea was staring at him. "You must have been hungry. You haven't said anything since we started eating."

"I'm sorry. I didn't mean to be rude." He suddenly seemed nervous. Not the man who had arrived confident and unconcerned. "Thank you for having dinner with me, but I think I'll be going."

"Are you sure?"

"Yes."

He caught the attention of the waitress and asked for the check.

Raising her eyebrows, Chelsea said as a question, "We've only been here an hour."

"I understand." He looked right into her eyes and she thought again that he wasn't even seeing her. "I gave you the card and I appreciate having dinner with you. It was worth it."

They sat in silence until the waitress brought the check and he paid it.

He stood. "Thank you again," he said, then left.

Chelsea got up to leave. She was cognizant of the waitress watching her, no doubt assuming the date hadn't gone well. As she walked to her car alone she thought about the man named Simon. Married. Cold feet. He'd never call again. No chance to fleece him. When she got to her car, she sat, reached into her purse, and pulled out the envelope. Opening it, she counted out thirty $100 bills. They had agreed on $2000. She was sure that was the last she'd see of him and was disappointed. A man who would pay more than asked for was a man who would have been willing to pay a lot for her ongoing services.

She looked again at the Hallmark card. It was a simple card that had a pre-written poem ending with a "heartfelt thank you." In very neat cursive he had handwritten on the opposite page.

I'm grateful for your time tonight, be it long or short.
With all sincerity, thank you. - Simon.

Chapter 2

One week later Chelsea was sitting in the same bar, but at a table near the back of the patio. It was more private and out of the way. Tonight she sat and watched the sliding glass door that led to the patio from the main part of the restaurant. There was no need to monitor the intersection. She'd already met Simon and knew what to expect.

Simon had called her that morning and made arrangements to meet with her again, same location, same amount. She wondered if he would overpay this time too. She had been sure after their last date that she wouldn't see him again. Men with cold feet didn't call for a second date. She supposed it wasn't as much about the money as it was about their fragile egos. Men didn't make a second date for a myriad of reasons. Cash would be the issue for some, fear of being caught was always another possibility. Facing the same woman after a failure was a certainty. This time, however, she was wrong. He had called again, and this of course made him different from other men. Not better, not worse, just different.

The contents of the Hallmark card had told her one thing, though. He had money. Men with no money didn't pay more than asked. She was satisfied at the chance to build a deeper connection and exploit him further.

Last week she had dressed in what she called sexy conservative. Tonight, she took it up a notch. She wore a white buttoned blouse with a push up bra and the top two buttons undone. A black belt and tan high heels completed her outfit. She'd spent her usual two hours on her hair and makeup. Overall sexier, but still not slutty. Definitely dressed to get his attention. Definitely dressed to exploit.

They had agreed to meet at six, so there were more people on the patio when she arrived. As an added bonus, the weather was nice. There would be someone, eventually, sitting at the table next to them. That wasn't good. In order to take advantage, she needed to get him talking about himself. She needed to stroke his ego. But to get him talking, he would need to feel a sense of privacy and not be concerned about his surroundings. He wouldn't want people to overhear any of their conversation. Experience had taught her that privacy helped. Married men can't afford to be caught.

It was unlikely he was from Folsom. A married man never met in the town where he lived. He was likely from Sacramento, or more likely from even further away. Possibly the Bay Area. Regardless, she needed to get him talking tonight.

The same waitress, Jamie, approached her table. "Hey..." she said with recognition, "welcome back. Can I get you started with something?"

"Just water, thank you."

"Are you meeting that same cute guy?"

The question irritated her. She was a private person and it was a private line of work. Normally she wouldn't have returned to the same restaurant, but he had asked, and she'd weighed his need to feel comfortable against her own. It was more important to put him in charge, and make him feel comfortable now, so he would be easier to manipulate later.

"I'll just start with a glass of water," she repeated, hoping the girl would get the hint.

"I'll be right back with that," Jamie replied happily. Chelsea was pretty sure the waitress had gotten the hint.

"Collide" by Howie Day started up on the sound system as Simon walked through doors onto the patio. He looked at the table where they'd sat the previous week and paused, not seeing her. In that moment, her brain was flooded with thoughts. First was how he looked. The same tan leathery skin. Same wavy brown hair. Same laugh lines on his face. A different suit, but still clean, tailored, and expensive. She thought he looked like a guy out of a movie. She never really thought of men as good looking, or ugly, or average. She usually just saw them as rich or not rich.

At that moment, however, she realized he was good looking. The more she looked at him, the more good looking he seemed. She reminded herself that he had money. These thoughts also coincided with the lyrics of the song that was playing....

"Even the best fall down sometime..." In the back of her mind she wondered if she was helping "the best" fall down as they collided with her. For a moment it bothered her. She'd never felt this way before and she chided herself for being soft. It was a transaction. He was willing to pay and it wasn't her business if he was married or not. He was responsible, not her.

Simon sat down and placed another envelope on the side of the table between them. He looked at the woman sitting across from him and decided she was beautiful. Normally he didn't care to see a lot of makeup on a woman, and Chelsea wore quite a lot, but the amount she wore accentuated her beauty without distraction or looking too gaudy. The way she was dressed was sensual, but he felt little towards her. Then the waitress interrupted his thoughts.

"Can I get you something to drink?"

Simon looked at Chelsea, waiting for her to order first.

"I'll have the Chardonnay, please," she said as she looked at the menu.

He looked a moment longer at the menu then ordered. "The hefeweizen please, Jamie."

"Can I interest you in any of our starters?"

Simon looked at Jamie, then at Chelsea, and said, "Nothing for me, please."

"Nothing tonight, thank you," Chelsea added.

There it was again, Chelsea thought. His use of her name. She recognized her own irritation at this man who was with her, but paying attention to another woman.

As they waited for their food he looked directly at her. He doesn't mind strong eye contact, she thought. She returned his gaze moment for moment. Normally she would have felt uncomfortable with them just staring in each other's eyes, but this time she didn't. Finally, he broke the silence.

"Can I ask you a question?"

"I'd love to answer anything. Go ahead," Chelsea replied, trying to be as warm as friendly as she could.

Simon glanced at her left hand and nodded, "The ring?"

She held up her hand.

"Do you like it?" Chelsea asked with a smile.

"That's not really what I meant."

"I know." She smiled again. "You want to know why I wear it. To tell you the truth, it makes my life a little easier. It also makes my customers' lives a little easier."

"How's that?" Simon asked, genuinely curious.

"Well, I often end up sitting in bars waiting for my date to show up. Wearing the ring is a repellant for some men. Some, not all. It also stops a lot of questions. Anyone who looks at us right now, they'll assume we are married."

Jamie returned with their drinks and then took their orders. Simon selected the Bistro Cobb Salad that Chelsea had the previous week; she chose a basic wedge salad.

Chelsea continued to talk, but decided she would open the door a bit for him. "If we decide to sit close, if you kiss me, if we do anything physical while in public, people dismiss it if they think we're married. If you aren't married, they seem to pay more attention. So I wear the ring."

"I understand," was all Simon said. They drank their beer and sat quietly for a few minutes. The temperature on the patio was pleasant and the music over the sound system was now playing some kind of jazz. The period of silence grew too long and Simon sensed they were both becoming uncomfortable. He thought through a number of questions he could ask her, finally settling on one.

"Last week you mentioned that you liked reading. Would you mind telling me what you like to read?"

"What would you like to know?"

"Well, what's your favorite book?"

"I don't know if I have a single favorite book." She knew she needed to turn the conversation to him. "The most recent book that I really enjoyed was *Wild*."

"I'm not familiar with that. What was it about?"

"It's a story about a woman going it alone and hiking on the Pacific Crest Trail. I'm not sure if it was fiction, or if the author was telling her actual story, but I enjoyed it." Chelsea took a drink and then feigned like she'd swallowed wrong. She made eye contact and coughed a bit.

"Ugh, I swallowed that wrong." She coughed lightly again. "What about you?"

She knew that he would naturally feel compelled to speak if she were uncomfortable. Her faked swallow and cough worked. He started in slowly.

"I've read a lot of fiction, I suppose." Then he listed off a number of authors. John Grisham, Michael Crichton, Ken Follett. "I don't really have a favorite," he concluded.

Their dinner arrived. "What was the last book that stood out to you?" she asked.

"I recently finished a book called *The Man Who Flew the Memphis Bell*, about the B-17 bombers during World War II."

"I'm sure it wasn't accurate, but did you ever see the movie *Memphis Belle*?" she asked. When Simon shook his head no, she continued. "You should, it's a pretty good movie. Not historically accurate for sure, but it was good."

Simon stared at her. The look was back. The corners of his mouth, almost always turned up in a slight smile, were now flat. She knew he was looking at her but not seeing her. He continued to eat, but his eyes were fixed in a blank stare.

⁊

It was Saturday morning October 27th, 1990. Memphis Belle was the most popular movie to hit the theaters. Simon called the number Allie had given him two days earlier. An unfamiliar voice answered. Simon assumed it was her roommate.

"Is Allie there?" His heart was beating like he'd just completed a race.

"Yeah just a sec," the roommate replied.

"Hello, this is Allie."

"Hey, this is Simon. I was wondering if you'd like to see Memphis Belle."

"Well, yeah, I would like to see it. Thanks for checking." He heard her laugh and then she hung up.

Caught off guard he stared at the phone for a moment. Then he got the joke and redialed the number. Allie picked up like nothing had happened. "Hello?"

"Hi, this is Simon." He played along. "Is Allie there?"

"Oh. Hi Simon, did you want to know anything else?"

"Would you like to see Memphis Belle, the movie, with me?" He emphasized the last two words.

"I would," she replied, then added, "Sorry I couldn't resist."

"That was pretty funny."

"When did you have in mind?"

"Tonight at seven?" he asked.

"Well, I think that will work, but can you pick me up earlier?"

"Sure. Would you like to grab dinner first?"

"I was thinking maybe you could come by at noon, but if you'd rather wait till 5 or 6 that's up to you."

He looked at his watch. It was 11am. "No, that sounds good. I'll be out in front of your dorm in an hour."

"I'll see you there."

An hour later he was in front of her dorm waiting. October in Seattle was usually wet and overcast, but today was a rarity. The sky was blue and the temperature was in the upper sixties.

As she left the dorm, she had been thinking, maybe her first impression was wrong. Maybe he wasn't as good looking as she thought. She also worried, maybe he isn't the kind person she was hoping he was. But when she saw him standing on the sidewalk in front of his car waiting for her, she knew her initial impression was right. He looked great.

Simon was even more taken as he watched her walk towards him. She was wearing a dark forest-green sweatshirt and jeans. Her auburn hair, the green sweater, the blue sky, and all Simon could think was that she looked like some kind of rare flower in the sun.

"Hey, thanks for coming a little early," she said. Unable to control herself, she reached up quickly and ran her hand through his wavy hair.

He smiled and his whole face lit up.

"Do you curl that or is it natural?" she joked.

"Oh, I spend hours with a curling iron," he joked back.

He was standing in front of his ten-year-old Honda Accord.

"Is this your car?"

"I was going to bring the Porsche but it's in the shop," he said with a shrug.

"Well, honestly..." her voice no longer joking. "I'm glad you don't have a Porsche. I'd be uncomfortable. This is more my speed."

"It gets me from here to there," Simon replied. "Speaking of getting from here to there, the movie doesn't start for a while. Actually, it doesn't start till 7. Did you have something in mind for the next seven hours?"

"Can we start with lunch?"

A guy on a Harley Davidson drove by, the sound so loud it drowned out Simon's voice. He waited for a moment then said again, "I was going to ask you if you'd like to get lunch, that sounds good. I've got an idea."

He took her to a Subway where they both ordered sandwiches to go, then drove to Discovery Park along the ocean. They parked and found a place to sit and eat.

"This is perfect," Allie said as she unwrapped her sandwich. "Tell me about yourself, Simon." He wanted to tell her everything he could. He wanted to impress her but felt that would be impossible. He'd told her so much that first night, in the Starbucks, that now he didn't know what to share.

"What else do you want to know?"

"You said you grew up in the country?"

"Yeah." He told her a bit about being raised on a farm in the Willamette Valley in Oregon. The idea of telling her about growing wheat, beans, and berries felt boring to Simon.

Allie found the idea of him working on a tractor and growing things with his parents wonderful, almost noble. She'd noticed how muscled his arms were and realized it was from being raised doing manual labor. It was completely different than her upbringing.

Even more than he disliked talking about himself, Simon wanted to hear about her. The more he asked questions, the more she shared, and the more she shared the more he wanted to just listen to the sound of her voice.

Anything Allie talked about seemed exciting. She spoke with exuberance and passion about everything. He watched her as she ate the chips that she had ordered with her sandwich. She wasn't making eye contact with him, but just eating one chip after the other, looking out at the ocean, and talking about herself.

She was telling Simon about her younger sister when he found himself staring at the freckles across her nose and cheeks.

Seeing him just staring at her, not thinking he was listening anymore, the usually confident girl was suddenly self-conscious. "What? What are you staring at?"

He smiled that warm smile and replied, "Your freckles."

"Oh God, I hate them. If I had the money I'd consider plastic surgery and have them all removed."

"Wait a minute. Look at me," Simon said suddenly and very seriously. He reached up and turned her face so that she was no longer looking out at the ocean. She stared at him while he looked directly into her eyes. After a moment of intently looking at her, he said, "Changing anything on your face would be a huge mistake. Your freckles match you perfectly." From only a foot away he continued staring intently at her face. His eyes moved from her nose to her cheeks to her mouth, and back up to stare into her eyes. It made her uncomfortable, but she let him continue to look her over.

As his eyes moved from feature to feature, he said, "You have a beautiful mouth and your lips and smile make it perfect. You have spectacular blue eyes. They suit you flawlessly." Then he looked to her hair, and added, "And your hair is so red. It's an awesome color." His eyes moved to the center of her face. "Your freckles are perfectly placed across your face and make your cheeks and your nose, your entire face... They make your face stunning. That's the best word for when I first saw you. I was stunned."

There was only one thing about herself that she hadn't liked and it was those freckles, but now she suddenly loved them. She just sat, overwhelmed, and stared back at him.

"I'm serious," Simon said. "If you removed your freckles it would be like removing the center of a famous painting. It would be like taking the Mona Lisa and cutting out the face. I know I said it already, but that's what it is. Your face is perfect."

She found herself tearing up.

"I'm sorry, did I say something wrong?"

"No, you made me so happy I want to cry," she replied.

Simon laughed. "If that makes you cry, remind me not to make you happy."

She leaned in and they kissed. No part of their bodies touched but her lips and his. Then her hand came up and she touched the side of his face before she backed away. "I'm always happy."

They spent the rest of the day walking though the immense park. As they walked, her hand found its way into his, and she felt his strong calloused hand hold hers gently.

They talked about everything they could think of to talk about. They found a quiet spot and sat in silence watching the sun set over Puget Sound. For a while there was nothing to say so they just sat comfortably next to each other, hand in hand, watching until the first stars began to appear.

Finally Allie broke the silence. "I'm getting cold and I'm hungry. Can I buy you dinner?"

"No, but I'll buy you dinner, if you know where you'd like to go."

"Well, I assume since you are a college student, you are as broke as me. So how about McDonald's?"

"It wouldn't be my first choice but I can afford that."

"I love their French fries."

"Okay, McDonald's it is."

They drove to a McDonald's that was between the park and the college and sat for another hour talking. Neither were concerned about the time. Both were enjoying every moment. He loved watching her dip her French fries in her chocolate shake... something he'd never seen before. He loved watching her face light up as she talked about her childhood dog. Each moment they spent together he felt his desire for her grow.

Suddenly Simon's eyebrows shot up and he looked at his watch.

"Hey, we missed the movie."

"That was my plan," Allie replied. "To be honest I didn't want to sit in a dark room and ignore each other for two hours." She reached up again and tussled the hair over his forehead. "I just wanted to hang out with you and talk."

Later that night he walked her from the car to the front of her dorm. Simon knew that *the* moment had arrived. Inside his head a voice was telling him to reach for her, to kiss her, to embrace her. Another voice was saying slow down, don't freak her out. She turned to look at him.

"So should we go see that movie another time?" he asked.

"If you ask me to a movie, I'll say yes, but I'll probably ask you to pick me up early and try to get us both to forget about the movie." She smiled.

He was mesmerized by her smile. She paused for a moment and then turned to head into the dorm. He reached for her and she turned back towards him. They embraced and kissed passionately. Neither wanted it to stop, but he realized they were standing in front of the dorm, where people were coming and going, and he broke away from her. She reached up and tussled his hair again.

"Thank you, Simon, that was the best date I've ever had," she sighed, then turned and entered the dorm.

e/3

"Simon?" Chelsea had eaten her entire meal in silence while watching him do the same. Not a word was spoken. Even when the waitress had asked if they wanted more beer, she had answered for them both.

"Simon?" she repeated.

He was interrupted from his memory. He never did see the movie Memphis Belle. He stared across the table at the blonde woman and felt raw emotion. Not love or lust. Not hatred. He couldn't even place his feelings. It was a combination of despair, anger, and disgust with himself. He looked down at his salad. It was gone. He'd finished his dinner without even realizing it. He looked at his wedding band again. He shouldn't be here and said as much.

"I think we should be going."

She gathered her purse as he paid the bill and they both exited the restaurant together. Outside the restaurant, he turned to her and stopped.

"I'm sorry. You don't deserve to be ignored like that. My mind wandered."

"It's fine." Chelsea wanted to turn the night to her advantage, but dinner both nights was like nothing she'd ever experienced and she couldn't figure out how to take advantage, or feel in control. She felt like she was in a car that he was driving but she had no idea where they were going. Nevertheless, if he wanted to pay for her to eat and sit in silence, who was she to complain. It was costing him plenty.

Then, she thought, when we get back to my room, he'll come out of his shell. After that I'll be able to take the driver's seat.

"Last week I left you to walk to your car alone." He looked directly into her eyes as he spoke. "That was not like me. Let me walk you to your car, please."

She realized they weren't going back to her place. "Are you sure? Is there anything wrong?"

"Yes. I'm sure. And no, there isn't anything wrong. I should be going."

He walked her to her car silently. It was a newer BMW. He couldn't tell in the dark parking lot if it was blue or black. When she put the key into the door to unlock it, he reached and opened the door for her, keeping the door between them.

Maybe she could turn this around, she thought. She didn't get into the car, just stood there facing him. Was he going to ignore her? Didn't he understand she was giving him an invitation? Didn't he realize that he was paying for her and didn't need any invitation?

Simon didn't move towards her. Instead, he stepped slightly to the left, putting the door further between them. She stared into his eyes and he matched her gaze.

"Thank you for the company, but I really should be going." He stood for a moment longer until she gave up and climbed into her car. He closed her door, turned, and walked into the dark.

Chelsea sat for a moment. Her own emotions were confusing her. She couldn't figure out how to turn the situation around. She was pretty sure she'd struck out again. How would she manipulate or take advantage of a guy she couldn't figure out? It was probably over; she'd never see him again. Of course, she'd thought that the week before. She'd been certain. She opened the envelope. It was another Hallmark card. Inside the card was another thirty $100 bills. She smiled. One thing was certain. It was easy money. There was also another handwritten note.

Chelsea,

Thank you for your company at dinner tonight,

Simon

Chapter 3

Three weeks had passed and Chelsea was sitting in her condo in Citrus Heights. In front of her was a Scrabble board. She had three racks of tiles and was alternately playing each rack as if she were three different people. At the moment she was stuck on rack number 2. U, O, I, I, E, E, and Z. No matter what way she looked at the board, she couldn't find a place for a decent word to play. She thought about which tiles to put back into the bag. Hopefully shaking up the tile bag and getting different tiles would fix rack number 2.

It was 10am Friday morning and she was putting off her workout at Cal Fit. She lacked motivation. Not just motivation for the gym, motivation for anything. She looked around her condo. A white leather couch sat on a real Persian rug which in turn covered most of the hardwood floor. A painting hung on one wall, a 60-inch flat screen TV hung on another. A laptop computer sat on a small antique wooden desk under the painting. Even the Scrabble board sitting on the glass coffee table was the collector's edition, with real wood tiles... not plastic.

In her kitchen was a Gaggia coffee maker. It came from a maker in Italy, made great coffee, and she'd justified its $500 purchase price because, she told herself, "she wouldn't be spending that money at Starbucks." She frequented Starbucks anyway, but probably not quite as much. All the appliances and the dishes were things she was proud to own.

The condo was in a gated community and, although expensive, she had paid it off. The entire neighborhood was under a homeowners' association which maintained the immaculate landscaping, community pool, and common sidewalks and biking paths. There were visitor parking spots but all of the condos had their own garages.

She always had a great view from her patio on which were potted roses, gardenias, and palms. It was where she sat most mornings, drinking coffee and enjoying the warmth of the morning sun. The condo was at one of the highest points in the neighborhood and the view west extended all the way to the Sierra mountains, when air quality was clear enough to allow it.

Each day she swept the floor, vacuumed the rug, did the dishes, and made her bed. She did her laundry every 3 to 4 days and washed the windows of the condo once a week, along with the bathrooms. Her meticulous routines were not borne out of a desire to better herself or from some military-like desire to get things done. She did them because they kept her from being bored, and being bored reminded her she was lonely.

Her condo was clean, organized, well furnished, and overall beautiful, inside and out. She had wanted nice things and when she got them she took care of them.

When she was 26 she'd told herself she deserved "the finer things in life" and quit working as a hairdresser, a job she had done since high school. She had completed two years of college but when the money ran out she couldn't finish the degree she'd been pursuing as a nurse. Unable to find any other work she had returned to the salon.

After five more years of working in the salon she grew tired of the long hours. Tired of being controlled by the women who wanted their hair done at 6:30pm on a Thursday night, or at 9am on a Saturday morning. She was tired of seeing those married women come in and get their hair done, the manicures, the pedicures, all while spending what seemed an endless amount of money. Most annoying of all were the women who didn't work. Their rich husbands paid for it all, while they sat in the chair being tended to like royalty and complaining about how busy their days were. At the time she could barely afford to pay for her broken down Ford Taurus or her rent in the seediest part of Rancho Cordova.

So she took up a different career. A career where those same rich husbands would give their money to her. She pursued the things she wanted. The BMW, the beautifully furnished apartment, the vacations. At the time she was motivated. She saw men, old and young, rich and not so rich. She learned well how to ply her trade. Those things she wanted, things she believed would make her happy, she acquired. She had *the* car. She had traveled to more countries then most people ever see. Her apartment was furnished beautifully. Each of those things once acquired, however, did nothing to provide a lasting satisfaction.

For the first two months after buying it, the BMW was fun and exciting. But the thrill was fleeting. The furnishings in the apartment were all fun to purchase at the time but the satisfaction borne from getting something new always wore off. Soon she realized that the more expensive the item, the longer the satisfaction lasted. The less expensive the item, the quicker the enjoyment left her. But no matter how much she spent, the emotional reaction rarely lasted longer than a month. Travel was the worst. Travel was expensive, but the joy only lasted until the day she was back home in her apartment. Then her emotions swung the opposite direction towards loneliness and depression.

The only exception to this diminishing return on her spending was the art hanging above her antique desk. A print entitled "A Mother's Happiness" by a Russian named Vladimir Volegov. She'd seen the original while walking through a gallery on a date with a client four years earlier.

The painting captured a beautiful young woman in a pink low-cut tank top and a blue-green full-length skirt. The woman was sitting next to, and watching closely over, a small child. The room they sat in was filled with potted flowers and bathed in sunlight pouring through white linen curtains.

The next day she went back to the gallery, purchased a print, and had it framed professionally. The artist didn't matter to her and she thought the name "Mother's Happiness" was wrong. Over the next year she'd played her own game and written down titles for what she would have named the painting. She finally settled on a new name for the painting, "The Color of Warm." It was the only object in her condo that she never grew tired of looking at. Everything else was money spent for short-lasting satisfaction.

As time went on she became more selective in who she saw, and charged more for her time. She took meticulous care of her health and physical shape. She ate well, stayed away from drugs entirely, and only drank wine when she was on a date. Even when she drank, it was at most two glasses in an evening. Eventually, she was down to less than five dates in a month, ranging from $2000 to $5000 each. A few of her dates had paid more. Some of them gave her gifts or gift cards. It was a cash-only business. There were no taxes. She owed no one. All in all she made enough to do, and buy, the things she'd always wanted. It was, however, never enough to create lasting enjoyment or satisfaction.

She was 35 when she'd first realized the satisfaction was ebbing away. She also realized that her work was tied so closely to her age and appearance. She didn't like to think about it, so she didn't spend a lot of time analyzing her own thoughts. But each time she did contemplate her future, it became more bleak. She had no real plan. In the back of her mind, she knew that when her looks were no longer her number one asset, the money would dry up. "Aging out," she called it. No one would pay to go on a date with an old woman. Worse, she'd seen some of the older ladies in her profession. It wasn't pretty.

She was realizing now that no matter how many men she met, no matter how well she manipulated or how much she took from them, it would never be enough. It was unlikely she'd ever make enough money to buy the things to create lasting satisfaction. She felt trapped.

Irrationally, what she now attempted, without even consciously realizing it, was to make one great score. One man with a lot of money manipulated enough to fix everything. Trapped people try the impossible. Trapped people aren't always rational.

So she sat in her apartment, unmotivated, listening to The Price is Right play on TV. She stared with disinterest at the fruit and oatmeal she'd prepared for breakfast.

The laptop was getting older. She stared at it, thinking she should get a new one. At least she should update its systems and change the passwords again. She only had nine active customers at the moment. There were other names on the computer. Clients from the past, and the occasional "one time only" date. Privacy was imperative to them all. She had read enough to know that changing her passwords often and keeping them random meant even better security. People's lives could be ruined if she didn't. She should change them again now, but was unmotivated to do so.

She thought about those nine customers. Aside from Simon, her newest, and she suspected the wealthiest, it was an eclectic group. Her thoughts stopped her for a moment. Simon. Why did she think of him as Simon? All the others she thought of in terms of their careers, not their names.

There was the bald insurance salesman. Not very creatively, her name for him was Insurance Salesman. Married but, according to him, in a relationship where there was no longer love; he would leave his wife but she'd end up with so much money he couldn't. Insurance Salesman paid her the most per visit and saw her the most often.

There was the professional athlete. Also not very creatively named, the Jock. His wife refused to move from Dallas when he was traded to Sacramento. So he lived the season here, seeing her when his needs dictated. He paid her very well, but she knew he would move on when he was traded again.

There were the two politicians. The Democrat and the Republican, those were her names for them as well as their jobs. Sacramento was full of politicians. They were both eager to meet her, and willing to pay extra to ensure their privacy. She probably could have extorted either of them just to keep their privacy, but thought better of it. Who knows what some desperate politician was willing to do, including having her arrested or beaten or... worse. What would either one of them do if they suspected she would out them? She should assure them that would never happen. When she saw each of them again, she would drop a few not so subtle hints that she would always maintain their privacy.

Two other married men were seeing her currently. Their names were Electrician and Cardboard Guy. Cardboard Guy was named because he worked in some plant that made cardboard and was always talking about it. She knew that neither had much money or they'd have visited her more often. When you don't have much, spending $1,000 to $2,000 for an hour or two of pleasure is not easily done. That kind of money is also hard to hide from a spouse, unless you make significantly more.

Then there was a teacher at UC Davis. Her nickname for him was the Professor. He claimed to be single, but she was pretty sure he was lying about that.

Then there were two single guys. The first was around 30, a nerd working at Intel in Folsom. He was some kind of programmer. He was either from India or his parents were. Not that his race mattered to her. She just noted it because his accent was so strong and at first she thought it cute. Clearly he'd not been around many women. No doubt it was easier for him to pay for companionship than to develop a mental algorithm or program necessary to get women to date him. Her name for him was appropriately Computer Guy.

The other single guy was okay at first, but lately she had found herself becoming more and more uneasy dating him. Construction Guy. Several times he arrived straight from his construction job un-showered, which was unacceptable to her. He'd also become increasingly curious about "who else" she was seeing. He as much as told her that if he saw her twice a month at $2000 a visit, there was no need for her to see anyone else. In reality, he only saw her about once every other month. He clearly had no idea how much she made.

She needed to do two things. She needed to reset the passwords on the computer and she needed to tell Construction Guy that she wasn't going to see him anymore. But she lacked motivation and did nothing.

There was one more thing. She needed to stop referring to the rich guy in the suit as Simon, and just use the name Rich Suit Guy for him.

The phone rang and interrupted her thoughts. She looked at the caller ID. It was Simon.

"Hello Chelsea?" he said when she picked up. "This is Simon."

"Hello Simon. It's great to hear from you." She tried to sound interested, but she was not sure how to approach him.

"I know it's been a few weeks but I was just wondering if you would like to meet me for dinner again?"

"I'm glad you called. When did you have in mind?"

"Tonight, I was thinking." He sounded distracted, probably at work, she thought. "At the same place."

"Tonight would be fine, but Simon, could we possibly meet somewhere else?" She used his name, still trying to make a connection. Without a connection he would be uninterested. Without his interest in her, she'd be unable to take advantage of him. She hoped suggesting a new location would create an opportunity. Maybe she could turn the tables by doing something, anything, and get him talking to her.

"Did you have someplace in mind?"

She thought of the restaurant with couches. Maybe they could sit on a couch and she could get closer to him, physically and emotionally. There was no guarantee she could get one of the two tables with couches, but it was worth a try. Like tossing your rack of Scrabble tiles back into the bag and shaking them up. Hope for change.

"Are you familiar with El Dorado Hills, just up Highway 50 from where we've been meeting?"

"Yes."

"There is a restaurant called Milestone, in El Dorado Town Center."

"I know the place, yes. I'll meet you there. Will six o'clock work?"

"Yes, six will be fine."

"Thank you."

"Thank you, Simon." Then, trying to sound excited she added, "I look forward to seeing you again."

He hadn't hung up, but didn't respond. She knew he didn't know what to say. She continued, "Simon, is there anything in particular that you'd like me to wear tonight?"

"Nothing in particular. No need to dress up."

"Okay, I just thought I'd ask."

After a brief awkward moment he said, "I'll see you tonight then," and hung up.

Chelsea dressed for the gym. Yoga pants and a sports bra with a loose T-shirt over the top. It was warmer out today and there was no need for a sweatshirt. She needed to work out and look her best for the evening.

It was crazy, but she always felt like she looked more fit and trim after working out. It's not like it was true. In the last five years, in spite of working out nearly every day, she was exactly six pounds heavier. Actually she'd gained the five of those pounds in the last two years. At 35 she'd been 140 pounds. She was exactly 145 pounds today.

Nevertheless, she told herself she'd have to work out more. She dreaded the thought of gaining three pounds a year for the next ten years. She caught a sideways glance of herself in the full-length mirror on her closet door. She still looked great, and judging by what she could see and her increased bra size over those last two years, some of that weight was in the right place. She wondered if Simon thought so.

As quickly as the thought came to her, she chided herself for it. She reminded herself of what she knew. Relationships are transactional. Take what you can from them and move on. Besides, Simon wasn't even interested.

She couldn't help but think about him some more. Why was he asking to meet her again? What was he getting out of this? Clearly he, of all people, as the one paying her, knew that it was a transaction. But what was he getting? She didn't understand him and it bothered her.

She was still thinking about all of those things when she pulled her BMW through the gates and out onto the public road. She didn't notice the pickup truck parked on a side street just down from the gated entrance, and she didn't notice it pull out and follow her, two cars behind.

Chapter 4

Like Back Bistro, and like many restaurants in California, Milestone Restaurant in El Dorado Hills had an outdoor dining area. There were metal tables and chairs, but also two couches around shorter tables like coffee tables. In the middle of each coffee table was a cutout area with a gas burner hidden beneath crushed rock. Flames danced up from the rocks, creating a warm and inviting look. Harder to eat at, but easier to drink and visit.

Simon saw Chelsea sitting on one of the couches as he approached the restaurant. Avoiding a walk through the front doors, he entered through a wrought iron gate and made his way between several groups of people. He sat on the opposite side of the table in a chair, leaving her alone on the couch.

"Simon, please join me." She looked at him with almost a look of hurt. "It feels a little weird sitting on the couch by myself. Besides, if you sit over there, I'll feel like we have to practically yell across the table."

For just a moment she thought he was going to ignore her. Something few men did. But after a pause, he stood and moved over to the couch. She noticed, however, that he didn't sit close. He did lean forward and set an envelope on the table. She picked it up and dropped it into her purse.

"Thank you for sitting over here, I just felt like that would be easier to talk this way."

He looked at her and again she felt like he was looking through her, with the corners of his mouth turned upward in an ever so slight smile.

Simon looked at the woman sitting on the opposite end of the couch. She was quite beautiful. Her blonde hair dropped just below her shoulders, although he noticed for the first time tonight that her roots were dark. He didn't really care about the details of how a woman styled her hair. Maybe it was dyed blonde, maybe it was some kind of look a naturally blonde woman would pay to have. It really didn't matter to him. It fit her. She wore bright red lipstick that he'd have thought too bright in any other case, but she wore it well. Under her full dark eyebrows, she had large brown eyes that seemed enlarged by the dark eyeliner and eye shadow. A woman of her beauty was rare. He wondered how she'd ended up choosing this as a life and was about to ask her, then decided against it. But the thought persisted. He wanted to know.

She was wearing blue jeans and a basic T-shirt style top. He thought about his own suit, and realized that by telling her "not to dress up" that she may be feeling underdressed.

"I didn't have time to change after my meeting," he said. Then he added, "You look very nice."

"Thank you, Simon," she replied. "I was feeling a little underdressed when I saw you arrive."

"No, you look just fine."

Her dark eyebrows rose and she tilted her head as she looked at him. "I usually try to look more than 'just fine.'" There was a hint of truth in her words, but also a bit of sarcasm.

Unsure of what to say at that point he just left it alone.

The waiter approached their table. "Hello, I'm Rob. I'll be serving you…" he started then, recognizing Simon, said instead, "Hey Mr. Murray. It's been a long time. It's good to see you."

"Hello Rob. Please call me Simon. It has been a while since I've eaten here. How are you?"

"I'm still here," Rob replied. "The menu's changed. The cooks have changed. But I'm still here."

As they interacted, Chelsea thought to herself. Most men she met with didn't want to meet at a restaurant they frequented in their day-to-day lives. They usually preferred a location far from their normal haunts. She wondered about that and settled on the idea that maybe he'd lived in this area in the past. That would make sense. He would know the area enough to feel comfortable and meet her, but not worry about being seen by friends and family.

"Can I get you any drinks to start off?" Rob asked.

Simon looked briefly at the drink menu on the table. "I'll start off with a glass of the Malbec."

"I'll have the same," Chelsea said when Rob turned to her.

"I'll get started with these and be back to take your order."

Chelsea looked at Simon.

"You've eaten here before?"

"Yes, it's been a couple of years, but I used to come here quite a bit."

Chelsea was cognizant of the fact that Simon still seemed as if he were even more distant than the far end of a lengthy couch. It wasn't that long of a couch but his aloofness added to the feeling. Most men would have sat down right next to her, touching her.

She'd invited that. He hadn't sat against the far end of the couch, but definitely further than necessary. A casual observer might think they were having a business meeting. She was thinking things needed to be private to progress and was grateful for the music and general noise. Other people were filing into the restaurant and nearly every table on the patio was now full. Between the music and conversations, it was almost loud, at least loud enough to drown out their conversation and keep it private.

They sat in silence until Chelsea became uncomfortable. "Simon, we've been out now three times. Why don't you tell me a bit about yourself?"

Simon smiled, "I was thinking of asking you the same question."

"How would you feel if we trade questions?" she suggested. "I'll answer a question you ask, then you answer a question from me."

He took a drink of wine. Before he could answer, a couple approached their table.

"Simon?" The man and woman looked to be the same age as Simon. Both were wearing wedding rings.

"Hello Brian... Kim." Simon didn't stand. He didn't introduce Chelsea. Not so subtle hints for the couple to go away.

The woman didn't get the hint. "Simon aren't you going to introduce us?"

"Kim, Brian, this is Chelsea."

"Hi." Kim looked from Simon to Chelsea as if for some explanation.

Chelsea knew the situation. Her job was to follow his lead. She remained seated. "Hello. It's nice to meet you both." Both Simon and Chelsea remained quiet for a moment, until the hint was taken.

"Well, we just finished an early dinner. We're headed up to Tahoe for the weekend... it's a long drive so we should be going," Brian said.

Then with a last curious glance from Simon to Chelsea, Brian added. "It was nice seeing you. We should catch up sometime."

"Sure thing, Brian, call me anytime. We'll get together."

As the couple walked away Chelsea looked at Simon. He didn't look uncomfortable or worried. At most he looked irritated, but what most surprised her was that he just seemed unconcerned.

Simon noticed her watching him. "I know him from work."

She was good at reading people but Simon seemed a list of contradictions. On one hand he kept calling her and asking for a date. On the other hand was the wedding band. He was confident and sure of himself. The men she usually met were not. On nearly every "date" the man wanted to meet in an out of the way place and avoid being seen. Simon seemed unconcerned and even agreed to meet at a restaurant he'd frequented. Even when he ran into someone he knew, he hadn't responded with the inevitable lie. He had avoided conversation about her, but didn't make up some elaborate story, like this is my cousin, or this is someone being interviewed for a job. No, he seemed unconcerned. That wasn't normal.

She was thinking all this when she realized she was just staring at him. He noticed it at the same moment, looking back at her in silence. Then the corners of his mouth turned up into kind of wry smile. She couldn't read him. She tried to figure out his affect. Then she placed it; his face and his eyes. He wasn't worried. That hollow blank stare that he'd had the last few times they'd eaten dinner carried a look of sorrow. She wasn't positive, but he seemed sad.

Even so, when he looked at her, and his face broke into a smile, it was almost like he had no choice. It was like his smile was so much a part of him that even if he were sad, his natural reaction was to smile when speaking with someone.

The waiter returned and took their order. Simon suggested appetizers, figuring a light fare of finger foods would be easier to handle while sitting on a couch. They sat in silence for a while. The appetizers arrived and they both ate slowly while sipping wine.

Still trying to figure a way to turn the relationship to her advantage, Chelsea started in where they'd left off. "Well, what do you think about my idea? I'll answer your question, you answer mine?"

Simon tipped his head in a quick half nod, "One question, go ahead."

"What do you do for fun, Simon?" she asked and just like that it was as if he'd left her. He was still there but his fixed stare told her he was no longer even hearing her.

や

It was mid-November, their freshman year in college. They had just finished a Saturday lunch at McDonald's and were making the long walk back to campus. They had been silent for some time. Even though she was wearing cotton gloves, he enjoyed the feeling of her small hand in his.

"Want to keep walking around?"

"Sure," she replied quietly. She too was simply enjoying the moment.

"Are you warm enough?" Both were wearing coats over sweatshirts and jeans. Allie had a blue knit scarf wrapped around her neck and a matching hat.

"Yeah. As long as we keep moving." Her breath created a white cloud in the cold.

They made their way to a concrete walk along the south side of the campus. It followed the edge of Portage Bay and was dotted with benches. Though it was nearly 2pm there was still a heavy frost in the shade caused by the many fir trees along the path. Few pedestrians were out in the frigid temperatures.

Across the Bay were boathouses and beautiful homes along the shore. What little warmth the sun provided hit them from over the water.

"I love how a perfectly sunny day like this with the sky so blue can be so cold."

"It's beautiful." Simon didn't want to walk her back to the dorm and end the afternoon with her. They stopped and took in the view.

"I'd say let's sit on a bench but I think we would freeze out butts off."

"Agreed," she said and turned to him.

With her free hand she reached up and tossed the wavy hair over his face. "No hat, no gloves... are you warm enough?" she asked.

"Yeah."

"Simon, what do you do for fun?"

"I'm doing it."

"You know what I mean." She reached out and with her free hand took his so that they were now facing each other, both of her hands in his. "If we hadn't met, what would you be doing right now?"

"Probably wrestling."

"What?" She'd only known him for a month, but it seemed incongruous with the gentle person she knew.

"You mean like on a wrestling team?"

"No, I'd just be going to practice with the U of W team."

"What are you talking about?"

"Most afternoons I go wrestle with the team."

"But you aren't on the team?"

"No. I wrestled in high school and I was recruited to wrestle in college but I gave it up."

"Why?"

"I just wanted to focus on school, on my programming classes, and being on the team would have meant tons of time. It's a huge commitment. It also meant cutting weight which I hated doing and decided I could still do it for fun without hassles."

"So you just go practice?"

"Well, it's really not just practice. I mean the team is practicing, but when I go we actually spar. It's just like a wrestling match except for the scoring and the pressure."

"And that's what you do for fun?"

"Yeah, I really like it. It's a contest. I compete against the other guy. I push myself to the limit physically. It really is fun, and by not being on the team, I have none of the negative."

"Can I come watch?"

"I think you'd be bored."

"No really, would you mind?"

The sun was shining in her face, lighting up her red hair into a dazzling effect. The contrast of the blue knit hat, her red hair, the freckles on her nose, which was turning slightly red from the cold, and the sunshine was too much for him. He leaned towards her and kissed her. Their hands released, his finding their way around her waist, hers up over his shoulders and behind his neck. They kissed for a moment, then she backed away as her breath came out in a white cloud in front of her. She smiled at him.

"Kissing me is nice, but if this is your way of changing the subject it won't work."

"What?"

"What nothing." She continued to press, "Can I come watch you wrestle?"

"I guess."

The following week Allie was sitting in the bleachers watching Simon. Next to her was Simon's gym bag, water bottle, and a towel. The gym was loud with whistles, and with coaches barking at the wrestlers. Multiple pairs of wrestlers were fighting. Some had coaches standing over them, yelling instructions. Others were simply sparring without coaches, stopping themselves and starting again, practicing particular moves and straining against the strength of their partner.

The gym smelled of mats and sweat. She was surprised by everything she saw. She still couldn't get over the fact that Simon was a wrestler. Somehow she'd always thought of wrestlers as kind of stupid jocks. Now she was watching the person she knew who was kind and gentle. Who she'd thought of as a kind of computer nerd. This person was standing 25 feet away from her in wrestling tights.

In the month she'd known him, Simon was either wearing a sweatshirt, a T-shirt, or a coat. She'd noticed his muscular arms but had chalked that up to his working on a farm. She didn't think of him as an athlete. She'd never really thought of him as strong physically, but now she could see he was ripped.

For his part, Simon was about to spar with a U of W athlete. He was cognizant of Allie watching but put it out of his mind. One thing he'd learned wrestling in high school was to focus. Without that focus on his opponent he would be pinned, and he really didn't want her seeing that happen. So he took a few deep breaths and stepped up on the mat.

The U of W wrestler's name was Ron, and Simon had sparred with him several times before. Ron was in the 145 pound weight class and cutting weight to stay there. Simon weighed 147 pounds. They both faced each other and shook hands. One of the coaches stood between them, whistle on the lanyard about his neck.

"Okay, guys, you ready?"

"Yes."

"Yeah."

The coach blew the whistle and Simon instantly dove at Ron's legs. Caught off guard by the suddenness of the move, Ron was lifted off the ground and found himself with no leverage at all. Simon quickly twisted and after a few moments of struggle, pinned Ron. The coach blew the whistle and they untangled and stood.

"Dammit, Simon." Ron was irritated. He had sparred with Simon multiple times. He had lost several and won several, but never had he lost this quickly. "What the hell was that?"

"Ron!" The coach barked his name. "Let me get this straight. Are you upset because he kicked your ass, because he did it so quickly, or because you were totally unprepared and lacked all intensity?"

The coach launched into a lecture about being intense, focused, and ready at all times. Simon knew it was not really Ron's fault. He knew it wasn't the suddenness of the attack. With Allie watching, Simon had never wanted to win so badly. They had sparred before, but this was different.

"Okay, let's go again," the coach said.

Ron was angry, but still unaware of Simon's motivation. The second session lasted significantly longer but in the end Simon pinned him again. They went at it a third time with neither getting pinned. All in all they wrestled for nearly 30 minutes. At the end, both were exhausted when they shook hands.

"Good god," Ron exclaimed as they shook. "You kicked my butt today."

"You were just off, and I was on. Next week you'll kick my butt," Simon promised, then started to make his way over to Allie.

Allie was completely mesmerized by the entire situation. She'd never even been to a wrestling match and found herself thrilled as she watched Simon fight and beat his opponent. She was still shocked by his obvious strength as she watched this sweaty guy who she felt like she hardly knew walk towards her.

Simon felt a little rush of self-consciousness as he approached her in his wrestling gear, still breathing hard, sweat pouring off his face. He grabbed the towel and wiped the sweat from his face then took a long drink of water.

"Well, a little boring, right?" he asked her.

"Nuh uh," she replied, grinning at him. "That was pretty awesome."

The coach who had been overseeing the sparring approached.

"Hey Simon, got a second?"

"Sure, Coach."

"Simon, I really wish you would reconsider my offer. You are an exceptional wrestler and you could be a starter on our team."

Allie was surprised. She didn't know anything about wrestling but she figured if a college coach was offering him a place on a team he must be more than just good.

"I appreciate it coach. I really do. But like I said last week, I'm really here to focus on my degree. I love learning to fight better but it's not my end goal."

"Nothing I can do to change your mind?"

Simon smiled and shook his head. "No. But I'd still like to come and wrestle with the team now and then."

"I'll get you a printout of our schedule. It has all of our matches and our practice times."

"I'll come as often as I can. I really enjoy it."

"Well I wish I could talk you into joining us, but if I can't you are welcome to come to practice any time you like. There's no better practice for the guys than wrestling a better opponent."

The coach retreated back to the mats and began barking instructions to a couple of other wrestlers. Simon wiped himself off again with the towel. His breathing was slowing and he was starting to cool off. Sitting next to the gym bag, he opened it and pulled out a hoodie and sweatpants.

Allie sat on the opposite side of the bag.

With a degree of amazement in her voice, she said, "The coach just asked you to be on the team?"

"Yeah, he's been pestering me about it."

"Why aren't you?"

"Because everything I like about wrestling I can get by showing up at practice. I like really making the effort. I like working hard and the competition. I like fighting against the other guy. But I don't have to put up with all the things I don't like. Being committed to every single day. Traveling to other schools for days at a time. Cutting weight."

"So you actually like fighting?"

"Yeah, I guess I do. But I think all guys do to some extent. I've always felt like fighting, wrestling, boxing, whatever it is, just prepares us for that 'what if' in life."

"What if?"

"Yeah, what if I'm forced to really fight someday? What if I get in a situation I cannot walk away from, or that I have to protect someone and there is no other way but to fight? I think all men kind of feel deep down inside that we should be ready."

"Have you ever had to fight anyone?"

"Not for real."

Allie smiled and looked right at Simon. "And if you had to protect me, would you fight for me?"

"If there was no other way. Sure." Simon thought of it more as a philosophy, not as chivalry, and tried to explain it further.

"Look, if I'm on a street corner and a brute of a man attacked a small child, do I just wait? Do I call the police while he kills her? Or do I get involved? Pacifism is great as long as everyone obeys the law. But for some reason I've always felt like wrestling would prepare me, at least in part, to be ready if needed. If the police and law aren't available, we should all know what we can do, what we are willing to do, and what we should do."

"And what am I supposed to do if this dude attacks the little girl and I'm the only one around? Beat him up?" Allie said with her eyebrows raised.

"No, but I'm sure not opposed to women who are armed."

"You think I should carry a gun?"

"I said I'm not opposed to it. Again, it's about being ready. For those who carry a gun, hopefully they never have to use it. Hopefully I'll never fight anyone in real life other than in friendly competition and practice."

"I still say you should join the team."

Simon smiled at her. "Not interested."

He finished putting on his sweats over his wrestling tights and looked at her. She seemed somehow disappointed. "Besides, If I join the team, we probably would only see each other about once every other week. Are you saying you'd like to get rid of me?"

"Nope," she said with a grin. Then she reached up and started to run her fingers through his hair.

"Oh gross... sweaty." She wiped her hand off on his sweatshirt. "You made the right choice."

⁊

"Simon?"

He looked up and saw Chelsea at the other end of the couch staring at him. She was nothing like Allie. Brown eyes, not blue. Blonde hair, not red. Her complexion was flawless, there were no freckles. Her body was spectacular, but in a different way from Allie's. Allie had been thin and athletic; she could eat anything and she stayed thin. Chelsea, on the other hand, was voluptuous.

Why was he comparing them? There was no comparison. He would never love anyone the way he loved Allie. He was here with Chelsea for only one reason, but it didn't matter... nothing mattered.

"Simon?" Chelsea repeated, "is everything all right?"

"I'm sorry. Maybe we should be going."

Hoping she could move things forward, she pressed, "Where will we be going?"

"I'm sorry. I should be going. I'll walk you to your car first."

They made their way to her car and he again held the door open, putting himself behind it. She faced him and paused, trying to give him an opening. Then she thought to herself, what the hell. I can kiss him. She started to move around the car door towards him but he backed ever so slightly away.

"Thank you again," Simon said with finality.

She realized it wasn't going to happen. Then she thought, who cares? I have the money... move on. She gave up and sat down in her car. He shut the door for her, then turned to leave.

He heard the BMW start and pull away then he saw an older model pickup start up and leave the parking lot. The truck was primer grey and had a dented rear fender on the passenger side. The only reason he noticed it was because it reminded him of the farm. He knew the truck well. A 1973 Ford F-150. He'd caught a few hours of sleep on the bench seat of that truck many nights during the harvest years ago. He'd loaded it and unloaded it with equipment a thousand times. His brother now owned the farm and Simon wondered if he still had the truck. He'd have to ask him.

As she drove back to her condo she was irritated at the thoughts in her head. Men didn't ignore her. Was she losing her looks? Was she "aging out"? She looked in the rear-view mirror at her face. Surely not yet. She worked out hard at the gym. Her figure, yes with the help of the right clothing, was still enough to turn heads. Why didn't he want her? His lack of interest made her feel even more lonely and unwanted. This was worsened by the fact that she wouldn't have turned down any advance he made. He was paying for her to physically be there with him, but he was uninterested. The thoughts kept repeating, unwanted, lonely, until she pulled through the gates of her complex.

Then, as she was pulling into her driveway, she said aloud, "No more dates for you, Simon—Rich Suit Guy."

She got out of her car and entered her condo. As she tossed her purse on the couch and sat down, she saw the envelope. She opened it. She counted the hundred dollar bills. Thirty of them again tonight.

"Okay, Maybe another date for you, Simon." she said aloud to her empty condo.

She didn't read the card.

Chapter 5

For the last two years Simon's life had been a dull monotony. Unable to sleep he usually got up around 4:30 or 5am. Not hungry, he drank coffee and forced himself to eat. Toast with cottage cheese, an egg or two, or oatmeal was about all he ever had. By 11am he usually went to In-N-Out or Chick-Fil-A.

He knew he had to keep active to maintain his sanity and health. As a result, at 1pm each day he was at the gym and working out. On a day where he felt a complete lack of motivation he would run for 30 minutes on a treadmill. On days he felt slightly more alive he would warm up on the treadmill then work his core and lift weights. Then in the later afternoon, he would head to the high school to wrestle and coach, or during the times of year they were not practicing he would head to a local judo studio. Judo engaged his mind in a way that helped him forget the past. He had only been studying it for six months but the instructor had been encouraging.

The judo studio was located in an older strip mall in Folsom and fronted by windows. It sat between a DMV office and a

Chinese restaurant. Inside, the center of the floor was covered in mats. A huge square mat covered the majority of the massive room and extended to within 10 feet of each side wall. The front 20 feet of the place was a wooden floor and had a rack for shoes as well as a display table with promotional material about the gym and upcoming tournaments. The wooden floor extended to the back of the building where there was an office as well as men's and women's bathrooms.

One wall held shelves for people to place gym bags or anything else. Above it were posters of pictures of fighters at past events. On the opposite wall was single long shelf which was filled with trophies, mostly won by the instructor.

Once wrestling season ended Simon had arranged with the instructor to come at a time of day before younger students arrived and receive private lessons. And so it became routine, but it also added to the monotony of Simon's life. Every day, 3pm, he and the instructor, Tim, would practice.

The routine today was slightly different because he was meeting Chelsea for dinner, but he was still at the judo studio at 3 for his lesson.

"I've got to be done at 4 today, Tim, so I won't likely stick around any longer, sorry."

"Simon, if every young person that came in here had your consistency and drive, I'd have a few Olympic hopefuls in my school."

"I just have more time than most."

"No, it's more than that. For a guy your age you are remarkable."

"It's all my wrestling."

"But that's what I mean. Most guys your age don't actually wrestle."

"I don't know how much longer I'll be able to," Simon said as he stretched and twisted his upper body. "Last time I was wrestling one of the boys at the high school sure got the better of me."

"Pinned you?"

"Yes, but he was a heavyweight and probably outweighed me by quite a bit. I guess I shouldn't be practicing against higher weight classes anymore."

The instructor laughed. "Maybe you shouldn't be wrestling against 18-year-olds anymore."

"Well, that's why I'm learning judo. I like learning the fighting skills, but this seems like something that lines up more with my age."

"You made a good choice. Judo is a lot easier on your body as far as fighting goes. You've heard me say it before, in judo you use their weight, momentum, and leverage and your skill to your advantage. In my opinion it's the perfect fighting skill for someone your age."

"Okay, now I feel old."

They finished another session and Simon left promptly at 4. He had plenty of time to drive home, shower, clean up, and head to dinner.

❧

Two hours later, Chelsea was again making her way to Milestone Restaurant in El Dorado Hills to meet Simon. The air conditioner of the Black BMW was on high as the temperature was in the 90s. She'd decided to wear something a little more risqué and had dawned a red dress that was short and form fitting. The tight dress stretched over her push up bra in an almost unreal way. As always, her loose curly blonde hair flowed down around her shoulders. She pulled into the parking lot and turned down the visor to check herself in the mirror.

Pulling lip gloss out of her purse she reapplied the wet gloss over the red lipstick that matched her dress. Perfect, she thought.

No way he could resist this. She opened the door and stepped out into the heat. Despite the evening temperature cooling, the parking lot was still boiling hot with residual heat from the sun beating down on the pavement all day. The patio at Milestone had trees, she thought, it would be cooler in the shade.

She didn't notice the Ford Pickup. It had pulled into the far side of the parking lot. The driver rolled his windows down and parked in the shade of several large trees, turning off the engine. He watched her as she walked towards the restaurant and out of sight.

Chelsea felt her dress hike up a bit as she walked in her high heels. She smiled to herself. They'd again be sitting on the couches. She could face him and with her dress as short as it was, maybe she'd let it hike up just enough so that he would see the black lace underwear beneath. It would be accidental; she would watch his face and only allow it for the briefest second. She'd done it before. Seduction was a skill, an art, and she was excellent at it. He wouldn't be able to resist.

But an hour later she wasn't so sure. Simon had arrived similarly to their nights before. He wore a suit, was cordial and kind, but as before, he seemed aloof. She'd tried yet again to get him to talk about himself, but he didn't. She made eye contact and tried to flirt with him. His response had been to ignore it. And when she tried the trick with the dress, he never even once looked down.

They had the same waiter as the week before, Rob. Simon seemed to have a better conversation with Rob than with her. She was frustrated. She was convinced Simon had money. She was sure that this man would pay her more and more if she could only manipulate him, but he seemed to ignore everything she tried.

A family was sitting at the table nearest them, and the two children, done eating way before the parents, were up and running around their table. It was loud and annoying but it allowed Simon and Chelsea a distraction from the silence between them.

She was about to give up trying to figure Simon out and then she thought of their conversation the week before.

"Simon, last week you agreed to answer a question of mine and I was going to ask a question of you."

She took a sip of wine and continued. "Well, so far, we've eaten several dinners together. I'm not complaining but I think you've yet to share a single thing about yourself." She smiled at him, trying to disarm him, trying to make him feel at ease, trying to make him notice her and want her.

Trying to be fun and flirty she went on, "How about we continue that game?"

He smiled at her and replied with a simple "Okay," but then said nothing more.

"I need to ask a good question, so I'm going to think about it for a minute." She took another sip of wine. "Would you like to ask your question first?"

Simon thought for a moment. "Sure. I don't need to think about it." But then he paused, not wanting to ask the question that again came to his mind.

She asked it for him. "You want to know how I came to be in this line of work."

Simon's eyebrows shot up and he replied, "Yes."

"Eventually everyone wants to ask that. Most are too afraid to ask, or they don't want to know the answer."

The waiter returned and interrupted them. He placed the salads they had ordered on the table in front of each of them.

"Can I get you anything else?"

"Not right now, thank you, Rob," Simon replied.

They began to eat quietly. She looked at him. His smile was gone and he ate a few bites without comment. She couldn't get over the fact that he seemed sad.

"Are you sad, Simon?"

He looked at her, directly. Normally eye contact was a thing she used to flirt, but with him it wasn't a flirty thing, it was like he was just being genuine and present.

"That sounds like a cartoon character. Sad Simon." He seemed to force a smile and then took a drink. "Do I seem sad?"

"You seem a lot of things," Chelsea responded honestly.

"I'm curious. What things do I seem?" Simon replied.

"No, that wasn't the deal," Chelsea said. "We're both supposed to ask one question of each other."

"Well aren't you going to answer my question first?" Simon countered.

"Technically, you haven't asked me a question. You started to, but I asked it for you," Chelsea chided.

One of the children from the table next to them, still running around the patio, bumped into the coffee table. As heavy as it was, the jarring was enough to tip over Simon's glass of wine. It spilled across the table and across his legs, covering his suit pants.

The child's father looked exasperated and angry. "Dang it, James. Look what you did."

"I'm sorry about that," the father said to Simon. Then he turned to his son, "Now apologize to this man and get over here and sit."

The boy looked at Simon, worried by both his father's anger and the unknown response of the stranger. "I'm sorry I tipped over your drink."

"Thank you for saying that," Simon said. Then he grinned and bent towards the boy. He beckoned with his finger and the boy walked closer. "Here's a little secret," he said. Intending to be only loud enough for boy to hear, he went on, "They'll give me a free drink so you don't need to really worry about it."

Simon smiled again, fully, lighting up his entire face. "And these pants, they were old and dirty anyway, I was going to either clean them or throw them away. But thanks for saying sorry." The boy grinned back and then returned to his table, now more worried about the anger of his father than that of a stranger.

Chelsea was close enough to hear the interaction. The suit wasn't old or dirty and it definitely wasn't cheap. She guessed the wine wouldn't come out no matter how well it was dry cleaned. Now she knew a couple more things about the man, Simon. He wasn't prone to overreact, and he was good with kids.

The waiter showed up and saw the mess.

"Hey, Rob, we seemed to have had a little accident here. Can I get another glass of wine?" There it was again. Simon treated everyone as if they were his equal. As soon as the thought popped into her head, it was followed by another thought. People just don't do that.

"Sure thing, boss," Rob replied, then added, "I'll bring you a towel for your pants. I'm very sorry about that."

"Not your fault," Simon replied. Then, as he had already used the cloth napkins that were on the table, he added, "A towel would be nice, and maybe some more napkins."

Simon and Chelsea returned to eating silently. Simon didn't really want to share anything and Chelsea didn't really want to answer the question of career choice.

Finally, Simon broke the silence. "What things?"

Chelsea looked at him, confused.

"You said earlier that I seemed 'A lot of things.'"

She wondered how to turn the moment to her advantage. Normally she would have lied about a number of his traits and accomplishments. Stroking egos had almost always led to more money in the past. They made eye contact. He will know if I'm lying, she thought, besides she didn't really know enough about him to stroke his ego. She took a drink of wine and decided to tell the truth, especially since the truth was likely to stroke his ego anyway.

"Well, if I had to guess. You are good with children. You are kind to others around you regardless of their position and yours. You dress nicely, but seemed unconcerned about the wine. Based on that and how you overpaid for our last two dates, I would say you make a very good living. Am I right so far?"

"Go on."

"I would say the most noticeable thing is that you have smiled a lot in your life."

"Why would you say that?"

"Some people call them laugh lines. Your face is marked with that more than anything else. You laugh and smile a lot, Simon. Or at least you have in the past. You can't hide that."

His face changed and he was now looking past her with his blank, almost sad stare.

∁

Allie was sitting in front of Simon at McDonald's, dipping her French fries in her chocolate shake again. They had both taken their last final earlier in the day. They hadn't counted the number of dates they had been on, but they had spent nearly every free moment together their entire freshman year. In a few moments both would leave for the summer; him to Oregon and her to San Diego by way of SeaTac airport.

"Do you know what I love about you, Simon?" She didn't look at him as she spoke. She was busy dipping another fry in her shake and said it almost absentmindedly. "I love that you are always smiling. Even when you aren't smiling, you have a little smile."

He stared at her. Neither had used the word "love" before in connection with each other, and he didn't know how to react. After an entire school year together he was still amazed by her.

Simon felt he had to say something. "I guess I'll confess something to you," he started, tentatively.

She stopped eating and looked directly at him.

"I thought you were beautiful the first time I saw you." He paused.

"And now you've changed your mind!" she said with a laugh.

"No, seriously. The more I get know you, the more beautiful you are." Simon then added, "I thought you were so pretty the first time I met you. I still love how you have just the right amount of freckles and that they are perfectly lined up across your cheeks and nose. I love your blue eyes and your dark eyebrows. Your hair isn't red, it's a cross between brown and red, and I think most women would pay to have hair that color."

Feeling uncomfortable, Allie began to say something, but Simon stopped her. "Wait, let me finish. I thought you were beautiful when we met, but now after getting to know you, I think you are more beautiful than ever. You have a great sense of humor. You are always happy and upbeat. You don't seem to care about what others think of you. You're smart. You're kind. I've never heard you speak about someone else in the negative. You see the good in everyone. I want to be more like you."

She waited for a few seconds then replied, "Are you done?" Then she smiled and added, "If you want to be like me, I'd suggest you come to San Diego this summer and meet my family. Since they raised me and made me this way, it would be the only way to help you with that."

"I'd love to, but summer is the busiest time for our farm. I know my parents will be needing my help more than ever. I'm sure since I've been gone they've had to do more and some of the work has piled up."

She replied with sarcasm, "Really, you'll be too busy to visit me even once?"

"I would love to visit you, but I know that this time of year, I won't be able to get away. I'll get home and my summer will be filled with work."

"What does a day at your farm look like?" she asked without the humor or sarcasm. She genuinely wanted to know.

"Well, we get up about 5:30 and have breakfast. We start working at about 6:15 or 6:30. Every day is a little different. Some days it's riding in a tractor plowing or planting. Some days it's tying back canes."

She looked confused by that but rather than get into the boring details he continued, "Some days it's moving water pipes in sugar beets or beans. As the summer progresses it changes to berry picking season, then running the bean pickers, or combines."

"Do you have a least favorite job or hardest, or a favorite job?"

"Well, least favorite, and probably one of the hardest, is moving water pipes in the sugar beet fields."

"What makes it so hard?"

"A water pipe is 3 inches around and 40 feet long. I don't know what it weighs, but they are heavy enough. You have to walk through the sugar beets which grow kind of like corn to about 5 or 6 feet high, pick up those pipes where they had been watering, and move them about 70 feet over so they can water the rows that need watering next. It's hard because, unlike corn, they grow into each other at the bottom, so you're walking through a bunch of vines that have grown together. Kind of like walking with your shoelaces tied together. And because they are so tall, you have to hold the pipe over your head. To top it off the pipe has a 4 foot high sprinkler attached to one end, so when you pick it up, you have to hold it so that sprinkler stays in an up position; otherwise, when you are walking it catches in the plants. The pipe is wet and it constantly tries to turn in your hand because of that sprinkler head, so you have to grip really hard to keep it from falling over."

Allie realized that wrestling wasn't the only reason Simon looked so strong. It was actually a lifetime of working on a farm. His arms were defined with muscles and when she held his hands they were thick and calloused.

Simon continued, "And then you're moving them from where they had watered, so everything is extremely wet and you get soaked, but you move them into the area that needs to be watered so it's dry. The minute you walk into the dry area, the plants are covered with a long-seeded top that just explodes pollen so when you run into the dry plants it's like someone threw yellow baby powder in the air. And because you are wet, it all sticks to you. By the time you are done with moving 100 or 200 pipes, you look like you are caked with yellow flower. Then we leave it to water for about 4 hours and we do it again."

Allie grinned, "Okay, that sounds bad, but I'm going to need a picture of you looking like that."

"I don't think so." He smiled back.

"Can't you even take a weekend off and visit me once?"

"I'd like to, but we work every day, even Sundays, when we harvest. Each day we work until around noon and stop to eat lunch. Then we work until dinner. When it's time to combine wheat or run the bean pickers, we sometimes do that all night."

"Wait... all night? When do you sleep?" She thought maybe he was joking.

"We get sleep here and there. Usually my brother or I will run the combine until 1 or 2am, then we either take a break or switch. But when it's time to harvest most things, it needs to be done as fast as possible. Rain can ruin the wheat or grass seed. Canneries want the delivery of the beans at a certain time. It just all has to get done.

"It's not that I wouldn't like to come see you," he added, "it's just that I won't have any time. When we are working nights, I won't even have time to call or write."

Just for a moment Allie's face changed. For a moment she looked worried. It was the first time all year Simon had seen her other than happy.

"You are coming back next fall right?"

"Tell you what..." Simon said. "When you come back this fall semester, I'll pick you up at the airport."

"Deal. When I get my tickets I'll call you and let you know when I arrive."

ↄ৲

"Simon?" Once again Simon was transported back to the present. He hated everything at that moment. He hated that he wasn't with Allie. He hated that he couldn't live the rest of his life in a dream. He wished he could transport back in time and relive every moment he'd had with her.

He looked down at his plate. He'd eaten his salad, and Chelsea had finished hers. His wine was gone. He looked at Chelsea, really looked at her. She was quite breathtaking. Any man would be thrilled to be with her. He was aware of how rude it must seem, ignoring her for nearly an entire meal.

"I apologize." Simon took a deep breath and looked directly at her with eye contact that seemed so sincere. "It was rude of me to ignore you while we ate. I'm sorry for that." She believed he really was truly sorry and meant every word. She decided to try again to turn the situation to her advantage. She stared back at him, matching his gaze.

"Simon, why don't we go back to my condo for the night?"

"No." Simon never broke the stare as he spoke. "I'll walk you to your car."

For a moment she felt cheap and embarrassed. Then he continued and used her first name. When he did that, the embarrassment faded as if he was not judging her in the least.

"Chelsea," he seemed so kind at that moment, as if he was trying to explain his actions and at the same time put her at ease,

"I want you to know I appreciate just sitting here and eating dinner with you. I need nothing else."

She didn't know what to say but tried, "Okay. I was just offering to..."

"I know, but I want nothing else. Sitting here with you and not eating alone is enough."

Thankfully Rob came and interrupted the uncomfortable moment. "Can I get you two another glass of wine or dessert?"

"No, thank you, Rob," Simon replied and handed Rob his credit card. "I think we're done."

Rob left and they sat quietly. It was pleasant on the patio under the trees. The temperature had dropped with the setting sun. There was still a bright glow to the sky and a few small birds flitted about the patio, landing here and there to pick up a crumb of food or the occasional French fry. Fields of Gold by Sting was playing over the sound system on the patio and they both watched the birds and listened until Rob returned with the check.

"No hurry, stay as long as you'd like," Rob said as he handed the bill to Simon.

"Thank you, Rob."

"Thank you, Mr. Murray... Simon."

Simon filled out the credit card bill and laid it face down on the table. Then he stood.

"Can I walk you to your car?"

Chelsea had given up. "Yes, thank you."

They made their way to her car and once again he opened the door for her, stepping behind the door. She sat and he closed the door. She started the BMW and drove away. Simon was parked in a lot on the other side of the Town Center. As he walked there he failed to see the pickup pull out and follow her out of the parking lot.

Chapter 6

Two weeks later, Chelsea was in a holding pattern. She'd told herself that she would only take one more date with Simon, but she hadn't heard from him. The Democrat and the Republican were in Washington DC for some kind of session. The married men hadn't called, nor had Computer Guy. Construction Guy had called but, feeling uncomfortable, she had told him she was booked and couldn't see him that week. He wasn't happy about it and, after a lengthy conversation and an increase in her rate, she'd agreed to see him the following week. Relationships were a transaction after all, and her bank account had dwindled a bit.

Going to the grocery store after working out, she'd purchased two fresh flower arrangements. She split the pink chrysanthemums into two vases. Their fragrance filled her condo. She'd also purchased an arrangement of tulips and daffodils. The flowers weren't necessary but they made her empty condo feel warm and alive. Less lonely.

Her workout that morning had been longer than usual. She had lifted light weights and followed it up with a cardio session.

Instead of 30 to 45 minutes on the elliptical, she had stayed at it for an hour and a half. After the last couple of weeks it made her feel accomplished, something she needed.

Her condo was as immaculate as ever, her chores were done. Her workout was over. She was bored. She looked at the computer and decided to change her passwords and update the system. It was time. She needed to be safe. Then the phone rang. She looked at the caller ID and didn't even realize her spirit had lifted. It was Simon.

She picked up, "Hello Simon."

"Hello Chelsea. I was wondering if we could meet for dinner again."

"Just dinner?" she replied, hoping that maybe with a little obvious encouragement she could turn a dinner into an entire night. More time, more money, and hopefully more of a connection to exploit.

Simon didn't respond directly to her comment. "Would the same restaurant, The Milestone, at 6:00 be okay?"

"I think that would be wonderful."

It was 12:30 and she thought about the rest of her day, working backwards. She wanted to arrive early. Possibly as early as 5:15. It meant sitting around, but she wanted to get one of the couches. Hopefully she could coax him into sitting closer. Hopefully some "accidental" physical contact from sitting next to each other would move things forward.

If she arrived at 5:15, she'd need to leave the condo at 4:45, which meant she needed to start putting on her makeup and doing her hair 2:45. She looked at the clock again and decided to shower and start getting ready now. She hadn't spent an entire afternoon getting ready for something like this since high school prom, but she rationalized that there was nothing else to do. Once again, she forgot about the laptop and its security.

After showering and blow drying her hair, she dug through her closet, looking at clothes. She spent nearly an hour laying them out on her bed then putting them away, not happy with her choices. Jeans and sports jerseys. Blouses of all colors. Stretch pants and skirts. Evening dresses. From slutty to classy, from girl next door to dominant businesswoman.

She kept thinking about Simon and no outfit seemed to be right. She was frustrated. She thought about going and buying something, but when she thought about what she would buy, she already had it in the closet. Then when she pulled it out, somehow it didn't seem right.

Finally, she chose a casual summer dress. Short enough so he could see plenty of her legs, and low-cut enough to be provocative but still look like something the "girl next door" would wear. Hopeful that this evening would progress, she chose a white lace lingerie body suit for underneath.

She checked the time and realized she'd spent over two hours trying things on. Time was flying. Her hair took time as she put in a few extra brushes, a few extra curls. She spent even more time on her makeup, perfecting her brows, lashes, eye shadow, blush, everything. Finally, she chose a more natural-looking lipstick. Still glossy, but not the bright red or the deep mauve she normally wore.

Making her way to the door, Chelsea took one final look in the mirror. Attractive and appealing on the outside, seductive underneath. Mission accomplished.

Milestone Restaurant sat at the intersection of a street that ran through El Dorado Town Center with a paved walking path. The path circled a small lake, or what one might call a large pond. The street ran past the restaurant, crossed over the lake on a quaint bridge, then after passing a number of other shops all in one building, it dead-ended at a movie cineplex.

Parking seemed easier near the cineplex, so Simon showed up early and walked the quarter mile back down the street to the restaurant. As he crossed over the lake, he faced the patio and was able to spot Chelsea sitting on one of the couches again. He wasn't sure he liked the couches. It was fine if you wanted to sit, talk, and drink, but was difficult to actually eat a meal while leaning over a table not much higher than your average coffee table.

He supposed it didn't really matter. If she wanted to sit on the couch and eat, that was fine. She didn't seem to eat much anyway. Nor did he for that matter. To Simon, for the last couple years food wasn't so much a pleasure as it was a necessity. Sometimes he felt he couldn't even taste it.

He entered through the wrought iron gate again and smiled at her. She was sitting near the middle of the couch, which posed a problem. Did he sit on the couch right next to her or in a chair on the opposite side of the table?

Chelsea saw him. "Simon, it's good to see you." She put her hand on the couch next to her. "Please sit here with me."

Well, that answered that, he thought, and sat where she indicated. Now he felt awkward; it seemed too close. He reached into his suit pocket and pulled out another envelope. She took it and placed it in her purse as before.

A waitress approached, "Hey folks, thanks for joining us tonight. I'm Mary and I'll be serving you. Can I get you started with anything? Drinks? Something off our starter menu?"

Simon looked right at her. "Thank you Mary. It's nice to be here. No appetizer for me, please." Then he turned and nodded for Chelsea to go first.

"I'll have the Cali-Chicken salad."

Mary didn't write anything down, but replied, "Okay, and anything to drink?"

Chelsea looked at Simon who again nodded. "A glass of the Chardonnay please."

Mary then turned to Simon. "And for you, sir?"

"Please no Sir. My name is Simon." He said it nicely and without thinking all while looking at the menu.

"Okay, Simon, what can I get you?"

"I'll have the Basic Caesar salad."

"And to drink?"

"What do you recommend, Mary?"

"To be honest, I'm not 21 yet so I really don't know, but I'm told if you order a salad and ask, to recommend a white wine."

Simon looked up at her and smiled warmly. His laugh lines, his smile bearing witness to his genuine engagement in the conversation. "You look old enough to drink. Are you new here?"

"Yes, I'm a student at Sierra College and just started working here."

"Well I'm glad you have the job and glad we have you serving us tonight." Simon continued, "What are you studying, Mary?"

"I've just started. I took a year off after high school and now I'm trying to decide what to major in while I get my general ed stuff out of the way."

"Good for you," Simon replied. "Tell you what. I'll have the Pinot Grigio."

Again Mary didn't write it down. Simon inquired. "I'm just curious. I've been here before and the staff have always written down the orders, but you haven't. Do you just have a great memory?"

"Oh, no it's nothing like that." Mary replied. "Apparently it's a new thing. The owner just changed it. Some of the people working here didn't like it, but it was that way since I started, so it's no big deal to me. I just had to memorize the menu to make it easier."

"I was just curious."

"I can handle it, unless it's more than four people. Bigger groups are harder."

"I'm sure you'll do fine. Thank you, Mary."

"Thank you." Mary replied, seeming very much at ease. "I'll get this started for you."

As she walked away Chelsea was running through a few thoughts in her mind. Why was he so interested in Mary? Simon had spoken to the teenage waitress more than he'd spoken to her on their first date. Another thought popped into her head. Why doesn't he notice me? He didn't even compliment the way I look and I spent hours getting ready. And now a waitress says "Can I take your order?" and he already knows her story?

She couldn't help herself. "Simon. I'm curious. You always use the waiters' and waitresses' names. A few weeks ago you seemed to know our waiter personally, or at least he knew you. Just now you meet this waitress and you ask her to call you by your first name. You use her first name. You talked to her about college."

She didn't really ask a question but let the observation hang there.

"I guess it's a habit. I read a book a long time ago by a guy named Carnegie. *How to Win Friends and Influence People.* The book made an impact in several ways. Treat others with respect. Use their first names. Connect with everyone around you. Things like that. I've found over the years that those things matter and I guess it's such a habit now that I don't even think about it."

He looked at her and sensed she was ill at ease. "Does it bother you?"

"No. Well, maybe a bit."

"Why?"

"I arrived here tonight and you didn't say anything to me about how I looked. I just feel like you are more interested in the waiters and waitresses than me." Even as she said it she was thinking, Why am I saying this to him?

"I'm sorry. It was never my intention to ignore you or make you feel that way."

"Why don't you talk with me more? What are we doing here?"

"I'm uncomfortable around you. I'm not uncomfortable around them. It's as simple as that."

"Ah," she acknowledged. She wanted to ask why he was uncomfortable but she already guessed she knew the answer. He wore a wedding band. That was enough to make any man uncomfortable the first time.

"But Simon, we've been out four times now. Aren't you a little more comfortable now?"

He sat silently for a few moments, and she supposed she had her answer. He wasn't.

Their wine arrived and they sipped in silence. Shortly after, their food arrived.

"I guess I am more comfortable now than when we first met," he volunteered suddenly.

"And by the way, you do look beautiful. There isn't a man alive wouldn't agree with me. I could run through all the things that make you beautiful, but trust me, you are that."

"Thank you, Simon. I was starting to doubt myself."

At a nearby table a young man was suddenly on his knees and proposing to a young girl. The girl, crying and nodding yes, hugged him tightly. Simon and Chelsea joined the other diners on the patio in applause for the happy couple.

It reminded Simon of the summer after his freshman year.

❧

Simon was at SeaTac Airport waiting at gate C5 for Allie to arrive. In his pocket he carried an engagement ring. He was excited, but unsure when he would give it to her.

Crowds of people waited around the gate. Some waiting to board the next flight, some like him, waiting for friends and family to arrive.

Then he saw her. She exited the ramp and began looking around for him. She was very tan and her hair seemed lighter, a bit more red than brown.

Allie saw Simon and ran the twenty feet into his arms. She kissed him firmly then stepped back.

"I missed you." She looked at him as she spoke. "Oh my gosh, you're so tan. And your hair, it's practically blond." She reached up and ran her fingers though his bangs.

"I was working outside all summer."

He was wearing a T-shirt and he looked like some of the guys she'd seen on the beach who worked out daily. The difference to her was that those guys worked out like peacocks. They were narcissistic and wanted to be seen. Simon looked great accidentally, unintentionally, as a result of hard work. It made him somehow even more appealing to her that he was working so hard to help his mother and father. He was "old fashioned" in an endearing kind of way.

"You're pretty tan yourself," he commented. Then he stepped forward and reached up and took her face gently in his hands. He stared deeply at her face for a moment, his eyes moving from her mouth, back and forth across her cheeks and nose, and finally to her eyes. "God, I just love your face. Your freckles are darker."

They kissed again and then broke apart, her hand finding its way into his.

"They get darker in the sun. I used to hate them, but if you like them..." she said.

"I love 'em. Let's go get your bags and get out of here."

They made their way to the baggage claim, then out to his car. It was Saturday morning and they had two days before school started.

"You hungry?" he asked.

"I could eat. But let's get my bags into my room first."

They got to her room, dropped off her bags, then went to eat. The rest of the afternoon was spent talking about the summer. She wanted to know everything about the work on the farm, even though he thought it completely boring to talk about. Her enthusiastic interest was enough to get him to share about the entire summer. When Simon ran out of things to say about the farm, he asked Allie about her summer.

She shared about her family and the fun she'd had with her sister. "We've always gotten along, but being gone for school last year I didn't realize how much I missed her, and I think we get along even better now. All those little things that irritated us when we lived together for 18 years seem like they are gone. We had so much fun all summer just catching up and hanging out at the beach."

Eventually they made their way to dinner at a burger joint next to the college. Simon delighted in watching her dip her fries in her shake and not even looking at him as she shared about everything she'd done that summer.

After they'd finished eating, Simon found that she'd been talking nearly 30 minutes without a break. He realized she was nervous.

He interrupted her. "Allie, is there something wrong?"

She looked back at him and didn't say anything. She looked nervous or worried or even scared.

"Seriously, Allie, what is it?"

She took a deep breath in. "Simon. I hope you don't take this the wrong way, but I found out yesterday that my roommate isn't coming back."

"Okay, why would I take that the wrong way?"

"Well," she paused and took another deep breath, "I was wondering if you'd like to come spend the night?"

When Simon didn't respond immediately she blurted out, "Just forget it, I'm sorry. That was totally inappropriate."

"No... No..." Simon reached across the table and grabbed her hands. "I want to, but I need to tell you something first."

Now Simon took a deep breath. "I was raised in a small community, in a little town, and attended a tiny high school. I also feel a certain way about things."

She started to speak and he stopped her. "Just wait, let me finish.

"There are a whole bunch of things in my head right now I need to say and I'll just throw them all out there. First, I've never told anyone outside of my family that I loved them."

He was uncomfortable and avoided her eyes as he spoke. "The reason I don't say it to just anyone is because my parents taught me that love, real love, is a commitment more than a feeling. I think that's true. So I don't want to say it unless I'm committed to someone. Really committed."

He paused again, but she didn't know what to say so she waited. "And the other thing is the way I was raised, too, that if you aren't committed you shouldn't sleep together."

Allie's heart sank and she felt weak. She forced herself to let go of his strong hands and she wanted to run, but she didn't think her legs would work.

"So before I come to your dorm tonight I want to give you this." Simon reached into his pocket and pulled out a ring.

"Allie, I knew the minute I met you I loved you, but my brain told me I couldn't commit to someone I'd known for only a short time. But I know now. Being away from you all summer just made me want to never be apart again. I know I love you. I don't know how you feel, and I know this is sudden, and maybe you should think about it. I need you to feel the same way about love that I feel; otherwise, I think I'd be making a mistake. I think you'd be making a mistake.

He was finally able to look at her again and said, "I wasn't even planning on giving it to you today. I especially wasn't planning to give it to you at Bob's Burgers."

She reached over and grabbed both his hands and took the ring. "Simon, I love you... and I mean it the same way you do." Then she stood up and leaned over the table and kissed him quickly. "I really do love you."

They were quietly walking back to the dorm when Simon said, "I'm not sure if you understood everything I told you."

"I think I did. You told me love and commitment were the same to you. That to you love means your committed and that you wouldn't sleep with anyone unless you were committed."

"Yeah, and I've never told anyone I love you."

She laughed and stopped walking. She turned and hugged him warmly and whispered in his ear. "I think I understood you perfectly."

While still embracing each other she leaned back and looked him square in the eye. "Simon, I've never been with anyone either." She kissed him again, and as they made their way back to the dorm she kept looking down at the ring.

❧

Simon woke to find Allie's head on his chest, his arm around her body. She felt small, soft, and warm next to him. He looked down to see her eyes were open. She was staring down at the ring prominently displayed on her finger. Sensing he was awake she looked up at him and smiled.

"That was awesome."

Simon laughed and kissed the top of her head. "If I'd have known, I probably wouldn't have been able to wait so long."

"There were times I felt like I was the only one left in the world that didn't sleep around," Allie commented. "I'm glad I waited."

"Totally worth it," he replied.

She went back to staring at her ring for a few more moments. "Did you have a date when you want to get married?"

Unthinking, Simon replied, "I don't really care."

"What do you mean, 'you don't care'!?" She looked up at him quickly, then with confusion in her voice she continued, "Last night you said you wouldn't sleep without commitment and now you don't care when we get married?"

With one hand he turned her head, still on his chest, so his eyes met hers. "What I said last night I meant. To me the best way to measure love, to define love, is summed up in the word commitment. I refused to say 'I love you' without knowing in my mind that I was committed to you, no matter what. I love you. I'm committed to you 100 percent. Therefore I'm willing to have sex with you."

"I think it's the computer programming side of me. I'm not willing to say I love you unless I am committed to you, and I'm not willing to have sex unless I am committed."

She laughed as she thought about that. "A computer flow chart. That's romantic. I can see it on paper now. First IF THEN statement, IF you love, THEN you must be committed. Next IF THEN statement, IF committed, THEN and an arrow on the flow chart to SEX."

She said the word sex with emphasis and a giggle.

It was his turn to laugh. "I guess that's about it. My kind of logic."

"That can be the title of the next paper for one of your computer classes, Simon's Logical Love Flow Chart."

"Too long."

She tilted her head up and kissed him, then said, "How about Simon's Love"?

Then she sat up on one elbow next to him, and the blanket that was over her shoulder fell down across her waist. Her chest, no longer covered, was distracting and he had a difficult time thinking about more than just grabbing her and making love again.

"So you just don't care *when* we get married?"

"I guess what I'm saying is I don't even care if we get married. I'm 100 percent committed, and I didn't want to sleep with you unless you felt the same. But as far as marriage goes, it doesn't really matter to me."

Then he added with a smile, "I guess to me it's an unnecessary part of the flow chart. I don't care if a justice of the peace, a pastor, a priest, or anyone else for that matter says we're committed to each other. I love you and I am committed to you no matter what."

"Simon's Love," she joked, again referring to the flow chart. "So why the ring?"

"I bought it this summer when I realized I was really in love with you. I guess I expected that you would understand my commitment to you better with a ring. I just didn't think about having this long flow chart conversation."

"My flow chart has another arrow and it points to marriage," she replied.

"Your flow chart works for me too."

"Let's stop calling it a flow chart."

"Okay, I just wanted you to know how much I love you."

"Simon's love."

"Referring back to the flow chart?"

"No, I'm referring to your definition of love. Simon's love."

He was again mesmerized just looking at her face. He kissed both cheeks just below her eyes, one then the other. Then she laid back and pulled him towards her. No longer able to resist, he began to kiss her passionately.

❧

"Simon?"

He was staring down at the floor. He looked up and saw Chelsea and felt despair.

"Is something wrong?" Chelsea asked.

He looked again at the young couple just engaged. They kissed. He missed that. They were staring at one another. They were holding hands. They were smiling and happy. He missed all of it.

"No. I'm sorry, I was lost in a thought."

"Care to share it?"

"No."

He suddenly felt sorry for Chelsea. Even though he was paying for her time and he owed her nothing, he knew that she had feelings. Earlier that night when she had shared briefly how she'd felt neglected, he'd wanted to just leave. He'd wanted to go home. But he couldn't. Compassion and kindness wouldn't allow it. He realized he needed to do this for her. He took a deep breath in and shook off the despair.

"Would you like to take a walk around the lake with me?" he asked.

"I would love to."

Simon couldn't tell if she were saying that because she really meant it, or if it was because he was paying her. He proceeded with the idea that she really meant what she said.

He paid the bill and they exited through a side gate directly onto the paved walking path that circled the lake. For a while they walked in silence. He was keenly aware of how close she was to him. He could smell her perfume and occasionally she'd brush up against his side as they walked. The sun was just setting but the path around the lake was lit with short ground lights. Other people, either walking dogs, jogging, or strolling along like they were, passed in both directions. Simon sensed the silence growing and felt he needed to speak. To be nice. To be kind.

"You asked me once if I was sad, and even though I didn't directly ask it, my question for you is 'Why this? Why this as a career?'"

Chelsea kept walking alongside him. "Would you like me to answer that question now?"

Simon thought about that for a long moment. He couldn't lie but he also couldn't tell her he was uninterested in her answer. That he was uninterested in her. Even though she kept brushing up against him, giving him such obvious signals, he had no desire to sleep with her. He was uninterested in everything.

"Why don't you just tell me about your family instead?"

"I don't have a family. I was an only child. I knew my mother, but never had a father. My mother died when I was 17." Chelsea said it flatly without emotion. Then she quickly moved on.

"I think it's my turn to ask a question. Why are we only eating out these last few weeks?"

He knew what she was implying. How could he tell her that he just didn't want to eat alone? How could he tell her that he just wanted to use her to avoid his own loneliness?

He took a slow deep breath and said, "Honestly? I'd like to just listen to you talk."

She thought about that for a moment. He wants you to just talk to him. What do you say to a guy you know nothing about? How do you just say something when you don't know what to say? They had at least another half mile to go to complete the circle around the lake and then back to her car. It would take a half hour at this pace. She could make something up, but she felt very much like he would know if she were lying. Could she talk to him, no lies, just speak honestly for 30 minutes? And then she decided she didn't care, she would try.

"Well, let me start with something simple," she began. "I like Scrabble."

He stopped and turned to her, surprised. "Scrabble?"

"Yes Scrabble." She was irritated and let it show. Not a good idea in her line of work. Not good for cultivating a repeat customer. She didn't care. Was he making fun of her? Did he think she was too stupid to play Scrabble?

"You know, the game? Little wooden tiles with letters? You spell words?" Her words came out bitter and harsh.

Simon laughed. It was disarming. "I know what it is, you just surprised me."

"Why?" she wanted to say. Because a girl like me can't possibly like a cerebral game like Scrabble? But instead she just said, "What is so surprising about that?"

"I guess it's just that I didn't know what you were going to say," Simon replied. "Maybe after you posed the question I was thinking... you know... 'How'd you get into this line of work,' I was expecting something more serious."

He was still smiling, and in reaction to her anger, he raised his hands up as if to say, don't shoot.

"I like Scrabble. It's a great game." Then he added, "It says a lot about you."

She was looking at him and realizing again how his face lit up when he smiled. Her comment about Scrabble had drawn the biggest smile out of him since they'd met.

More relaxed now, she turned to continue their walk around the lake. Another couple, walking faster, came up behind them intrusively. A jogger was coming in the opposite direction preventing the other couple from going around them. Simon reached out and lightly took Chelsea's arm just below the elbow.

He led her onto the grass between the path and the edge of the lake. Other than her attempts to make physical contact, it was the first time he had touched her. She felt as if there were a shot of electricity in his warm hand on her arm.

The couple passed them and the jogger continued in the opposite direction. They stepped back onto the path and resumed walking.

"So what do you think playing Scrabble says about me?" She was no longer defensive. Just curious.

"I'd say that if you like Scrabble, you probably like reading. People who like Scrabble usually have a pretty good vocabulary and can spell. Those two things really only come from reading. Am I right so far?"

She nodded her head, "Okay, go on. What else?"

"I may be wrong but I think playing Scrabble takes a little bit of an artist. You have to see the word even though it's not written in front of you. Kind of like a sculptor who chisels a statue out of stone. They say the statue was already there, they just chipped away the extra pieces."

Simon stopped talking as another couple caught up to them from behind. They stepped off the path again, letting the couple pass. The sun had set, leaving behind a pink and orange glow in the west. The color faded into a deep blue directly above them and that in turn turned to a dark blue, almost black, in the east. The stars were beginning to shine and they stepped back onto the path.

Simon continued his thought. "I'd say Scrabble is like painting a work of art. You have to see it in your head before you paint it, or in the case of Scrabble, spell it. I'll bet you like art more than anything else. I'll bet you have some paintings or art in your house."

Chelsea thought of the painting hanging above the antique desk, "The Color of Warm." It was almost like he'd been in her home the way he described it all... she shivered.

He noticed her shiver. "I'm sorry, I'm wearing a coat and you didn't plan on walking around after sunset wearing only a dress."

He took off his coat and turned to place it on her. She thought about telling him she wasn't in the least bit cold, but decided better of it. As he placed the coat over her, his hands landed lightly on her shoulders. She shivered again.

"That should help." He stepped back and they continued walking.

"So was I right? Do you read? Do you like some type of art? Or is my Scrabble prediction totally off base?"

"Yes," she replied quietly. This man, knowing something so personal about her, left her with a feeling she couldn't describe. She wasn't sure if she liked it. Somehow she felt vulnerable like he knew something about her no one else knew. Then she placed the feeling... it was intimacy. Her mind quickly recoiled from the thought. How could that be? She'd never as much as kissed him. She couldn't even get him to sleep with her. How could she feel like they were intimate?

They continued walking silently again. The light in the west was now nearly gone and the path wound around back towards where they started. She tried to put the thought out of her head. She couldn't feel intimacy with a man she was going to fleece. Then she reminded herself, relationships are transactional. Intimacy is not a part of any relationship, just a momentary feeling.

Finally she broke their silence. "What about you Simon? Do you like art?"

"I like Scrabble," he said as if that explained everything.

"So does that mean you have a special painting that you love hanging on one of your walls? Or is it a sculpture?"

"Actually, I have a guitar."

"A guitar?" she said, curious about the revelation.

"That surprises you?"

"Yeah, I guess it does."

"Why?"

"Well I've only seen you wearing a suit, and it's led me to only think of you as a businessman." She stole a glance at him. She couldn't imagine him on a stage playing in a band.

Then she quietly added, "I guess I just don't really know you."

"Earlier tonight you guessed some things about me." She noticed him taking a deep breath, as if talking about himself was difficult. Then he continued, "You were right about those things... And I like Scrabble."

They walked in silence for the remainder of the circle around the lake. Simon realized he hadn't thought about Allie for nearly their entire walk. He was grateful to Chelsea but said nothing. Then, as he thought of Allie, he felt as if a weight was dropped back down upon him.

"My car is over there," Chelsea said, and led the way to the lot where she was parked.

The feeling was back but it was a bit different. At first it was a feeling of closeness because he knew something about her. Now she felt she knew something personal about him.

They arrived at her car and, once again, she unlocked the door and he held it open for her, keeping the door between him and her. No opening to kiss him. She immediately climbed into the car and he shut the door. She started the car and drove away.

Simon stood there watching her go, then turned and noticed the pickup. It had just started up and was moving out of the parking lot. Same 1973 Ford F-150. Same dent. It was at the far end of the parking lot but it was unmistakable. It was too dark to see the driver. Must be a worker at the restaurant or another store in the area, Simon thought.

Chapter 7

Two weeks had passed and Simon was walking through the Palladio towards the Back Bistro. Springtime was rushing towards summer and Sacramento was growing very hot. If they had agreed to meet for lunch it would have been too hot to sit on the concrete patio. Even 5pm may have been uncomfortably warm. It was now almost 6:30 and the delta breezes had kicked in so the patio would be pleasant.

As he approached the restaurant, he saw Chelsea coming from the opposite direction. The corners of his mouth turned up ever so slightly. It was ironic, he thought. She was a head turner. Any man alive would see her approaching, dressed like that, and take a second look. Yet he was uninterested.

She wore a very low-cut green tank top style shirt or body suit, he couldn't tell which. It was form fitting and tucked into a full-length skirt. The tight material across her toned stomach only served to make her breasts seem larger. The white and green floral patterned skirt had a slit that reached her upper thigh and revealed a very long, tone, and tan leg which was made longer by the high heels she was wearing. It was a very revealing outfit and it made Simon uncomfortable.

She reached the front door where he waited.

"Hello Simon, it's good to see you," she said.

He could smell her perfume as she stood close to him. He felt awkward and didn't know what to say. The simple word "hello" was too formal, but "hi" would be too casual.

"Thanks for meeting me." Even as he said it he realized it sounded like a business meeting. He wanted to say something else, but stood uncomfortably, looking at her, for a moment. A compliment, he thought.

She had changed her hair. It was very curly, and significantly lighter blonde. He had no idea if the curls were something permanent or not. It made her look young and playful.

"You look nice tonight."

"Thank you, Simon." Then she added, "I didn't think you'd notice."

Was she being sarcastic? Was she just trying to joke around or actually making fun of his compliment? Not notice her dressed like that? He gave up thinking about it and turned towards the restaurant. He opened the door to allow her to walk in before him.

Inside, nearly every seat at the bar was taken and there were only a few vacant tables left. There were multiple TVs above the bar; one had an NBA game between the Spurs and the Pelicans, another an MLB game. There was no sound from the TVs, but had there been, no one would have been able to hear it above the general noise. The music playing over the restaurant's audio system was just loud enough to be heard.

"Welcome to Back Bistro." The host greeted them. "Table for two?"

Several tables near the middle of the dining area had been pushed together and a large group of women sat together. Black mylar balloons, shaped in the number 40, floated above the middle of their tables, tied to a black centerpiece. The women were laughing loudly and could be heard throughout the restaurant.

"Yes, but on the patio," Simon replied, wanting to escape some of the noise.

As they walked towards the patio Simon was keenly aware of the men looking at Chelsea. With the low-cut tight shirt and the skirt with the slit reaching nearly to the top of her thigh, it was no wonder. Even some of the women at the party stole a glance at her as she walked by.

Though still crowded, the patio was significantly quieter. The hostess led them to the only remaining empty table. They sat as she placed the menus on the table.

"Your server will be with you in a moment."

"Thank you, Bobbie," Simon replied.

Chelsea looked up and saw that she was wearing a name tag.

It wasn't quiet on the patio, but it wasn't loud either. The expanse of the outdoors made that a reality. The myriad of conversations, laughter, and silverware clinking on plates would make it impossible for others to listen to their conversation. Plus some rock music from an older generation was playing in the background.

Now that she was sitting, Chelsea drew a lot less attention. Simon relaxed a bit.

Simon took an envelope from his suit and once again placed it on the table between them and once again she took the envelope and dropped it into her purse on the floor next to her.

"Thank you for asking me out again, Simon."

He found it odd that she spoke like they were on a date but she thanked him much like he had thanked business customers in the past.

"I'm glad we could eat dinner together again," he replied.

There it was already, Chelsea thought. He was as much as saying "dinner only." It was only the beginning of the date, but she was certain at the end the car door would be between them again and he would be closing it with her inside.

The waiter approached and set a glass of water in front of each of them. "Hey folks, can I get you something to start off with? Drinks or an appetizer?"

Simon, ever the same, took a quick glance at his name tag and responded, "Hello Jim." Then he took an obvious look around at the crowded patio. "It looks like a good night to be working."

"Yes, I suppose it is. I'm not so sure why it's this crowded. Must be something going on in town."

Simon noticed the wedding band on Jim's finger and asked, "Are you married, Jim? Got kids?"

"Uh yeah, I'm married." Jim was a bit hesitant. It wasn't a question most patrons asked. "No kids."

"Well, I appreciate you are willing to serve us tonight. Maybe as crowded as it is you'll have a great night. Maybe make a little extra for you and your wife."

"Yeah, hopefully." Jim realized that this man in the suit was pulling for him and added, "Thanks man, but before I worry about everyone else, let's get you two started off with something."

Simon nodded at Chelsea to go first.

"I'll have the Pinot Noir," Chelsea said.

"I'll have the same."

"Okay, two Pinot Noirs coming up," Jim replied and left them.

They sat quietly drinking water. Two women sitting at a table next to them were talking about a man. The conversation was just audible enough to pick up bits and pieces. "... it was your second date?" "... he seems so nice..." "... I'm not sure if I'd trust him...." It went on and on. Neither Chelsea nor Simon were intentionally listening, then one of them whispered loudly, "Oh my god you slept with him?"

"SSSHHH." The other woman looked in Simon and Chelsea's direction. Both were looking at each other as if not to have heard a thing, and the woman looked back at her friend. "Shit. Not so loud." Then they continued their conversation.

Chelsea looked at Simon and smiled. Simon smiled back but said nothing. It got her thinking. Would they ever sleep together? Why was he so uninterested in something every other client wanted? Should she ask him? That felt risky. Then she decided she had nothing to lose.

"Simon, may I ask you a more personal question?"

"You can ask me anything you'd like, but I'll decide if I want to answer it or not."

"Fair enough," she said.

She kept her voice very quiet, making certain not to be overheard by the other tables.

"We've been out a number of times. Each time you've paid money for a four-hour date. Each time you've overpaid. And each time you've left early, as soon as dinner was over. Our first date you were barely there an hour."

Simon took a sip of water and paused, thinking about his answer. "I just don't want to eat alone. I wanted a conversation that was all."

She sat for a moment taking that in and wondering if she should ask more, but decided against it. She had tried being sweet and sexy. She'd tried being obvious. Tonight she went for a completely sultry look. Nothing had worked. She looked at the ring on his finger and wondered if that was the reason. With nothing to lose she tried another question.

"Tell me about your wife."

"No." His response was instantaneous and left no room for questions. For the first time since meeting him he seemed harsh, almost angry. It left an uncomfortable silence between them. After a moment each reached for their water as a way to mask the empty moment.

Thankfully, the waiter arrived with their wine and took their orders. He left and the silence resumed. Chelsea's mind returned to her original purpose for dating him. To fleece him. In order to do that she had to get closer to him. The only way that she knew to do that was to sleep with him. To sleep with him and get him to need her so much that he was willing to pay more and more. But he wasn't cooperating. He wasn't interested in what she had to offer, and it left her without her only weapon.

She took a sip of wine and didn't like her own thoughts. Use sex against him as a weapon? Suddenly it seemed very distasteful. He was a kind person and paying her for a conversation. He wasn't asking for anything anyone wouldn't give. So why did he choose her?

"So why me?"

He looked at her, confused.

"Why pay me for a conversation? You are personable. You obviously have no problem carrying on a conversation with random people. Why me?"

He didn't answer and at that moment his face changed. Even when he was stone-faced the corners of his mouth were usually smiling, but not now. The laugh lines were still there, but suddenly he looked as sad as anyone she'd ever seen. It was his eyes. There were no tears, but the way he looked at her almost made her want to cry. Why did he look so sad? What had she said?

Simon swallowed hard and looked away. An eternity seemed to pass in silence.

"It's just easier this way," he said as if that explained everything.

Chelsea was frustrated. One moment she thought he was opening up, the next there was nothing from him. Maybe she should just give up trying to take advantage of him. Maybe she should just enjoy getting paid a ridiculous amount to eat dinner with him and call it good enough. Maybe taking advantage of him was wrong; after all, she liked him.

That thought stopped her in the middle of a sip of wine. She'd never liked any of the men she'd met before. Why did she like Simon? Why would she develop any feelings for the one man who clearly had no feelings for her?

The waiter arrived with their food and placed their plates in front of each of them, a salad for her and a small flat iron steak for him.

"Is there anything else I can get you?"

"No thank you, Jim," Simon answered for them both. "I think we are good for now."

Jim left and they both began to eat. Van Morrison's song Crazy Love began to play over the restaurant's sound system and Chelsea listened for a few moments. She thought about how much she liked the song and desperately wanted to end the silence.

"I've always liked this song," she started. "Do you like it?"

Simon didn't respond and she looked up to see his blank sad stare. He was sitting right in front of her and he hadn't even heard her. He was no longer even eating. He was just sitting, looking down, staring at nothing.

❧

It was March 5th, the night before the wedding. The wedding party and both families were all sitting at Buca Di Beppo, an Italian eatery in San Diego. The rehearsal for the wedding was over and everyone was a bit more relaxed now that they'd finished a meal.

Simon's mother and father had made the trip down. The farm work in Oregon at this time of year was lighter and it was often too wet to actually work the fields. Simon noticed his father, stern of face, looked out of place in the city. His mother, always smiling and happy, looked at home no matter where she was. They were engaged in a conversation with Allie's parents that no doubt went as deep as possible for people who really didn't know each other.

Simon's brother Paul and his wife Diane sat at a table with their three-year-old son. Allie's younger sister, Angela, and Allie were at the same table. Both were laughing and playing with the three-year-old. Angela had a small bottle of bubbles and was blowing them to entertain the boy. Where she got the bubbles Simon had no idea.

The rest of the wedding party, friends of Allie's and Simon's from high school as well as college, sat around visiting and filling the room with stories and jokes. Each had been given an invitation that included a plus one if they wished. Generally, local friends had brought a date or a friend; those flying in from out of town had not. Simon's friends were greatly outnumbered by Allie's, not that it mattered to him. Grandparents, the minister, and the wedding coordinator rounded out the group of nearly 35 people. It made him nervous knowing what he had planned.

Simon nodded to Paul who quietly got up and left the room. A few minutes later he stood and made his way to a spot where everyone could see him.

"Hey, if I could get everyone's attention," he started in. The room went from a loud mix of conversations to totally silent. His heart was racing and he took a couple deep breaths and tried to relax. Then he looked right at Allie's parents and addressed them.

"Bob and Marie, I want to start off and just say thank you. Thank you for giving us your blessing to marry. Thank you for bringing this amazing person into the world so she and I could find our way to each other. She is the most amazing person I've ever met. I think she is the most beautiful person in the world inside and out. She has the most wonderful personality of anyone I've ever met in my life and I know that you are the major reason she is who she is. I promise you that for the rest of my life I will do everything I can to make her happy and in turn make you proud that she chose me as her husband."

He had spent almost no time with her parents and felt he had to assure them that he wanted nothing but the best for her. It was an awkward speech but he knew no words would convince them. Their confidence in him would only come with time and success but at least it was a start. Then he turned to Allie.

"Allie, I've kept a secret from you. A big secret." He let that statement hang for a second, just to build a little suspense. Paul walked back into the room at that moment carrying a guitar and handed it to Simon.

"I've never told you that I like to play a guitar."

Everyone laughed and Simon continued.

"Allie, the first time we met we spent the night together..." As he said it there was an audible gasp in the room and people started talking.

"No, wait wait... that's not what I meant," Simon nearly shouted over the noise. Allie just laughed.

"What you should all know is that the first time we met we sat in a Starbucks TALKING all night."

Allie and her sister were laughing and Simon looked at her parents who were now smiling at the misstatement.

"Okay, I need to start over." Simon began again, "Allie, that first night when we met, and we spent the entire night talking," Simon emphasized, "I am sure I fell in love with you that first night. I fell in love with your laugh. I fell in love with your voice. I love that you are kind and filled with hope. I saw all of that the first night. Do you remember talking about your freckles that day we were in the park?"

Allie looked at Simon nervously and simply mouthed the word "yes."

"I started writing this song the day after we had that conversation. I cannot imagine anyone ever bringing such a brightness to my life. I know we've talked about love. I expressed to you that the best definition of love, to me, is a commitment, and Allie I'm committed completely to you for the rest of my life."

He took another deep breath, "So I wrote this song. Allie, I love you." With that he started playing.

> *The moment we met*
> *I knew I loved you*
> *Sudden loneliness*
> *Was a life without you*
>
> *The moment we met*
> *I saw in your eyes*
> *My future was clear*
> *Like a morning sunrise*
>
> *You're my light, a radiant sight,*
> *   a snowcapped peak, a star at night*
> *You're my light, a radiant sight*
> *   A noonday sun hitting waves on high*

Simon was close to choking up and knew he wouldn't be able to keep singing and playing if he looked at her so he kept his eyes fixed on his own hands and continued.

> *The moment we met*
> *And heard your light laugh*
> *From that moment forever*
> *I was caught in your path*

The moment we met
I saw perfect loveliness
The world has no treasure
No gem to compare

You're my light, a radiant sight,
  a snowcapped peak, a star at night
You're my light, a radiant sight
  A noonday sun hitting waves on high

As he sang the chorus the second time he looked up and saw Allie. She was staring at him and laughing. Tears and mascara were running down her face. She had a napkin, soaked with mascara, and she knew her face was a mess. Angela was trying to grab napkins from around the table and help. When Angela handed Allie a few more napkins both laughed.

Crying and laughing, with mascara and tears running down her face, he thought she was more beautiful than at any other time he'd seen her. His voice started to break and he looked back down to gain his composure and continued with the bridge in the song.

A living rose that lights my life
There is nothing else in the world to see
No artist the world has ever known
Could contain your beauty in a masterpiece

You're my light, a radiant sight,
  a snowcapped peak, a star at night
You're my light, a radiant sight
  A noonday sun hitting waves on high

You're my light, a radiant sight,
        a snowcapped peak, a star at night
You're my light, a radiant sight
        A noonday sun hitting waves on high

When he finished, everyone started clapping and yelling. Simon and Allie looked at each other, and in the same moment they both mouthed silently I love you. Allie stood up and quickly made her way to him and hugged him. With the guitar pressed between them, they kissed.

જ

"Simon?" Chelsea said a second time. "You there?"

Simon looked up and saw her and the despair sank into him again. He hadn't eaten his food but he wasn't hungry. He wanted to leave, but it could be construed as mean, or rude. He just couldn't do that.

He forced himself to breathe in, almost a shuddering breath.

"Sorry," Simon said and forced himself to take several bites of his steak. After a few moments he calmed down and looked at her, forcing a smile.

"Did you ask me a question?" he asked.

"I did, but I have a different question." She was just making small talk when she asked about the song. She decided that she wanted to ask him the other question on her mind.

"Simon, don't you think it makes people uncomfortable when you use their first names all the time?"

"I guess I didn't even think about it. You asked me about it before," Simon replied. "Does it bother you?"

"No. Well, at first it did. I thought you were doing it for some reason to impress me or seem important. But once I realized it was just what you do naturally... no it doesn't bother me."

Simon smiled. "What makes you think I'm not trying to look important or impress you?"

"Are you?"

"No." Simon smiled. "As I said before, it was just something I learned."

"But you always greet them by name. And you talk, not just about the food, but about their lives. Your conversations are personal to each person you talk to. I guess I just figure if you put that much effort into your conversations with complete strangers..."

"Then you wonder why I don't put in more effort with you," Simon said, finishing her thought.

"Well, yes."

"Tell you what, Chelsea," Simon said, intentionally using her name, "I'll do better."

Simon smiled that small smile where the corners of his mouth turn up slightly. For just a moment he hadn't thought about Allie, and what a relief it seemed.

Then Simon said, "Thank you."

Chelsea looked up from her salad, confused. "Thank you?"

Simon looked directly into her eyes and paused. "Yes, thank you. Thank you for being here and providing me company. Thank you for being honest and pointing out that I can be more attentive. Thank you."

In her life Chelsea had never felt liked she had been thanked in a more heartfelt way and yet she had no idea why. It was hard and it was wrong but she liked Simon, and if she liked him she couldn't take advantage of him.

The waiter stopped by and refilled their waters. He saw the half-eaten steak and asked, "Was everything okay with your meal?"

"Yeah, Jim, it was fine. I guess I just wasn't very hungry."

"Can I get you a box to go?"

"No, I think we are finished. If you could bring the check I'd appreciate it."

"Sure," Jim said and left them alone.

"We've not been here very long." Chelsea said. Without pointing out that he paid for more time, she added, "Would you like to do anything after dinner?"

Simon thought about it and decided against it. "No, but thank you again."

He paid the check and walked her out of the restaurant and to her car. She noticed that, exactly like the previous dates, he moved so the car door was between them.

"Thank you again for the date, Simon," she said as she got into the driver's seat.

"You're welcome," was all he said. But this time he surprised her by not closing the door. Instead, he leaned over the door a bit and looked down at her.

"Chelsea could we just go ahead and plan on dinner again next Friday?"

"I think that would be nice, Simon. Did you have a place and time you'd like to meet?"

"How about 6:00 at Sutter Street Steakhouse?" Simon asked. "It's located in Old Town Folsom."

"Yes, that would be fine."

Simon closed the door and she started the engine. As she drove away, he stood for a moment before beginning to walk back towards the shopping area and his car on the other side. Once again he noticed the Ford F-150. It was the same pickup. Same year. Same make. Same dent. It pulled out of the parking lot just a moment after Chelsea's BMW had left.

Funny, he thought, the same pickup three weeks in a row on a Friday night. What are the odds, he wondered. Twice it was a shopping center just up the hill. Then tonight it was the shopping area here. Then he told himself there was really nothing strange about it. It was kind of nice, he thought, that he kept seeing the same pickup he'd grown up with.

Chapter 8

Chelsea sat in the living room of her condo and stared at the painting hanging above her desk. She smiled at her renaming of it, "The Color of Warm." She had matched the paint in the condo to those in the painting. Sitting beneath the painting were flowers purchased the day before. Now sunlight showered in from the morning sun through her white sheer curtains. Curtains that also matched those in the painting. "Nailed it," she thought. Her condo captured the warmth of the flowers and the sunlight as the painting did. There was one thing it didn't capture. There was a little boy in the painting. Chelsea had no child and no family. She put the negative thought out of her head. What she needed was a longer run this morning. That meant getting breakfast and getting going.

The man in the pickup had parked just down from the locked gates on a side street 90 minutes earlier. From his vantage point he could just see between two of the condominium units to her door. If she exited her front door he would see her; if she drove out he couldn't, but in that situation he would see her BMW moments later as it exited the gates. He had called her several times over the last few weeks and only gotten her voicemail. She hadn't called him back and it pissed him off. Didn't she know who he was? It wasn't like she'd been on a bunch of dates. As a matter of fact, in the last few weeks, she'd only been on a few dates with the guy in the suit. He wasn't even sure if those were dates. They never kissed, they never went back to her place or a hotel after dinner. Maybe he was just her brother or a cousin or something. It didn't matter. He was patient, he could wait.

In her mind, Chelsea was busy planning her morning. It was beautiful outside, but likely to be hot by the time she finished her run. So, along with her Greek yogurt and granola, she drank extra water. She felt particularly good so she planned to make the long run all the way up the American River to Folsom Lake. On a Thursday morning it wouldn't be crowded so if she decided to walk even further she would have the lake to herself. She wondered about the distance and decided it didn't matter. She would take her phone and Uber back.

She caught a glimpse of herself in the full-length mirror on her closet door. How many 37-year-old women could wear a sports bra and Lycra shorts and still look like they had the body of a teenager? She turned sideways and put her hand on her stomach and looked again. Okay, not a teenager. Not many teens had the curves she had, but they were in the right places. She put on her running shoes, drank another small glass of water, and grabbed an armband that could hold her phone. She stuffed her key, her driver's license, and a credit card in the armband behind the phone and grabbed her headphones. She headed out the front door with an iTunes workout mix playing loudly in her ears.

He saw her exit the condo from the front door. Good, she was going for a run along the river. He started his truck and pulled out slowly. He knew exactly where she was going.

For the first half mile Chelsea decided she would walk and let her breakfast settle a bit. The music was motivating, and she was ready to run, but figured she'd wait until she got to the paved path along the river first. Her mind was going nonstop from one thing to another so she started organizing her thoughts into three categories. There were things she needed to do, things she probably should do, and then things she wanted to do. She needed to get her oil changed. She wanted to book a trip to Hawaii or maybe someplace in Europe. Maybe she should dye her hair a different color. She needed to tell Construction Guy she was no longer available. She'd been avoiding his calls. For that matter, she'd been avoiding most of her customers' calls lately. She didn't feel like going out with anyone. On the other hand, Simon was different. She was hoping he would call.

That reality sunk in for a moment as she made her way down the path. It was a stupid thought. There was nothing to be gained by limiting herself to dating only one man. And this particular man seemed to almost ignore her at times. But when he was present with her and not zoning out in some kind of weird quiet moment, he was kind. When they did talk he seemed genuine and attentive. What stood out most to her was his smile. She loved his little smile, where his mouth turned up ever so slightly at the ends and the corners of his eyes wrinkled. And those rare moments when he actually broke into a full smile made her feel as if he was the most warm and honest person in the world. When he smiled like that he would look right at her and it felt like he was welcoming her into a moment in time where the two of them shared the greatest inside joke in the world. Just the two of them, smiling and sharing that moment.

She told herself she had to stop thinking about Simon as she stepped out a back gate, leaving the condo units. The gate swung shut and locked behind her. In order to make her way to the river trail she had to travel down a dirt path that ran through a green belt.

He pulled his pickup into the parking area for the trails and got out. There was no one around. If someone had been, he'd have waited for another day. He thought about the brush along the path and the unusual route she took. It was not the main path. The route she chose took shortcuts off the paved, well-traveled path and onto dirt trails that very few used.

The cooler morning air was being driven away by the sun. He felt the sweat roll down his back beneath his shirt and he wiped his hands on his jeans. He thought about what she was wearing. It pissed him off. A running bra and tight spandex like volleyball shorts. He walked the paved path for a short distance from the parking lot then saw the dirt trail. The shortcut she took so often. He looked in both directions. No one was in sight. He quickly stepped off the pavement and made his way up through the brush.

Chelsea headed down the path towards the running trail along the American River. It was funny that people referred to this as a green belt. In actuality it was a swath of land about two to three hundred feet wide where nothing was built due to the overhead power lines. The communities around Folsom Dam had numerous "green belts" with so many power lines running from the dam. Beneath the high-tension wires was unkept land, overgrown brush, growing sometimes to 15 feet in height, and tall grass that was starting to turn brown with the summer's heat, making the term "green belt" inaccurate. It was, however, a little bit of wild in an otherwise urban setting. Occasionally, she saw rabbits, deer, and every now and then a coyote. Overgrown brown-bush-belt would have been a better term for it, but the path through it gave her quick access to the nicer paved trail along the river; otherwise, she would be walking along a heavily trafficked road for almost double the distance. The dirt path was quicker and easier, and she could travel along under the power lines in the quiet, listening to her music.

Her mind returned to things she needed. She probably should buy a new computer. She needed to update her computer if she didn't buy a new one. She looked down at her shoes as she walked. Did she need new shoes or just want them? She decided she needed them.

She reached the paved trail and let a biker pass, then she started to run. She wasn't running fast but it was enough to get her heart rate up and she knew she could keep up the pace for at least five miles. Really, she had no idea how long she could keep up the pace. She'd never tested herself. She simply ran until she didn't want to run anymore. Some days she'd run three miles; others she'd run five. When the weather was perfect and she felt good she'd run her normal route up this path then cut through another green belt to another running and biking path. She felt great today. The sun felt hot against her skin. So much the better. She would get a tan and exercise at the same time.

She came up to the dirt path that led through another green belt and stepped off the pavement. She didn't run though this area. The trail was uneven, and rocky at times. The brush sometimes grew so close together that she had to push it back like a door to pass through.

She walked through a particular area where the brush grew right up to the trail on both sides. The music was loud enough that she heard nothing, but in her peripheral vision she saw a quick movement from the brush on her right. Startled, she swerved. The opposite side of the path was thick with brush and she ran into it. She never really saw him before his arm slid around her neck. She started to scream for help but it was cut off as his other hand clasped over her mouth. He was behind her and she felt herself being jerked off her feet. The arm around her felt like it would crush her throat as he held her a few feet off the ground. She kicked and fought like mad but he was behind her and simply carried her backwards across the path and deeper into the brush from where he came.

The hand clasped over her mouth was huge and for a moment she thought how it was disgustingly sweaty. The wet hand felt like it covered her entire lower face. She tried to scratch and claw at it, but felt her fake nails tear off. Well off the path now, he suddenly twisted with immense violence and slammed her face first down on the ground, his huge body landing with all its weight on top of her. The air exploded from her lungs. She felt like her insides were shattered. His hand released from her mouth but she had no wind to scream or even struggle. Pain erupted in her sides and she couldn't breathe. Then he hit her across the back of her head and suddenly things were fading. She felt him punch her repeatedly in the back and sides. He grabbed her by the hair and smashed her face into the ground repeatedly. She felt her forehead slam into a large rock. Smaller rocks and dirt tore into her face as he continued to repeatedly slam her face down. Blood was dripping down into the dirt, pooling into mud beneath her face.

She went nearly limp beneath him, but he didn't stop. He turned her over and put both hands around her throat and squeezed. She looked up at him, her eyes wide in panic. Everything was cloudy and hazy. The pain was no longer as intense and she realized she was close to passing out. Between the blood and dirt in her eyes and the concussive blows she no longer saw anything but the bright light of the sun behind a dark form squeezing her throat.

She was now fading into nothing. Her arms felt heavy and she was no longer able to move. He continued to squeeze his hands around her throat. He was excited and thrilled at the same time. Never in his life had he felt such rage and power and control all at once. Watching her eyes grow wider, almost pleading with him, he shoved her head down hard one more time. For a brief moment his mind told him that if he stopped now he would be able to control her. That she'd have to do what he said. Her eyes were still begging him. With his hands still around her neck he jerked her up and slammed her head into the ground once more. Then he watched her eyes slowly close. He squeezed a moment longer then slowly took his hands away.

Sweat dripped off his brow into the dirt next to her. He felt as if his heart pounding in his chest would burst. He simply wanted to scare the shit out of her, but it was over now. Somehow those eyes, wide and pleading, had created a rage in him. She'd made him do it. He had only wanted to scare her so bad that she'd agree not to see anyone else, but now as he looked down, he saw she was laying motionless. He looked around, making sure he was unseen. Her body was well back from the trail. He thought about burying her but his heart was racing. He had to get out of there in case anyone else came by. He was still on his knees, straddling her.

He got up quickly and made his way back down the dirt trail. Just before he got to the paved path he stopped. He looked down at himself. There was some blood on his knuckles from where he'd struck her. He tried to wipe it off but it was dried on. He brushed the dirt off the knees of his jeans and looked out from the brush in both directions. No one was coming so he stepped out onto the path and made his way to his truck.

❦

At 6:30pm a couple was walking the dirt path between the condos and the river trail. They had both worked that day and had come home to a quick dinner. Now they were trying to get in some exercise before the day was done. The husband stopped and turned to his wife.

"Dang it, I should have used the bathroom before we left. I gotta go."

"Dummy," she said. "You want to go back?"

"No, I'll just go back here a ways in case anyone comes." He stepped off the path and made his way back into the brush to relieve himself.

The woman waiting on the dirt path heard him suddenly exclaim, "Holy shit!"

"What?"

"There is a dead woman's body. Holy shit. Holy shit." The man half yelled it. "Don't come back here."

He came out of the brush back onto the path with his wife. "Got your phone?"

She nodded yes, her eyes wide. "Are you sure she's dead?"

"Call 911." The man's face was white. "Yeah, you don't want to see that. Holy shit, holy shit. Looks like she was beat to death. Fuck."

Twenty-five minutes later Detective VanDyke walked up the dirt trail to where several people had now congregated. He felt the sweat already running down his back and hated the department's standard that he wear a suit. It was bad enough that he had to spend money on suits. Then soaking the suits with sweat meant he had to spend money on dry cleaning way too often. The whole situation added to his irritation.

He looked at the folks in front of him. Two patrol officers, a couple that looked like they had been out for a run, and coming up behind him a couple of guys from the fire department with a gurney.

One of the officers was keeping a few folks back farther up the trail. No surprise, the looky-loos were already showing up. The other officer was standing, white faced, alone as VanDyke approached him. He'd never met the officer before and checked his nameplate.

"What do we got, Officer Hinson?"

"A body, sir. Female. She's back off the trail over here." He pointed in the general direction and started to lead the way. When they stepped through the brush, Hinson stepped to the side, allowing VanDyke the opportunity to see and approach the body.

"First time finding a body, officer?"

"Yes sir."

"How long you been on the job?"

"Only two weeks, sir."

"Well, tell me what you know so far." He figured the rookie would get over his squeamish demeanor quicker if he started acting more like a cop.

"Sir, the couple back there found the body at approximately eighteen thirty. They called it in."

"You interview them?"

"Yes sir."

"What's their story?"

"They were both walking for exercise and the guy needed to take a leak, so he stepped back off the trail here and found her."

"Pretty big coincidence him stepping off right here don't you think?"

"Maybe."

"So they found her at eighteen thirty and called it in immediately?"

"I assume so, sir."

"Don't assume." VanDyke hated the sloppy approach he was already seeing. "Did you check with dispatch? What exact time did the call come in?"

"I'm not sure."

The crime lab guys had now shown up and were now starting to tape things off. The guys with the gurney waited while a tech took pictures.

"All right." His irritation was growing. "Does she have ID?"

"I don't think so."

"Dammit, does she or doesn't she?"

"Well, I didn't want to touch the body, but I could see she was wearing those running stretch pants and no pockets so I don't know where she'd have ID on her."

VanDyke looked at the body. Blonde hair, grass, and weeds were tangled in blood and mud, caking over most of her face. He saw the armband with the phone, and the headphones.

"Did you look under the phone?"

"Sir?"

"For the ID." VanDyke was starting to think Hinson was an idiot. "Did you look under the phone?"

"No sir."

VanDyke reached into his pocket and pulled out a pair of latex gloves. Then he walked over and carefully began to remove the victim's phone from the armband. Beneath the phone was a credit card, a key, and a driver's license. Her noticed her arm was warm and soft. Even though it was still warm outside, her arm was too warm. He looked at her chest and stomach and saw the slight rise as she breathed in.

"God dammit." Now he was just pissed off. "Hinson were you the first here?"

"Yes."

"Did you take her pulse or do you just assume people are dead? Fuck."

Hinson made no reply.

"You guys get over here." He called to the men with the gurney.

Chapter 9

Simon was sitting in Sutter Street Steakhouse waiting for Chelsea. He was sure he had said 6pm the previous week but it was 6:30 and she hadn't arrived. Simon figured that she had mixed up the time and was going to arrive at 6:30 instead 6:00.

At 6:35 the waiter stopped by to fill his water glass. It was the second time in the last half hour. "Can I get you a glass of wine while you wait?" he asked.

"No, thank you, David," Simon said, reading the name tag. "I'd rather just wait."

"No problem, let me know if you change your mind."

He hated sitting in a restaurant alone. To Simon, eating food was a necessity, but eating at a restaurant was a social event. If he were going to eat alone he'd just assume stay home. It was why he was paying her. He was tired of his own cooking and had tried eating out alone a couple of times. He hated it. It was lonely. It was more lonely than eating alone in an empty house. It was somehow more conspicuous and, he felt, everyone could see that you were by yourself. The loneliness was also accentuated by the fact that everyone else in the restaurant was noticeably with other people.

He looked at his watch. 6:45. He decided to call her. Maybe she'd forgotten, or something came up and she wasn't coming. He dialed the number. After five rings he was about to hang up when a different woman's voice answered.

"Hello, this is Brenda's phone," the voice said.

"I'm sorry I was looking for Chelsea," Simon said, "I must have dialed the wrong number."

"Oh wait. Don't hang up." The person on the other end sounded urgent. "I didn't realize she uses her middle name. This is Brenda Chelsea Lee's phone."

"Could I speak to Chelsea?"

"Is this a family member?"

"I'm sorry, who is this?" Simon asked confused by the conversation.

"I really can't talk about patients, but we've not been able to get a hold of anyone. I'm a nurse at U.C. Davis Medical Center. Chelsea was in an accident. Do you know her family?"

"Is she going to be okay?"

"I really can't say anything about her," the nurse replied. "But if you could help us reach her family, I would really appreciate it."

"She doesn't have any family." Simon said, and without a thought he added, "I'll be down there as quick as I can."

He hung up before the nurse could reply. He stood and caught the waiter's attention. "I'm sorry. Something's come up. I've got to leave."

Twenty minutes later he walked into U.C. Davis Medical Center off Highway 50 and Stockton Boulevard, near downtown Sacramento. He had never liked hospitals. They smelled sterile.

In high school a close friend had been in a car accident. At first, Simon had visited because it was his friend. But his friend never regained consciousness and there was nothing he could do, so he stopped visiting. Then at the behest of his friend's parents, he returned. He spent nearly every day for three weeks in the room. His friend looked horrible, covered in bruises, cuts, and casts all over his body. It was hard to see his friend, a three-sport athlete, with monitors and needles hooked up all over him, his leg with metal pins attached, and tubes in his mouth and nose. He died four weeks and two days after the accident. That day seemed as bad as the day of the accident as Simon watched his friend's mother screaming and crying as they tried to revive his friend yet again.

That had been his first hospital experience; there had been others. His father had passed away from cancer just four years ago. His entire life he had seemed so strong and unmovable, but those last days in the hospital he looked nothing like himself. Simon was present when his dad passed away, this time comforting his weeping mother.

He made his way to the front desk.

"Can you please tell me the room number of Brenda Chelsea Lee?" He used her full name but it seemed strange, knowing her only as Chelsea.

"She's in the ICU, room 2116, but you'll need to check in at the ICU desk first," the elderly woman replied. "If you walk down this hallway and take a left the elevator can take you to the second floor."

"Thank you," Simon said then made his way down the hallway. There was a coffee shop and flower store but both were closed. He took the elevator to the second floor and followed the signs to the ICU.

"May I help you?"

"Yes, I got a call that Chelsea was here."

"Are you a family member or her husband?"

Simon was about to say no when another woman, not dressed as a nurse but more like a young candy striper, appeared from around the corner. She heard the word "husband," at the same moment bells and alarms sounded in a nearby room.

The nurse stood quickly, and the younger girl said, "Hey, JoAnn, thanks for covering for me, I've got it now."

JoAnne moved to the room where the alarms were sounding, leaving Simon alone with the aide. Her name tag read Dawn, and as she sat, she looked up at Simon.

"Can I help you?"

"Yes, Dawn," Simon started over again. "I'm Simon. I got a call 30 minutes ago that Chelsea… Brenda was here. I got here as quick as I could."

The nurses and aides had talked about Chelsea. She was wearing a wedding ring so they'd assumed she was married. After hearing the nurse use the word husband, and hearing him address himself as "Simon" like she should know who he was, she made an assumption. After all, he was wearing a wedding ring and talking about rushing down here as soon as he got a call from the hospital. Dawn made the completely reasonable conclusion that this man was her husband.

"Your wife is three doors down on the right." She looked concerned and then continued, "Has anyone spoken to you about her condition?"

Simon had started toward the room but stopped. "No. Is there something I should know?"

"Her face is cut up and bruised pretty badly, but it looks worse than it is. I just didn't want you to be frightened when you saw her."

"Thank you. I'll be okay," Simon replied, then asked, "Is there anything else I should know?"

"I'll get a hold of one of the doctors. A nurse or attending doctor will be along as soon as they are able and tell you more. I'll let them know you're here."

"Thank you." Simon made his way to the room and entered. He stepped around a corner and saw Chelsea. Her face was swollen and misshapen. There was a large cut over her right eye and another beneath it on her cheekbone. The right side of her face was swollen so badly that it was grotesque. Her right eye was completely swollen shut, her left nearly so. Smaller cuts were on her nose and chin, and on her left cheek. Her entire face seemed different shades of purple, deep blue, and greenish yellow.

Her right arm was in a cast from the elbow down. She had a breathing tube in her mouth and IVs in her left arm. Monitors above her beeped regularly, checking her heart and breathing.

Simon stepped closer and looked at her, then got very dizzy. He felt the room spin and put both hands on the foot of the bed to steady himself.

"Oh, hey." The nurse's aide had come in behind him, and saw the blood rush from his face. She'd seen people pass out before. "You better sit down."

She took him by the arm and led him to a seat next to the bed. "Sit here."

Simon sat down and the aide continued, "I'll get you some water. You better stay seated for a few."

"What happened? Was it a car wreck?"

"I'll let the doctor fill you in." Then, wanting to comfort him, she said, "She's going to be okay."

The aide left the room and returned a few moments later with a glass of water. "Here. Drink this."

Simon took a sip but found it hard to swallow.

"I'll be right down the hallway if you need me." She stepped between Simon and Chelsea. She took the control box that was wired to Chelsea's bed and positioned it on the side of the bed next to Simon.

"You don't need to get up. You can just push the call button if you need anything." She pointed to the button he should use, then left.

Simon had a hard time looking at Chelsea, so he just closed his eyes and did nothing. The remainder of the night he sat in the chair as different nurses came and went. At one point a nurse came in and said nothing but checked the equipment then administered some kind of medicine intravenously. She looked at Simon who had nodded off, reclining back in the small chair. He looked uncomfortable and it was cool in the room. She took a blanket and gently laid it over him then returned to her work.

The following morning in the hallway, Dawn, JoAnne, and two other nurses were standing at the nurse's station talking. It had been a quiet night in the ICU, a rarity for South Sacramento, and the four ladies were drinking coffee and listening to Dawn, the nurse's aide.

"I feel so bad for him. Seeing his wife like that. If I hadn't walked in and got him to sit down he'd have passed out. When I walked in, his face was completely white and he was holding himself up with the end of the bed."

"Does he know what happened to her?"

"No. He asked if she was in a car accident."

A young doctor approached. His skin and dark hair spoke to his Indian heritage. He greeted the four nurses.

"Hello, ladies," he said with an unmistakable accent. "How's everyone today?"

"Good," one nurse replied

"Almost done with my shift then I'm off for three days," said another.

"I got a call that the husband was here?"

"That was me," Dawn replied. "Thanks for coming. The husband is in there with her now."

"What?" the doctor exclaimed. "Is anyone in there with him?"

"Well no, it's her husband."

"Look, I don't care if it's the Pope." The doctor made it clear he was irritated with the situation. "That lady was beaten up badly. We aren't going to leave her alone with ANYONE who could have done that to her."

One nurse immediately grabbed a chart off the desk and made her way into a different patient's room. A second nurse turned her back to get a cup of coffee from the pot on the counter behind the desk. As soon as she filled her cup she disappeared around a corner. That left Dawn and JoAnne, the nurse who had been working with Chelsea much of the night. The doctor was already moving towards the room.

Dawn followed down the hallway, replying defensively, "If you saw his face when he first saw her, you'd know he didn't do it."

The doctor approached Chelsea's room and let Dawn feel the anger his voice. "I'm glad you have such a keen understanding of facial expressions, but I'd rather trust my experience. And that experience tells me that about ninety-nine percent of the time it's the husband that beat the wife, not someone else. DO NOT leave her alone in there until we know what happened."

"I'm sorry," Dawn replied. "I won't."

When they got to the door of the room it was open. The doctor turned and looked at JoAnne, who was following along behind Dawn.

"Has she shown any change?" he asked in a quieter voice.

"No, she hasn't woken up."

"Okay then," the doctor replied.

The doctor entered the room and saw Simon sitting on the chair next to Chelsea. He was leaning forward with his elbows on his knees and his hands clasped together.

He is either praying or half asleep, the doctor thought. He had seen too many battered women in his career. If you are praying, good for you. Maybe you didn't do it. If you are asleep then you are probably a real sonofabitch.

Just as the doctor finished this thought, Simon opened his eyes and stood. Simon saw the doctor's ID badge, Dr. Reyansh Anand. He wasn't sure how to pronounce the name and at the moment he didn't really care.

"Doctor." He reached out his hand to shake but the doctor just nodded so he dropped his hand back to his side.

"Mr. Lee, do you know what happened to your wife?"

"When they called me they said it was an accident. I assumed a car accident."

"Someone beat her up," the doctor said, watching closely to judge his reaction. "She was assaulted."

Simon turned and looked at Chelsea. He felt a welling up of emotion, sadness and pity. It was followed just seconds later by anger at anyone who would do this.

All the doctor saw was a stoic countenance and he thought to himself, this is the sonofabitch that did this. He said nothing but hoped that Sac PD would nail his ass.

Simon stared at her face. She had been beautiful, now she was hard to look at.

"Will her face...?" Simon left the question unfinished.

"It will take some time, but the swelling will go down," the doctor said, hiding his feelings toward Simon. "The plastic surgeon was here and took a look. He thinks the scarring will be minimal. The cut on her forehead is the worst but it is just under her hairline and won't be visible. The cuts on her face should heal or can be fixed."

"So she'll be all right?"

"In time her face will be fine," the doctor replied. "But she had other injuries. In addition to the fracture in her arm, she has internal injuries that I am more concerned about. She has several fractured ribs, and a collapsed lung."

"Shit," Simon responded, starting to feel dizzy again. The monitors, the sterile smell of the room, her face, and the tubes going into her mouth all left him feeling lightheaded and sick.

The doctor saw the color drain from his face. A better reaction, he thought.

Simon sat back down in the chair.

"Will she be all right?" he asked again.

"The ribs will heal. The lung has inflated and we are keeping close watch should she develop a pneumothorax." The doctor saw Simon's questioning look at the last word and continued. "Basically, the biggest risk of a collapsed lung is air leaking into the chest cavity."

Simon closed his eyes for a few long seconds.

"Is there anything I can do?"

"No. It's going to take time for her to recover fully." The doctor was in more of a clinical mode now, looking at her chart and thinking more about the patient than the man who may have done this to her.

"When she wakes up I would suggest she not see a mirror immediately. Seems to me it would be an unnecessary shock," the doctor continued. "It will look its worst over the next couple days and the swelling may actually increase. She will look significantly better as the swelling goes down and the discoloration goes away."

Simon saw the doctor hesitate and decided to address him head on. "I heard what you said to the nurse." He looked the doctor square in the face. "I didn't do this. I would never do something like this."

He could see the doctor was unconvinced. "Would you be more comfortable if I sat in the hallway outside her door?"

"I think that would be a good idea for now."

"That's fine. Unnecessary, but fine." Simon picked up a smaller wooden chair from the corner of the room and carried it just outside the door. The doctor followed him out.

"Thank you," the doctor said. "I think until we know what happened everyone would feel better like this."

"Will you be her doctor going forward?"

The doctor misinterpreted the question, thinking because he suspected Simon that Simon would want him removed from her care. "Is there any reason I shouldn't be?"

Simon recognized the adversarial tone and decided to try a different approach.

"Doctor, let me ask you a question," he said flatly. "Who is the best trauma doctor in this hospital?"

The doctor answered as Simon guessed he would with a simple, "I am."

"Then you are the doctor I insist she have."

He wasn't sure if it helped, but it seemed the doctor lightened up a bit.

"There will be several doctors attending to her, but I will be the primary."

Simon looked at the name badge and said, "Do you go by 'Reyansh'? Is that how you pronounce it?"

"Yes, that's close enough, but most people around here just call me Dr. Rey."

"Okay, Dr. Rey." Simon again reached out to shake his hand. "I'll sit out here for now. In time you'll realize I didn't do this but I understand your doubt."

The doctor shook his hand almost inadvertently and said, "For her sake, I hope you're right."

Simon ignored the comment as the doctor headed back down the hall. At the nurse's station he lowered his voice and handed Dawn a Sac PD business card. "A detective with the police department left this card. You need to get a hold of him and let him know that her husband is here."

Dawn took the card and set it next to the phone on the desk. "I'll take care of it as soon as I can."

"In the meantime," the doctor continued, motioning towards Simon, "he's going to sit in the hallway unless someone else is in the room."

Dawn thought it was ridiculous but said nothing and nodded her head. The doctor left and she got up and made her way down to Simon. His suit looked disheveled, and overall he needed a shave, but what could she expect? The guy had spent all night by his wife's bed.

"Can I get you anything?"

"No I'm okay."

"If want to go and get some sleep we can call you the minute she wakes up."

"I think I'll wait here for now. But thank you."

She looked at the wooden chair. If he was planning on spending all day here it was going to get uncomfortable.

"I will ask the nurse if I can move her to the room right outside the nurse's station. If I do, then you can sit inside with her and I can see in from my desk."

"That would be nice of you, Dawn," Simon smiled. "I appreciate it."

It took several hours with the other work she was doing, but Dawn made the room change. Simon walked alongside Chelsea's bed as they rolled it to the new room. Soon, the bed was in its place and the monitors were beeping and flashing again.

The door opened directly across from the nurse's station, and just inside the door was a curtain that was pulled open.

"Thank you again," Simon said to Dawn. To Simon, everything seemed sterile and void. He really didn't like the room and realized he hadn't eaten or used a restroom.

"I think I will run downstairs to the gift store. Can you call me immediately if anything changes?"

"Sure, let me make sure I have your number."

They walked out to the nurse's station and she wrote down his cell number. A few minutes later Simon entered the gift shop on the first floor. A large walk-in flower case was fronted with glass. When Simon opened it, he was immediately greeted by the cool air and the smell of flowers. At least he could do something about the sterile smell and empty room. He identified four of the largest—and he hoped most fragrant—bouquets: a large yellow rose arrangement, one that had daises, and two that were a combination of flowers. Unable to carry all four vases at once, he exited and then pointed them out to the cashier.

"Could you have those four arrangements sent to room 2112?"

"Sure thing."

She entered the flower cooler and grabbed the tags off all four arrangements. After ringing them up, she asked, "Will there be anything else?"

He looked around at the stuffed animals, candy, cards, and other knickknacks.

"No, that will be all, Janice," he replied, noting her name from her hospital ID badge.

"Okay, that will be $317.92," she said and waited.

Simon was tired and simply zoned out for a moment. Thinking he thought the price way too high she read off the tags.

"The roses were $89, the daisies were $49, and the other two arrangements were each $76. With taxes that comes to $317.92."

Simon looked realized she was waiting for him to pay. "Oh, sorry. That will be fine." He handed her his card.

He stopped by a restroom on his way back. He also realized he hadn't eaten or changed clothes for close to 24 hours. He needed to eat but he really didn't feel hungry or care about eating. Over the last two years he had lost significant weight, and part of the reason was because he was never hungry. The lack of shower, shave, and fresh clothes were another matter. He thought about heading home to change but decided to wait.

Dawn made eye contact with him when he entered the ICU and smiled and nodded as if to say hello.

Simon nodded back and entered Chelsea's room. He sat in the more comfortable chair next to her. For a while he just sat. She was hard to look at and each time he did, it made him sick to his stomach. She had been beautiful. He wondered if she ever would be again. He pulled out his phone and scrolled through a number of emails, responding to one, deleting the rest, and sent a text. A young man rolled a cart to just outside the door, the four flower arrangements on top of it. He walked in with the first.

"Where would you like these?"

"Just on the counter would be fine."

The orderly left the flowers, and Simon stood to spread them out. The color livened up the room a bit and the fragrance helped. Dawn entered later in the afternoon.

"Mr. Lee..." She began.

"Please, Dawn, call me Simon."

"Okay, Simon." She looked critically at him. He was still wearing the same suit he had been wearing the night before, and he was unshaven. She also knew he hadn't eaten.

It was 1pm and nearly the end of her double shift. Two ten-hour shifts in a row and she knew how much she wanted to leave, shower, and sleep. She suspected he felt the same.

"If you'd like to head home and get some rest, we can call you the minute she wakes."

"No," he said, looking at his watch. "I think I'll just stay here for a while longer."

Dawn returned to her desk. She looked at the policeman's business card. One hour left in her shift, she thought. She picked up the phone and was happy when there was no answer. She left a message.

Just before 2, she returned to the room with a tray of food.

"I'm pretty sure you have to eat," she said, setting the food on a small rolling cart next to Simon. "I'm off till tomorrow, but Jeannie will be taking my place. Let her know if you need anything."

"Thank you." He looked at the food after she left. A turkey sandwich, some raw carrots, celery, and broccoli, a small cup of apple sauce, bottle of water, and a cookie. He picked up a carrot and ate it. He was hungry, physically, but had no appetite. Each time he looked at Chelsea he was nauseated, and the hospital, like all hospitals in his past, left him not wanting to eat or do anything other than get out.

After a while he ate the sandwich. The afternoon stretched into the evening. The hallway grew quieter. The sun set and the light from the windows was gone. The lights were dimmed and Simon grew tired. He left the room and saw the new nurse's aide sitting at the desk. She was a heavyset woman who looked to be in her early 60s.

"Hello Jeannie, I'm going to run home and get some rest."

"No problem." Jeanie was busy at the computer and barely glanced up. "We'll take care of her, no need to worry."

Simon couldn't tell if she was brash, rude, or overworked. He decided she was probably just confident and busy.

"Jeannie, I know you'll all take great take care of her but..." He left took a piece of paper from a notepad on the desk and scribbled down his cell number. "If she should wake up would you please call me?"

Jeannie finally looked up from her computer as she took the number from him. "Sure thing," she said.

Chapter 10

At 4:30am the night sky was just beginning to lighten. A yellowish grey grew in the east over the Sierras, chasing away the darkness in the west where the moon was fading. Simon pulled into the parking lot at UC Davis, stepped out of his car, and looked up. There were a few remaining stars fading away and the air was cool. He took a deep breath in. It would be hot today, he thought. Probably in the 90s. Typical for June in Sacramento.

He stood in the parking lot, enjoying the moment of quiet. He had gone home, showered, shaved, and managed to get a little sleep. After four hours he had woken, his mind thinking about too many things. As was his habit, he drank a cup of coffee, showered, got half-dressed, then made himself a breakfast of two eggs, a slice of toast, and another cup of coffee. He finished putting on a suit and left the house.

Now he stood looking at the hospital building in front of him not wanting to go in. The morning air was fresh and clean. The parking lot was quiet. He liked the outdoors in the morning and was dreading his return into the sterile smells, the fluorescent lights, and all that went on inside. Taking one last breath of the morning air, he forced himself to go in and up to the second floor.

She was still sleeping when he walked into her room. Doctor Rey had been correct, she looked worse. Her face was even more discolored and swollen. He felt the dizzying effect of being lightheaded and sat in the chair next to her. For the next two hours he alternated between nodding off, staring at the flowers, and looking at different news articles on his phone. It was difficult to look at her. The sun rose and the room was bathed in light from the outside. He made a mental note to ask the nurse if there was a way to get some kind of radio in the room for Chelsea. He contemplated whether people recovered quicker if they listened to music and even wondered if the recovery would be accelerated if they listened to a particular type of music, like Mozart or rock, or if it would be better if the patient was listening to their favorite music. If anyone had ever done such a study he'd never heard of it, and for now he was forced to listen to the generic sounds of the hospital room.

Yet another nurse entered and checked on Chelsea. She wrote a few things down on the clipboard before returning it to its hook on the end of Chelsea's bed and leaving. Simon got up and paced around the room, just to stretch his legs, then returned to the chair.

Chelsea's breathing remained constant along with the beep of a monitor and the lights tracking her oxygen levels and other vitals. He had no idea what he would say when she woke. He had no real tie to her and felt no emotional connection. He thought about his feelings towards her. He didn't love her. He didn't even really know her. The only feeling he did have was anger. He was very angry.

It was the first strong emotion he'd felt, other than depression and sadness, in nearly two years. It gave him resolve without direction. In his mind he thought about what he would do if he could somehow find the person who'd done this to her. It wasn't kind. He daydreamed about it. The last time in his life he'd had this kind of resolve had been when he started his business. The resolve grew as the business grew, and when he finally sold it he felt nothing but utter satisfaction. Now he felt that same determination. The desire to do something, but it was directionless. Do what? He had no way to seek justice. No way to exact revenge. It was resolve without direction.

It was nearly 3pm when a man walked in followed by Dawn. Dawn began to fuss around Chelsea at the bed. The man stood and looked at Chelsea then at Simon. He was several inches taller than Simon's 5'10 and significantly heavier, maybe 250 pounds or better. He wore a cheap dark grey suit. He reached inside his coat pocket and pulled out a badge.

"I take it you are Mr. Lee?"

Simon stood and reached out his hand to shake. "And you are?"

"I'm detective VanDyke." He offered the view of his badge but didn't shake hands.

"Nice to meet you, detective," Simon replied. "Do you know who did this too her?"

"I was kind of hoping you'd maybe be able to help me with that."

"I'm not so sure, but if I can help I will." Simon disliked conversations that beat around the bush. He disliked them in business, and in relationships. The more important the conversation the more important that it be straightforward.

"Would you mind telling me where you were Thursday?"

"Detective, I don't mind telling you anything. I can pretty much describe my entire day. Thursday, I spent the morning at the home of Natalie and Ron Hansen. In the afternoon, I went to work out at the gym in Folsom, and after that I spent an hour at a judo class until 4. Then I was at Natalie's and Ron's house again, where I ate dinner and hung out until about 9. Then I drove home and went to bed alone."

"How long were you at this..." he looked at the notes he was writing, "this home of Natalie and Ron?"

"I got there around 8am. We had breakfast. I didn't leave until around 3pm."

"What were you doing there?"

"I was helping them out watching their daughter. Ron works and Natalie wanted to do some shopping and errands. I offered to help."

"You weren't with your wife?" The detective said, tipping his head towards Chelsea.

"That's another thing you should know, Detective. Chelsea's not my wife."

"What?" Dawn interrupted. Her voice rose in volume with her anger. "You told us you were her husband."

"No, I never told anyone that. You all assumed it," Simon replied. He realized this was going to be a long conversation and with Dawn's voice raised, he thought it better to move out of the room. "Can we talk in the hallway?"

Simon moved towards the hallway.

"You shouldn't have even been in here in the first place!" Dawn said, still angry at the situation.

"Again, let's talk out here."

With them all standing in the hall outside Chelsea's room, Simon reached back and closed the door.

"No use disturbing her." Simon looked at Dawn. "I'm sorry Dawn, I never meant to deceive you. I never told anyone Chelsea was my wife."

"Well, let's back up then." The detective tried to continue his questioning, "Who are you and why didn't you tell them the truth?"

A woman's voice interrupted them from the entryway of the ICU. "His name is Simon Murray."

The woman was wearing a dark blue business suit, and a hospital ID badge hung from lanyard around her neck. She walked up and said, "Hello Simon, what are you doing here?"

"Hi Kate. I'm just here visiting a friend."

She reached out with both of her hands and Simon did the same. She took them and greeted him warmly. "It's good to see you. How are Natalie and Ron? I hear they had a baby."

"Yes," Simon replied. "They have a baby girl, Emma. They are all great."

"All right, can we all just stop a minute?" The detective interrupted. He was growing irritated.

"Look, I've got a job to do. There is a woman in there who's been assaulted. I've got a guy out here claiming to be her husband and now you say you aren't."

The detective looked at the woman in the business suit with the hospital ID. "I take it you work here?"

"Yes. I am Dr. Kate Williams. I am the Chief of Staff here at the hospital."

The detective continued, "And you know this man?"

"This man is Simon Murray and I'm quite certain that if he said he never claimed to be her husband he didn't. I've known this man for a long time and liar isn't a word I would ever use to describe him."

"I'm sorry, Dr. Williams," Dawn interrupted. "But he did tell us he was her husband."

"No, Dawn," Simon looked at her. "I didn't. When I called her phone and someone here at the hospital picked up, they assumed

I was her husband. When I showed up you all thought I was. I probably should have corrected you but I didn't."

The detective tried to get control of the situation. "Can everyone just stop for a minute? I'd like to ask a few questions and get them answered. Then you all can talk about who said what and who lied to who later."

Everyone stopped and looked at the detective for a moment. Then he pulled out his notepad and started writing. "You are Simon Murray?"

"Yes."

"You spell that M.U.R.R.A.Y?"

"That's right."

"Your phone number and address?"

Simon listed them out while detective VanDyke wrote them down.

"And how do you know Mrs. Lee?"

"It's Miss Lee. She's not married and I know her because I have taken her on several dates over the last month."

"Simon!" Kate exclaimed somewhat surprised.

The detective gave her an admonishing look as if to say please don't interrupt.

"Okay, everyone was saying married, now you say not married. Anyone know the truth?"

"She's wearing a wedding ring," Dawn interjected.

"Again, she's not married," Simon replied. "She told me she wears it to keep men from hitting on her."

"Okay, so she's not married. And these people you mentioned that you saw on Thursday. They will collaborate your story?" As Simon nodded yes, the detective continued. "Can I get their address and phone number?"

Simon pulled out his phone and read off the information. As the detective was writing down the number, Dr. Anand approached and joined them. Simon felt like the large crowd was all getting a little to close and personal.

"Okay." The detective finished writing down the information and looked at everyone a moment, thinking. Then he said, "Any idea who would want to hurt her?"

"No."

Dr Anand interrupted. "He didn't want to hurt her; I would say whoever he was was trying to kill her."

The detective looked at him skeptically. "You have a theory on this doctor?"

"Well, yes. She suffered massive bruising around her neck and throat. Based on the bruising, I would say he had very large hands. Whoever did this squeezed her entire neck and cut off the blood to her brain. In effect he caused her to pass out. If he'd had smaller hands, or if he knew what he was doing, he could have easily crushed her larynx or her windpipe. She would have died from lack of oxygen. As it was she passed out. He probably thought she was dead and left her."

The detective tried to find a flaw in the doctor's theory but couldn't. He didn't like anyone to identify something about a crime that he didn't come up with first, but he also liked the theory. He put that little bit of information away in the vault of his mind. If he ever saw the same situation again, he would be the one to present that theory.

"Okay, Doc, sounds plausible. But again, who and why?" He looked at Simon's hands as he asked. They weren't small but they weren't particularly large either. Average is about all he could say about this guy, No one answered him. Then he asked no one in particular.

"Does anyone have a number for any of her family?"

"She told me she was an only child," Simon replied. "That her mother died when she was in her teens, and that she never had a father."

"Any friends that I can talk to?"

"I'm sorry, Detective, I didn't know her that well at all." Simon continued, "As I said, we've only been out a few times."

"How'd the two of you meet?"

Simon thought about how to respond for a moment, then said simply, "online."

The detective was good at his job. He noticed the hesitation in the response and followed up. "Like one of those dating sites?"

"Yes."

The detective made a note on his pad to check out her online profile.

"So you said you called the hospital and then you came here?" The detective asked.

"Chelsea and I were supposed to have a date last night, or was it the day before?" Being up all night and the whole day without much sleep he was getting confused. "I'm not sure what day it is."

"It's Sunday," Kate replied.

"It doesn't matter." Simon went on, "Chelsea and I were supposed to have a date Friday night. I sat at the restaurant waiting for her. When she didn't show up I called her phone. Someone from the hospital picked up and told me she was here. I came directly here after that. When I got here people just started calling me Mr. Lee and I figured it was easier than to explain who I was."

"Listen, I'm going to check out your story and I may want to talk to you again. You aren't planning on leaving town or going anywhere?"

Simon smiled. "I'm not going anywhere."

"I guess that's all for now." The detective stuffed the notepad back into his inner suit pocket and turned to leave, then stopped.

"Oh, uh, one more thing. Why didn't you correct the staff? Why'd you let them think you were her husband?"

Dawn was still standing next to them, angry at the situation. She too wanted to know.

"To be honest. They told me on the phone she'd been in an accident. I thought they meant a car accident and I came to the hospital fully prepared to plead my case to let me visit. I understand they have rules, so I was certain they would refuse. When the mistake was made I didn't say anything. It was easier. She doesn't have anyone and I didn't want her to be alone."

Dawn interrupted again. "Well you can't visit her anymore until we get hold of her family or someone who knows her."

It was Kate's turn to chime in. "Simon, will you excuse us a second?"

"Sure, Kate." He walked down the hall and around a corner out of earshot.

"Okay, let's get something straight." Kate turned and addressed Dawn. "First, that man is one of the best men I know. He's donated more money to this hospital than all of us will earn in our lifetimes, put together. The south tower that is now being built, HE paid for it. So if he wants to visit one of our patients, and he says he knows her, until that patient has an objection we are going to extend to him EVERY courtesy. Got it?"

"Yes ma'am," Dawn replied contritely.

Kate was a nice person, and didn't really want to scare her. She smiled warmly. "It's Dr. Williams or Chief... not ma'am. Why don't you go find Simon and tell him he's welcome to visit."

"Yes ma'a... uh, yes Chief." Dawn hurried off to find Simon.

Kate turned to the Detective. "Officer, as I said, he is one of the best men I know. There is not a chance he would hurt her or anyone else for that matter."

"I appreciate that but if it's all the same to you, I'll just check his alibi," he patted the notepad in his breast pocket. "If it checks out I'll feel better."

"You do that, but trust me. You're wasting your time."

The officer left and Kate stood for a moment trying to recall why she had come to the ICU in the first place. Then she remembered the administrative issue she was working on. She was also curious about Simon. Dating someone, he had said. She wanted to ask him, but he was nowhere in sight. She turned to one of the nurses sitting at the nurse's station.

"JoAnne, listen, I've got to take care of some things, Will you call my cell and let me know if Simon returns to visit Miss Lee?"

"Sure thing, Dr. Williams. The number in the system?" she asked referring to their computer directory.

"Yes, and thank you." She headed into another wing of the ICU, still wondering about Simon.

The gift shop smelled of flowers, caramel corn, and candy when Simon entered. He considered buying something else to brighten up Chelsea's room and perused the store looking at stuffed animals, flowers, and cards, but finally decided against it. He wondered if his visiting privileges were going to be over and decided if they were he would just send more flowers and leave well enough alone. He made his way out into the wide hospital hallway.

It was the time most people were eating dinner so he walked across the corridor and entered the coffee shop. There was a cafeteria on a lower floor, but the coffee shop was closer to Chelsea's room. As usual he was physically hungry but had no appetite. Eating was about sustenance. It was like breathing. You had to do it. Unlike breathing, however, he had to force himself to eat.

Simon ordered a sandwich and a cup of water. The young girl at the counter asked for his name and rang up his bill. He paid and sat at a round table in a corner. The chair was small, wooden, and uncomfortable, and he hated eating alone, but he had to eat something.

The girl brought the sandwich and set in on the table. "I guess I didn't really need your name. It's not busy so I just brought it over to ya." She was talkative and continued, "I am used to working the morning shift and it's busy with everyone getting coffee, so we are shouting out names all morning."

He glanced at her ID badge and replied, "No problem, Marina. Thanks for bringing it over."

The sandwich came with a small bag of chips and he broke it open and started eating a few. He didn't want to eat. Several friends had recommended marijuana. "It makes you hungry and want to snack," they'd said. "It also relaxes you and you can just chill and take it easy after all you've been though." His doctor had recommended a glass of wine and had been willing to prescribe anti-anxiety medication to help him.

But Simon had never been tempted to take drugs in his life and didn't want to start now. Wine he drank with meals but not as a way to suppress the pain. He thought about his friends and wondered if they would think him odd for choosing to live with the emotions and pain.

He had taken only a few bites of the sandwich when Dawn found him.

"Mr. Murray, may I sit down?" She indicated the other chair at his table.

Simon smiled at her. "You can if you stop calling me Mr. Murray and just call me Simon."

She sat down and started in hesitantly, "I'm sorry about what happened upstairs. Dr. Williams told me to find you and let you know that you can continue to visit Chelsea for now."

"For now?"

"Well, Dr. Williams said as long as no family members are going to object, or Chelsea for that matter, that it would be fine."

"I see," Simon replied. "But it's me that should apologize. I didn't want to deal with the headache of trying to explain why I wanted to visit. And I'm pretty sure no one would have let me if I'd told the truth."

"Yeah, we wouldn't have," Dawn continued. "But Dr. Williams said it's okay and she's the boss."

Dawn got up from her seat. "Speaking of bosses, I need to get back to work. Please come on back up whenever you'd like."

"Thanks, Dawn, I'll be up after I eat."

Dawn returned to the nurse's station and sat down. She felt like couldn't really win. One minute she was trying to protect the patient and the next the chief of staff was dogging on her. Overall, the chief was pretty nice about it but it still left her a bit frazzled. A few minutes later the phone rang and she picked up.

"ICU, this is Dawn," she answered.

A man voice greeted her pleasantly, "Hi Dawn, this is Bill Johnson, I'm a friend of Chelsea's. Did I reach the right desk?"

"I can't talk about patients, I hope you understand."

The man had already called the front desk of the hospital and knew the room number. Now he was just looking for information. "I just wanted to ask how she was doing."

"I'm sorry Mr. Johnson but I really can't discuss a patient care. Is there anything else I can help you with?"

"Is it possible you could transfer me through to her room so I could talk with her?"

"No. I'm sorry, she hasn't woken up yet, so that wouldn't really help you."

Dawn realized as she spoke, she probably shouldn't have even shared that but figured at this point there was no way to take it back.

"Well, no problem. I guess I'll call back another time," the man said.

"If you like I can get your number and have her call you when she wakes up," Dawn suggested.

"No, I'll just call back. Thanks."

The man sitting in the '73 Ford Pickup hung up the burner phone and started shaking. How the hell was she still alive, he thought. If she woke up he was ruined. At first fear gripped him; he actually felt for a moment like he was losing everything. Then he was angry. The thought that this whore could somehow ruin him infuriated him. He told himself to calm down. He would deal with her, he just had to have a plan. He started thinking about solutions. Each possibility had to be weighed and seriously judged. He knew he'd find the perfect solution. He always had in the past.

Chapter 11

The next morning, Simon was sitting next to Chelsea's bed. He'd spent another uncomfortable night in the club chair. One of the nurses had supplied him with a pillow and a blanket. It hadn't done much for his actual comfort but he appreciated the gesture. He stood and folded up the blanket and set it on the counter next to the flowers. The flowers had drunk up the water in the vases, so he refilled each one by one. They were starting to wilt. No stopping that, he thought. He'd run down and get some more today.

He had been sitting for a while, sending a few texts, when JoAnne the nurse came in with a tray of food. "Dr. Williams told us to make sure you ate."

She set the tray on the rolling cart in front of Simon. He looked at the scrambled eggs, sausage, fruit, toast, orange juice, and coffee. He didn't really want it but he knew he needed it.

"Thank you." He picked up the coffee and started sipping it.

The nurse checked on Chelsea. "She looks better today."

Simon still had a hard time looking at her. The bruises were turning from a deep dark blue and black color to a greenish yellow. Not better, worse.

"Any thoughts on when she'll wake up?"

"She's been through it," JoAnne said, not looking at him. "Each day her body is healing, so that's a positive."

JoAnne left as Simon stood at the foot of the bed looking at Chelsea. Did she really look better? He couldn't tell. The more he looked at her the angrier he got. Once again there was the feeling of resolve with no direction, but in the back of his mind an idea was forming.

He sat and ate most of the breakfast and spent the remainder of the morning sending emails, texting, and finally buying another flower arrangement for the room.

"You're going to run out of room for all those flowers," JoAnne joked as she came in to check on Chelsea again.

"I'll throw out the old ones tomorrow."

"I was just kidding. They look great."

"Yeah, I felt the room was kind of empty."

"Well, if you like you can bring down some of her personal items. I'm sure she would appreciate it when she wakes up."

Simon didn't want to tell her that he had no idea where she lived or how to get any of her "personal items," but after a few moments he got an idea.

"JoAnne," he started, trying to sound nonchalant, "did Chelsea have her purse with her?"

"No, but she did have some things. They're all at the nurse's station out there. Let me go grab them."

A moment later she was back with Chelsea's belongings. "This is all she had on her."

JoAnne handed it all to Simon. "Were you looking for something in particular?"

Simon was looking at her address on her ID. He was happy to see the key and assumed it was to her apartment. "Yes, this," he said, holding up the key. "I thought I'd go over to her apartment and grab a few of her things for the room."

JoAnne said, "I probably shouldn't be giving you all of her things, but the Chief kind of vouched for you. Plus, if she has no family and you are willing to sleep in a chair next to her for several nights, then that's at least something."

"Thanks," Simon replied. "I'd really just like to help her out."

Joanne misinterpreted his concern. "It's obvious you really care for her."

Simon didn't know what to say, so he simply nodded.

"Well that's good, because she's going to need someone to help take care of her for a while, I'd guess." JoAnne said it while tending to Chelsea, tucking a blanket around her and checking her IVs.

Simon took a moment to punch in Chelsea's address on his phone, then handed the credit card and driver's license back to JoAnne. He kept the key and Joanne took the items back to the nurse's station.

A moment later a beautiful woman walked in. She had deep reddish-brown hair and freckles splashed across her nose.

"Hey, love you." She walked up to Simon warmly and hugged him.

"Love you too," Simon replied.

"How're you doing?"

"I'm okay." He kissed her on the forehead.

Then they both stood side by side and looked at Chelsea.

"How's she doing?"

༄

The first thing Chelsea heard was the quiet beeping of a monitor. She tried to open her eyes but it hurt so much she just sat lay there trying to figure out where she was. There was a tube in her mouth and her throat ached horribly. A woman and a man were talking. At first it was all garbled. Then, like a switch was turned on, she clearly heard the woman's voice.

"... and if you are willing to sleep in a chair next to her for several nights, then that's at least something."

"Thanks." It was a man's voice. Simon's voice. "I'd really like to help her."

Then Chelsea remembered the attack. It all flooded into her mind. She was hurt. Now she added to that the fact Simon had spent several nights with her. At her side.

Then the nurse's voice said, "It's obvious you really care for her."

There was no reply and Chelsea wondered what Simon was doing. Was he agreeing? Disagreeing?

Then the nurse's voice again, "Well that's good, because she's going to need someone to help take care of her for a while, I'd guess."

Chelsea wished she could open her eyes but it was like they were taped shut, and any attempt to open them hurt. She started to talk, but felt the tube in her throat and mouth. She felt like a giant heavy blanket was on top of her, stopping her from moving even a finger. It was as if she were drugged and unable to control any part of her body. She felt helpless.

In the back of her mind she cherished the idea that this man may actually care for her. Maybe there was some possibility with him. Maybe he was different than the other men in her life. It was a hope she'd barely cultivated before but it was there like a tiny seed.

She heard people walking, someone left, someone entered, and another woman's voice sounded.

"Hey, love you," she heard the woman's voice say.

"Love you too," Simon replied.

"How're you doing?"

"I'm okay," he said, and Chelsea heard a what sounded like a quick kiss.

Then they both stood side by side and looked at Chelsea.

"How's she doing?" the woman's voice was asking. Chelsea was confused but then she passed out again.

Simon looked at the beautiful young red-headed woman. No matter how much he loved her it was difficult to look at her sometimes.

"Would you like to go downstairs and get some lunch?"

"Sure, but I've got to get back home by 2:30 so I don't have much time."

"No problem, I've got a few errands I want to run myself."

Two hours later Simon was opening the door to what he hoped was Chelsea's apartment. He entered and looked around. Other than the dead flowers in the vases the inside was neat, clean, and orderly. There was a Scrabble game out on the coffee table as if three people were playing, but the tile racks were all facing the same direction. He wasn't sure what "personal items" to get so he just walked around the condo taking it in. He looked in the refrigerator, just out of curiosity. Then, because it needed to be done, he took the dead flowers from the vases and tossed them in the small garbage can he'd located under the kitchen sink. He rinsed out the vases and left them to dry on the counter.

He walked into what he could only assume was a spare bedroom. It wasn't connected to a bathroom and had only a daybed and no chest of drawers. The closet had a few dresses and several pieces of luggage all of different sizes. He took a smaller duffle bag and left the rest. The room was pretty sparse and barren of anything that looked appropriate to take to her hospital room.

Next, he made his way into her bedroom. There was a book on the nightstand next to her bed, *Eat, Pray, Love*. He'd heard the title but was not interested in reading it. Nevertheless, he put the book into the duffel bag and laid the bag on the bed. He felt uncomfortable doing what he did next, but thought it was what Chelsea would have wanted. He opened the clothing chest, one drawer at a time. He was looking for what would be comfortable and yet wearable. He found some pajamas as well as some sweatpants. He found a couple oversized T-shirts and stuffed those in the duffel bag as well. Then he found socks and the most basic bra and underwear he could find. There was plenty that was far from nondescript, and he was already worried about the conversation he may have to have with her. He could only imagine. "You went through my underwear?"

He stuffed those things all in the duffle bag and went into the bathroom. There he also grabbed the most basic things. A comb and a brush, not sure why she'd have both or which was right. He grabbed a toothbrush, deodorant, and laid them all on the bed next to the duffle. Then he went back to look in the closet in the first bedroom. He found what he was looking for, an overnight bag, and returned to put the different toiletries in it. Last but not least, he grabbed some makeup. Not sure what to get he just tried to put a variety of things together. Lipstick, eye liner, rouge, mascara, eye shadow, and some small tubs of things like foundation and cleanser. The more he grabbed the more he realized there was such a large variety. He stuffed it all in the overnight bag and placed that next to the duffle.

He took one more look around the bedroom and saw a long, comfortable looking blue robe hanging on the inside of the closet door. He grabbed it and shoved it inside the now overfull duffle. No more, he thought; no more room.

He went back into the living room and took another look around. He noticed the painting on the wall of a young woman with a boy. It was a print but it drew his eye. He stood for a moment taking it all in, then he took the duffle and the overnight bag out the front door and to his car. Then he returned to her apartment and took a picture of the Scrabble game with his phone. He packed it up and carried it and the laptop to his car. Finally, he came back and stared at the painting for a moment longer, thinking about it. He made up his mind and took the painting down, and brought it with him, too.

When he'd arrived 45 minutes prior, he had waited until another driver had come and opened the gate. Then he had rushed his car though before the gate closed. Knowing how those gates worked he was not worried about getting out. As his car approached the gate it triggered a sensor and he drove right through.

He thought about taking everything to the hospital immediately, but thought better of it and headed home first. He pulled into his driveway and parked. He looked over at the passenger seat. The laptop was there. It would be an invasion of her privacy but an idea was forming in his head. He picked up the laptop and turned it on. It was password protected. He smiled to himself. Twenty-plus years of work in computers and cyber security and what it all came down to was that he was now breaking into someone else's computer. He did so with ease.

Within an hour he found what he was looking for. A list of men's names and nicknames, where they worked, and in a few cases whether they were married or not. Along with those names were some descriptive sentences. Likes and dislikes. Things he didn't want to read but did anyway. He reached into his glovebox and dug out a small yellow notepad and a pen. He copied the names, their addresses, their phone numbers. The anger he'd felt earlier whenever he looked at her face now changed. He felt the same strong resolve, but now he had a direction.

Then he received a phone call.

"This is JoAnne at the Med Center. Is this Simon Murray?"

"Hello, JoAnne. Yes this is me. What's up?"

"I just wanted to let you know that Chelsea is awake."

"I'm a ways away, but I'll be down as soon as I can."

"There is no rush. She's doing fine and the doctor is seeing her now."

"Okay. Thanks, JoAnne."

He hung up and quickly entered his home to shower and change. Twenty minutes later he was driving back down Highway 50 again. It was rush hour traffic and it took a bit longer to get to the hospital, but he pulled into the parking lot just before 6:30pm.

He stepped out of his car. The asphalt parking lot and concrete sidewalks and buildings were all radiating the heat from the nearly 100 degree day. It was stifling hot but he stood and looked at the hospital. Maybe he should just drop off her things. He worried that the doctor or nurses were going to leave it up to him to tell her about her face. The possibility that he would have to answer any of her questions left him at a loss. He hated hospitals but made up his mind to go in.

He was unable to carry everything to her room in one trip so he left behind the computer, the painting, and the Scrabble game. He placed them all in his trunk out of sight and took the duffle and overnight bag to room 2112.

Chelsea was sitting up slightly when he walked into the room. The tube had been taken out of her mouth. Her left eye was open, the right still swollen shut. He dropped the duffle bag at the end of her bed and left the overnight bag on top of it, both where she wouldn't see them. He didn't really want to explain to her right now that he'd been in her apartment.

She looked at him, unmoving. Simon thought for a moment. His only reason for being there was out of kindness. At a time like this she needed someone. He cleared his throat and smiled.

"You missed our date."

She said nothing.

"Under the circumstances I forgive you for standing me up."

Again silence.

"Are you okay? Has the doctor spoken with you?"

"Simon, why are you here?" She was unable to speak with more than a hoarse whisper, but even then her voice was harsh and angry.

"I just felt like you needed someone to be with you."

"Why was your wife here?"

Simon looked at her with complete confusion on his face. "What are you talking about?"

"Earlier today I started to wake up. I couldn't open my eyes and I still had that damn tube in my throat. I heard a nurse and you talking. That you'd spent the night here with me. Then moments later I heard your wife come in. She said she loved you and you said you loved her. And she asked how you were and how I was. What is going on?"

Simon broke into a broad smile. His whole face was wrinkles and laugh lines under shining blue eyes. "Chelsea, that wasn't my wife. That was my daughter."

Then the smile left. "My wife passed away two years ago."

The sun was just setting and the sky outside the windows was turning all colors of pink against the deepening blue. The moment Simon told her that, several memories flooded back to Chelsea. Their dates, when he refused to talk about himself. He'd told her he just wanted to listen to her. Then the time when she'd asked him if he was sad. His reaction when she'd asked him to tell her about his wife. He was sad. He was hurting.

"I'm sorry," she said.

"How did she die?" When she asked the question Simon shook his head ever so slightly as if to say no, then he turned toward the window so she was now looking at his profile. From the side she could see his smile was gone completely and he almost seemed to shudder.

Her voice was a still a hoarse whisper and it hurt to speak. She reached over and took a cup of water on the tray next to her bed and slowly sipped from the straw. It felt like heaven as it trickled down her raw throat.

"Would you like to tell me about her?" The last time she'd asked the question he had almost seemed angry, but somehow things seemed different now.

Simon turned and looked at Chelsea. In that moment he was finally ready to talk about it. Hell, he wanted to tell everyone, for everyone to know all about Allie. The feeling welled up inside of him.

"I think I'd like that."

For the next two hours Simon told Chelsea everything about Allie. He shared the story of how they'd met that first day in Seattle. He told her about the fish hitting her and knocking Allie into him. He told her about how they'd spent the entire night talking in the Starbucks and he went on to tell her about how they'd spent the nearly every free moment together that first year in college.

Chelsea's voice was in no condition to speak. She could see that somehow this was cathartic for him so she just listened. He told her about the first time he told Allie he loved her and how he'd spent the night in her dorm room. He didn't share any details but just that it had happened. He shared the fact that neither had ever been with anyone else. As Simon spoke, he stared out the window. It was as if Chelsea were not there. She got the distinct impression that Simon needed to share these stories. Not necessarily with her but with anyone.

He told her about their first few years of marriage and how they both finished college and started their careers together. He told her how difficult it was as he started his business and the struggles that they faced financially and emotionally. And yet he continually came back to how much fun it was to be with her and together through it all.

"Allie was always so upbeat," Simon said at one point. "We lived in the crappiest little studio apartment. I made nothing with my work and she supported us wholly from the money she made nursing."

He paused, staring out the window, then added, "We had so much fun together. I remember coming home after another failed business pitch and she was waiting for me. She had a picnic basket with peanut butter and jelly sandwiches and a couple of water bottles. We drove to a park and just sat and ate. I remember looking at her as she shared about her day working at the hospital. We ate those sandwiches and sat talking and there was the most amazing sunset. She was sitting with her back to it and as the sun went behind her it lit up her hair like it was on fire. I'll never forget that moment."

He grew quiet and said nothing for a few minutes. Then Chelsea felt a desire to know more about this man. She wanted to know more about his life, about Allie, about everything.

"What kind of work were you doing?" Chelsea asked.

"It was really the beginning of computers in the world. Early on I realized there was going to be a huge need for security. I was basically building programs designed to keep computers safe."

He was still looking out the window and talking about Allie when Chelsea fell asleep.

Chapter 12

The first thing Chelsea saw when she woke the following morning was Simon, asleep in the chair next to her. Even with a blanket partially covering him he looked terribly uncomfortable. The chair was too small to lay in and he had one leg up over the arm of the chair to keep from sliding out. There was a pillow in his lap but his head simply hung there, supported by his chin on his chest.

She pressed the button on the bed to raise herself up to a semi-sitting position.

The second thing she noticed was the room. Yesterday she hadn't really noticed the flowers but the room was full of them. She actually smelled them and started to smile but it caused her to wince. Her face hurt.

Then she saw her things. Her laptop was on the counter. On a small end table next to Simon was a Scrabble board. But it wasn't just a Scrabble board. It was her Scrabble board, and even more it was set up like three people were playing. She stared at it. It was exactly how she'd left it in her condo.

She stared past her feet at the end of the bed. On the counter across from her, her painting was leaning up against the wall. For some reason it frightened her. Someone had been in her condo. She felt like her privacy had been violated.

She looked around the room again and then focused on the painting. Then she thought about the similarities. The flowers in the painting and the flowers in her room. The morning sunlight streaming in through the hospital window and the sun streaming in around the woman in the painting. She'd noticed such similarities in her own condo many times. She had tried to create them. Somehow in this hospital room they were once again created, only this time she wasn't alone. Simon was next to her, in the chair, the sun like a spotlight cascading down on him... and her.

For nearly fifteen minutes she sat in silence. She listened to him breathe as he slept. She didn't want that moment to end. It was as if the essence of the painting was captured more than ever before and any interruption would take that away. She tried to take a deep breath in but was cut off by the sharp pain of her broken ribs. So she sat, unwilling to even move, more for fear of waking him than the pain. Then a nurse came into the room and the moment was gone.

"Good morning," the nurse said, seeing her awake. "You look better this morning. Can I get you some breakfast?"

"Thank you," she replied. Her throat felt better but was still raw as she spoke. "Maybe just some yogurt and juice."

"I'll see what I can do."

"Thank you."

Simon's head came up off his chest as Chelsea was talking to the nurse. The sun was warm against the back of his neck and head. He looked around the room. He had brought in her things the night before and had used the picture of the Scrabble game on his phone to reset the board exactly how it had been in her condo. Covering his mouth, he yawned and managed to say, "Morning."

"Good morning, Mr. Murray." The nurse replied. "I was just about to call down and get Chelsea's breakfast. Is there anything I can get for you?"

"Simon, please. And a cup of coffee would be great."

"I think I can make that happen." She left the room and Simon felt the awkward silence.

"Good morning," Chelsea said. "That doesn't look like a very comfortable bed."

Simon stood and looked at the chair. "It's better than it looks."

"You were in my condo." It was almost an accusation.

"Yes." Simon looked around at Chelsea's things. "The room was empty and felt cold. I just figured you might want some of your things."

"How'd you get in?"

"You had your ID and your key on you when they found you. I used it."

Chelsea was silent.

"I hope you don't mind. I was only there a moment or two. I just grabbed things that were easy and I thought you would want."

"You thought I'd want a painting?"

"Well, I was also thinking about the room and when I saw it I figured maybe you'd like it. Anything to brighten up this room a bit."

"It's not actually the real painting. It's just a print, but I'm surprised they let you haul this stuff into my room."

"I kind of have some pull around here. My wife used to work here," he added awkwardly, as if that explained it.

Chelsea wasn't sure how to respond so she let the subject drop.

"I brought your laptop, the Scrabble game, some clothes and stuff."

One of Chelsea's eyebrows shot up. "You went through my clothes?" She really did feel like he had stepped over the line but wasn't sure how to say anything without coming across as ungrateful.

"I just grabbed a few things. I've seen women's clothes before," Simon said.

She thought about all the lingerie she had, all the sexy items, the outright slutty stuff. She was embarrassed thinking about him going through her things.

"It's just that..." she started but didn't finish.

"You feel kind a like I broke in? Like I invaded your privacy?"

"Yes."

"So did I." Simon looked at her and smiled. "I felt like at any moment you or a cop or someone would show up and I'd get arrested for theft."

She realized he was actually embarrassed and found that humorous.

"So what exactly did you pick out for me to wear?" she teased. "I have some wild outfits and pretty risqué lingerie."

"Honestly, I tried to get in and out of there as fast as possible. I grabbed some sweatpants, T-shirts, a robe; some pretty basic stuff." He grabbed the duffle bag and set it in her lap. "I'm sorry if I overstepped."

She realized he was more uncomfortable with the situation than she was as she unzipped the bag with her good arm. "No, it's fine. Thank you."

She dug around and saw the clothes. It was mostly stuff she would never wear on a date, that was for sure. "You did get pretty boring stuff, but thanks, it's what I would get if I was packing for this." Then she said, "Do you mind?" motioning for him to take the bag from her.

"Oh, here." He took the bag and returned it the counter.

A middle-aged man entered the room pushing a cart with food trays on it. "Breakfast anyone?"

Simon saw the cup of coffee and took it first. "Thanks."

The man moved the food from the cart to a tray that was designed to sit next to Chelsea's bed but with an arm that reached out in front of her.

"Can I get you folks anything else?"

"No," Chelsea replied. "Well, actually. Do you have a radio or anything so I can listen to some music?"

"I'm pretty sure there are some music channels on the TV but no radios around that I know of."

"Okay, thank you."

The man left and Chelsea began to struggle with the orange juice. It was in a disposable plastic drinking cup but the top had a foil lid that was glued down. With one arm and hand in a cast, she couldn't hold the cup in one hand and grasp the lid to pull it off with the other. She looked at Simon, "Would you mind?"

"Sure." Simon opened the juice and set it in front of her. Then he took the plastic lid off the top of the platter, revealing her yogurt and granola. In addition, there was a bowl of fruit, scrambled eggs, and toast.

"I didn't order all of this."

"I'm sure the nurse ordered just in case one of us wanted more."

"If you'd like it you are welcome."

Simon reached over an took a piece of toast off the tray.

"Anything in particular you'd like to listen to?" He asked as he set his coffee down on the window ledge and took up the TV remote.

He flicked through until he found the list of channels that played music and selected classic country.

They both ate in silence while the TV played Alabama, then Randi Travis.

Simon finished the toast and sipped the coffee. "I was thinking about leaving for a bit to take care of a few things today." There wasn't anything in particular that he needed to do, but he wanted to get back to the gym and work out. "Would you like me to get anything in particular from your place, or can I pick you up anything?"

"No." Chelsea replied, once again feeling uncomfortable at the idea that this man would just enter her condo. "How'd you get in the gate?"

"Hmm?"

"The locked gate at my place." She asked again, "How'd you get past the gate?"

"Oh. Most of those gates are pretty slow. I just watched someone else enter and when they did I saw the speed of the gate. When the next car entered I just followed through right on his tail. Does it bother you?"

"I just feel like my privacy is gone right now," she replied.

They sat listening to the music, the sun climbing higher in the sky. Simon looked outside. He hated hospitals but knew it was worse for the person confined in them. He looked at his phone and wondered how much longer he should stay for Chelsea's sake.

Then Kate stood in the doorway. "Mind if I come in?" she asked politely.

Seeing her hospital badge, Chelsea assumed she was another doctor come to tell her something about her health. "No. Please come in."

"Hello, Kate," Simon said as she entered further.

"Hello, Simon."

Chelsea looked from one to the other. "You know each other?"

"Yes, Simon is one of our benefactors."

Chelsea saw Simon's face. He looked uncomfortable at the title.

"Simon," Kate began, "I hope you understand that the comments in the hallway yesterday weren't specifically directed at you for any reason."

"Kate, it's fine. I understand and I know you were bending the rules just to allow me in here."

Kate looked at Chelsea, "Well, Miss Lee, as long as you are okay with it, we will continue to allow Mr. Murray visitation."

"It's okay," Chelsea replied.

"All right, then." Kate continued, "Simon, could I speak with you for a moment?"

"Sure."

Simon and Kate stepped just outside the room. Curious, Chelsea turned the volume on the TV down and listened. In the hallway Kate addressed Simon.

"Simon, I just want to thank you again for your donation to the hospital."

"It was Allie's idea." Sometimes just saying her name was painful. "It's nothing."

Kate laughed. "Simon, 65 million isn't nothing."

"It was what she wanted and I'll never use it. I'm glad it's going here."

"I just wanted you to know that the board has voted and we are going to name the building after Allie."

Thinking he might tear up, Simon turned away, trying to hide the pain and hurt. "It isn't necessary."

"It's the least we can do." Kate saw his reaction. It had been two years but she realized that he was still far from over her death. "I'm sorry again for your loss, Simon. We all loved Allie."

"Thank you" was all Simon could manage to say. The loss Simon felt came in waves. Some days he was remembering and laughing; other days he felt he could barely breathe.

"The wing will be completed in a few months, or so they say," Kate continued. She could see his pain and tried to move the conversation in a more positive direction. "I would love to walk you through it before it's open. We can do it after, but I think it would be nice for you to see it before the public opening."

"When is the official date to start?"

"There are always delays but the contractor says we will be in by October 1st."

October, Simon thought. The month he met Allie. Everything seemed to remind him of her.

"Tell you what. If I'm up for it, I'll call you in early September and we will walk through it."

"That would be fine," Kate said, then she remembered another issue and paused, not wanting to bring it up.

"What?" Simon asked seeing her hesitation.

"Simon, the architect has planned for a memorial fountain just outside the main entrance of new wing. It's nearly complete but there is a plaque that will honor Allie. We have several drafts of what could be written on it, but I really think you should decide what it says."

Simon took a deep breath. "Kate, maybe you could call my daughter and ask her." Then he decided it would be just as painful for her. "Actually, you decide. You knew her. I'm sure whatever you choose will be good."

"Call me if you change your mind."

"I will."

"I'll also send you a copy of what we put on it beforehand. Just for your approval."

"That would be okay." Simon replied

"I've got a meeting in just a few minutes," Kate said, looking at the time on her watch. "If you need anything, let the nurses know and we can make it happen."

She smiled at him warmly and took his hand in hers. She wanted to comfort the man. "Simon, we all loved Allie. Hang in there."

Then she remembered there was a woman in the room behind him and she nodded her head towards the door. "I'm sorry for what's happened to her, but I'm glad I got to meet her. It's good to see you are dating."

"Kate it's not like that. She's a friend."

"Well whoever or whatever she is, go back in there and take care of her."

"Thank you."

After Kate left, Simon stood for a long minute, thinking.

Inside the room Chelsea had heard the conversation. She was thinking about the comment he had made at the end. He had called her a friend. She felt like somehow, at that moment, that the term friend was more intimate than if he had told Kate they were dating.

Chelsea looked at Simon as he walked back into the room. She realized the TV volume was off and quickly turned it back up. They both looked at each other, understanding what had happened. She was embarrassed but Simon was curious.

"How much of that did you hear?"

"I'm sorry. I was just curious so I turned the TV down."

"It's fine, but seriously, how much of it did you hear?"

"Pretty much all of it." Chelsea felt badly, "I'm really sorry. I shouldn't have..."

Simon interrupted her. "No. If it needed to be private we should have made it private. I prefer that some details of my life not be known to the public for specific reasons, but nothing was said that I would hide from my friends or family."

There it was again, she thought. He'd called her a friend. She felt closer to him than ever before.

"Thank you," she said.

"What for?"

"For calling me a friend."

Simon smiled again with a warmness that she'd never seen in anyone else, then returned to Chelsea's room.

Jeanne came in the room a moment later with a small cup, a couple of pills rattling in the bottom, and handed it to Chelsea's good arm.

"If you don't feel like you need it, I can lower the dosage, or pretty soon we will switch to ibuprofen. One is for the pain the other is for infection."

Chelsea took the pills and the nurse held a glass of water with a straw so she could drink from it.

"Thank you," she said, then took another sip of the water. "I feel better today. It makes me so sleepy; maybe I'll switch tomorrow."

The nurse left the room and Chelsea looked at Simon.

"Can I ask you a question?" she asked. Simon nodded. "I know it's none of my business, but you donated 65 million dollars to this hospital?"

"Yes."

He looked uncomfortable so she decided not to ask anything more. She stared out the window, thinking about the number. It was crazy. Sixty-five million dollars that he'd given away. How much money did he have? Then she realized that even though she wondered how much he had, she was only curious. A month and a half ago she would have been excited to try to fleece him, to take as much of it as she could. She felt guilty now even thinking about that, like somehow it was his business and not hers.

She was still staring out the window when, without thinking, she said aloud what was in her mind. "How does anyone make that kind of money?"

"I guess I got kind of lucky," Simon said.

She realized she'd said it out loud and looked at him. "Oh, I'm sorry, I was just thinking that; I didn't mean it as a question for you."

"It's okay." Simon sat in the chair and seemed to drift into thought.

"Like I said, I got kind of lucky. Allie and I had only been married a couple of years. She was working here at this hospital and I was working from our apartment. It was a terrible little studio apartment above a Thai restaurant in Rancho Cordova." He smiled as he said it. "God, I'd give anything to go back and relive my life at that time. I wouldn't change anything. Our circumstances were terrible but we had so much fun just being together."

And then Simon began to remember again, but this time he told Chelsea.

☙

Allie walked into the studio apartment. It was tiny and everything smelled of Thai food. The only thing new in the apartment was the mattress lying on the floor in the far corner away from the door. Simon had hung a six-foot dowel in opposite corner. It stretched from one wall diagonally to another. Most of their clothes hung from it. What wasn't hanging was in a few plastic totes beneath. Allie had three and Simon had one filled with socks, underwear, and whatever else wasn't hanging on the dowel. All the totes were the same size and color and each had a label written on them with a Sharpie: "Simon's underwear and socks," "Allie's underwear and socks," "Allie's T-shirts," and "Special."

Between the mattress and the corner with the dowel was a tiny desk. Two screens sat on the desk with a tower beneath. Behind that was the only window in the apartment, which was open, partly to keep the computer cool but more to help with the temperature. There was an AC unit but Simon was not sure if it really worked, as once the outside temperature got over 100 the apartment began to heat up unbearably regardless of whether the AC was on. They kept the door propped open on hotter days, but the restaurant below opened their door on those same hot days and the smell and the noise from the place sometimes became too much for Simon to concentrate.

Opposite the bed was a tiny kitchen with a small counter that extended out into a bar. There was no stove, but they had a single electric burner plugged into a wall socket. The kitchen counter was plastic Formica, the cabinets were painted a lime green by some former tenant, and the walls in the entire place were a light purple. To Simon it looked like a fun house in a carnival.

Just to the inside of the front door and next to the kitchen was the only other door in the place, and led to the bathroom that was barely bigger than a closet and contained a sink with no counter, a toilet, and a tiny stall shower.

Other than two stools at the bar, there was only a wooden chair, which was where Simon was working at the computer when Allie walked in the open door. She was wearing scrubs and looked tired, but she was smiling when she saw him.

"Hey honey, you been working at that all day?"

"Yeah." Simon stopped and turned in his chair to watch her. She looked more than just tired. She looked like she was worn out. Her face looked thinner and he would have said she'd lost weight, but looking at her he thought her breasts looked bigger. Probably wearing a push up bra, he thought. It bothered him that she was working so hard and supporting them. He felt guilty that he was not supporting her fully and hoped that would all change soon. Today's news may change that and Simon was excited to share it with her.

"How about you and I go somewhere and eat?" he asked her.

"That sounds great," she replied. "PB and J at the park?"

"No, I was thinking somewhere we can get a burger."

Allie had shut the door and made her way over to the clothes. She stripped off the scrubs, revealing her lithe body in only a bra and underwear.

"Okay, I'm not going to get any more work done now," he said, standing up and moving to her. He put his arms around her from behind. "How do you expect me to do anything with this kind of distraction?"

She turned and kissed him. "I love you, but I've got baby vomit and a day's worth of sweat on me. Let me take a shower."

She extracted herself from his arms and reached to grab a pair of jeans and T-shirt from the dowel. She threw them on one of the stools then opened the tote that said special. Inside, it contained lingerie.

"I'll just wear something from here, how's that?"

Simon smiled. "Sounds great to me."

An hour later and they were at In-N-Out burger in Rancho Cordova. It was early October and the sun had set, but the temperature was warm. They sat on a concrete picnic table just outside the doors eating their burgers. The road noise along Sunrise Boulevard was loud but not so bad that they couldn't converse. Allie was dipping her fries in her shake, sharing about her day. To Simon it seemed she could talk endlessly with excitement about the things at the hospital.

"There are four kids right now in the neonatal ICU. Two are doing great. They just had some complications and are going to be fine. It's amazing the difference between the families. The two kids who are doing well, their parents are there all day long every day. The two kids who were born premature were drug babies. Those parents show up for an hour or two about every other day, or once a week. Jackie, the new nurse, says people should have to get a license to have a baby."

"Allie, I think Brian and I have done it," Simon interrupted, referring to his business partner, Brian Mather.

"Done what?"

"I think we've sold the program. Brian called me and told me he presented the program to several companies today. Before he got home from those meetings he had three calls. All three are offering to buy."

"I'm just happy we get to eat In-n-Out tonight," she laughed. "But really, I'm so happy for you. You've been working so hard on that thing."

He was still amazed at her beauty and almost childlike attitude about everything. Whether it was talking about babies in an ICU or about his business, it almost seemed secondary to her happiness.

"I don't think you understand," Simon said. "The first offer was for $800,000."

The French fry stopped halfway between the chocolate shake and her mouth. A large drop of the milkshake fell off the fry onto the table.

"$800,000?" Her eyes were wide.

"Yes." Simon smiled at her. "But don't get too excited yet. Whatever we get will be split between Brian and me. And after taxes that will mean even less."

"Like what?"

"Oh, I don't know, that would probably be around $250,000 each," Simon said, then continued, "But like I said, there were three companies interested. We need to see where the other offers come in and they could get into a bidding war."

"Simon that is incredible. I'm so proud of you."

"If we hadn't lived on your salary these last two years I'd never have made it happen." Simon looked at her. "I love you. Knock on wood but when this thing goes through I think we should look at buying a house or at least moving into a nicer apartment instead of the stinking hole we are living in now."

"I like our stinking hole," she laughed.

Simon smiled at her. "I just want to get you out of there."

She looked at Simon mischievously then looked around to make sure no one was watching them. Then she reached up and readjusted her shirt, revealing the top of her lacy black bra. "Well, maybe we should go celebrate."

There was no one else eating outside at the other tables and at In-n-Out you paid before you got your meal, but Simon yelled out loud, "Check please!"

They both laughed and got up to leave.

Two months later they had settled the deal to sell the security software for just over 1.8 million dollars. After splitting it with his partner he had earned $900,000. They set aside nearly half of that for taxes and put down $249,000 on a house in Folsom. The remaining $200,000 they put in the bank. For the first time since they had been married, Simon felt like he had actually provided for Allie. That he was taking care of her as much as she had taken care of them these last couple years.

♋

"Simon." Chelsea interrupted him.

He realized that he'd been talking about his life while looking out the window, and turned to Chelsea. She looked exhausted and he realized the pain meds had kicked in.

"I want to know what happened. I really do, but I'm sorry, I can't keep my eyes open."

"No, it's fine. I'm just droning on. I've never really talked much about it to anyone, so it felt kind of good to remember and reflect."

He looked at Chelsea and realized she'd faded off to sleep. He found the telling of his life tiring and depressing, yet somehow cathartic. He also knew the best medicine for him was to eat and be active. He looked at his watch and planned the rest of his day. He could eat, work out at the gym, then go and spend an hour at the judo studio training. He didn't want to, but he knew that it would take his mind off his despair.

He looked at the woman sleeping in the hospital bed and remembered his own wife in a similar position. The feeling of hopelessness returned.

"God I hate hospitals," he said to no one, then left.

Chapter 13

The next morning Chelsea woke to see a nurse looking down at her.

"You slept a long time," the nurse said when she noticed Chelsea's eyes were open.

Chelsea remembered waking a few times but each time it was the pain that had awakened her, and each time a nurse had brought her more meds, sending her back down into a spiral of deep sleep.

"How's your pain?" the nurse asked.

"Not as bad. I think I'll deal with it. I don't want to sleep more." Chelsea pushed the button on the bed to bring her up into a sitting position. "I'm more hungry than in pain."

"I'll go grab you a menu," the nurse replied and left only to return a moment later.

"Here ya go."

Chelsea looked at it and handed it back almost immediately.

"I'd just like fruit, yogurt, and granola if that's okay. And some coffee."

"We can make that happen," the nurse replied then left.

Chelsea felt alone. She couldn't remember Simon leaving yesterday, and only remembered him telling her a bit about his business partner and selling a business. Somehow it seemed like Simon wanted to talk to her about his life. That had not happened before and she wondered about his willingness to share. Maybe he was warming up to her. She didn't have a single friend to come visit and she hoped he would return and simply fill the void in what promised to be an eternally long day.

Her breakfast arrived and she began eating. Her arm hurt, her ribs hurt, her head hurt. As she ate, she considered calling the nurse for more meds. Maybe sleeping the entire day was better. Then Simon walked in.

"Good morning," Simon said as he saw Chelsea sitting up a little straighter and eating breakfast. Sun was streaming into the windows of the room bearing testimony to the fact that summers in the Sacramento Valley were rarely anything but hot. It was shining directly in Chelsea's face.

"You look better."

"I don't really feel any better."

"Would you like me to close the blinds?"

"No, the sun feels good. It will move and not hit me in the eyes in a couple more minutes." Chelsea was using her good arm to eat and squinting a bit. Simon moved to the opposite side of the room so she wouldn't be looking at him with the sun in her eyes.

"I must have fallen asleep yesterday, I don't even remember you leaving."

"It gave me a chance to get to the gym. I needed it."

"Thank you for talking to me."

"That seems a strange thing to thank me for," Simon said.

"Simon, we went out multiple times and you've never really shared anything about your life. And now I'm stuck choosing between complete boredom and pain or a drug-induced sleep. So yes, thank you."

The corners of Simons mouth turned up ever so slightly as he looked at her.

"Will you tell me more about your business?"

"I think it would bore you."

"More boring than sitting in a hospital room with nothing to do but wait for bones to heal?"

Simon was silent. Chelsea no longer cared if it seemed she was prying.

"Yesterday you told me you sold your business. But you said you sold it for about $2 million. How in the world did you donate so much to the hospital?"

"Well, I got another idea for a computer program. A better idea. I partnered with Brian and we went to work and sold that business for a lot more."

"That's it?"

"Yes, basically."

"Simon." She looked directly at him. "I'd really like to know. Please tell me about it. What did you do?"

"You really want to know?"

"Yes."

"Well I got an idea, like I said, and I invited Brian and his wife over to see if he wanted to partner again."

Simon began to tell Chelsea the story.

❧

Simon stood in the backyard with Brian drinking a beer. Burgers were grilling and they both talked while watching the grill. Kim and Allie were inside visiting. The blue sky belied the colder air which was normal for early December.

Brian was a large man, a bit overweight. Nearly everyone called him Big-B. When not working, and often even when at work, he was filled with a sense of humor that constantly spilled out of him. His laughter was contagious and Simon noticed that whenever they were around groups, Brian attracted people.

"So what's next, Simon? You gonna start the most successful pizza company in the world?" Brian asked. He was joking but it spoke to his confidence that whatever Simon wanted to do, he would do.

"Actually, that's why I wanted to have you over," Simon replied. "I'm thinking everything we did will be completely obsolete in about two years."

Brian laughed. "Yeah, you are probably right, if not earlier."

"So I have an idea and I was wondering if you'd like to partner with me again."

"Man!" Brian exclaimed. "Simon, I owe you everything. You didn't need to split things 50-50 with me. You did all the heavy lifting on that program. I pretty much just sold it."

"That's funny," Simon replied. "The program was the easier part in my mind. I would never have wanted to meet with those execs and present our program. I wouldn't have known where to start. I wouldn't have known how much to ask."

Simon paused to turn over the burgers which had begun to flame up as the grease dropped from them.

"Dang it, these are gonna burn if I'm not careful." He moved them off the flames to a different place on the grill and continued.

"Seriously Brian, without your personality in meeting with people, we wouldn't have sold. I don't have what it takes to make people listen to me like you do."

Brian stopped mid-drink and laughed. "The art of bullshit? Is that what you mean?

"No. You know what I mean. You connect. You know how to get the meetings. You network. People want to be around you and when you talk, they all listen."

"Simon, the entire process we were one stupid sentence coming out of my mouth from failure." Brian said it with a huge smile and Simon thought for a moment how much he liked this giant, jolly man with his sense of humor and welcoming personality.

"Doesn't matter. We did it together. I told you we'd be partners and splitting it 50-50 was never a question for me."

"When we met in class at U of W and you said one day you were going to start your own company I thought you were an arrogant idiot. Then you crushed every class we took together. You flew through every class and completed everything like it was a first grade spelling test. When you called and talked me into moving down here to work with you I thought maybe I was the idiot." Brian took a sip of the beer he was holding.

"Then I met Kim and got married. That whole year seemed like I barely had a chance to think. If I hadn't moved south to work for you I'd have never met her. I'd have never helped you sell the business. I'd never have a bank account the size I have, with a house that's paid off. I'd probably be unmarried and working for Microsoft up in Seattle."

"So it's my fault you guys got married?" Simon joked.

Brian smiled. "No. What I mean is I'm pretty grateful. Hell, Simon, in a sense we were both idiots. Think about our business partnership. We didn't have one. We talked about it. You told me we'd be partners and split it 50-50. We had no written agreement. Hell, I worked that first year and a half at Best Buy just so I could afford to live. You did way more work than me at that point."

"I guess I never saw it that way," Simon said. "We were both 100% invested in the business. We were both committed to it. You just didn't have a wife to pay the bills yet."

"I do now," Brian said.

Simon held up his beer bottle. "To the wives."

"To the wives," Brian said and clinked his bottle against Simon's.

Both knew the effort their wives had made in supporting them while they spent countless hours working on the computer program. Sometimes they would work nearly all night only to get up the next day and keep at it. All the while Allie had been working as a nurse and Kim had worked as a barista at Starbucks.

"But seriously, Simon," Brian said, "about six months ago Kim asked me about our contract. When I told her I didn't have one, that we were just working together, she thought I'd lost my mind."

Simon laughed. "I suppose you're right. It wasn't too smart. But it worked out pretty well, don't you think?"

"Damn good."

"So want to do it again?"

"What do you have in mind?"

"Look, we both know that computer security is going to be a major issue going forward. Right?"

"Yeah."

"I have an idea. Right now everything is about a wall. Everyone puts up a wall on their computer or system. A password gets people in the door. Once in the door everything is vulnerable."

Allie walked outside with a plate. "Hey, here's the cheese. Kim and I both want it, so you can put it on all of them unless one of you doesn't want it."

Simon put cheese on three and looked at Brian, "Cheese?"

"Sure." Simon put it on the last burger and shut the lid to the gas grill.

"It's too cold out here, I'll be inside with Kim," Allie said, and Simon continued talking to Brian.

"So I have this idea that we can build not just a better wall, but a defense. I was thinking about it like an army defending a barricade. They don't just stand there. They fight back. They do recon missions. What if we build a security program that does recon missions?"

"What do you mean?"

"Imagine a security system that, when you try to log in, it needs to see where you are logging in from. It not only needs to see your ip address, it needs to have access to your computer and look inside. Our program needs to rummage around in your computer before it grants access so it can determine if you are legit. It would be like a recon mission."

Simon continued. "Most hackers spend time just trying different passwords. A good defensive system would see that for what it is and immediately reject them. But not only would it reject them, it would see their computer and all that is on it. It would learn and reject that computer every time moving forward because of its recon.

"Hackers also steal the password and there is no defense for that. But what if there was a defense? What if, even though you had a password, the program looked at your computer, at everything on your computer, and could discern if you were friendly? That's what a recon mission does."

Brian watched Simon as he excitedly continued sharing without stopping. "What if our security system looked at your computer and said 'wait a minute this isn't a friendly'? What if the system learned to identify friendlies and reject hostiles? I think we can do that."

"I wonder if anyone would even go for something like that," Brian said. "That means that employees, customers—hell, anyone logging in would be giving a company the right to see their computer and everything on it. Sounds like a privacy nightmare."

"Not if they agreed to it. Most people are logging in from company computers anyway. And if they are logging in from a home computer they'll have to agree to the terms."

"Why would they agree to let their boss's computer look at theirs? That's the way people will see it."

"Think of it this way. You are an employee, you want to work from home. Or you are a CEO or exec and you need to log in remotely. First, you may be using a company laptop or computer. So it shouldn't be a problem there. Second, a warning could pop up and tell you the security system will now scan your computer for security threats. It could even state something like, 'everything on your computer is now being looked at.'"

Simon continued. "And we can write it so that even the loser with a computer full of porn would not be an issue. Privacy isn't the issue. Our program isn't going to care if your computer is filled with garbage. Our program would be looking at efforts to hack other computers. Again, go back to the idea of a recon mission. When the military sends out a recon team they are looking for threats. They aren't interested in friendlies or locals that don't pose a threat."

Simon opened the grill and saw the cheese was melted on the burgers. He went inside and grabbed a plate and came back out only to continue.

"Think of it more like a cop who runs through your house looking for something illegal. He finds nothing, so when he ends up on a witness stand he shares nothing about what he saw."

"Okay, well what if he did share it?"

"It's just a bad analogy. It's a program not a cop."

"But what if our system is scanning someone's computer and it finds kiddie porn or something like that?"

"What our program will look for is going to be the most difficult part. We can't just code it to look for one or two things. We have to take it up a notch. I think the program has to incorporate AI. It has to be learning. Since hackers and those who pose security threats will be changing all the time, our program has to learn and change. Our program needs to see inside a computer. It needs to see what is on it, it needs to learn, and to look at other computers with the same thing it learned. I'm telling you, man, we can do this. We are going to need to hire a couple ex-hackers just to help us create test computers so our system can learn."

"Slow down, buddy," Brian said. "I like where you are going with all of this, but I'm not even sure if it will work."

"Look, I know I can make it work. You just need to help me hire programmers. We need some of the best guys out there in the area of AI. Then we need some of the best hackers out there. Then, just like before, we sell it to someone like Cisco, or Microsoft."

Brian found Simon's confidence encouraging.

"Simon, if we do it right, it won't be obsolete the year after we sell it. We could sell it for a lot more."

Simon transferred the burgers to the plate. He shut off the grill and looked at Brian.

"How much more?"

"Man, I have no idea. Done right? A lot more."

"Well?"

"Well what?"

"Do you want in? Partners?"

"Seriously? Hell yes!" Brian replied.

"Good, because I already started. I started thinking about it the minute we sold the other program. When we moved in here three weeks ago I started working on it."

"Geez man, you need to take your wife and go to Hawaii or someplace and relax like we did. Take at least one day off."

"Okay, I will when we are done with this one."

"Simon, I'm in but on one condition."

"What's that?"

"We write up a contract. And this time we do it 60-40. This is your idea. You are way better at this than me. You write the code way faster than me. You need to take the lion's share."

"Why not just keep it 50-50?"

"No man, seriously. I didn't do half the work you did on the last program. I'll work harder but you really should take more. Hell, you already started without me. It's your idea. You could do it without me and take it all."

"No. And this time will be different. We are going to need to hire people who know AI. Former hackers, which pose issues right there. I'm not excited about hiring guys who are already prone to ethical and moral lapse. We will also need programmers. Hopefully, Tim and Sai could join us again."

"I've kept in touch with Sai, but not Tim. But I'm sure after the bonus money you paid them they will jump at the chance."

"I'm going to focus on writing it. You are going to hire everyone we need, you are going to manage things, and you are going to sell it all when it comes time. 50-50."

Brian shook his head. "60-40. It's your idea. It's your baby."

"Okay... will you do it for 55-45?"

Brian paused and looked at him. "Okay. 55-45."

Simon reached out his hand and they shook. Then he joked, "55 percent for you, 45 percent for me... you drive a hard bargain, Brian."

They both laughed.

"These burgers are getting cold, let's get inside."

❧

Simon looked at Chelsea. "I'm sorry. I'm probably boring you with all that."

"No, it's interesting. How'd it work out with you and Brian and the next program?"

"We kept creating programs and selling them, but for years we never actually made the defensive system I wanted to create.

Internet and computer security changed so fast we barely had time to create the basis of the system. Each one worked but each time it seemed it was nearly out of date by the time we had it finished, but we sold them all. Each time was slightly more lucrative than the first, but it was the AI, the learning part of the program that continued to prevent me from getting it perfect."

"Then, about eight years ago, cybercrime really got out of control. I'd been working on the defensive nature of my idea and we hired a few new programmers to help us. They were better in the realm of AI and we were successful. We finished the system in 2016 and sold it, but this time it was different."

"How?" Chelsea asked.

"This time we had a program that was more about the defense and fighting back than about just a wall and a password. Several of the largest companies out there went after it. We had to sign all kinds of non-disclosures and agree to all kind of secrecy. I think the company that bought it was worried we'd built some kind of backdoor into the system, or that we'd be a security risk. At first they wanted all of us to go to work for them. It was ridiculous but three of the guys did. Brian and I didn't really care if our guys took a job with them since we sold the company for more than we ever imagined. Technically, selling the business meant selling the employees too."

A nurse entered with a cup of water in one hand and a small cup of pills in the other.

"These are for pain and to control infection." The nurse said as she handed Chelsea the pills. Then she handed her the cup of water so Chelsea could wash them down.

"Thank you," Chelsea replied after taking them. The longer she'd been without the drugs, the more the pain seemed to be increasing.

Simon paused, waiting for the nurse to leave. Then he looked at Chelsea. "So we sold it all and made more money that either

Brian or I could ever have dreamed of. That's how I gave so much to the hospital."

Chelsea couldn't imagine. She wondered about the numbers and the non-disclosures. "You can't tell me?"

Simon looked at her. "Well, the non-disclosures are mostly about the company that bought us. I can't disclose that. As far as the money goes, both Brian and I structured our company as best as possible to keep our names private. We had as much reason for secrecy as the company that bought us did."

"We both structured the lion's share of the money into irrevocable trusts. So technically we don't have the money anymore."

"Why?" Chelsea didn't understand.

"That kind of money makes anyone a target. By putting it in a trust I removed my name from the money, at least for the most part. It makes me much less of a target."

Simon could see Chelsea was still confused so he continued.

"Let's just say, if someone sued me, they'd not get it because it's no longer mine; it's the trust's money now. I can get any of it I want as one of the executors but I will never need it. I left enough money outside the trust and it's invested and will earn me enough for the rest of my life."

"Aren't you worried about me?" Chelsea asked.

"Should I be worried about you?"

She'd spent her entire adult life manipulating others for her benefit. She'd justified her actions. Her father had left her mother. Her mother had died her sophomore year of college. Only two months after her mother's death, when she needed someone the most, she'd been date raped by a guy she'd known for nearly a year. She'd just wanted someone close to her. So she let it happen and continued to let it happen. She used those events to justify her actions. Life had taken from her and now she would take from others.

She looked at Simon. She knew she wasn't going to use him; she couldn't. She liked him. She wouldn't use the word love, since she had no idea what that really meant. But he had called her a friend and she felt a fondness for him that she'd never felt for a man. She felt very tired and closed her eyes.

"No, you don't need to be worried about me."

"I wasn't worried." Simon put down his empty cup of coffee and stood. He took a long look at her. Her arm looked like it was out of sci-fi movie, pins sticking out of the hand with rods attached on the outside extending up and then attached to more metal that looked like it was driven into her slender arm. The cuts on her face were better but the color of the bruises had turned to a yellowish blue and green. The blood causing the bruising had also moved and spread, causing nearly her entire face to be colored like she was wearing some grotesque mask.

Each time he paused to look at her, it angered him. Then he looked at the time on his phone.

"Chelsea I have a few things I've got to take care of today, but I'll stop by later if I can."

He looked at her and saw that she had fallen asleep. The pain meds had kicked in. Simon left the room and made his way down to the parking lot.

In the hallway outside Chelsea's room the phone rang. Nurse JoAnne picked up and a man's voice asked for Nurse Dawn.

"I'm sorry there is no Nurse Dawn, but we do have a Dawn who is a nurse's aide."

"Oh, I just made a mistake, it was the aide. Is she there?"

"I'll grab her for you, just one minute."

JoAnne got up and walked down the hallway. Dawn was straightening up a patient's room when she found her. "Hey, you've got a call on line 2."

"Okay, thanks." Dawn left the room and headed for the phone. JoAnne decided that since she was already at this end of the hallway she'd check in on her patients.

"Hello, this is Dawn," the young aide said when she picked up the phone.

"Hi Dawn, this is Bill Johnson, Chelsea's friend. I don't know if you remember I spoke to you the other day?"

"Oh yeah, I remember. What can I do for you?"

"Has Chelsea woke up yet?"

"Yes, she woke up a couple of days ago. Would you like to talk to her?"

The man on the other end was trying to think quickly. If she'd been awake, why hadn't she called the police? Why hadn't they come to question him or arrest him? Was she keeping his identity to herself in order to blackmail him? What was her game? He decided the most obvious answer was that she was going to try to blackmail him.

"Mr. Johnson? Are you there?" Dawn asked, wondering about the long pause.

"Oh yeah, sorry, I think we had a bad connection there for a minute."

"Would you like to speak with her?"

And then an idea presented itself. It seemed perfect and he ran with it. "No, actually, there is a group of us, friends of hers. We want to throw her a welcome home party and I was wondering if you could call me on the day before she is checking out so we can be ready."

"Well, she's not checking out anytime soon, but I'd be happy to help."

"That would be great. I'll leave you my number."

Dawn scratched the number down on a notepad and repeated it back to him.

"Yeah, that's it. Thanks a bunch, Dawn. I really appreciate it."

"No problem. It will probably be a couple weeks, but if I'm not here I'll have one of the nurses call you."

"That would be great." The man's voice seemed happy and excited at the same time. "Oh hey, I just thought of something. Don't tell her I called. I'm kind of the guy in our circle who always plans the surprise parties. If she knows I called she'll suspect us all."

"I get it. No problem," Dawn replied. She wished someone would throw her a surprise party.

"Thanks again," he said and they both hung up.

Chapter 14

Simon left Chelsea's hospital room and took the elevator to the first floor. He had been debating between eating at the hospital's cafe or grabbing fast food someplace off the freeway when his phone rang. He looked and saw it was Natalie.

"Hey, honey," he answered. "What's up?"

"Hey Dad, we just had a policeman call us and ask about you. Is everything okay?"

"Yeah, it's fine. Just tell him the truth."

"I did. He wanted to know if you were here last Thursday."

"Yeah, that was the day Chelsea was beaten up."

"Oh." There was a pause. "Dad, is everything okay?"

"Everything is fine. No need to worry."

"I hope you are being careful."

"Honey, I told you everything. No secrets. I just wanted someone different to talk to and eat with. Sometimes I just don't want to eat alone."

"You can always come here. Ron and I want you to come any time you want."

"I appreciate it, and I know that. I just needed a change."

"Do you love her?"

"If you are worried that I'll replace your mother..."

"No Dad, it's nothing like that. I'd be happy if you found someone. I just don't want you to get hurt."

"Natalie, I'm fine."

"I know it's not my business."

"No, I'm glad you asked. You can talk to me about anything, you know that."

"I know, Dad. I always have. I love that about us."

"I do too." Simon walked out of the hospital towards the parking lot. It was extremely hot for only noon.

"Would it make you feel any better if we got together and talked about everything?"

"Well, is anything different than what you told me a couple weeks ago?"

"Nope. I told you everything about her, about me, about what's going on."

"Okay. If things change just promise me you'll tell me."

"I will honey. I love you." Simon approached his truck and pulled out his keys. "I've gotta run."

"Okay, Dad. Love you, too."

When he opened the door of the Toyota Tundra, heat blasted Simon in the face. Rather than get in, he walked around and opened the door on the passenger side. The heat penetrated his suit coat. He'd be sweating in no time if he stood in the sun much longer. He made his way back around to the driver's side, reached inside the truck, and started it. He stood outside, both doors open, and reached in, adjusting the AC to high. After a moment he walked around and rolled down the window on the passenger door, then closed the door. He walked back around and climbed in and shut his door. He opened his window and put the truck in gear. Two minutes later he was driving down Highway 50 away from Sacramento towards Rancho Cordova. At 60 miles per hour with the windows down the air circulated quickly.

He rolled up the windows. It was silly, his process for cooling off the car, but it was the only one that made sense to him. The outdoor temperature was in the upper 90s and climbing. He had no idea what the temperature in the truck was when he opened the door, but he wondered if it was in excess of 150 degrees. Getting in and immediately shutting the doors was idiocy. Even turning on the AC was pointless as it blew hot air for the first 30 seconds. By opening everything up it vented the car and got the temperature down somewhat. Then by driving for a minute or two with the windows open, the temperature in the truck no doubt dropped even faster. Only when he guessed that the temperature in the truck and outside were nearly equal did he figure it made sense to roll up the windows and let the AC do its thing.

A few miles down the freeway to the east Simon exited. It was cooler in the truck as he drove up to a Chick-Fil-A drive-through window. He ordered a chicken sandwich and a lemonade. He sat in the parking lot to eat, and pulled out detective VanDyke's business card from his wallet. He dialed the number.

"This is Detective VanDyke," a voice answered bluntly.

"Detective, this is Simon Murray. We spoke at the hospital the other day. I don't know if you remember me..."

"I remember you," he interrupted. "What can I do for you?"

"Well, I take it you checked out my story?"

"Yes."

Even with that said, Simon felt like it was almost an antagonistic conversation. He tried to alleviate that.

"Look Detective, I know I'll be a suspect until you either find who did it or until you can be one hundred percent certain I didn't. I appreciate that you are thorough, and I want you to know

I appreciate what you guys do. I have the utmost respect for police and the things you guys have to deal with. Especially these days."

"Why are you calling? I'm sure it isn't just to thank me."

"I just wanted to know if you'd found any suspects or leads regarding Chelsea."

"Look, Mr. Murray, you're right. We do have a lot going on right now. We've got enough on our plates just dealing with the riots, the protests, and our regular work."

Simon heard the irritation in the detective's voice but said nothing. VanDyke continued, "You are aware of Miss Lee's profession, I take it?"

"Yes."

"So you'll forgive me if I don't spend a lot of time looking for someone who beat up a prostitute, or worrying about what one of her Johns thinks."

"Detective, I suppose you won't care or believe that I wasn't a John. But regardless, I was just trying to follow up."

"You are right. I don't believe you. But like I said we have way more important things to deal with right now. If Miss Lee wants to live in safety tell her to quit and get a real job."

Simon realized the conversation was pointless. "Sorry to bother you, Detective. I was serious when I said I respect what you do. I don't suppose it matters, but I hope you realize there are plenty of folks out there like me who feel nothing but positively towards law enforcement. Plenty of us in the country support you, unlike what the media and protesters present. I'll not bother you again."

"Thank you," the detective said, and hung up.

VanDyke was frustrated with himself. He recognized the mounting pressure in his own life. The riots against police, the fact that many of his fellow officers were quitting, and the mounting stack of cases on his desk spoke volumes. At the same time, he knew he shouldn't have spoken to the guy on the phone that way.

It didn't matter who she was, or her profession, whoever had done this had clearly tried to kill her. He made a mental note to look into her case and get back to Simon. Or, at the least, to let him know the next time they spoke that her case wasn't being ignored.

Simon looked at the chicken sandwich in his lap and thought about what he would do next. He had hoped the detective would be moving forward with the investigation but had to accept that wasn't happening. He felt the entire country went crazy every few years as protests and hostilities towards police departments grew with each mistake made by a few bad cops.

He finished his chicken sandwich and pulled his laptop out of the briefcase on the passenger side floor. It was hot from sitting in the car all morning and he hoped it would turn on and function properly. While it was coming on, he reached inside his coat pocket and pulled out a piece of paper. He opened it and looked at the names of the men he'd written down. The names he'd taken from Chelsea's computer.

One by one he put the names in his computer and did a basic Google search. Plenty to go on already, but he wanted more. He paid for a search engine that promised to give more. He wanted addresses, phone numbers, criminal backgrounds. He did a search for the first man on the list and wrote down the address. Then he continued through the list.

Two hours later he was still sitting in the parking lot, his truck idling to keep the AC cool. He now had a list of nine names, nicknames, and their addresses. He looked down at his list and thought about his next step. He pulled up Google Earth and entered the addresses. Then he rearranged the list starting with the closest and going in as close to a circle as possible. The men didn't live in a circle but it would allow him to drive from one to the next without backtracking repeatedly. He looked down at his list.

Paul Ryerson "Insurance Salesman" 784 Vista Drive Rancho Cordova

Prad Nadkarni "Computer Guy" 12812 Old Glendon Hwy Apt 18 Orangevale

Steve Maston "Republican" 1129 Golf Club Drive El Dorado Hills

Oja Vladkowski "Jock" 3382 Lakeview Drive Granite Bay

Bill Constantine "Democrat" 7171 Sunset View Dr. Rocklin

Allen Anderson "Electrician" 19789 Country Lane Woodland

Richard Hills "Professor" 6737 University Drive Davis

Mike Millson "Cardboard Guy" 346 Laurel Lane Elk Grove

Ron Crusiano "Construction Guy" 3195 Jamie Drive Modesto

Three of the addresses, Modesto, Woodland, and Davis, were outside the Sacramento area significantly enough that they would need additional time if he was going to drive to them.

He plugged the address for the first name from the list into his phone. It was 3:15. Why waste time? He could be at Paul's house in a matter of 20 minutes. He pulled out of the Chick-Fil-A lot and followed the directions on his phone.

As he drove he wondered if it would be that easy to identify who'd attacked her. It wouldn't be proof, but he remembered the truck from each of the last three dates. Would the '73 Ford be in the driveway? Could it be that simple? At first he thought it was coincidental but now he wasn't sure. If one of these guys drove that truck, it would be beyond coincidence.

He turned onto Vista Drive and found the address of Paul Ryerson. Simon parked across the street and several houses down and waited. The clock on the radio read 3:55. He hit the scan button and listened to the radio as it switched stations every five seconds. Scan... Boston sang their classic, "I hear my Marianne walking away..." Scan... "Traffic on Highway 50 is slow between the downtown interchange and just past Sunrise..." Scan... "I've got friends in lowly places where the whisky drowns and the beer chases my blues away..." Scan...

Radio station after radio station. Simon played name that tune in his head and opened his laptop again. He googled Paul Ryerson and began looking for everything he could find about the man. For nearly an hour the Tundra idled. At 5pm the digital temperature gauge showed the outside temperature to be 104. Simon watched the heat waves dance up off the street in the distance. Several cars passed and by 5:30 one car pulled into the driveway of the home next to him. The garage door opened the car drove in and it closed.

Ten minutes later a Ford Taurus approached him from behind and slowed. As it passed him the garage door opened at Paul Ryerson home. The Taurus pulled into the garage and parked. Simon pulled forward so he could see into the garage. A bald man in a suit climbed out of the car and walked to the door leading into his house. He hit a button to close the garage door and went inside.

Chapter 15

The following morning Simon was drinking a cup of coffee and waiting for the toaster to pop up. Other than the sound of the refrigerator's compressor running, the house was silent. At the moment it sounded loud. Had two people been in the room talking no one would have heard or even noticed it. He looked around the massive kitchen. Only three years prior he had surprised Allie and had the home custom built without her knowledge. He was nervous about so many of the decisions during the building process that more than once he almost gave up and told her what he was up to. But it would have ruined the surprise. The only thing he was certain of was the kitchen. He closed his eyes and could see her standing there the day they moved in.

೮๑

"Ooohhh." Allie nearly screamed with delight. "Simon, it's perfect."

She went first to the Williams and Sonoma stove and oven. It was a red stove with six burners and a grill. She turned each one on then off.

"We can have our friends over, and look," she turned on the grill. "We can even barbecue inside if we want."

She opened both of the oven doors beneath the grill. "Holy cow, on Thanksgiving, I can bake a pie and cook a turkey at the same time."

She reached up to the side of the stove and flicked a switch. Lights beneath the cabinets came on. She flicked another switch, the massive copper hood that covered the entire six-foot-wide stovetop started up.

"Say goodbye to the fire alarm going off every time I burn something," she laughed.

"Oh my gosh, look at the fridge," she exclaimed. It was actually two units side by side. A full-sized fridge and a full-sized freezer built directly into the wall. She opened the doors and looked inside. They were empty, which made them seem even more massive.

"They're huge!" She shut the doors and went to the island. It separated the main kitchen from the great room.

"I love the island. I love the granite countertops... and the color. Did you pick everything?" she asked him.

"Yeah, I hope you like it."

"I love it!" she exclaimed. "The stove is my favorite. I love the red, I love the old-fashioned look."

She stopped and looked around, then she turned to Simon and he could see she was tearing up. "Simon, I love it so much."

No longer able to keep the tears from flowing, she hugged him, "Oh..."

Simon laughed. "I hate it when you cry. Can't you be really happy without crying?"

"No." She stepped back laughing and wiped away the tears. "Remember that apartment over the Thai restaurant?"

"I'd rather forget."

"I'll never forget. I liked it there. I like our home right now. But this... I love it. Let's never move again."

She laughed some more. The tears had stopped but the mascara was a mess on her face. She hugged Simon again. "Thank you so much."

"Sounds good to me. We can stay here forever."

⁖

The toaster popped and shook Simon out of his daydream. The kitchen seemed quiet and cold. He looked at the stove and tears came to his eyes. It was hard for him to even use it. He looked into the great room. Dust was gathering on the coffee table and end tables. He knew he couldn't stay here but at the same time he couldn't sell the place. Everywhere he looked he saw her.

He buttered the toast and spread some jam on it. Then, with coffee in hand, he walked through the sliders onto the deck overlooking the backyard.

He looked up at the stars overhead. It was still early, the coolest part of the day. He took a deep breath, trying to forget. A faint yellow in the east was just beginning to signal the coming sun. Sitting in a lawn chair, he drank the coffee and ate the toast. Staying here reminded him of Allie and he hated it. But he didn't want to forget either. It was like a vicious cycle. Each memory was precious, but each also came with a sword that seemed to cut into his chest. Suddenly out of nowhere he thought of the Aerosmith song, "Sweet Emotion." He wasn't sure of all the words of the song... but that's what it was. A sweet emotion. It was the only thing that made him feel alive.

He finished his coffee and toast. The sky was only slightly lighter as he washed the cup in the sink and left the house.

Twenty-five minutes later and the Tundra was sitting in a visitors parking space at the Orangevale apartments. He could see unit 18 out his rearview mirror with its garage unit beneath. There were all kinds of covered parking spots. They were numbered and no doubt for the residents. Most were full of vehicles. None was a '73 Ford Pickup.

It was significantly lighter out but the air was still cool. Simon sat with the windows down listening to couple of guys clowning around on a morning radio program. The cool air felt almost like drinking water. His entire life, mornings like this reminded him of the farm and getting up early to work. There was almost a feeling of pride that he was doing something, accomplishing something, hard at work, before the rest of the world. He figured anyone who grew up on a farm felt that and it never went away. Now he was trying to do something. He wasn't even sure what he would accomplish, or how. But for now, he was at least acting on something. He was trying to accomplish one thing. Figure out who did it.

Nearly an hour and a half later the garage door opened. A young man emerged pushing a bike. He had a helmet in one hand and leaned his bike up against the wall of the apartment unit. He went back into the garage to shut the door. The door started to slide down and the young man ran and stepped over the invisible line to clear the garage door.

Simon had a clear view into the single car garage. Inside was a tiny car not much bigger than a golf cart. Simon had no idea what the make or model was and he didn't really care. It wasn't a Ford Pickup. The young man strapped the bike helmet over his jet-black hair, stepped onto the bike, and rode out of the apartment complex.

Simon looked at the list of men. Check off Prad Nadkarni, Computer Guy. He looked at the next name on the list and started the engine.

It was before 8 when he arrived at the hospital so he went to the cafe and ordered a cup of coffee. He sat drinking it, waiting for time to pass. Odd that he had spent several nights sleeping in the chair in her room, but now that she'd woken and was healing he felt like he couldn't go in so early.

By the time he finished his coffee the gift shop across the hall had opened. He picked out another arrangement of flowers. He looked at the mylar balloons. They felt celebratory. Nothing to celebrate about the beating she'd taken so he passed on those, paid for the flowers, and made his way to her room.

Dawn and JoAnne were both at the nurse's station when he arrived at the ICU.

"Oh Mr. Murray," Dawn began, "They've moved Chelsea out of ICU to a recovery room on the third floor."

"Thanks. Do you have a room number?"

Dawn clicked away on the computer for a moment, then looked up at him. "She's in room 3127."

He started to leave, then turned back to the ladies. "Thank you both for caring for her."

They both thanked him then JoAnne came out from behind the counter. "Mr. Murray, yesterday Chelsea saw her face for the first time. The doctor came in and talked to her about it. He assured her that she'd heal, but when he handed her a mirror she was pretty shook up. I just thought you might want to know."

"Thank you, JoAnne."

Simon made his way up to the third floor and followed the signs. He made his way through the hallways, past several nursing stations, until he got to room 3127. The door was only open about six inches, so he knocked.

"Yes?"

He heard her voice and he pushed the door open a bit more but didn't enter. "It's Simon. Okay if I come in?"

He looked down at the flowers in his hands and waited.

Inside the room Chelsea sat in silence. She couldn't stand the idea that anyone would see her face, let alone this man who was a complete enigma to her. It seemed like he was the least attracted to her of any man she'd known. And now, for the first time in as long as she could remember, what he thought, how he felt, his attraction to her, and his friendship; it all mattered. She didn't believe he loved her, but the possibility that someday he could weighed on her. She looked horrible and he was here to see her.

It wasn't even a conscious thought but she'd always used her looks to attract men, and now that it mattered, now that she really wanted to attract someone, she felt she'd lost her ability to do so.

Simon's voice came from outside the room again, "Chelsea?"

What the hell, she thought, he'd already seen her. "Yeah, come in."

She watched him as he entered holding the large vase filled with purple, red, and yellow flowers of all different types.

"I thought the old flowers were probably getting a little wilted," Simon said. She noticed that he hardly looked at her. He placed the flowers on the counter next to her bed. He took the most wilted of the flowers that had come up from the ICU, pulled them from the vase, and dropped them in a small garbage pail in the corner. He put the vase in the sink and rinsed it out. The entire time he never looked at her. She was reminded every second he didn't look at her of the face that she'd seen in the mirror.

Simon finished cleaning out the vase and turned and looked at her. He made that direct eye contact with his blue eyes. The crow's feet at the edges of his eyes deepened and he smiled.

"How are you doing?"

Chelsea turned her face away but felt like she had no ability to hide. "God how can you ask me that?"

"Ummm..." Simon fought for words. He knew it was her face. What he didn't know was if she was embarrassed, hurt, or worried. He had no idea what she was feeling. He wanted to comfort her, to tell her it didn't matter. He wanted to tell her the doctor had said she'd be back to normal in time, but he worried if he said that he'd be acknowledging that she looked bad. Or that it mattered all that much to him.

"I wish I knew exactly what you felt," Simon started. "I don't know what to say."

"Maybe you should leave."

"I'd really rather not." He paused and suddenly the music seemed louder. "Days Like This" was playing. It seemed perfectly appropriate, and Simon smiled.

They listened to the song, neither speaking. How could she tell Simon what she really felt? How could she say that at this very moment she was embarrassed? She felt like every decision she'd made since high school was a colossal mistake. She was ashamed of her life. She started to cry silently. Her body shook as she tried to hide it and remain quiet.

"Chelsea, you're going to be okay. The doctor said it will just take some time to heal."

Tears flowed down her face. "I know."

Simon felt at a complete loss. He had no idea what to say, what to do, or how to help her. He felt like maybe his presence was making it worse.

"Do you really want me to leave?"

"Do you want to leave?" she asked quietly.

"No." He saw her shudder and he continued, "What I want is for you to know how much you've helped me over the last two months."

"I'm not sure what you mean."

"You've helped me."

She turned and looked at him. "Is that supposed to make me feel better?"

"I hope it does," Simon said and moved closer to her.

"Just a few months ago I could hardly eat. I felt I had no one to talk to and I didn't want to talk to anyone. I didn't want to be in my home, but I had nowhere to go." Simon paused and looked at her.

She looked back at him. As ashamed of her life as she was, it made her happy to know that she'd meant something, anything, to him.

"You've helped me and if that helps or not, I want you to know."

"It does." She wiped the tears away with her good hand and looked around for a tissue. "Can you please find me some Kleenex?"

"Sure." Simon walked out and returned a moment later with a box. "They had some at the nurse's station."

"Thank you, Simon."

"It was just a box of tissues." He smiled at the joke.

"No... thank you for everything."

Suddenly they both felt awkward. Chelsea decided to change the subject.

"The doctor told me I could go home soon."

"That's good news."

"Maybe."

"You don't want to go home?"

"No."

"Why?"

For a moment Chelsea was quiet. Simon looked at her. She was staring out the windows. The sun was streaming in and the TV was giving the mid-morning traffic report. The bruising had gone down significantly and although the discoloration still remained she looked a bit more like the beautiful woman she was. It was then Simon noticed the look on her face. It was worry.

"You don't want to go home because you're afraid," Simon said out loud to himself, but also with a note of realization. "Whoever did this won't do it again."

She turned and looked at him.

"How can you be so sure?"

"People that do crap like this will be stopped."

"You can't know that."

"I do know it. Whoever did this will get caught and pay."

Chelsea thought again about her attacker. Was it someone she knew? She thought immediately of Construction Guy. She had told herself she wasn't going to see him anymore and she'd hinted at it with him. He had become possessive and demanded that he only see her. She realized now that she had become fearful of him. Simon was still talking and it snapped her back from her thoughts to the present.

"... Whoever did this will get caught and pay."

"How can you be so certain?"

Simon changed the subject.

"When did they say you could go home?"

"Tomorrow or the next day."

Simon didn't know what to say. He couldn't very well tell her to not be afraid. Anything he said would be pointless. There was some wack out there who did this and he hadn't been caught. Her fear was real and nothing he could say would change it. He wasn't even sure if it was fear of who'd attacked her or something else.

"It's not just that I'm afraid of who did this," Chelsea began as if sensing Simon's question. "I'm not sure what I'm going to do. It still hurts to breathe. My arm is stuck in this god-awful contraption. And my face..." She continued, "I can't go shopping. I can't go to the gym and work out. I can't..."

She couldn't work. Simon knew she was thinking it but didn't want to say it. He wondered if she had enough money to get by or if she was going broke just being here and not working. He was thinking about how to ask her about her finances but then had a different idea.

"I've got some work I've got to get to today, but if I get a chance I'll stop back by tonight."

"I thought you were done working. What do you do Simon?"

"Well, It's not really work. Normally I spend a couple days a week watching my granddaughter. It's only for a few hours a day, but it helps my daughter out and I love to see the little squirt. There are a few things I also like to keep consistent in my life, and one of those is working out. I usually go to the gym almost every day." Simon also thought about the list of men's names, but he didn't want to tell Chelsea anything about that. Instead, he just said, "I try to keep myself busy."

A nurse entered with a couple of towels in her arms. She looked from Chelsea to Simon. "I'm here to help Chelsea with a few things but if you'd like I can come back."

"No, I was just leaving," Simon said. "I'll try to stop by later today. Is there anything you need?"

"No."

Simon left the room and made his way down to the gift shop. He paid for another arrangement of flowers to be delivered then walked into the cafe. He ordered a coffee and sat down at a table. After a couple of sips he pulled out his phone. He scrolled down on his contacts and stopped at Dr. Kate Williams. He looked at her name for a minute debating whether he should call her or go see her. Then he hit the button. A moment later he was connected.

Kate answered the phone. "This is Dr. Williams."

"Kate, this is Simon Murray."

"Simon." She greeted him warmly. "I needed to call you but I'm glad you beat me to it. What can I do for you?"

"Chelsea told me this morning that she'd be checking out in the next couple days and I was wondering if we could delay that."

Kate wanted to make sure anyone like Simon got his way, but also wasn't sure what the reason was so she pried a bit.

"Well… we like folks to leave as soon as possible. I hope you understand, we run a great hospital, but there are reasons we want people to leave. The risk of infection, catching something else, from others." Kate continued, "It's typically healthier if folks are at home as soon as possible. Is there some reason she shouldn't be going home?"

"She's scared. The police haven't caught anyone and may not."

Without a pause, Kate said, "Let me check into her insurance and see how long we can keep her."

"I'm not even sure if she has insurance. But can I just ask you to bill me directly if she doesn't or if they stop paying?"

"I can do that."

"And can you have the doctor make up a reason why she should stay? I'd prefer she not know that I'm doing this."

"I'll probably not get Dr. Arnand to lie directly to her, but I'll come up with something."

"Thank you, Kate."

"Simon, one of these days you're going to have to tell me what's going on."

"I'll do that. Thanks again."

Simon hung up and pulled the list out of his pocket. He looked at the next two people on it. Republican and the Jock. He finished the coffee, left the shop, and headed for the parking lot. Once in the car he got out his laptop.

It took him little time to pull up information on the politician beyond his name, his party, and his office address. It also didn't take him long to realize that he was out of town. In Washington DC.

He pulled up the next name on the list. The Jock. Same situation. The team he played for was out of town.

Simon looked at his watch. It was still early in the day and the next two people on the list were both out of town. There were the three that were out a ways. Woodland, Davis, and Modesto. His mind worked like always, grasping for a logical approach to his next step. He ruled out a few choices then made his decision. Construction Guy. Modesto.

It made the most sense. First, he was the furthest away and it would take a longer time to get there. It was early in the day so this choice made sense. Second, construction workers usually started early and got off closer to 4pm. If so, he needed to be at the Modesto address by 3:45. And last, the other addresses still fit a bit more into a pattern that he could drive to; this was the most out of the way, so checking it out today made sense.

Simon planned out his day, working backwards. He would be at the address at 3:30, it was about an hour drive. He would need to stop and eat at some point, which meant he'd have to leave whatever restaurant he was at by 2:30. That meant being at the restaurant around 1:45, which meant leaving the gym a few minutes before that. If he gave himself two hours at the gym he would need to be there at 11:45. That would give him time to lift, run, and shower and clean up. He looked at his watch. It was 10:45. Enough time to go home grab his gym clothes and stop by to see his daughter.

Since Allie's death, Simon had only kept two habits. He went to the gym and he went to wrestling or judo practice. He didn't want to go. He wasn't always motivated to work out hard. But he went. Something inside himself told him if he didn't he was giving up. So he went. The time in the gym and the interaction during wrestling took his mind completely off his life as did the judo.

It was the physical effort that allowed him to get to sleep at night. For two weeks after Allie's death he nearly gave up. Sleep rarely came and finally, exhausted by his own mental state, he started the physical routine and sleep at least came a little more quickly in the evenings.

He had a workout room at the house. There was a treadmill as well as other equipment. Allie had wanted it. For her it was easier to balance her schedule with working at the hospital and taking care of Natalie. But for Simon he had always preferred a gym where others were working out. There was something about having others around and working out that motivated him.

So this morning, he grabbed his clothes and stopped by Natalie's house. She wasn't home. He tried calling her but there was no answer so he left a message. He arrived at the gym and worked out hard for nearly two hours. He showered and dressed at the gym. The hard workout and the tiny breakfast left him feeling almost lightheaded. He drove to The Habit and ordered a burger. He sat in the Tundra and ate slowly.

The sun was heating up the day and he thought back to the old pickup he drove on the farm. If he'd have left that truck in an idle it would have overheated in temperatures this high. It didn't even have an AC unit. He'd sat many a day in that truck, windows down, at the side of a field eating his lunch alone like today. Back then he never felt alone. It was just a rest between jobs on the farm and it was relaxing, even in the heat. Today, he felt very alone. Finishing his sandwich, Simon turned on the radio and tried to shake himself out of the funk he was slowly drifting into.

Time to focus on the immediate, he thought. He looked at his phone. It was only 1pm. It was early but he plugged the Modesto address into the map on his phone and began the 60-minute trek. Driving from Folsom to Modesto, he had several choices. Simon chose the more rural route. Grant Line Road south of Folsom until it hooked up with Highway 99, which he took the remainder of the way into Stockton.

He never understood why people made the decision to live in areas of high crime and rampant social issues. It seemed like in the last 10 years not a night went by that he didn't turn on the evening news and hear of a murder, a shooting, a gang-related issue, or some kind of violence in Stockton or in the surrounding areas of Lodi or Modesto.

If he was looking for a violent person, a person who could attack someone and nearly kill them, he felt it would be ironic if that person was from Stockton or Modesto. He wondered if he shared that thought someone would come to the erroneous conclusion that he was racist. The idea of treating someone better or worse based on the color of their skin was simply ridiculous to him. His father had hired immigrant workers from Mexico nearly every summer. He had worked alongside them moving water pipes, combining, and doing a million other tasks on the farm. Most were incredibly hard-working people, completely opposite of the stereotype. Without a doubt his father had fired many more white people for their laziness. Simon guessed that over the years his father had hired at least double the number of people with Mexican heritage simply because they were more willing to actually work.

His experience helping out with the wrestling team in college had exposed him to even more people with different racial backgrounds. He was convinced there were simply good people and not so good people and race had nothing to do with it.

He exited Highway 99 and followed the directions to Jamie Drive, noticing more and more graffiti on buildings. As he drove past a gas station on a strip mall the retail stores gave way to a residential neighborhood. It looked like any other neighborhood built 25 or 30 years ago. The houses were typical ranch style, most likely three bedrooms and two baths. Most had either one- or two-car garages. Many of the yards had brown grass that was dying in the summer heat. The occasional green well-manicured yard told the rare story that its homeowner still took pride in its appearance, or had the funds to pay the ever-increasing water bills the municipalities in California charged. Cars were often parked in the yards and the once straight concrete sidewalks were often cracked and uneven.

Simon turned onto Jamie Drive and was greeted by the sight of multiple police cars as well as two news vans. Nearly a dozen police officers both in uniform and plain clothes were standing in front of a house. The iPhone app in the seat next to him said, "Your destination is on your right." He pulled over a couple houses away behind one of the TV news vans. A line of police tape stretched out and blocked the growing crowd of people from approaching the home.

Both news crews were setting up and preparing to film with the home and police in the background of their shots. Simon shut off his truck and got out. It was stifling hot and for a moment he considered getting back in the truck with its air conditioning. Instead, he walked near the news crew that looked like they were about to start shooting.

A suited young news reporter stood in front of a cameraman who hoisted the camera up and began peering through the lens. Simon didn't know his name, but recognized him from one of the local Sacramento TV stations.

"How's this look?" the reporter asked, not yet holding the mic up to his face. "You got most of the crime scene in the background?"

"Yeah, that looks good. We've got it."

"Okay then, on me in three, two, one..."

The reporter's voice changed as he started to record. "A killing today represents the third person this week to die from gun violence here in Modesto. Modesto Police have not yet identified the victim but TKUU has been able to identify that the killing took place at the home owned by a Ron Crusiano. We have tried unsuccessfully to reach Mr. Crusiano. Neighbors reported hearing several gunshots just before 3pm. More at 5 on TKUU."

"How'd that sound?" the reporter asked and turned to look at the home. "Get some B-roll of the victim being carried out, or anything else you can, and we'll get back to Sac before rush, hopefully."

"Sure thing." The cameraman moved to get a couple different shots of the home.

Simon moved to get a better look too. The garage door was up and he could see an older pickup in the garage. It was a Chevy, probably mid '90s. He saw several police officers standing off to one side. He bent and untied one of his shoes, then proceeded at a quick walk as if to pass the officers. When he could make out what they were saying, he stopped, knelt down, and started tying his shoe. He could just hear the conversation and tied slowly, then made out to tie the other shoe as if one were loose, the other might be as well.

"We don't have a positive ID yet, but it appears the victim was a Ron Crusiano." One officer reported to the officer in charge.

"Not positive?"

"Vic took at least one shot to the face. The DL in the wallet says it's him but we'll need the coroner to confirm."

Simon straightened up and turned to look back at the house. A gurney with a covered body was being rolled out to an emergency vehicle. There were now three TV crews spread out on all sides of the crime scene. Most of the cameramen were filming as the body being rolled out was likely the only "action" they were likely to get. Simon took one last look around then climbed into his truck. He pulled out the list. Scratch one more off.

He looked at his watch. He'd be ahead of rush hour traffic and he considered his choices. He'd already worked out. There was nowhere he had to be. He thought about going back to the hospital. He looked at the other names on the list and smiled to himself. His original plan had been to be efficient and take a look at each of them while make a big counterclockwise circle around Sacramento. That hadn't happened but he was still getting through it. The next name on the list that would be most efficient was Mike Millson. An Elk Grove address would be on his way back to Sacramento if he took the interstate. He could likely be there before 5pm and catch the guy coming home from work. He started the truck and began the trip back to Sacramento.

If everything went well he could scratch another name off the list and make his way to the hospital and see Chelsea. He justified that thought by telling himself that she needed the company, but in reality he didn't want to go home to the empty house and just sit there. A conversation, even in a hospital room, was better than home.

He read the address into his iPhone as he drove and was sitting in front of the "Cardboard Guy's" house 45 minutes later.

Cardboard Guy, Simon thought. Some kind of job with cardboard, which might mean he was working in a warehouse or in manufacturing. Jobs that were outside in this heat or in warehouses without air conditioning that he was aware of had earlier start times. Guys started between 5 and 7am and were off in the late afternoon before the heat became unbearable. It was possible the guy was already home or had come home and gone back out again. Simon looked at his watch. It was 5:05pm. He decided if he saw no one by 6, he would leave and try again later.

A variety of signs bore testimony to the fact that it was an older neighborhood. Large trees in the front yards meant the homes had mostly been built at least 25 years ago. The homes were of older design and not the more modern track homes like so many other places around Sacramento. Mostly they too were ranch style, probably three bedroom two bath homes common for homes build in the '80s and early '90s. The lots were larger too, which was uncommon today. Builders today would squeeze three homes into the same space of two of these lots.

Simon parked in the shade under a large sycamore and turned on the radio. He listened to the traffic report followed by a five-minute news brief on the happenings of today. The killing in Modesto didn't even make it into the lineup. The news ended and turned to rock music. Boston, The Cars, Joe Cocker, and a song he had never heard before. A few cars made their way onto the street. He looked at his phone. It was 5:25.

He was listening to Don Henley's "Boys of Summer" when a car slowed in front of the home he was watching. The garage door lifted and what looked to be a Honda CRV pulled into the driveway. Simon pulled the Tundra slowly forward as the driver finished parking. There were no other vehicles in the garage.

Simon pulled over at the house on the opposite side of the street. If the driver was a woman then he'd not be able to check Mike Millson off the list. He waited until he saw a man exit the Honda. Check another person off, he thought as he pulled out and headed for the hospital.

He thought of Chelsea and wondered if she was okay with him just stopping in so often. He had assumed she was, but he wasn't sure. It was an odd relationship. He had not wanted to be alone so he had paid her to have dinner with him, but it was different now. Now that he was not paying her, maybe she didn't want him around.

His phone, tethered to the Tundra as he drove, rang and he looked at the caller ID on the truck's display. It was Natalie. He hit the answer button on the steering column.

"Hey Honey, what's up?"

"Hey Dad, are you doing anything?"

"Just driving at the moment, did you need something?"

"Yeah, well, Ron and I were just thinking we'd go see a movie tonight and were wondering if you could watch Emma."

"It will take me about 45 minutes to get there. Will that be okay?"

"Are you sure it's okay?"

"No problem."

"Thanks, Dad."

"See you in a bit."

He hung up and thought about Chelsea. Should he call her room and let her know he wasn't coming? Then he thought better of it. After all, she wasn't expecting him. He'd stop by tomorrow morning.

Chapter 16

Chelsea lay sleeping in the hospital bed when she felt a massive pair of hands grasp her throat. She struggled but felt her head slammed up and down. She opened her eyes but couldn't see who it was. The sun was directly behind the man's head, blinding her, and yet at the same time everything was blurry and dark. She panicked and tried to scream but the hands continued to squeeze, preventing her from doing anything.

Everything in her was screaming for help, but no help was coming. Everything in her mind wanted to be free from the hands. Free to breathe. Yet she felt herself slowly drifting away and knew she was dying.

Then she woke up. Sweat dripped down her forehead. She looked around the hospital room. Her heart was racing and she fought against the panic. She reached for the nurse's call button and a moment later a nurse entered.

"I'm sorry, but could I get something cold to drink?"

"Sure thing." The nurse looked at the beads of sweat on her forehead. "Are you okay?"

"Yeah, I just had a nightmare."

"Sometimes that can be caused by a fever. I'll be back in a minute with the water and to check ya out."

"Thank you."

The nurse returned a moment later with a large cup of ice water and an electronic thermometer. She put it up to Chelsea's forehead and held it until it beeped.

"Well, you don't have a fever. That's good," the nurse said, looking at her. "Anyone that went through what you have has every right to have a nightmare or two. If you'd like we can probably get something to help you sleep better."

Chelsea looked at the clock on the wall. It was 4:30am. It was still dark outside but she didn't want to go back to sleep after that dream.

"No. It was the only one," Chelsea replied. "If it happens more maybe I'll change my mind."

"Well, you may also want to know. You don't have to leave as soon as we'd thought."

"What changed?"

"Doctors orders. They decide everything around here." The nurse replied. "He probably wants to see you heal a bit more before leaving us."

Chelsea decided not to ask anything else. She felt as if a little weight had been lifted and didn't care why. The nurse left the room and left Chelsea alone, still feeling the lingering panic from the nightmare. She turned on the TV and watched the remainder of an old Andy Griffith rerun. She wasn't really watching it, but wanted it on to distract her from the dream.

The sky outside was just beginning to glow at 5am when the local news came on. She played Sudoku on her iPhone and glanced at the news, wondering what time they would bring breakfast. She thought about buzzing the nurse and asking for a snack but had just decided against it when she heard the name. "Ron Crusiano." She looked up from her phone and grabbed the remote. She turned up the volume and watched.

"... the victim of yet more gun violence in Modesto. This marks the third killing this week. Police have asked for anyone with any information to please call the crime stoppers hotline on the screen. Again, the victim was identified as Ron Crusiano, age 42..."

Chelsea watched as the video cut to a picture of a stretcher being rolled out of the house to a van. Suddenly Chelsea grabbed for the remote and turned up the volume. She watched as the video played and in the background she saw him. Simon. The suit, the hair. It was all quick, but he looked to be kneeling down and tying his shoe. As the camera followed the stretcher being rolled down the driveway Simon was standing back up and facing the camera.

Chelsea wondering what was going on. She remembered their conversation earlier and how confident Simon had seemed when he had said, "He will pay."

Her mind raced from thought to thought. Had Simon killed Ron? How could Simon know who'd attacked her? How could he even know of Construction Guy's existence? She told no one of her list of clients. It seemed preposterous yet it was unmistakably Simon in the news footage.

For nearly an hour she kept thinking through all the possibilities but no reasonable answer came to her. Then she looked at her computer. She turned off the TV and stared at the laptop. Simon had brought her things; he'd had the laptop with him. Simon made security programs for computers. Had he gotten her list of clients from her computer? Was he capable of not just breaking into her laptop but of killing Ron? And once again, how would he know it was Ron? She thought of Ron and realized that her own conclusion was that if the attack had been someone she knew it would have been Ron she thought of first. Had Simon somehow connected the attack to Ron?

She thought of Simon's smile and the wrinkle lines at his eyes. She thought of the way the corners of his mouth turned up ever so slightly even when he wasn't smiling. She remembered the kindness she'd felt whenever he spoke to her. Could he have killed someone? Was he some kind of sociopath who was smiling and nice while at the same time capable of killing someone? It creeped her out, imagining his face, that smile, while he pointed a gun and shot someone. And how could he know that was the person who had attacked her? She didn't even know that.

Three hours later she was still thinking all these random thoughts. The only positive thing was that she'd forgotten the nightmare and had eaten a good breakfast.

Two floors beneath her Simon entered the front doors of the hospital. He stopped by the cafe and grabbed a coffee then made his way across the hall and ordered yet another arrangement of flowers to be delivered to Chelsea's room. This time he took the flowers with him and rode the elevator up to her floor. His mind was preoccupied as he continued thinking about the different men on the list.

That morning he had scratched two more names off the list. At 3am he had woken up and couldn't get back to sleep so he decided to make the drive to the home of the Electrician. It was a long drive, 30 miles northwest of Sacramento in Woodland. It was very early when he arrived so he pulled out his laptop and Googled the "Jock's" name. He was a baseball player and it took very little time to pull up the team and look at the games and the box scores of those games. On the day of the attack, the Jock was in the middle of a six-game road trip where they played in Chicago and then in Texas.

Simon pulled up the game that was played on the Thursday night of the attack. The Jock had walked once, got a single, and struck out twice. Not bad, not great, not noteworthy as they had lost the game.

The Electrician's house had a work van in front of it. Anderson Electrical was stenciled on the side of the van with the telephone number. By 10am there was no movement at the house. The sun was now high overhead and Simon grew tired of sitting in the truck. He waited another 20 minutes and gave up.

Now Simon was taking the elevator up to Chelsea's floor, still thinking about the list. There were only four left. The Republican, the Democrat, the Electrician, and the Professor. What would he do if the truck never appeared in anyone's garage? What if he was wrong? Then he reminded himself, one thing at a time.

A male orderly was wheeling a cart out of Chelsea's room when Simon arrived. He left the door open so Simon entered. Chelsea was sitting up and struggling to put on makeup with her one good hand.

Simon stood staring at Chelsea for a moment, flowers in one hand and coffee in the other. She looked better each day. The swelling was definitely going down and the discoloration from the bruising was better. Or, he thought, it could be the makeup. But then he decided it didn't matter. She was healing and that did matter.

"You seem better today," he said as a matter of greeting.

"I am," Chelsea replied.

"Big plans today?" Simon said it with a smile, trying to be funny, but Chelsea didn't reply. She was thinking of a question that would help her understand what was happening, without sounding like an accusation.

Simon set the flowers on the counter and took up a flower arrangement from one of the first days he'd visited. Tossing the old daisies in the trash can he dumped the water into the sink in the bathroom, rinsed out the vase, and refilled it with fresh water and the new tulips.

"There you go," he said, then as he arranged the tulips he added almost to himself, "I've never really liked daisies as much as other flowers. Somehow they remind me almost of weeds. I guess it's because they grow wild pretty easily and were basically a weed around the farm where I grew up."

Chelsea remained quiet, watching him and wondering about the news footage. Finally she thought of a question that she could ask.

"Simon what did you do yesterday?" She tried to sound casual but she knew the question was out of nowhere and awkward.

Simon looked at her for a moment. "Well, I visited you for one."

"Yes, but I'm curious. You left here around noon. You don't work. What did you do with the rest of your day?"

"Well, I worked out. I told you before, I usually visit my daughter and granddaughter pretty often. I usually fill my day up pretty well without work."

"Nothing special yesterday? Nothing unusual?"

Simon looked at her, wondering what she was getting at. "No not really. Did you want to know something in particular?"

"No." Chelsea didn't know what to think. He was hiding the fact of his whereabouts and the only conclusion she could think of was that he had somehow for some reason been involved in a murder. It seemed incongruous with the man she knew, but how well did she really know him? She looked up at him, trying to read him. She made direct eye contact and tried to see into him. He smiled back and at that moment she thought of him killing Construction Guy. Goosebumps raised up on her arms. She just wanted him to leave. "Look maybe you could give me a few days. I have no privacy here and I think I could use a few days to myself."

"Is there something I can get you or do?" Simon asked.

"No." She said it more harshly than she meant too. "Just don't visit me anymore."

Simon could tell she was upset but had no idea why. "I can give you all the time you need. Did I do something wrong?"

"I just want to be left alone."

"Okay." Simon made his way out of the room, leaving Chelsea alone with her thoughts.

She realized she was angry and hurt. He was lying and it felt like the one thing about him she'd always sensed, his sincerity, was gone. The anger seemed like a natural reaction to being lied to. But why was she hurt? She had no right to think he was any different than any other man she knew. Who was she kidding? She cared for him and if he cared for her, too, he would be honest with her. Lying was just further evidence that he didn't care about her. She tried to tell herself it didn't matter but it did.

A myriad of random thoughts flooded into her mind, overwhelming her. She knew she'd have to go back to her condo, and it scared her. She still didn't know who'd attacked her. What if it was one of her customers? In the back of her mind, she thought of Construction Guy and wondered if it was him. What if it was a former customer? Would he return to finish the job? What if it was just a random attack?

She was afraid to return to the condo if there was someone out there trying to hurt her, but it could be that no one was trying.

More thoughts flooded into her head. Returning to the condo and having her arm held up in this metal contraption like a broken wing. She couldn't see how she could even drive like this. One of the few constants in her life, working out daily, was impossible. How would she keep in shape for her job? Then she realized she didn't ever want to go back to her job. Anything but that, she thought, but how would she live? She thought about leaving the hospital and felt trapped. An overpowering sense of hopelessness overwhelmed her. She began to cry. Tears started to flow and she wiped them away and saw the mascara on her hand.

"Dammit!" she said aloud. It was the first day she'd put on makeup and it was a mess.

She took a deep breath and forced herself to stop crying. Taking a few tissues from a box next to the bed she dabbed her eyes and the running mascara. While she worked to fix her makeup she tried to separate the facts that she knew from feelings that she was having. She listed the facts in her head. She didn't know if he'd killed anyone. All she knew was that he was at the location and that he had lied to her about it. Try as she might she had no idea how he could have come to be there, but maybe there was a reason. How could he possibly know Construction Guy? She decided that she'd ask him the next time she saw him.

Ironically, and in the back of her mind, when she thought of her attacker, she had wondered if it was Construction Guy, and that had her even more worried. If Simon had known it was him was he under the impression she would want him dead? Did Simon kill him because of that? Her mind was racing to all kinds of conclusions again and she had to take a deep breath and try to calm down. She didn't know anything.

Chapter 17

At 5:30 the next morning Simon poured himself a second cup of coffee and made two slices of toast. As he was waiting he pointed the remote control across the great room and turned on the TV. The early morning news was on, mostly showing clips from the day before and some human interest type stories. He fried an egg and put it on one of the slices of toast, then put jam on the other.

He set the plate of food on the island that separated the kitchen part of the great room from the living room. He finished the egg on toast and saw prominently displayed on the screen were the words "Steve Maston, Rep. Town Hall." He turned up the news broadcast.

"Representative Steve Maston, Republican from California District 4, held an open house last night in Auburn. Polls show Maston leads by a wide margin and most expect him to hold on to his seat. Maston told News 10 that he plans to continue serving the people of California and hopes that the voters will help him by defeating the radical agenda of democrat Tom Sterney."

The short audio was clipped over video shots of Maston during the town hall meeting and visiting with people afterwards. He was a good-looking man with dark hair and a wide smile although he was a bit overweight. No doubt being good looking helped him get elected. Simon knew the reality. Probably 60 percent of voters read at a sixth grade level. Most of them never read any real news, but instead listened to the politicians' talking points, regardless of the fact that those talking points were in fact pointless. Politicians were the same the world over. Say things that don't matter, tell people you stand for something that everyone would agree with, then make it appear your opponent does not.

Simon could hear them in his head saying something like, "We must have clean drinking water. If my opponent gets elected he will vote against the very environmental safeguards we must have." They were all liars and narcissists as far as Simon was concerned.

The news clip ended as the media shouted questions at Maston as he walked out and around to the driver's side of his pickup. It was a newer F-350. The truck looked to be elevated a bit and Simon saw it plainly. The camera angle caught Maston as he stopped and looked over the top of his truck and answered one of the questions being shouted at him.

"It's as simple as this: a vote for me is a vote supporting freedom, quality education, and law enforcement. My opponent would abolish what we hold true and love."

Simon smiled. Another pointless statement. He may as well say something like, "I am for humans" or "I support breathing air."

Nevertheless, Simon saw the truck and realized that was one fewer person he had to go check out, at least for now. He knew the Maston could have, and likely did have, multiple vehicles. He also knew it was not as likely that he had two pickups. The term

Occam's razor popped into his head, the problem solving principle that his father had taught him. "The simplest explanation is most likely the right one." Simon had learned to use that theory in computers as well as in wrestling. He was using it now. Until he went through the list and saw what vehicle each man was driving, he would operate on the principle. If they weren't driving the truck, it probably wasn't theirs. Once he worked through everyone on the list, if he didn't see it, he would circle back around and look in more detail. For now he simply used Occam's razor and ruled them out.

He walked to the entryway where he'd set the list of names and looked at the next name on the list after Maston. Bill Constantine, Democrat. Another politician. The Rocklin residence wasn't far. He looked at the time. Maybe.

At 6:30am Simon was sitting several houses down from the home of Bill Constantine. Unfortunately no one came or went all day. Close to noon Simon left, ate lunch, and worked out at the gym, but by 4pm he was once again sitting in the same place. The next day the same exact thing had happened, which was nothing. Simon decided that the politician must be out of town or on vacation. Rather than waste another day he looked at the next name on the list.

Simon spent the next two weeks getting out of the rut he had been in since Allie's death. Looking for Chelsea's attacker was not only time consuming but it took his mind off himself and focused it on a problem. When people weren't home he moved on and came back later. Several of the remaining names on the list were people who lived out of town so the driving was more time consuming.

He ruled out the Professor in Davis. From all he could tell the man may not even own a vehicle. He lived adjacent to the campus and walked every one of the three days that Simon watched him.

He couldn't be sure he didn't have a vehicle, but Simon checked him off the list for now. He could always circle back around, but there was no point in looking for a truck that wasn't there if that was the situation.

After several more tries at the home of Bill Constantine with nothing happening he had found the phone number for his office and called. He learned that the Democrat was indeed on vacation and wasn't scheduled to return until the day after tomorrow. Simon then drove out to the home of Allen Anderson and sat for an entire day with no luck. No one came or went.

Simon looked at the list. Of the nine names, he had crossed off seven. The final two, Allen Anderson and Bill Constantine, were not home. He tried to think of other ways to figure this out, but he was stumped. If he had access to the DMV records he could find out who owned '73 Ford Pickups, but he didn't have access. Even if he did there were probably hundreds still being driven around in California today.

For the first time he began to accept the possibility that one of her current clients didn't own the truck. He wondered what a real private investigator would do. With a greater appreciation for the work of detectives, investigators, and the like, Simon decided to take a few days off.

Natalie had been calling and he'd not responded so he left the home of Allen Anderson in Woodland and drove the hour and a half back to her house, calling her when he was still 30 minutes away.

"Hey Dad," Natalie greeted him as she picked up the phone.

"Hey. What plans do you guys have tonight for dinner?"

"Nothing much. I was just about to figure something out."

"Can I take you all out?"

"Let me check with Ron and I'll call ya back."

A few minutes later the phone rang and Simon answered.

"Hey Dad, I talked to Ron. Sounds good. Where'd you want to go?"

"You guys decide. I'll just stop by your house and we can go when you are ready."

"Okay." Then Natalie paused. "Hey Dad, can I ask you a question?"

"Sure."

"This lady you were seeing for dinner, you said she was in the hospital, is she okay?"

"Yeah, I think so."

"Do you like her?"

"It's not like that."

"I know, I know. But I just want you to know Dad, it's okay with me if you want to see someone."

"I know, honey. Chelsea is just a friend, that's all."

"Is she still in the hospital?"

"I'm not sure. I haven't seen her for a while. She asked me not to visit her anymore."

"Why?"

"I don't know."

"Okay, well, sorry."

"It's okay. She's been through a lot."

"Yeah, you told me." Natalie continued, "Well, Ron should be here in about 10 minutes, how long till you are here?"

"I'm coming up to Rancho Cordova now. I'm probably about 20 minutes away."

"All right. See ya soon."

Simon took the family out for dinner that night, then took the next several days off from his searching. He spent the time getting back to the things that mattered most to him. He spent time each day at the gym, 15 minutes of cardio, followed by weight training, then he followed it up with 30 to 60 more minutes of cardio.

He enjoyed the gym and liked switching the cardio workout daily. One day he'd go hard on a rowing machine, the next would be the StairMaster, then running on a treadmill, and finally the bike. Likewise, he rotated his weight regimen, hitting each muscle group every other day. Every day, he worked his core with sit-ups and planks. Overall, he felt that he was in as good shape as any 50-year-old man could be.

High schools were back in session and Simon visited the wrestling coach, Lance. They'd become friends years before when Simon had assisted in coaching, and Lance welcomed him back each year. Simon looked forward to sparring with the guys on the team. Even at 50 years old, he still enjoyed the competition. At first, Lance thought Simon was crazy, but had grown accustomed to watching this middle-aged man not only wrestle some of the best young men on his team, but beat them.

"You still plan on sparring this year or you going to hang it up?" Lance asked him as they sat in the teachers' lounge.

"I'm going to wrestle," Simon said. "When I'm too old to actually wrestle then I'll hang it up."

"Don't hang it up as long as I'm coach. You are a great help to the team, whether you are sparring with the guys or not. You are a better coach than I am. We need you around here."

"Thanks, but for me the fun is more about testing my skills against theirs. I don't mind teaching them till they are better than me, but I like the effort and the test."

"Suit yourself."

Simon left the high school and decided to continue looking for Chelsea's attacker. At this point there were still two names left on the list and it didn't feel right until he crossed them off.

He drove to the home of the Democrat and sat for several hours. Unfortunately, there was no movement at the house. He tried looking up information on the Democrat to see if he was still out of town, but could find nothing. Eventually, he drove home.

The next two days he continued the same routine. Working out, wrestling practices at the high school, and sitting on the street of the Democrat. Finally, on the third day, the garage door opened. A Lexus pulled out driven by a man with grey, almost white hair. Simon pulled forward and saw that the only other car in the garage was a Mercedes. He drove forward a few blocks then pulled over and did a quick Google search to see what the Democrat looked like. The search pulled up a 67-year-old man. Married. Grey almost white hair. It was the same man. Check another off the list.

Chapter 18

Two days later, Simon's daughter Natalie walked into Chelsea's hospital room. Chelsea looked at her red hair and freckles. She was beautiful in a unique way. Both women stared at each other for a moment before Natalie spoke.

"Hi Chelsea, we haven't met. My name is Natalie. I'm Simon's daughter."

Chelsea was irritated. She decided she didn't want the speech she knew was coming, so she spoke before Natalie could say anything more.

"Look, I know what you are going to say, you can just save it. I asked your dad to leave the other day and not come back."

"I'm not sure why you did that but I suppose that's your business." Natalie said and at the same time looked truly confused. "I just came by to speak with you for a moment. I'm not sure what you thought I was going to say."

"Look, I'll leave your dad alone, That's what you want right? Stop taking his money. Stop seeing him. Stop sleeping with him."

At that last statement Natalie's eyebrows shot up. "Please! I don't want to know about that."

Then she looked at Chelsea, smiled warmly, and actually laughed a bit. She moved over next to the bed and sat in the club chair next to Chelsea. "I think you are making a mistake. I didn't come here to ask you to leave Dad alone. I came here to thank you."

It was Chelsea's turn to be confused. Several times in her life women had come to her and demanded that she leave their husbands alone. Never a daughter, but several wives. Hell, she thought, she was after their money and no doubt this red-haired girl didn't want Chelsea taking it all. But now she was thanking her?

"Thank me for what?"

"Look, my dad is a grown man, he can do whatever he wants. I came to thank you for helping him."

"I'm not sure how I've helped him."

"Since my mother died my dad has been depressed. And if you really knew my dad you know that is not normal for him. He's always been upbeat, driven, positive, and fun. My dad used to smile more than anyone I knew. And then my mom died and for a while I thought it had destroyed him. He barely ate, he stopped doing almost everything, and ceased to be the father I grew up with. If it wasn't for his habit of working out, and seeing his granddaughter nearly every day, I don't know if he would have survived. I know he started seeing you a few months ago."

This time Chelsea's eyebrows shot up and, seeing her questioning look, Natalie continued. "Yes, I knew. He told me."

"He told you about me?"

"Well yes. We've always talked about everything. When mom died he stopped communicating and then about two months ago he started talking with me about things again. I asked him what was going on and he told me."

"What did he tell you?"

"Well, to be honest, that's between us." As she said it she sensed Chelsea's demeanor change, that she was somehow disappointed.

"But I suppose I can tell you," Natalie said and Chelsea's eyes met hers. "I asked Dad what was going on, and he told me he was seeing someone but it was kind of different. When I asked him what he meant by different, he told me he was paying a woman he met online to meet him for dinner. He told me he wanted someone to talk to that didn't remind him of my mom or the past. He said he just needed this and hoped I was all right with it."

"And you don't mind?"

"Why would I mind?"

In spite of the words Chelsea didn't believe her.

"You are okay with me taking money from your dad? You are okay with your dad paying a woman like me?"

Natalie looked at her. "A woman like you? You seem kind. You made my dad smile again. You're not obtuse or we wouldn't be having this conversation. Knowing my dad, he wouldn't have seen you more than twice if you didn't have at least average intelligence."

Natalie looked at her and continued, "My dad always taught me to treat everyone with kindness and fairness. I'm not sure what you mean by a woman like you."

Chelsea refused to think Natalie really understood. "Look, I'm not a counselor who gets paid, I'm an escort."

"I understand what you do, but that isn't who you are. You can be anyone you choose to be."

"So you are okay if I continue to take money from your father?"

Natalie let out a light, airy, warm-natured laugh. "Well, first understand this. There is no amount of money that you could take from my father that would make a difference. He can afford to do anything he wants to do."

"So you really want me to believe you are all right with this?" Chelsea asked.

"My dad is talking to me again. He is eating, at least something. I've seen him smile again. Yes I'm not only okay with it, I was serious when I said I was here to thank you."

"What if I took all of his money?" Chelsea didn't even know why she said it, but felt like she was checking to see if this girl was for real.

"Then you take all he's got in his bank." Natalie answered matter-of-factly. "My dad gave me more than I'll even need when he sold his business, and he has protected his assets in a trust. My father gives away money all the time. He won't give away money unless he wants to and that's his business."

"So you want me to think you are all right with this?" Chelsea pressed, still unconvinced.

Natalie stood up. She placed her hand lightly on Chelsea's good arm and looked directly into her eyes.

"I'm all right with it. I'm all right with anything that makes my father smile again."

Chelsea saw Simon's face in Natalie's, the direct, honest, sincere trait he'd passed to his daughter. Chelsea said nothing, somehow feeling embarrassed by her entire life in front of this younger woman.

"Look, I'm going to be going." Natalie reached into her purse, pulled out a business card, and handed it to Chelsea. "Here is my number, if you need anything let me know."

Natalie started for the door and then stopped, turned, and looked at Chelsea with a smile. "And as for your comment earlier. I know you aren't sleeping with him."

"How...?" Chelsea stammered.

"I told you we pretty much talk about everything." Natalie laughed lightly. "We don't talk about his sex life, ew. But he wanted me to be comfortable with your situation and he told me he just wanted someone to talk to. He felt I needed to know he wasn't sleeping with you."

Natalie thought she saw disappointment in Chelsea but couldn't be sure. Then Natalie added, "To be honest, I think he didn't want me to feel he was betraying my mom somehow."

Chelsea nodded but was not sure what to say.

Natalie turned to the door. "Just don't hurt my dad. He is a great guy." She said it almost as an afterthought thrown over her shoulder as she left.

Chelsea sat in silence.

Chapter 19

The next day Simon found himself with a sense of excitement. There was only one name left on the list. He looked at his watch and decided to hit the gym early so he could make the drive out to Woodland. At 3:30pm he was sitting a few doors down from the home of Allen Anderson, the last name on the list.

He knew he was too early, but he had been eager to complete at least this leg of the journey. His workout had been hard and long and now he felt the muscles in his body relax as he drank water and tried to recuperate.

He looked back at the list. Paul Ryerson, the insurance agent, had driven a car and had no pickup. Prad Nadkarni, the Computer Guy, had ridden a bike and had a tiny car. The only vehicle he'd seen Steve Maston the republican drive had been a Ford truck, but it was new and the wrong model. Ora Vladkowski, the jock, had been out of town playing baseball on a road trip. Bill Constantine, the Democrat, drove a Lexus and looked too old to pull off the kind of attack Chelsea had suffered. Richard Mills, the Professor, seemed to not even own a car. He was also a tiny man that made Simon doubt he could pull off the attack on Chelsea. Mike Millson, Cardboard Guy, didn't drive the right kind of vehicle and his garage had no Ford truck. Ron Crusiano, Construction Guy, who was now dead, also didn't drive a Ford F-150. So that left Allen Anderson, Electrician.

Simon drank more water and waited. He thought about what he should do if he saw the old Ford. He could call the police, but it would all be circumstantial. He could confront the man, but that could result in so many possible outcomes that even Simon's logical brain could not immediately comprehend the results. He took a centering breath. A long deep breath in, held it, then released. One thing at a time, he told himself. First identify who the attacker was, then come up with a plan of action. One thing at a time.

At 5:15 the Anderson Electrical van pulled up and parked in the driveway. The garage door opened as the man climbed out. Simon pulled his truck forward and looked in the garage as he went buy. No truck. Only an old Volkswagen. Simon drove on past. It was a letdown.

As he drove home he realized that he had failed and that didn't sit well. Then his phone rang. He looked at the caller ID, saw that it was Natalie, and picked up.

"Hi Honey, what's up?"

"Hey, Dad, I just wanted to you know I stopped by the hospital yesterday and saw Chelsea."

Simon wasn't sure where this was going so his reply was a short, "Ooo-kay."

"Dad, go back and see her, will ya?"

"Did she ask for me to?"

"No, Dad, but just do it."

Simon didn't reply.

"Dad, did you hear me?"

"I heard you."

"Well, will you go see her?"

"Why the sudden interest?"

"Dad, listen, will you just go back and see her?"

"Okay, but tell me why."

There was a pause. "Two reasons. You need it, and she needs it."

"Those aren't really reasons."

"They are my reasons. Trust me, she'd like you to come by."

"But she didn't ask for me to."

"No, but I know she would like it."

There was a long pause. Finally Natalie broke the silence.

"Tell me you will."

"Okay, I will."

"Thanks, Dad. Gotta run, bye."

"Bye."

Simon hung up and drove home. His mind was no longer on the attacker; he was now thinking about when he would go visit Chelsea. Even though he'd told Natalie he would go see her he decided he would wait.

Chapter 20

Several days passed and each grew more monotonous for Chelsea. On one hand, being in the hospital room provided her with the ability to heal as well as feel safe after the attack, but her privacy was gone. People came and went, disturbing her sleep, her rest, even the few moments she found herself relaxing. At first having a menu to order from, and having nurses there to care for her, had seemed nice. Now the food seemed to all taste same and the nurses, while kind, were a constant interruption. There was also a growing concern, within her, about the cost of the room.

She knew most hospitals didn't turn away emergency patients, which she had been, regardless of their insurance coverage or ability to pay. However, now she was no longer "an emergency" and the cost had to be paid by someone.

When she inquired, at first the nurses just said, "don't worry it's being taken care of," as if that explained everything. She pushed Doctor Rey when he came in and got no further with him than them. Finally, after pushing hard one day, one of the nurses winked at her and said, "You don't need to worry about, it. I'm not telling you who is paying for the room, but let's just say a nice good-looking man is helping you out."

Chelsea knew that could only mean one thing. Simon. Not only did he have the money, he was, no doubt, paying for her room. She hadn't seen him since she'd asked him to leave, and now she felt that maybe she'd jumped to a conclusion. She'd seen him in the news, but what did that really mean? She remembered his face, the kindness, the warmth. She wished he would come back and see her. She looked at her phone and thought about calling him. She picked up the phone and began to dial his number, then hung up. She wasn't ready to call him.

That evening as Chelsea watched the news, she caught a story about an arrest being made in the murder of Ron Crusiano. She went to her phone and Googled the news and read all she could. According to the report, the murder had been drug-related and a gang member had been arrested. It still didn't answer why Simon was at the scene of the murder, but she no longer cared. She thought about calling Simon but was embarrassed by her own treatment of him.

Another week passed and, even though she had anxiety about being alone in her condo, she knew she couldn't stay at the hospital any longer. She informed the hospital staff she was going to leave the following day.

The day before, the doctor had finally removed the metal monstrosity that had been attached to her arm, and she now had a cast which ran from just below her elbow down to the palm of her hand. She was able to breathe in without the stabbing pain. Her face had healed significantly, and with makeup, she was able to look almost normal. It was time to leave.

She looked at her phone, and as she had done countless times over the previous week, she thought about calling Simon. She picked up the phone and texted him instead.

Thank you for all you've done for me. I am leaving the hospital today. I just thought you should know.

Simon's phone "pinged" as he was leaving his driveway. As he pulled out he thought about the text and fact that he told his daughter he would go see Chelsea days earlier. Instead of driving to the gym, he headed for the medical center.

Ten minutes later Dawn walked into Chelsea's room.

"I hear you are leaving us today?"

"Yes."

"Well, I'm here to help."

Dawn helped her get packed and now all of her things, the painting, the laptop, the Scrabble board as well as her bags were on a cart near the door.

"Do you have someone meeting you to drive you home?" Dawn asked.

"I'm just going to call an Uber. Which reminds me..." Chelsea unlocked her phone and opened the app. She saw that several cars were near but decided to wait to select a driver until she was in the lobby.

"Okay, well, I've got another patient I have to take care of, but I'm going to call an orderly to take you down."

"Okay, thanks."

Chelsea was left sitting in the room alone. Now that she was all packed up it felt much less personal and back to a cold sterile hospital room. She sighed. It would be good to just sit in her condo and eat the food she wanted.

Dawn called an orderly, then dialed the number on the notepad in front of her.

"Hi, Mr. Johnson? This is Dawn at U.C. Davis Medical Center. You asked me to call when she was checking out. I left you a message last night but I wasn't sure you got it so I wanted to call you again and let you know..."

"Yes Dawn, I remember you. Thanks. I did get your message. I've already called our friends, we're planning the surprise party for her. She doesn't know, does she?"

"No, I remembered you guys wanted to surprise her. I'm sure she'll love it."

"Thanks. I'm sure she'll love it too." Then the man said, as if an afterthought, "Oh hey, I don't remember who is picking her up. Do you know if one of us needs to come get her?"

"No she's taking an Uber."

"Great. Thanks so much."

"Sure thing. Have a great party." Dawn hung up the phone.

"What was that about?" JoAnne asked.

"Oh, a friend of Chelsea's had left me his number a couple of weeks ago. Her friends are planning a welcome home party for her and they wanted me to call when she left so they could be ready. It's a surprise party."

JoAnne thought it odd. Friends? No one had visited her except Simon. She was about to comment when a bell went off. She looked at the screen. It was Mrs. Hanson in room 3131 again. The woman wanted to be attended to constantly. It was as if the woman was thinking of ways to push the button and call for a nurse. A bottle of water, clean pillowcase, a snack, the TV didn't work right.

JoAnne headed for Mrs. Hanson's room, forgetting about Chelsea and the phone call completely.

The man hung up the cell phone and started to sweat. The night before the girl at the hospital had left a message on the burner phone. After a few minutes he'd made a decision that the best time to enter Chelsea's apartment was between 3 and 4am. People leaving the bars at 2:30 would be home by 3 and people who got up early rarely left before 5.

At 3:15 that morning he'd parked the Ford Pickup on an unlit side street nearly a quarter mile away from Chelsea's condo. As he walked he considered how he would enter the property. He could wait and sneak in behind a car after it drove through. He felt like that held the highest risk of being seen and didn't like that idea. He knew there were trees and bushes surrounding the property and decided the safest way in was to climb the fence, away from any gate and hidden by the greenery. In the end, when he arrived, he noticed a pedestrian gate had failed to fully shut. A rock had been placed there to block it by someone, maybe kids riding bikes had gotten tired of stopping to use the keypad, or construction workers had left it there. Regardless, he simply walked through the gate and once inside the property moved into the shadows between a tall hedge and a large electrical box.

He was hidden in the dark looking at all the condos. He wanted to make sure he was unseen before he approached her unit. There were no lights on and no one was coming or going, but he waited until nearly 3:50 before he moved out of the shadows. He took the stairs two at a time until he reached the fourth floor, then opened her door with a key.

He didn't have to break in, he had done that nearly a year ago. At the time, his obsession with her had been growing and he felt almost an irresistible compulsion to get into her apartment. He didn't know how to pick the lock but after watching multiple YouTube videos online, buying the right tools, and practicing on his own home, it was fairly simple. The first time he had waited for a night where she was out with another client. He picked the lock and entered her apartment. The rush had been intoxicating when he walked around her bedroom. Then, in fear that she would return, he left quickly. A few weeks later, he broke in again. This time he rummaged around and found a key. Trying it on her front door, it worked, so he pocketed it and made a copy the following day.

Since that day he had snuck in several times. He'd returned her key, but now that he had his own, entry was simple and quick.

The excitement was incredible, but each time he returned it waned just a bit, and so he grew more bold. The last time he had stolen a bra and a pair of her underwear. It was a trophy and he knew he should get rid of them but he hadn't. They were in a bag behind the seat of his truck and sometimes he took them out just to look at them and touch them.

Now he was in the familiar apartment again. He noticed the painting that had hung on the wall was gone, but other than that everything was the same. It had the feeling of a place that was unused, which made sense with her time in the hospital.

He walked into her bedroom and looked out the window. From here he could see the last two steps of the stairs she would walk up to get home. While he waited he pulled the black ski mask out of his pocket. He considered not wearing it at all. Wouldn't it be better that she see his face and know that it was him? He remembered the day on the trail and her eyes as they bulged in fear and panic while he squeezed her neck. His heart raced as he remembered it and now he was glad she hadn't died that day. He was going to get to do it again and the excitement was overpowering.

☙

Chelsea looked at her bags and the things in the cart, wanting to leave. Nurse JoAnne had told her that there'd be an orderly along to take her to her car, but she was growing tired of waiting. She'd finally made the decision to leave and now she longed for the privacy and comfort of her condo. At 9am, a young man wearing scrubs finally showed up, pushing a wheelchair into Chelsea's room.

"Hi, I'm here to take you down to the front doors."

"I really don't need the wheelchair."

"It's kind of policy." He said it matter-of-factly, and turned the chair around in a way as to encourage her to sit.

Chelsea figured why not. She could play the invalid card one last time. Once she was in the condo she'd be back to being alone and doing everything herself. She sat and as he started to push her forward she looked and realized he was pushing her with one hand and pulling the cart with her things with another.

"I really can walk if you'd just bring my things."

"It's no problem, I've done this a million times."

He wheeled her to the elevator and down to the front door just as Simon was coming in.

"Well, hello," Simon greeted her. "Going somewhere?"

"Home... finally." Chelsea said, avoiding eye contact. Inside she was happy to see him, but she was embarrassed to say anything because of their last conversation.

The orderly asked her, "Is this your ride?" referring to Simon.

"No, I was going to call an Uber."

"I got your text and figured I would come see you. Can I give you a ride home?"

"I'd like that, thank you."

Twenty-five minutes later Simon pulled the Tundra up to the gate at the condominium. Chelsea told him the four-digit code and he punched the numbers for the gate to open. He pulled into the parking lot and she directed him to the nearest visitors parking space which was just around the corner from the front door to Chelsea's condo and just below her bedroom window.

"Why don't you go ahead and head up?" Simon said. "I'm going to make a call to Natalie and then I'll bring up your stuff."

"Thank you. I will," Chelsea said. She got out of the truck and headed for the stairs leading to her front door.

Simon dialed Natalie's number. In Chelsea's bedroom four floors above, the huge man watched Chelsea get out of the truck and head around the corner to the stairs that led to her front door. He couldn't see the man in the truck because of a glare from the sun on the windshield, but he could tell he was using his phone. Made sense, the man thought. The Uber driver was looking for his next ride. The man let the curtain drop and turned away from the window.

He still didn't understand how she'd lived nor did he know why she hadn't reported it. It didn't matter. This time he'd make sure. She'd made the mistake of not identifying him and now she had to die. If she told anyone, it would ruin him, so he had to make sure she didn't.

He decided to wait in her bedroom. Let her get all the way in. Maybe he'd have one last bit of fun. He was sweating and his heart raced as he waited.

Chelsea unlocked the door, walked into the condo, and flicked on the light. The place had been empty and locked up for too long. She looked at the vase of dead flowers on the coffee table and thought the place smelled unfamiliar. Probably the dead flowers or something long rotten in the fridge, she thought, and walked over to the sliding glass door leading to her deck. She opened it to let in some fresh air and walked out onto it. The sun was setting on the opposite side of the condo and, she thought, it must be a spectacular sunset because it was lighting up the foothills in the east.

She looked critically at the plants. Two were in pots hanging by ornamental chains another two were sitting on the deck. All were dead. One thing about a potted plant in the summer in California, it had to have water every day. Oh well, she thought. She could replant something.

She took a deep breath, thinking it felt good to be home. A chipmunk chattered away down below and she looked over the railing at the rocks four stories below. As always, the height gave her that feeling of vertigo, like she was going to fall even though she was safely behind the sturdy wrought iron railing.

She turned to go back inside but left the sliding door open. It was still too stuffy in the apartment and it needed the fresh air. She needed to use the bathroom but realized Simon would be coming up so she walked over and opened the front door just an inch, then headed for her bedroom.

In the Tundra below, Simon called Natalie. He'd seen that she'd left a message and wanted to get back to her.

"Hey Dad, thanks for calling me back."

"No problem, what's up?"

"Hey Dad, just curious. Did you go see Chelsea?"

Simon paused, not sure what he wanted to tell her. "Yes."

"Yes? And?"

"I'm with her now. Helping her get home. I'll see you tonight."

Natalie chuckled on the other end. "Thanks, Dad. See you tonight."

He hung up the phone and got out of the truck, grabbed her two bags, and shut the door with his hip. He didn't lock it but he'd be coming right back down to grab the painting and the Scrabble board. Then he made his way up the stairs.

Chelsea had just cracked the front door and made for the master bathroom in her bedroom. She opened the bedroom door and everything seemed to happen at once. First, the door didn't open all the way. Because it didn't, she hesitated instead of walking all the way into the bedroom, and at that moment a massive man in a ski mask came out from behind the door.

Chelsea screamed as he grabbed her good arm. Instinctively she swung her free arm, the hard cast hitting his head like a piece of wood.

The man let out a yell of pain and released her. Chelsea fell backwards onto the floor. She yelled, more like a moan, as he came at her again. Scrambling to her feet, she backed away, but the only place to go was the deck. Thinking she could get out and somehow shut the balcony door, she ran onto the deck. Only too late did she realize her mistake. There was no way to lock the slider from the outside, and though she tried to hold it closed, the man was much stronger and easily forced it open. Chelsea screamed as he pushed it aside.

Thinking it had worked before, she swung her casted arm at his head as hard as she could. But this time he was ready for it. The man simply blocked the blow and, enraged, shoved her as hard as he could. He slammed both hands full force into her chest at the shoulders. Chelsea felt as though she'd been hit by a truck. The force not only flung her back but actually lifted her off her feet.

She felt the wrought iron railing hit her in the butt as she slammed into it. Her head hit one of the hanging pots. Then for an awful moment that seemed to happen in slow motion, her upper body went slowly over the rail. She reached out and her hands grasped the ornamental chain, causing the pot to spill out and fall the four stories, crashing to the jagged rocks below.

She struggled for a horrid moment to grab the chain with both hands. Her knees were still over the rail with her body hanging out, only held up by the chain. Then the hook that was holding the chain to the ceiling gave way and with a scream she felt herself fall. She tried to grasp the rail with her lower legs but as she flipped upside down she felt the tenuous hold her legs had fail, and she went over.

Simon heard a scream as he approached the door. He dropped the bags on the landing and ran through the partially open front door. Unlike Chelsea, who had felt that it all happened in slow motion, for Simon it all happened too fast. He saw the man slam Chelsea backwards and over the railing. He saw her try to stop herself with her legs. Then the man, unaware of Simon, moved forward to make sure she fell to her death.

Simon yelled in a panic.

It attracted the man's attention and he turned quickly and faced Simon. Simon could see past the masked man and watched as the chain pulled out of the ceiling and Chelsea screamed again and fell out of sight. He was momentarily sickened to think about her body falling four stories into the boulders below, then a rage welled up in him.

The huge man slowly advanced towards him, but wrestling was not just a game to Simon. All those years of wrestling had made him aware not only of the sport, but also of the illegal moves, the choke holds, the ways you could twist a body part and break it. And growing up on the farm he had wrestled his brother, who was much bigger than him, more than once. Now all he could think of was tying this giant in a knot and slowly breaking every bone in his body.

The man lunged suddenly and every instinct and skill Simon had was heightened by the massive rage and adrenaline pumping through him. Like lightning, he countered the lunge and almost instantly had the man on the floor, face down. Now on top of the man, Simon heard Chelsea suddenly scream for help. Shocked, he turned to look, and in that moment the larger man threw him off.

Simon could think only of Chelsea and the larger man could only think of escaping. With both of their desired objectives in front of them, that's what they attempted to do. The man sprang up and fled out the front door and Simon turned and ran to the deck.

He rushed to the railing and looked over. The ornamental chain had wrapped around Chelsea's good arm as she had tried to keep herself from falling. Now it was digging hideously into the skin around her forearm and wrist. The other end of the chain was somehow caught on the wrought iron railing. Simon reached over and grabbed Chelsea's wrist and she gasped in pain. He leaned forward and grabbed her upper arm with his opposite hand. Even with the adrenaline and his strength, he was barely able to pull her up.

Chelsea clawed at the rail as he lifted her to the top and suddenly she was clinging to him in a panic, but Simon wanted to go after the man. He tried to untangle himself from her but as he pulled away she went hysterical, holding him even tighter. He gave up and held her, telling her over and over again, "You're okay" and "It's all right, you're safe," until she calmed down a bit.

"It okay. He's gone," Simon said again, but she still clung to him. After several more minutes and several attempts, he finally got her to let go. They both stood on the deck. Simon looked over the railing at the rocks below. The flowerpot had hit and exploded into a thousand shards of pottery. The dirt and dead plant were spread across a large boulder. All Simon could think of was if that pot had been Chelsea. The adrenaline was wearing off and the thought of her flinging over that rail made him shudder violently.

Chelsea saw him shake and wiped the tears from her face. "Are you okay?"

"I'm fine. Jacked up to be sure. Let's go back inside."

Chelsea was no longer clinging to him, but she didn't leave his side as he moved in and shut the sliding door.

Simon looked at her and asked, "Where was he?"

"In there." Chelsea said, nodding at the bedroom.

"I doubt anyone else is in there, but I want to be sure." Simon said and started for the bedroom.

Chelsea realized what he was saying and began to panic again, "Wait, don't leave me!" She began looking around for where someone could be hiding...

"I need to make sure." Simon was fairly confident there was no one else. "Come with me if you want. Like I said, I'm pretty sure we are alone."

"How can you be sure?" she asked as she followed him closely into the bedroom.

"Because if he had a partner they would have attacked me already. But just to be sure..."

Simon looked under the bed, in the closet, and then checked in the bathroom.

"I see no one."

"What about the other bedroom?"

"Come on." Simon went back into the living room and shut and locked the front door. Then he thoroughly checked the entire condo. All the time, Chelsea never more than a foot from him.

"See? We're good." Simon said when he was done.

But Chelsea was still in a panic. "Can you check again?"

Simon walked through the condo again. This time, Chelsea came but also looked for herself, trying to convince herself she was safe.

They both ended up in the living room again and Chelsea sat down. Simon sat but then stood. He couldn't calm down. The adrenaline that had pumped through him had left him wired.

Suddenly Chelsea started crying again.

"What is it?" Simon asked.

"It was him. It was the same man who attacked me before. I know it was." She was crying and shaking again. Simon sat next to her and put his arm around her, not knowing what else to say.

With a start, Chelsea looked up, eyes wide. "Oh my God! He knows where I live. We need to get out of here!"

"It's okay. He's not coming back."

"How can you be so sure?"

"Well first, he didn't come here with a plan to fight another man. And second, he was wearing a mask. He probably feels safe for now. He doesn't know I know who he is."

"You know who he is?"

"I'm not certain, but I think so."

"Who?"

"Wait. Before I tell you I want to make sure."

"Why don't you just tell that detective?"

"He won't believe me. And I don't think he is very motivated to help, but I'll call him regardless."

Simon got the detective's card out of his wallet and called the number. It went to voicemail. He left a detailed message about the events in the condo, including the fact that the man was masked. Then he asked the detective to call him back as soon as possible.

Chelsea looked down. "What are we going to do?"

"Let's start by fixing up your arm."

Chelsea looked down at her "good" arm. It was bleeding and beginning to swell from where the chain had dug into her. She suddenly realized how badly her arm hurt. Her shoulder also throbbed and the pain where the chain had caught her forearm and wrist was sharp and growing worse. When she tried to move her arm, there was a stabbing pain in her elbow too.

She stood up and followed Simon as he walked into the kitchen.

"Where are your towels?" Simon asked.

Chelsea stepped towards the drawer and nodded. "In there." She was now holding her "good" arm against her chest with the casted arm.

Simon took a towel from the drawer and wrapped it around Chelsea's arm gently. The slightest move caused her to gasp again.

"I'm sorry," Simon said as he finished.

"I think it will be okay. Thanks." Then looking around, she began to feel the panic returning.

"What am I going to do?" she asked

Simon thought she was talking about her arm. "I can take you to the hospital."

"No, that's not what I mean."

"Simon, I can't stay here. What if he comes back later?"

Simon thought for a few moments then replied, "We'll get you out of here to someplace safe."

Simon looked at her and smiled reassuringly. "Then once you are safe, I'll figure out a way to confirm my suspicions. I'm certain I know who it was."

"You said that before. Who is it?"

"I can't be certain, so let me think of a way to confirm it before I say." Simon's mind was working like he worked with computers. It was a series of logistics and prioritizing things.

"One thing at a time," he said. "First, let's get you out of here."

"Where are we going to go?"

"I have a place."

"But he's seen you. What if he knows who you are and where you live?"

"Well, I'm pretty sure he doesn't but we aren't going to my house. Grab some clothes. As much as you need for a week or so. And make sure you have some for all kinds of weather."

Chelsea started for the bedroom then stopped and looked down at her arms. "Can you come help me?"

Simon realized both of her arms were hurting and that she needed help. "I'm sorry, I wasn't thinking."

They walked into her bedroom together and Chelsea pointed out the clothes she wanted him to pack. He filled a duffel bag with clothes and then she walked into the bathroom to grab a few things in there.

"Where are my bags that were at the hospital?"

Simon had dropped them outside the door on the landing. He'd retrieved them and piled the three bags up in front of the door when his phone rang. It was a blocked number but Simon answered.

"Hello, this is Simon."

"Simon this is Detective VanDyke."

Simon switched his phone to speaker so Chelsea could hear the conversation.

"Thanks for calling back, Detective. I take it you got my message."

At the other end, the detective was walking up to a house with a dead body inside, in midtown Sacramento. There were police in and around the house and he wanted to get this call off his plate before walking into the crime scene.

"Yeah, I listened to your message. I just wanted to get back to you. I am really sorry, but I've got two active murder cases at the moment that I'm dealing with. I can send a unit over to take your statement and file a report."

"I'm not sure that will do any good."

"Why's that?"

"Well, for one, the guy was masked and there's no way to say for certain who it was. I could speculate, but in reality I can only tell you he was dressed in black, with a mask, gloves, and very large. I'd guess he weighed easily 250 or more and was around six and a half feet tall."

"Well, that's something to go with. But like I said, I am buried right now. I can send a unit over to at least take a report, or I can request aid from another agency and give them your number."

"I'll leave that up to you, Detective. Just have anyone you pass it off to call my cell and we'll do what we can."

"I'll do that. Thanks for understanding. We're just a little consumed right now with a few cases. I don't want to say they're a higher priority, your case is important, but..."

"I understand. I'll wait for you, or them, to call. Thanks."

With that, Simon hung up the phone and looked at Chelsea.

"You ready to get out of here?"

Chelsea looked around her condo one more time. "Yes, let's go."

Back in midtown Sacramento, the detective hung up the phone and made a mental note to contact another department for help. Then he walked into a particularly gruesome murder scene and, for the next few days, forgot all about Chelsea's attack.

❧

An hour and a half later they were driving west on Highway 80. They'd driven through the Sacramento rush hour traffic and were now coming up to Fairfield. The sun was setting almost directly in front of them, making for horrible driving conditions. Simon was calming down after what had happened in the condo and wondered if Chelsea was too, but he didn't ask. He felt a little like he felt in high school after an important but extremely difficult wrestling match that went the full nine minutes. Physically, he was drained and now he felt famished.

"I gotta get something to eat. I'm going to pull off at an In-N-Out up here and grab something." Then he added, "Besides, by the time we get back on the freeway, the sun won't be blasting me in the face."

"I don't think I can eat anything."

"Well, maybe just get something to drink." Simon didn't know how being attacked and nearly falling to her death had left her feeling but he figured the emotional rollercoaster was extreme. The fight with the man had been only seconds, but it had left him with an adrenaline rush that was impossible to deny. His body was only now starting to let go of the pent-up energy. He figured she might still be flying high with that same adrenaline.

They pulled into the drive-through and Chelsea ordered a Sprite but still insisted that she wasn't hungry. Simon ordered two burgers, two fries, and a Coke.

Chelsea looked at him after he ordered, "I'm really not hungry."

"I believe you. It's for me." Simon turned and smiled at her. "But if you do get hungry you can have a few of my fries."

After getting the food, Simon pulled over into the parking lot and turned off the truck. He pretty much devoured the first burger and then told himself to slow down as he ate the fries. Chelsea drank about half of her Sprite then reached over and started grabbing his fries. Simon noticed but didn't say anything. She continued until she'd eaten an entire order.

When she finished them she looked at the empty container and said, "Sorry, I ate your fries."

"I figured you would, I ordered that burger for you too," Simon lied. He really wanted more, but didn't want to go back through the drive-through. As she took it out of the wrapper and started eating, Simon started the truck up and maneuvered back onto Highway 80, still going west.

After a few moments, she set half the burger down on the wrapper in the center console.

"I don't think I can eat the rest. I'm hungry but my stomach is in knots."

"No worries."

She saw him look at it and guessed his thought, "Do you want it?"

"You sure you're done?"

"Yes."

Simon ate the other half of the burger while continuing to drive. The western sky in front of them turned from light blue to grey. Yellow and red clouds streaked across the horizon, lit up by the sun that had dropped out of view.

"Much better driving," Simon said, and lifted the visor up and out the way.

The food did them good and Simon thought they were both calming down, but the stress of the night caught up to Chelsea.

Simon soon realized tears were rolling down her cheeks. She looked out the passenger side window trying to hide it, but Simon asked anyway.

"You okay?"

"Yes," Chelsea answered, wiping away the tears. "I just don't understand why this is happening to me."

For a moment Simon thought, it's happening because of your job choice. But as quickly as he thought that he also said to himself, don't be an ass, you can't say that to her. He knew people made crappy choices in life for all kinds of reasons. Only the arrogant and conceited judged them. Simon was neither.

Trying to sound positive and encouraging, he said, "I think most people are pretty good people. Occasionally you come across someone and they aren't good. They make bad choice after bad choice. They choose bad."

Chelsea looked at him with a cold stare. "Are you talking about me?"

"No. Holy cow! No. Sorry if you thought I was." Simon smiled at her reassuringly. "I'm talking about the person who attacked you. Some people choose to live a life of lies and deceit and the longer they are allowed to get away with it, the more corrupt they become. They become so morally bankrupt that in the end they think they can get away with anything."

They sat in silence for the next few miles, listening to the radio. Simon was suddenly aware of the song playing, "Bad Day" by Daniel Powter. At first he thought about turning the channel, but the song seemed so crazy perfect for the moment and for what had just happened.

Simon started to laugh and turned to look at Chelsea.

"Man. This song..." was all he could say, still laughing.

For her part, Chelsea laughed, too. She looked at him through a hand that was partially covering her face.

"God, it's just not funny." But she laughed as she said it.

"You had a bad day," Simon said loudly and in his own voice but at the exact time as the song said it.

She was laughing and crying at the same time. Tears flowed down her face, but inside she knew that it was funny.

"You ass."

"Wow!" Simon laughed. "First time I've heard you ever say something like that."

"Well?"

"I guess you are right. I'm an ass for laughing. But you're laughing too."

Chelsea winced, "Yes I'm laughing but I'm also crying. And all of it hurts."

Simon changed the station.

"Okay. I'll stop. I don't care what happens in life, sometimes you gotta just laugh."

Chelsea just shook her head and wiped away more tears.

Simon exited Highway 80 and caught the 580 across the northernmost part of the bay. They drove the long open stretch of bridge across the water. It was dark now and Chelsea looked out at all the lights on the bridge and in the distance.

"Are you going to tell me where we are going?"

"I have a boat. That's where we're going."

Chelsea pictured a rowboat or a ski boat. "Just what are we going to do, go fishing? Are we taking the boat somewhere?"

"You'll see," was all Simon said. After crossing the Richmond Bridge he left the 580 and took Highway 101 south into Sausalito. A few minutes later he pulled into the parking lot of the Sausalito Yacht Harbor and parked the truck.

"We're here."

"What's here?"

"My boat is here."

They both got out of the truck and Simon grabbed Chelsea's large duffel bag. When Chelsea reached into the backseat to grab the second bag and her toiletries she let out a yelp of pain. "Ahhh!"

"What's wrong?"

"My arm. My good arm. It's really sore."

"Just leave it. I'll carry both bags and come back to get the other stuff."

Chelsea followed alongside Simon as he headed towards the water. The wooden dock was well lit and they passed a couple who seemed to be just taking a walk. As they headed down the wooden ramp and onto the dock Chelsea realized how wrong her picture of his boat must have been.

The boats were much larger than typical ski boats. There was the occasional smaller boat, but for the most part even those boats were still yachts. As they walked down towards the end she heard music coming from one boat. She glanced over and could see the lights on and what looked to be a half dozen people drinking wine and visiting onboard.

Simon turned and walked another 20 feet, stopping at a small ramp that led onto one of the larger sailboats. "Here we are."

"This is yours?"

"It is. This is 'The Natalie,' named for my daughter." Simon walked up the small ramp and turned and looked back at Chelsea. He set her bags down and turned to offer her his hand as she crossed the ramp. "Welcome aboard."

Chelsea stepped onto the ramp but when she reached for his hand she winced.

"You're not okay," Simon said.

"It's just sore."

Simon unlocked a door and walked down a few steps into darkness. "Wait there a sec while I get the lights."

Moments later the lights came on and Chelsea walked through the door and down five steps into a plush living room. In many ways it seemed like the inside of a giant RV, but it was bigger and everything seemed to be trimmed in a warm polished wood. The sitting area gave way to a small kitchen on one side.

"Sit down for a second and let me look at your arm," Simon said.

"Really, it's okay."

"No, I insist. Let me just look at it. I've spent years wrestling and coaching wrestling. Dropping all of your body weight onto your arm like you did could have torn it up pretty badly. Let me just look."

Chelsea sat down and tried to hold her arm out. The bleeding had stopped and her arm was turning all kinds of black and blue. The skin was broken in places where the chain had wrapped around it.

"Oh wow!" Chelsea said. "It looks worse."

"Yeah, that looks pretty rough."

"But nothing is broken."

"You know this?" Simon looked at her and added, "Are you a doctor now?"

"No, but I think I would have felt it, if it broke."

"I think your body was going through such a rush that you may not have felt it, even if it had snapped a bone." Simon gently moved her fingers around.

"Does that hurt?"

Chelsea shook her head no. Simon moved from her fingers to her wrist and moved it around in every possible position a wrist would move. Chelsea was aware that he was basically holding her hand. His hand was warm and rough with calluses. She liked the feel.

"Does this hurt?"

Again she shook her head no. He continued to hold her hand with one of his hands and moved his other hand to her elbow. He started to move the elbow.

"Ouch. Okay, that hurts."

"Okay. What about your shoulder? Can you move your arm at your shoulder?" Simon dropped his hands away and let her move on her own. She lifted her arm up to the front of her, "It's okay."

"Try lifting it to the side."

She did and winced again. "Okay, that hurts too but not like my elbow."

"Well, we could take you to a hospital. But if your elbow is actually broken they won't put a cast on it anyway."

"They won't?"

"Funny thing about an elbow. When you break them, they usually want you to keep up your range of motion or the elbow will fuse together and you'll end up with an arm that doesn't bend at the elbow anymore. Or one that doesn't have full range."

"That's not a funny thing." Chelsea replied.

"No, I suppose it isn't. And I'm not a doctor so we should probably take you to a hospital."

"No. I know it hurts, but I'm sure it's going to be okay. If it's not better tomorrow I'll go then."

"Suit yourself." Simon got up and picked up her bags. "Follow me."

He led her to a door and opened it, revealing a somewhat cramped bedroom that was mostly filled with a queen-sized bed. Simon tossed the bags on the bed while Chelsea stood in the doorway.

"There's the head, the bathroom," Simon said, pointing to a door at the other side of the bed. "Inside is a shower, a sink, and a toilet. I'll turn on the water pump. There are instructions on how to use the toilet on a sticker that's next to it, but it's pretty self-explanatory. You just have to fill the toilet with water before you use it. That's the main difference."

"Got it. Fill the toilet beforehand," Chelsea said almost sarcastically, then added, "If there are instructions, I'll figure it out."

"You can stow your clothes in the different drawers or the closet. There may be a few things in them. If you need more room just toss the stuff in them out into the main cabin on the couch and I'll take care of it."

"I'll be fine," Chelsea said.

"I'm going to run back up to the truck and grab the rest of your stuff."

Chelsea followed Simon up the stairs and out into the night air. As he stepped off the boat she was suddenly scared. "Simon, what if someone comes?"

"You'll be fine. No one is coming. No one knows we're here."

She knew that was true but as he walked away up the dock, she felt a panic rising in her. She went to her room and shut the door, locking it behind her. Unpacking her clothes was difficult with her arm as sore as it was, but Simon had seemed confident that she should keep using her arm. She stowed her things in the drawers that pulled out from beneath the bed and in the cabinets that were about head high along the walls of the little room. When she opened the closet she saw that it was filled with coats and rain gear. She had tossed one dress into her duffle bag as she was packing to leave the condo, so she hung it in the closet.

"Not much need for that," she said out loud to no one. She had kept herself busy but now that she was unpacked she felt the fear rising up in her again. Then she heard movement and footsteps on the boat above.

"Simon is that you?" she called out, trying to sound casual.

"Yeah."

A few seconds later he knocked on her door. "I've got your overnight bag, your laptop, and that painting."

She opened the door and took the overnight bag from one of his hands and the laptop out from under his arm. In the other hand he held the painting.

"Thank you." She nodded at the painting, "Anywhere you can put that?"

"Sure. There's room in my cabin." Simon started to move away from the door then looked back at her. "Get some sleep. If you need anything, I'll be in my berth."

Chelsea watched as he departed into the other cabin and then shut her own door. Two hours later she was still lying in her bed. Sleep was impossible. No matter what she tried to do, her mind kept going back to that moment where the giant masked man came out from behind the door. She'd put it out of her mind and close her eyes, then panic would start again, and she would feel like she was clawing for the hanging pot to keep from falling. Every terror-filled moment of the evening kept coming back to her. She looked at her phone. 11pm.

Then she heard movement in the main cabin and got up. As stiff and sore as she was, she managed to dress in a pair of sweatpants and a sweatshirt. She opened the cabin door and saw Simon standing in the galley with bottle of wine in one hand and an opener in the other.

"You couldn't sleep either?" she asked.

Simon shook his head no. He picked up a remote control and pointed it to a glass cabinet at the far end of the cabin. Rock music began playing and Simon clicked the remote, cycling through different styles of music until a soft jazz sound filled the cabin.

"I'm starting to wonder if I'm going to be able to sleep at all, but I figured this might help," he said, lifting the bottle a little. Then he proceeded to open it. "Would you like some?"

"Sure."

Chelsea moved to the opposite side of the kitchen counter while he poured them both a glass and handed one to her.

"Cheers." He held his glass up towards hers and they clinked them together.

"Not sure what we are supposed to be toasting," Chelsea said and took a sip.

"Well. Find the positive. There's always something."

"I'm not feeling that way at the moment. What would you say are the positives in this situation for me?"

"Well, you've got a nice glass of wine. That's a start."

Simon moved from behind the kitchen counter to the couch and sat down.

Chelsea took another, much bigger drink of the wine. "Are you saying all I've got going for me is a glass of wine?"

"No, I'm saying that at the least, at this very moment, you have a great glass of wine," Simon answered. "You look for the positive and you find it."

Chelsea let it drop. She could think of very little positive at the moment. For several minutes they were silent, drinking the wine. Simon on the couch, Chelsea leaning against the bar.

Looking down at her glass, she realized it was empty so she poured another glass then looked at Simon. "More for you?"

"Yes, thank you."

She walked over and though his wasn't all the way empty yet, she refilled his glass. Then she returned the bottle to the counter and continued drinking.

Another quiet few minutes passed. The jazz filled the cabin and the wine was relaxing them both. Chelsea was trying to think of something to say. Simon seemed content to sit in silence but it was uncomfortable for her. She wanted to go sit next to him. She longed to just be comforted and held, but he had never really given her an open door for that kind of physical contact. She remembered back to when he pulled her up from outside the railing on her deck. The tight embrace they'd shared and how safe she felt at that moment. She tried to remember how his body felt but couldn't.

The alcohol was already having its effect and she felt herself getting sleepy. Finally, she didn't care if he gave her an open door or not. She needed to be close to him, close to anyone. She needed to feel the safety and security, and standing across the cabin from him felt like she was as alone as being stranded on a desert island.

If the purpose of the wine was to relax her, well, why not, she figured. She raised the glass of wine and let the entire contents pour down her throat. She set the empty glass on the counter and walked across the cabin to the couch. Simon was leaning back into the plush soft leather on the end far end. The arm that held his wine was sitting on the armrest; his other arm was stretched across the back of the couch.

Chelsea climbed onto the couch, under his arm, curled up her legs, and leaned her head on his chest.

"I'm sorry I cried so much today."

Simon didn't know what to say. He was just trying to relax and now she was lying next to him with her head on him. That definitely didn't relax him. He took a drink of the wine and let his arm drop down so that it rested across her shoulder and arm.

"I don't know anyone who wouldn't have cried going through what you have."

His chest was warm and she felt comforted when he dropped his hand to her shoulder and let it rest against her. She was grateful for the physical contact, even if she'd practically forced him to do it.

For nearly an hour they stayed like that, motionless. At some point the wine and the music had finally calmed her enough and she fell asleep. Simon couldn't see her face but realized she was sleeping by the steady breathing which seemed to be deeper. Not wanting to wake her, he stayed there. He finished his wine and set the glass in the cup holder at the end of the couch. The arm he had around her was starting to fall asleep from the uncomfortable position.

Finally, not wanting to wake her but needing to move, he got up slowly. As he did, he held her head as best he could until he was up and then lay her down slowly. She moved slightly and he looked down to see her eyes staring up at him.

"I'm sorry I've got to use the bathroom," he lied. "I'll be right back."

He went to his cabin and grabbed a pillow and a blanket. Then he waited a few minutes and returned. Her eyes were still open. She lifted up to allow him to put the pillow under her head when he offered it. Then Simon covered her with the blanket and returned to the kitchen to pour himself another glass of wine.

When he returned to the couch she was asleep again. Simon shut and locked the door leading up to the deck. Then, figuring she might wake up, he left the jazz music playing and turned all the lights off but one. With nothing else he could do, he finished his wine, went to his cabin, and climbed into bed. Sleep didn't come easily since he kept thinking about the events in the condo. He was about to give up and find a book to read when finally, somewhere between 3 and 4am, he fell asleep.

Chapter 21

Chelsea woke with a start to the small sounds of a fork stirring in a bowl and something frying. Bacon. She'd slept so soundly that for a moment she'd forgotten where she was but as she sat up she saw Simon in the kitchen. She could smell the bacon and the familiar aroma of coffee. The clock on the microwave read 7:54am. She figured Simon for an early breakfast kind of person, but it was very early for her. Nonetheless, the smell of the bacon and the coffee made her realize how hungry she was.

She stood and realized her entire body ached. The events of the day before, being jammed in the shoulders and chest so hard that it had sent her airborne over the railing, hanging by one arm with the chain digging painfully into her skin, all of it was now resulting in feeling like she'd been hit by a car.

"Good morning." Simon said as she stood up. "How're you feeling?"

"God, I'm sore all over."

"Want some Advil?"

Simon sounded so awake and upbeat to Chelsea that she couldn't help her next comment.

"Ugh. You're a morning person," Chelsea said. "Yes, I'll take some Advil."

Simon produced some Advil from one of the cabinets in the kitchen then handed her a cup of coffee.

"How many?"

"Four."

Opening the bottle he shook four tablets out and handed them to her.

"Thanks. I'm going to clean up and change," Chelsea said after she'd taken the pills and had a couple sips of the coffee.

"When you're ready, I'll make you some eggs," Simon said as Chelsea made her way back to her berth.

She looked at herself in the small mirror and wished Simon hadn't woken before her. Her hair was a mess and she wanted time to clean up and figure out what to wear.

She looked at the tiny shower and decided to forgo that option, and instead just wash her face in the sink. The bathroom was tiny and not made for sitting and putting on makeup for two hours, as she was used to doing. There was a larger mirror on the back of the closet door and by sitting on side of the bed she was able to use it in the cramped room.

She threw on some makeup she considered essential and tried to run a brush through her hair for a few minutes. Unfortunately, raising her sore arm to brush her hair was painful. Using the arm in the cast, she could barely hold the brush, and putting it to her hair wasn't working. She found a band and used it to put her hair up into a ponytail. She switched out of the sweatpants she'd been wearing all night into a pair of leggings and an oversized T-shirt that hung down more like a dress. With her arms the way they were it was a painstaking process to put on clothes, but she managed. Then she brushed her teeth and exited her room into the main cabin.

She stood for a moment at the bar opposite Simon and watched him. The bacon and coffee smelled good and she retrieved the cup he'd given her and held it for him to refill.

"Thank you."

"Not a morning person?"

"Not until I've had a cup or two of coffee, but I'm doing better now."

"How's your arm?"

"Sore. I think it's going to get worse before it gets better but I think it's okay."

She turned and leaned against the bar and sipped the coffee quietly as she took a better look at the interior of the boat. The large room could really be broken into four sections. One corner was the large L-shaped couch where she'd slept. A reclining chair, a coffee table, and an end table filled out the space that was basically a small living room.

In the corner of the cabin, diagonally opposite the living room, was the kitchen where Simon was working. It was about the size of a kitchen you'd find in a very tiny apartment. All the appliances were smaller, and the cabinets, the stove, the sink; everything was packed in in such a way that it seemed very functional. She watched as Simon lifted the bowl of pineapple to the bar she was leaning on, basically offering it to her.

"Where'd this come from?" Chelsea asked but didn't take any. The coffee was still the only thing she wanted.

"I really couldn't sleep so I walked down to the end of the dock this morning and got some food for us."

Chelsea sipped her coffee and looked around more at the cabin. The room was completed by a kitchen table surrounded on three sides by a padded bench. She thought for a minute it was like an RV and that the table could be torn down and turned into a bed, but then decided it was more likely a permanent table locked into the floor.

The final corner of the room, flanked by the stairs leading up to the main deck, was an area that looked more like it belonged on a sailboat. There were electronics of all sorts. Radios, a stereo, and she assumed navigational equipment, among other things. It was flanked by the kitchen on one side. The stairs separated it from the living room. All in all everything was clean and beautiful.

She had no idea what something like this cost but decided it must be tons.

Simon interrupted her thoughts, "I hope I didn't wake you up too early."

"I slept so sound, I'm not sure when I would have woken up if you hadn't."

"I'm sorry, but I checked the weather and it's going to be a great day to take the boat out, so I wanted to get started. I hope you don't mind."

"I've never been out on a sailboat, should I be worried?"

"Do you get seasick or motion sick?"

"I never have, but I've never really been on a boat before."

"Well, you shouldn't be worried. If we go out and you don't feel good, let me know and we can come back to the harbor."

Cool morning air poured through the open door at the top of the stairs. Chelsea set her coffee down and ducked back into the bedroom. She grabbed an oversized sweater and threw it on over her lighter shirt. She took another look in the mirror, worried that she didn't look her best, but realized there wasn't much she could do about it now.

She re-entered the main cabin as Simon was setting plates down at the table.

"I made you an omelet. If you don't care for that I can fry eggs or scramble them and I'll eat the omelet."

"No, this is good," Chelsea said. "I usually just have yogurt and coffee."

"Well, I can help make half of that happen." Simon refilled her cup of coffee and set it on the table next to her plate. He finished making another omelet and set it on the table opposite her along with another cup of coffee. Before sitting down he brought over the bowl with the cut up pineapple and a plate with bacon.

"Anything else?"

Chelsea was halfway through chewing a third bite of the omelet and shook her head, "Hmm-mm."

Simon sat and they both ate for a few moments in silence. When his omelet and half the bacon was gone, he took a sip of coffee and ate a few pieces of the fruit.

It was very quiet, and Chelsea would have felt uncomfortable but for the meals they had eaten before when he sat in silence.

"Well, here is how this works," Simon began. "I'll clean up these dishes, then I'll take care of a few things on the boat. There are covers on the sails and some other things I'll need to get ready."

"I can do the dishes." Chelsea offered.

"No. You're sore and it will only take me a few minutes, then we will motor out of the marina until we can get clear enough to put up the sails and have some fun."

"Do I get a choice?" Chelsea feigned fear.

"No, I suppose you don't," Simon joked back. "Consider me a pirate and you've been taken captive." Then he added, "But seriously, if you do start to feel the least bit queasy, let me know. We'll come right back in. There's nothing fun about being seasick."

"Okay."

"I was told once by an old timer who spent his life on the ocean, if you eat something like eggs and bacon, greasy fried food, you won't get seasick. He swore if you eat sweet things like donuts or orange juice, then you would get seasick. Personally, I've never been seasick, but I've tried both types of breakfast and I can tell you when I've done the sweeter thing, I've felt a little less than great. When I have the eggs, bacon, and coffee I've never felt bad."

"Well, should I avoid the pineapple then?" Chelsea asked.

"I think you'll be fine." Simon got up and started on the dishes.

"It will probably take me 30 minutes to get us ready to leave, and then another 20 or 30 minutes till we are sailing, so you can just relax here and have coffee or do whatever you'd like."

"Thank you."

Chelsea sipped her coffee while Simon washed the dishes. She watched as he stowed everything away and realized that every cabinet, every dish, everything was either latched shut, or put in a way so as not to fall or come loose.

"If you are done with your coffee just set your cup in the sink. If you want more, bring it out with you. But don't leave it sitting or it will likely get dumped and spilled."

"Yes, Captain," Chelsea said with a grin.

"Hopefully it won't be too cold, but the wind will be blowing, so if you want a windbreaker there are several in the closet in your berth."

"Okay. This sweater is pretty warm but I may grab one."

Simon climbed up the steps to the main deck and out of view. Chelsea went back into her room and looked at the windbreakers in the closet. Not sexy, not fashionable, just black nylon windbreakers. She decided her sweater was a much better look. She put on a pair of tennis shoes and could hear Simon moving around on the deck above. Curious to know how this whole sailing thing worked, she left the windbreaker behind and carried her coffee up to the main deck.

Simon had just finished removing a cover from the main sail, though it was still furled. He stowed the cover in a bin and continued moving around. To Chelsea it seemed he was unhooking some things and hooking up other things with no rhyme or reason. She sat near the back of the boat on a bench and watched while she finished her coffee.

The sun was still low on the horizon and the cloudless sky was promising a beautiful day. There seemed to be no breeze in the marina and Chelsea was convinced that not only would she not want the windbreaker but that in a very short time the sweater was going to be way too hot.

Finally, Simon started the engines and while they idled he unhooked the bowline. Chelsea watched Simon as he seemed to effortlessly manage too many tasks for her to comprehend. In the end, he stepped to the stern of the boat and seemed to almost simultaneously unhook the last line that held the boat to the dock while putting the engine into gear and swinging the wheel over as the boat pulled away.

Chelsea felt a little excitement build in her. "Would you mind if I sat up on the front of the boat?"

"No, go ahead."

Chelsea stood and looked at her coffee mug.

"Just put your mug in the sink," Simon said, then he added, "Do you have any headphones for your iPhone?"

"I have earbuds in my room."

"Okay, first we're going to have to get you using the correct language out here. It's not a room; it's your berth. The bathroom is 'the head.' The kitchen is 'the galley,' and the living room, if you want to call it that, is the 'main cabin' or 'salon.'"

"Sounds kind of snooty to me," Chelsea said, joking with him a bit.

"Sailing is kind of snooty. But it's what we do out here."

"Okay. I've got earbuds in my berth," Chelsea said with an emphasis on "berth."

"Well, when you put your mug in the sink, grab your earbuds."

"For?"

"Just trust me."

"Okay."

Chelsea made her way below and a few moments later she returned with the earbuds.

"Can I pair those to my phone?" Simon asked.

"Sure, I forget how."

"Here hand them to me. I can do it."

She handed the earbuds to Simon and he took a few moments to pair them to his phone.

"Okay, there ya go."

"Am I listening to anything in particular?"

"Nothing yet," Simon said.

"Well aren't you a mystery."

"It's no mystery. I just want you to experience this the way I think you ought to."

Then Simon motioned to the front of the boat.

"As you move up front, the general rule is to keep three points of contact. Keep a hand on the deck, or on one of the stays or guy-wires holding up the mast. The rail around the boat is another point of contact, but some people feel more comfortable reaching towards the center of the boat as opposed to the cable railing on the outer side. It's a good habit to get into but you should be fine until we get out of the marina. A sudden wind can toss people over pretty quickly if they aren't ready for it."

Simon watched as Chelsea made her way to the bow of the boat. The sweater she was wearing was large, but only long enough to cover the top half of her butt. The leggings or yoga pants, or whatever they were called, left little to the imagination. Her legs were perfectly toned. Her figure was really amazing. For the first time since he'd met her, he really thought about the way she looked. It was ironic, he thought. Her face was still healing and he knew she couldn't look as pretty as the first day he'd met her, but somehow, now, he truly noticed. She was beautiful. Most women would kill to look like she looked; most men would be enthralled by her.

As soon as he realized he was thinking this, he thought of Allie, of her red hair, her freckles, her laugh, and the way her eyes lit up when she looked at him. Guilt, frustration, and depression sank over him.

He tried to force the depression out of his mind and focus on piloting the boat. They were just clearing the dyke that was protecting the marina now and the bow of the boat raised up slightly as the first wave passed under her.

After a few hundred feet, he spun the wheel to starboard and pointed the bow of the boat directly towards San Francisco. He increased the throttle until they were at least a half mile out from the harbor.

Simon had always felt that September through October were the best months to sail in the bay, and today was turning out to be one of those rare and spectacular days. There was no fog, the sun was shining in a completely cloudless sky, and the temperatures the last few days had been near record highs.

Belying reality, San Francisco looked clean and peaceful from out on the water. Sausalito was off to their right, and Angel Island was off to their left as they headed from Richardson. Ahead in the distance was Alcatraz. As they moved beyond Sausalito the Golden Gate Bridge came into view.

The water was choppier but the 60-foot hull was sleek and designed to cut through much worse. Simon killed the engine and moved forward. He grabbed a small cushioned seat with a back. Chelsea stood and started to make her way more carefully now as the boat seemed much less stable outside the harbor. The wind had been at their back but now she felt the breeze and was glad she had the sweater on.

"Wait there a minute," Simon called to her. He joined her at the bow. "I'm just going to ask you to do one thing for me."

"What's that?"

Simon handed her his phone. "I have a music mix called 'Sailing.' Just listen to it until we pass under the bridge. If you don't like it, you can turn it off then. And stay right up here on the bow as we sail under the bridge."

Simon set the cushioned seat down. "This will be better than sitting on the deck. You'll maybe want to keep your legs up and not dangling over now. Or you can, but they'll probably get wet."

"I'd rather stay dry for now." Chelsea sat in the seat, her legs crossed front of her.

"Okay, just start the music when we start sailing."

"I thought we were sailing."

Simon grinned. "That wasn't sailing. That's motoring. You'll know when we start sailing. If you have to unlock my phone to turn on the music, my password is 'SECURE.'"

Chelsea was surprised. He'd just given her his password without a thought. For the first time she felt like Simon had entrusted her with something.

Simon moved to the back and Chelsea looked down at the phone in her hands. She punched in the numbers that spelled out SECURE and the phone unlocked. She thought about looking at his picture album or his browser history. Then she felt almost ashamed that she would somehow take advantage of his trust. She clicked the button to close the window.

The seat Simon had brought was designed so she could sit back and she did. The morning sun was warm now. She relaxed and enjoyed the quiet. The view was gorgeous with the city in front of her and the bridge in front and to the right. She'd been in San Francisco many times but this was different. She'd always been keenly aware of the smells and the noise. Out here on the water it was crisp, quiet, and peaceful.

Then there was a loud, almost flopping sound. Chelsea turned quickly and looked back at Simon. He had raised the mainsail and it was now catching the breeze. He looked at her, smiled and waved, then busied himself with a line in one hand and the wheel of the boat in the other.

The boat suddenly leaned over and Chelsea looked back at Simon, worried. Simon was looking forward now. He looked relaxed and had both hands on the wheel. He saw her worried look at waved again, then motioned with both hands to his ears.

Chelsea nodded then turned and looked forward again and put in the earbuds. She punched in his password again and found the music mix entitled "Sailing." She hit play.

She knew the first few songs, Lionel Richie's "Easy" followed by Little River Band's "Cool Change," and then Christopher Cross' "Sailing."

The boat was sailing nearly straight for the point, where the bridge entered San Francisco. Then the boat suddenly swung around. Chelsea looked back at Simon who was busy spinning the wheel in one direction. The boat turned and suddenly the entire sail flapped loudly over, along with the incredibly large pole that stuck horizontally out from it. The entire apparatus moved over, almost violently, and the boat now headed in a direction that was pointing them straight out through the center of the bridge. The boat now leaned the opposite way. That wasn't as frightening. Still, she stole a glance at Simon. It was comforting to see him looking calm and relaxed.

Thirty minutes later they moved under the Golden Gate Bridge and out into the open ocean as great swells came under the boat. The swells were large and far apart. They lifted the boat up and down like a giant swing or rocking chair. It was exciting, with the wind in her face and the boat rising and falling. The power of the wind seemed to transfer through the sails and into the mast, stays, and lines. In seemed incredibly powerful and yet peaceful, all at the same time. Somehow she imagined it must be a little bit what flying felt like.

A song came on and she was completely transfixed by the music. It seemed the absolutely perfect song for the moment. She listened and when the song was over she opened the iPhone and looked to see what it was. She'd never heard of it, "Into the Mystic" by Van Morrison. She restarted it, then clicked on the app to make the song repeat.

Simon watched the back of Chelsea's head for nearly an hour. He didn't tack or jibe but took advantage of the offshore breeze as he sailed straight out of the bay. He kept his eyes scanning for other boats, but the perfectly clear day revealed fairly light traffic and only two large tankers, neither of which posed a hazard.

San Francisco is known as one of the most dangerous places to sail. Fog, large ships, rocky shores, islands, and varying winds and currents cause risks to the peril of many. Simon's meticulous nature combined with clear and perfect sailing conditions made for an uneventful trip out.

After nearly two hours Simon scanned the area. Seeing nothing around, he set the auto pilot on and made his way quickly to the front of the boat. He spoke out before he got right up behind her, not wanting to scare her.

"Hey."

Chelsea hit pause on the phone as she turned. "Hey."

"Just checking on you," Simon said and knelt next to her with one hand on the rail.

"I'm great. Thanks so much for taking me out here. It's amazing."

"Not many days like this but we sure got a nice one."

"I think I'll come back to the back." She started to get up. "I was getting cold, but it's so amazing I just didn't want to stop."

"Stay here then." Simon got up. "I'll bring you a windbreaker. You just need a little protection from the wind."

"I'd like that. Then I can stay up here a little more."

"I'll be right back."

Before going into the cabin below, Simon scanned to make sure everything was okay. He ducked below and emerged less than a minute later with a windbreaker. As he made his way forward he continued his watchful eye.

"Here ya go," he said and handed the coat to her.

Chelsea put it on. "That's a lot better."

"Okay. I'm not comfortable not being at the wheel so I'll head back there."

"How does the boat steer itself?"

"I have an auto pilot that will keep her straight, but really I shouldn't leave the wheel."

"Okay. I'm going to stay up here just a little longer then I'll come back and join you."

"Sounds good."

Simon made his way back and Chelsea started the music again. The wind was dying down now but the ocean swells still lifted the boat repeatedly. Chelsea turned and looked back. It had now been over three hours and it was amazing how far away land seemed. It was thrilling and frightening at the same time. She breathed in deeply. The air was so clean. No smells of the city. No smoke. No smog. No garbage. It felt like it was completely healthy breathing in, and she took another deep breath in just to experience it.

An hour later, the wind had stopped completely and now the boat just rose and fell with each swell. Chelsea got up and made her way to the back of the boat. She turned off the music on the phone, and sat down on a bench on one side of the boat.

"We're 'becalmed.'" Simon said as if that meant anything to her.

"So are we just stuck out here?"

"No, we have the engine if we need it, but there will be an onshore breeze that will start up soon. I checked the weather this morning. What was going to make this an amazing day was the fact that it was going to be clear and warm, but also we were starting off with an offshore breeze that's supposed to change this afternoon and blow inland." Simon got up and stretched his back.

"That offshore breeze this morning allowed us to get straight out here without a lot of tacking, and if that onshore breeze does start up, the same will be true for our trip back in."

"It's so beautiful." Chelsea looked around at the open ocean. "I think I could stay out here forever."

"It's not always this nice. Sometimes it's cold, with wind and waves splashing in your face. And fog can move in, making it very dangerous with the shipping that comes in and out of the bay. But today is beautiful."

"I don't think I'd mind the cold and wet. When we were moving with the wind it almost felt like we were flying."

"Yeah, I love it. I've sometimes wanted to head straight out and just keep going."

"That would make me more nervous." Chelsea looked out at the open sea. "Where would you go?"

"Well, I suppose I'd head south until I could catch the winds that were westerly and head for Hawaii."

"How long would that take?"

"Depends on conditions, but I'd guess somewhere between twenty to thirty days. You have to sail south first around the North Pacific High, and that means sailing down nearly as far south as the southern tip of Baja California, then west."

Chelsea sat silently, thinking about 25 days with no land in sight. The boat had seemed so large when she stepped onboard last night. Now it seemed small.

"I'm going to grab that pineapple, do you want anything?"

"No I'm great. Thank you."

"Stay back here for now. I've loosened the boom and it will swing hard to one side as soon as the wind picks back up. I wouldn't want to have it knock you in."

"That doesn't sound fun. I'll stay here."

Simon disappeared into the cabin below and returned a moment later with the bowl of pineapple and two forks stuck in it. He sat in the chair at the wheel and started snacking on the fruit, holding out the bowl to her at one point. Chelsea shook her head.

"No thanks. I can see why people own sailboats. It just feels so freeing."

"Yeah, I love it out here." Simon ate another piece then asked, "Did you like my music mix?"

"I loved it."

"We were sailing for quite a while. You must have made it through that mix a couple of times."

Chelsea laughed. "You're going to think I'm weird but I never got past about the fourth or fifth song."

Simon looked at her questioningly.

"I got to one song and hit repeat. I must have listened to it 100 times in a row. It has to be the perfect song for sailing. For today." She gestured to the ocean and sky. "For this."

Simon laughed. "What song?"

"Into The Mystic."

"Yeah, if I had to pick one song to sail to, that would be it."

"I'm not sure what was he saying about the foghorn, but it didn't matter. It was perfect."

"Here, let me see the phone."

Chelsea handed Simon his phone.

"Foghorns are used to warn of danger. Look back at the how far the land is." Simon swung around in the swiveled seat and faced the back of the boat and the land far away. "Imagine sailing right at that land but having fog so thick that you can't see more than ten feet in front of your boat. That's what wrecked so many boats before the day of electronics."

Simon clicked on the phone and turned on a control near the wheel and music began playing from speakers on the deck, flooding the entire boat in the sound.

"So on one hand he is singing about sailing, and likens that sailing to your soul and spirit. He says sailing is flying into the mystic. But then he sings about the fact that while most sailors fear the warning of the foghorn, he wants to hear it because it means he'll be coming home to see his girl."

Simon got quiet as they and they both listened to the song.

Chelsea was suddenly aware of the fact that the artist was also singing about "rocking" the girl's gypsy soul and making love and that their souls would "flow into the mystic." Simon was quiet and she wondered if he was thinking the same thing.

They both sat in silence as the chorus continued and repeated the lines that Chelsea now felt awkward about.

The sail flapped loudly and the boom slid over, slamming against the lines. Simon got up quickly and held the bowl of fruit out to Chelsea. "Can you hold this for a minute?"

Once again Simon was moving around the deck, tightening lines and spinning the wheel until the boat swung around, pointing back towards land. The boat began to heel over to one side slightly as it picked up more wind and cut through the water.

She wanted to stop time and return to that moment in the sun when the wind was calm and the boat slowly rose up and down without moving forward. As awkward as it was, she felt like she was finally growing closer to this man who had saved her and taken her away from the hell that was her life, if only for a moment.

She wished the wind would stop again but just the opposite happened. The wind picked up and on top of the swells the water grew choppy with whitecaps cresting across the waves. The boat heeled over aggressively and sped through the water back towards the bay. Simon was now completely focused on piloting the craft and seemed oblivious to the fact that the song was still playing on repeat.

Chelsea felt like the wind and the sea were living things bent on interrupting. That they somehow conspired to control and ruin a moment that felt somehow important. She wondered if there was ever a song that had been written about the wind interrupting someone's life. Finally, she shrugged off the feeling that the moment was lost and accepted the fact that she was still out here on this beautiful boat. It was still a wonderful day and she was with Simon at this moment.

The wind continued to increase and the boat heeled over further which now worried her. She was about to say something to Simon when he looked over at her. He could see the worry in her face.

"It's fine. No worries."

"What if we tip over?"

"Not possible. These boats are made in such a way that that can't happen."

She looked at him curiously and he continued, "First the keel on the bottom of the boat is the heaviest part of the ship, which is working hard to hold the bottom down. Then, even if the wind did blow hard enough to tip us over too far, the rudder would then slip out of the water and the entire boat would act like a weathervane. We'd instantly spin around in the wind and she'd right herself."

None of it made sense to Chelsea so she just said, "I'll take your word for it."

Simon looked at her and chuckled. "Just don't worry. Enjoy it."

"I am." And she realized that of all the days in her life that this was one of the most amazing. Not because of anything she'd done or accomplished, but just because of the sheer beauty of it all.

"Simon." She said his name so he would make eye contact and she could look right at him. "Thank you for taking me out here. I think this is one of the most beautiful and amazing things I've ever done."

"I'm glad we could do it."

Three and a half hours later they were docked back in the marina. It had been a very quiet ride in and Chelsea couldn't help but wonder if Simon had been thinking about the Van Morrison song. If he had been, he gave no indication.

After they were tied back up to the dock, Simon turned off the engine. The sun was now dropping over the mountains behind Sausalito.

"It will take a little while to stow the sails and batten everything down, but when I'm done, would you like to go get dinner?"

"Yes, I'd like that," Chelsea answered. "How long before you'll be ready to go?"

"It'll probably take me about 30 or 40 minutes."

"I think I'll clean up a bit," she said and headed for her berth.

The wind and the saltwater had left her face feeling almost sticky. She used the tiny shower, but made an effort to not get her hair wet. Sitting in front of the tiny mirror in the room she reapplied her makeup and combed her hair out.

She was glad she'd brought plenty of clothes onboard but it didn't seem to matter to Simon. Unlike so many other times getting ready for a date, she put on what she wanted to wear, not concerned about what the guy would think or say. Now that they were no longer sailing it seemed very warm so she put on a pair of comfortable jeans and switched out of her oversized sweater for a T-shirt.

She left her berth and found Simon was rinsing down the boat with a hose.

"You ready?" Simon asked when he saw her.

"Sure."

"There's a little Italian restaurant right up at the end of the dock. We can walk."

He turned the hose off and shut and locked the door into the cabin. She followed him as he stepped on the dock and walked alongside him till they exited the marina docks. The restaurant was literally across the street from the entrance to the dock and had tables outside along the sidewalk.

"You okay eating outside or do you want to go in?" Simon asked.

"No, this will be great."

They sat at a small table and a waiter brought menus almost immediately. "Can I get you anything to drink?"

"Just water for me for now, please." Simon said and Chelsea nodded in agreement.

"It's funny," Chelsea commented. "When I sat down I felt dizzy or like I'm still on the water rising up and down."

"Yeah, that's pretty normal." Simon opened his menu to look at his options. "Sometimes after spending a few days on the boat, I'll come ashore and the first time I lay in my bed I will swear the room is rocking and spinning like crazy. Sounds funny but I actually like it."

Chelsea looked up from her menu at Simon. "Thank you again for taking me today."

Simon returned her gaze. "You already thanked me. Besides, it was my pleasure. I love sailing, but I think it's even more fun watching someone sailing for their first time."

"Well, I loved it."

They ordered, ate, and talked. Chelsea talked repeatedly about the sailing. Watching her reaction to the experience was more fun for Simon than he'd had in months. He didn't realize it but for the first time since he'd met Chelsea he ate an entire meal without thinking about Allie.

Chapter 22

S imon lay on the bed in his berth thinking about the problem of Chelsea's attacker. He was almost certain he knew who it was, but now a different problem presented itself. How to deal with him. Movies are filled with heroes killing bad guys, and Simon had no doubt if it were 150 years earlier in history this may have indeed been a solution he would have considered. This, however, wasn't the movies or the 1800s.

Ideally he should simply go to the police. Unfortunately, everything was conjecture at this point. The man had left no physical evidence behind, unless it was some DNA from hair or something left in her apartment. Even if he could convince the police that the attacker was who he thought it was, the police would never get a search warrant on such conjecture.

Making the problem even more difficult was the detective who all but said it was not a priority. With the riots, the election, and all the other issues facing the police department today, it was no surprise the detective wasn't interested in pursuing the matter.

That left it to Simon. He would commit no crime but he was certain he could figure out a way to either prove who the attacker was or ruin the man's future, which would be just as good. The best possible scenario would be to do both. Prove his guilt and ruin him.

Simon had always believed that the best way to approach a problem was to think about it from all angles, to think about every possible solution and all the ramifications of such actions. Then throw out the solutions with greatest risk and continue to consider those solutions with the greatest probability of success. And, finally, to start over and think about it from a completely different perspective. Patience was key. If he attempted anything in haste it was likely to blow up in his face.

So he ran through possibility after possibility. An idea started to form in his mind and he continued to look for the flaws in his plan. Ultimately he looked at it from the attacker's point of view. Sometime after midnight he fell asleep still working through the possibilities of his idea.

The next morning it was Simon's turn to waken to the smell of coffee. He was surprised when he looked at his phone to find that he'd slept until nearly 7am.

Climbing out of bed he rinsed his face in the sink and got dressed in jeans and a blue polo.

Chelsea greeted him when he came out of his berth. "Morning."

"Morning," Simon returned. "I haven't slept that late in as long as I can remember."

"Well, you've done so much for me, I figured the least I could do was get up and make coffee."

"Well…" Simon paused. "Thank you."

Chelsea was still working with one good arm and one semi-sore arm. She set a cup on the counter and with the same hand filled it with coffee.

Simon sat down at the table and sipped it. His mind was already continuing the thought process he'd gone to sleep with the night before. He continued to look for the possible flaws in his plan, and all the potential outcomes at every step.

"Simon?"

"Oh, sorry, I was thinking."

"What about?"

"About the man in your apartment."

"You said you knew who it was?"

"I think so."

"How could you know?"

"Do you know what a 1973 Ford Pickup looks like?"

"No."

Simon pulled out his phone and typed the year and make into a Google image search. He pulled up a truck that looked similar to the one he'd seen and turned his phone around to show Chelsea. He handed her his phone as she came out from behind the bar of the kitchen and sat at the table.

"Do you know anyone who drives a truck exactly like this?"

"I don't think so."

"I'm not surprised, but it changes nothing."

"Simon what are you talking about? Who?"

"Look, I said I think I know. Let me do a little digging and I'll confirm it."

Chelsea looked exasperated so Simon tried to smile with all the confidence he could.

"How would you feel if I left you here on the boat for a day or two?"

"I'd feel alone."

"But would you feel safe?"

"I feel safe with you here," she said, looking down, as if embarrassed by the sentiment.

"Look, no one knows you are here. Almost no one knows I even own a boat, and I don't believe the man who attacked you even knows who I am. There's a market right up at the end of the dock, several restaurants. We can go up and stock the boat with food you like. I can leave you with some cash in case you need anything, and I'll be back in a very short time."

"When?"

"Well, I'm not leaving until I make a few calls. It may not be today or even tomorrow."

"What if I went with you?"

"Maybe, but honestly, I think it's better if I do this without you."

Chelsea realized that what he was proposing meant spending at least one if not two more days on the boat. She felt like Simon was finally warming up to her. He still made absolutely no effort to touch her or get close to her physically, but somehow it felt like if he did, it would mean so much more. Maybe another day or two and he would.

"Okay," she said. "I kind of feel like I don't have much of a choice."

"You always have choices." Simon smiled at her. "It's choices that make life an adventure. They make it interesting. Without choice we have no control and life would be meaningless."

"This sounds like some kind of philosophy class."

"Nope, you are on a boat." Simon looked at his phone and checked the weather app that he used for sailing. "Tell you what. How would you feel if I make those calls, you make us some breakfast, and then we take the boat out again?"

"I'd like that very much."

"Let's do it." Simon stood up. "I'm going to head up to the main deck I've got to replace a winch that's going bad. Make anything you want, I'll eat it."

He opened a cabinet and pulled out a small toolbox. Then yet another and produced a small round metal device about the size of a tin can. Chelsea assumed it was the part he was talking about.

"Any suggestions?"

"Personally, if I'm sailing, eggs and bacon. But there is oatmeal in the cabinet. We'll hit up the market and get some other food before we head out. I don't think there is much by way of lunch onboard."

"Okay."

Simon walked up to the main deck. The winch was held in place by eight screws that were counter-sunk in the deck. He pulled out his phone, dialed Natalie, and set the phone down next to the winch he was replacing. Then he hit the speaker button and took out the tools to unscrew the old winch from its spot.

"Hey Nat, how's the fam?"

Meanwhile, Chelsea started some water boiling in a teapot. She got out two bowls and spoons and set the instant oatmeal next to them. Since hot water was all she needed to make the oatmeal, and since she desperately wanted to know what Simon was up to, she made her way over to the bottom of the stairs and listened through the open door. Simon was talking about his granddaughter. She felt guilty for listening, and started to head back into the cabin, but then he changed the subject.

"Natalie, I need you to do a few things for me."

"Sure, Dad. What is it?"

"I need you to cut a check from the foundation for $250,000. I want it dated two days from now. Then I want you to find a way to get it delivered this afternoon."

"And who is the lucky recipient getting this money?"

At that moment the teapot began to whistle and drowned out the conversation. Chelsea quickly went back and moved the pot and turned off the burner. Then she quietly moved back to the door.

"… I'm not sure who you specifically make it out to but someone attached to them."

"Dad, what the heck? You can't stand those people."

"Still don't. But I need you to do this. I know I gave you and Ron the foundation to run, but just make that happen. When you are done, call me back and I'll fill you in."

"Okay, Dad."

Simon hung up. He did a Google search for an address and wrote the number down in his phone. Then he called Natalie again. Once again he put her on speaker phone as he continued to unscrew the old winch.

"Hey, Dad."

"I also got the address for his office. Hire a courier service to deliver the check so it gets there today. I also need you to include a note with that check. Handwrite that note. It will seem more personal. Like we care."

"Oookaaayyy." She said it slowly and without confidence.

"Here, write down this address." Simon shared the address with her and had her repeat it back.

"Perfect. Now here is what I want the note to say…" Simon paused as he thought about it. "Write this… 'I'd like to offer additional support but please call my assistant for details at this number'… nothing else."

Simon paused in thought.

"Your number, Dad?"

"No. I want you to go to a store and get a phone that you prepay so there is no ID attached to it. I'm not even sure where you do that. Then use that number."

"I can do that. But Dad, seriously, what's going on?"

Simon ignored her question and continued, "When the call comes in I want an appointment with him. This next part is important. Under no circumstances can he know my identity. Just tell him that one of the people who directs the foundation wants to meet and, if you can, imply that significantly more support is being considered. Tell him that he is welcome to bring one assistant but that I would prefer to meet alone. If he asks why just tell him the foundation keeps our activities as private as possible, especially when it comes to this kind of giving. He'll understand that."

"I'm writing it down. But what the hell?"

"Then set up an appointment at my house. Day after tomorrow, preferably. That would be Thursday, but no sooner. If Thursday doesn't work, then Friday or Saturday."

"Dad, first, the foundation's activities aren't that private. They'll be able to look up the name of the foundation on the check and see our activities. And second, if you set up the appointment at your house he can just look it up in the county records and find your name."

"Actually, he can't. The house was listed completely in your mother's name. And when she died it became yours."

"Dad!" She sounded frustrated. "It's your house."

"I understand, but I always figured I'd go before your mother and we always planned to leave it to you. Besides, it's not like it matters. I've been paying the taxes so you have no need to worry."

"When were you going to tell me this?"

"Hang on. As for the foundation, was the last major donation the wing at the hospital?"

"There's been a few other smaller donations since. Like I said, they'll be able to look that up and see."

"I'm counting on it. That will convince him to meet me."

"Seriously, Dad, what's going on?"

"Just wait. One more thing. I need you at the appointment as my assistant. So schedule it for a time you can be there."

"Is something wrong? Is all this legal?"

"Nothing illegal. Nothing is wrong. But if anyone asks your name, make something up. Keep our identities unknown."

"Okay, but you have to tell me what is going on the minute I see you."

"I will."

"Promise?"

"Definitely." Simon continued removing the last two screws with the screwdriver. "Natalie, if for any reason he can't meet call me back. If he won't meet at my house tell him that meeting any other way isn't possible. Accept nothing other than that. And if anything else happens that throws you a curve ball just call me. But I think this will work."

"What exactly are we doing that 'will work'?"

"I promised I'd explain it all when I see you and I will. Text me when the courier delivers the check and then call me when their office calls for the appointment."

"You sure they will?"

"250,000 dollars sure. Matter of fact, if they seem to balk at meeting, and if you think it will help to make it happen, offer another 50k. You can increase it to a half million if you must, but I think the 250 will work."

"You are killing me with this." Natalie shook her head and half laughed in disbelief as she said it. "I'll let you know."

Simon took the last screw out and put the old winch in the tool box then positioned the new winch and got two screws started to hold it in place.

Next Simon dialed his old partner Brian and put it on speaker phone again while he continued to work.

"Hey Brian, this is Simon," he said when Brian picked up the phone.

"Simon, what's up? It's great to hear from you," Brian said sincerely. Simon had almost disappeared since Allie's death.

"Brian, who do you know that would be able to get a room completely wired with hidden cameras and quality sound to capture every single thing said and done in that room?"

"Um… I know a couple of guys that could do that."

"Who's the best?"

"Guy's name is John Ronaldo. He owns a surveillance and security business in Sacramento."

"Could he make it happen with only a day's notice?"

"I'm sure he would if the price is right."

"Can I ask a favor?"

"Anything, man."

"Get a hold of John and make sure he is available tomorrow, then stand by."

"Any more information?"

"Sure. If I proceed it will be for the office at my house and I'll need it to be completely wired and ready to go by the end of tomorrow. And you know me, Brian. Make it simple. One switch. I turn it on and everything in that room is captured, audio and video. And every angle. I don't want to miss anything, no matter how small."

"Now you've got my attention." Brian laughed. "What the hell are you up to?"

"It's complicated, but I'll fill you in with all the details another time."

Simon thought over everything, trying to think if he was missing something.

"Listen, Brian. Just make sure he is ready to go. If he can't, find someone else, but they've got to be good. I'll call you as soon as I know if things are a go or not."

"Okay."

Simon thought for a minute and then realized how singularly focused he was being. "Brian, I'm sorry. I never even asked you if you had the time."

"Simon, I pretty much owe everything I have to you. I'd have made the time. But, just so you know, I do have time. The wife and kids are out of town at her mother's. I can get it all arranged."

"Sorry about the last minute notice. If it is a go, I'll call the security guards at the gate and let them know to expect you and John's crew."

"No problem, Simon."

"Thanks, Brian."

Simon reached over and touched the phone, ending the call. He realized that he was excited and his heart was actually pounding. He took a few centering breaths, a technique he'd learned from one of his wrestling coaches in the past. Too amped up and you're liable to make a mistake, even when fighting. This was definitely a fight he needed to be centered for and not over-amped. There could be no mistakes.

Simon once again thought of each step and where the risks were. He tried to anticipate every choice and action that the man could make and what he would do in each situation. He continued to contemplate as he headed back down to the cabin.

Chelsea was standing in the kitchen when he came down. As he returned the toolbox to the cabinet, he looked at her.

"What's for breakfast?"

"Oatmeal. I hope that's okay."

"Sounds good. Let's eat that, then go grab some groceries."

An hour later, Chelsea had showered, in what she could only believe was the tiniest shower in the world. She'd put on her makeup and combed her hair out. They were going to sail again, so a ponytail seemed the only option. She picked out jeans and a light blue blouse that buttoned up the front. She looked at herself in the mirror. Then she took off the blouse, put on a pushup bra, and put the blouse back on. She looked at herself in the mirror again. She hoped Simon would notice. She came out of her cabin and greeted Simon.

He noticed her revealing top immediately but said nothing. Together they walked to the end of the dock and stopped at a market. It was strange buying food together. They had very different tastes but they managed. In the end they had a basket with items Chelsea picked out—granola, yogurt, fresh fruit, and water. They also had eggs, bacon, lunchmeat, bread, and mayonnaise that Simon had picked out.

As they walked back to the boat they passed a couple coming from the other direction. They were holding hands and all Chelsea could think of was that she wished Simon would hold her hand. She switched the grocery bag into the hand that was not between them and brushed alongside him ever so slightly.

For his part Simon was thinking of nothing but when Natalie would call back, and continuing to dwell on all of the things that could go wrong and planning for every possibility.

They sailed that day but stayed inside the bay. The morning started off well. The sun was shining and the wind was strong enough to give them speed to maneuver. Chelsea realized that she loved sailing more than almost anything else she had experienced.

"I think I could do this forever," Chelsea said absentmindedly at one point. "I think I'd love to just go out and keep sailing towards the sun."

"She's built for that," Simon replied. "But most people get a little freaked out when they lose sight of land. Especially after a day or two."

"I don't think I would. I think if it were up to me I'd sail straight for Hawaii.

"That's a long time to be out there alone."

The front of the boat lifted up on a wave and then came down hard just as another wave met her. It sent a heavy spray across the boat, smacking them both in the face, and making Chelsea laugh.

"I think if I had the choice I would do it," she said. "I'd leave tomorrow and not come back. I think I'd love it."

Simon smiled, "Maybe you would."

Another wave sprayed across the boat, soaking them both. Knowing how things could be when sailing, Simon was already wearing a windbreaker. But Chelsea's light blue blouse was soaked. The water had turned the blouse disturbingly transparent and Simon tried to keep his eyes focused forward on the sailing.

Thankfully, the chill got to her quickly and she went below, returning moments later wearing an oversized sweater along with a less than flattering windbreaker over it.

The wind grew stronger throughout the day and the waves rougher. Simon enjoyed watching Chelsea's reaction to the waves and wind. She seemed truly happy even when getting drenched with the spray. Soon she was asking him how to turn and steer the boat, so Simon gave her a lesson in tacking and jibing. She seemed to pick it up quickly and eventually he let her pilot while he kept a watchful eye.

It was nearly 5pm when they returned to the harbor. Simon had just tied up the boat when his phone rang. He looked at the caller ID and answered.

"Hey, Natalie, what's the word?" Then, after a moment, he said, "Perfect. 2pm. I'll meet you at the house at 10am. Also, I'm sending Brian by to grab your key to the house. He's going to meet a contractor there to have something done for me."

He finished the call with Natalie then dialed again. "Brian, this is Simon. It's a go. You can run by Natalie's house and grab a key from her, she's expecting you... Yeah, I'll let the guys know at the guardhouse. Do me a favor, call me when that's done... You can have them send me a bill or pay it and I'll get you the money. And Brian, if you could FaceTime me and have John run me through where all the cameras and the mics are. Or you could show me. Also, if you or John could show me how to operate things, that would be great."

Finally Simon made one more call, this time to the guards at the gate to his community. When he hung up Chelsea was sitting on the bench near the back of the boat staring at him intently.

"Are you going to tell me what's going on?"

"Let's think of it as a surprise. I don't want to ruin a good surprise."

"Simon, please let me go with you."

"I'm not going anywhere till day after tomorrow, but we can think about it."

Chelsea sat in silence, letting the matter drop for now.

Chapter 23

That night Simon slept but his mind continued to roll through all the possible eventualities of his plan. He woke multiple times during the night thinking about what would and could happen. Eventually, unable to get back to sleep, he got up and made himself eggs and toast. Along with the coffee, it woke him up. He wanted nothing more than to keep his hands busy, and would have worked on the boat, but there was no sound from Chelsea's berth and he decided to wait till at least 7am before he moved about and started making noise. There was always work to do on a sailboat.

He drank several cups of coffee and checked out the local news on his cell phone. When it was finally 7am, he was quickly on deck unscrewing a broken cleat and replacing it with a new one.

It was light but a fog had moved in. The Bay Area was notorious for its fog, which made everything feel damp and cold. Not a good day to sail for sure. He didn't mind sailing in the cold, but the fog made circumstances significantly more dangerous. The shipping through the bay was extensive. For people on shore, a large container ship looks as if it barely moves, but in reality cargo vessels move with pretty good speed. They don't turn quickly and don't stop quickly. A small sailboat could be out in the fog, crushed and sunk without a trace, before it is even missed.

Besides the risks that exist in the fog, there was almost no wind in the forecast until the late afternoon or early evening. So Simon had made a list of things in his mind to fix or check on the boat and was busy working through them.

Chelsea woke to the sound of something being dropped on the deck above. She lay in bed listening and after ten minutes realized that Simon was moving around above. She got up and looked out into the main cabin. There was coffee and she poured herself a cup. She had no idea how long Simon had been up.

She had watched him grind the coffee beans and fill the coffee maker the night before, with enough to make 10 cups. There were only about 4 cups left, so Chelsea realized he'd been up for some time. She took a few sips of coffee, hoping he would come down and join her, but realized the futility of simply hoping. Topping off her cup she returned to her room and decided as long as she heard him up above she'd take the extra time to shower, do her hair and makeup, and try to get back into her routine of primping herself.

Almost two hours later she looked at herself in the mirror. She looked good. The cut on her forehead had almost completely healed and her hair hid what tiny scar was left. The bruises from the original attack were all gone. The bruises from the second were mostly on her arm and on her upper chest and shoulders. Other than the one arm still in the cast, and the other being sore, she was nearly back to normal. Realizing the noises Simon had been making above had stopped, she left the berth.

"Would you like some more coffee?" he asked.

"No thanks." She passed her cup over the bar to him. "I've had plenty."

"I've been working on the boat. There's always something to do so I figured I'd get a few maintenance things taken care of."

Chelsea hoped they would sail again, but Simon said nothing of that possibility.

"Did you eat?" he asked.

"No, but I'm really not hungry at all."

"Okay." Simon continued, "I don't want you to feel ignored or trapped on a boat, but I was going to take care of a few more things. Is there anything you need or want today?"

"No." Chelsea looked around the cabin and noticed for the first time that there were quite a number of books. She picked one up. It was titled Mr. Midshipman Hornblower.

Simon saw her pick it up. "That's a great book. Before I ever sailed, I read it. It made me want to learn how."

Chelsea walked over to the couch with it and curled up. "Well, if you can turn on some music down here, I'll read until you are done working on the boat."

Simon turned on the sound system and clicked on a mix of music he had on an old iPod.

"This is some music I usually put on while I'm reading. If you don't like it you can try something else or switch it to the radio."

Chelsea already liked the soft saxophone music playing. "No, that's fine."

For the next three hours Simon continued to work on the boat. He checked the oil levels in the engine. The water intakes, a crucial component to keeping the engines cool, were prone to plugging up with seaweed, and Simon checked to make sure they were working properly. Then he spent nearly three hours replacing and recalibrating the electronic compass that was needed for the autopilot. The old compass had been going bad, causing the boat to veer to the port. The propane tanks weren't empty, but he walked them to the end of the dock and topped them off.

Chelsea stopped her reading and Simon his work long enough to head up to a local diner to grab lunch just before 1pm. Afterwards, they returned to the boat and Simon continued working.

In the late afternoon, Simon got a call from his former business partner, Brian. The work had been done and Brian switched from a regular phone call to FaceTime and ran him through the system, where the cameras and mics were located, as well as the location of the computer, which was in the adjacent room in a closet. True to Simon's request the contractor had been able to make one switch to start it recording.

"You'll have 12 hours of storage all on a digital drive," Brian explained. "It will also be backed up instantly to the cloud so you can retrieve it if anything happens to the local drive. The actual computer is on and running now. The surveillance program is designed to start up when the computer starts. So really the only thing that will stop you from recording is a power outage."

Brian walked back into the den still using the FaceTime app and focused it on a light switch in an inconspicuous location next to a bookshelf.

"So, when you get here, just double check to make sure the computer is on. There is only one program running. It should be up on the main screen and you'll be able to see the five different cameras and the video feed of what they are capturing in the room. Then if you flip this switch it will start recording everything. That's about it, Simon."

"That looks good. Thanks, Brian. I'll be using it tomorrow. You said it's all stored and backed up? Where's it backing up to?"

"I didn't have any way to store it to your cloud, so I stored it to mine. Hope that is okay."

"Yeah, that's fine. I just don't want it lost."

"You gotta tell me what's going on soon man, it's killing me."

"I will as soon as I have time." Simon said. "If things go the way I expect, you should be able to see a video by tomorrow night and figure it out for yourself."

"All right then. I take it I have permission to check it out?"

"Fine by me, but don't do anything until you talk to me."

"Very cryptic man… very cryptic. I'll get your key back to Natalie. Talk to ya later."

❧

Simon continued fiddling on the boat throughout the afternoon, all the while his mind racing along with almost a computer-programming type process. A series of if-then statements ran through his head. If this happens, then that. If that happens, then this. Scenario after scenario he continued checking off in his mind, then he'd go back over them again and try to think of what other possibilities could occur. At each new discovery in his mind, at each possibility, he created a new reaction. A new if-then.

The sun was setting when Chelsea came on deck. "Simon, you've been working on this boat all day and I'm getting hungry. Would you like me to make something?"

Simon looked up from the job he was working on.

"No, don't do that. Salito's is right there at the entrance to the docks. They've got seafood, salads, and overall pretty good food. Does that sound okay?"

"Sounds good."

Simon looked at her. She looked stunning and he looked down at his dirty hands.

"You're ready, but I'm pretty dirty. Give me 30 minutes?"

"There's no rush."

"Thirty minutes is all I'll need."

In fact, 20 minutes was all he needed. Thirty minutes later they were already seated at the restaurant, with a glass of wine in front of each of them. Simon had ordered a petite cut of prime rib and an order of crab. Chelsea had ordered the shrimp Louie. While they waited for their orders to arrive, Simon was silent. The meeting was less than 20 hours away. His mind continued thinking about it intensely.

Chelsea grew tired of the silence. She'd been thinking all day and had come to a decision. She was never going back to her job. She wanted to tell him but she knew it also may mean that she'd never see him again once things got back to normal. It was stressing her out and she decided that telling him would relieve a great deal of that stress. But now, he seemed to almost ignore her and there was no way to introduce the topic. It seemed like she'd sat alone and in silence all day. Finally, between her worry and the quiet, she opened up.

"Simon, this is a nice place. The wine is great. The boat, the marina, the sailing. It's all been wonderful. But I don't think I can take sitting here tonight in silence. I need to tell you something and I can't if you are ignoring me."

"I'm sorry. I get caught up thinking about things."

"Thinking is fine. Ignoring me isn't."

"I'll try to pay attention." Simon smiled at her warmly. "What did you want to tell me?"

"When I get back home I'm going to look for a job. A real job."

"Okay," Simon said, somewhat tentatively.

"Okay? That's all you have to say?"

"I'm really not sure what to say."

"Well, say something more than okay."

"I think it's a good decision."

"Because you don't think the decisions I've made in life are good?"

It seemed to him like she was trying to argue or fight with him and he felt trapped. He paused, thinking about his response.

"Look Chelsea, the older I've gotten, the more I realize that people are too quick to dole out advice, judgment, and opinions. If you want my advice you pretty much have to pry it out of me. If you think I'm going to judge you for your choices, you're wrong. And as for my opinions, well, it's my opinion that it's a good decision. That isn't an opinion or judgment on any other choices in your life."

"Well, you clearly don't think I've made good decisions."

"What I think is that you can make any choice you want and I'm not here to judge. The truth is, I've made horrible decisions in my life and I have to live with the consequences. What I'm trying to do is figure out the positive and live with that in mind."

The waiter arrived with their food. For Simon, it was a much-needed interruption. After setting down the two plates of food, the waiter asked, "Is there anything else I can get for you?"

"No, thank you, Wade," Simon said, of course using the waiter's first name. "I think we are good."

He looked down at his food as the waiter left, hoping Chelsea would change the subject or at the least not seem so argumentative.

"So, what are the positives?"

Simon looked at her a bit confused. "What do you mean?"

"You said you are trying to figure out the positive and live with that in mind." Chelsea repeated his statement back to him, then added, "What are the positives of the horrible decisions I've made in life?"

Simon hated this conversation. He felt like anything he said could be construed as an attack on her. All he wanted was to have a dinner and relax.

"Look, can we just drink this wine and have a nice dinner?"

"No. What positives do you see in my choices?"

Simon looked up from his meal and made eye contact. "Chelsea, I meant what I said. I do think we all make bad decisions in life. Nobody is perfect, me least of all. But there are always things that are positive."

"So what do you see in my life that is positive?"

He suddenly realized that this wasn't about her past choices. This was about her current circumstances. He looked at her. She seemed small and vulnerable. He knew she was afraid to go back to her apartment. Someone had almost killed her. She was scared and feeling helpless.

"I will tell you the most positive things I can think of, but give me a moment. Please eat something."

He took another bite of his meal and tried to organize his thoughts. Then he looked directly at her.

"Okay. Positive. The most positive thing I can think of," he paused for a moment, then still looking at her, continued, "Your choices in life allowed me to meet you. You have helped me in ways I don't expect you to understand. You have no idea how thankful I am for that. I hope that is a positive thing for you."

She suddenly felt closer to Simon than she could ever remember feeling. Actually, to anyone, ever. It was overwhelming. She didn't know how to respond. She wanted to throw herself into his arms, but she was pretty sure he wasn't looking for that closeness. She felt a tear running down her cheek and wiped it away.

"Thank you," was all she could manage to say.

"There are always positives, Chelsea." The wrinkles formed at the corners of his eyes and he beamed. Chelsea thought at that moment he looked happier than ever. Then he nodded at her arm in the cast. "People with broken bones know they heal back stronger. People with broken lives overcome and are stronger too. You are stronger than most people I know."

They both stared at each other a moment longer, then Simon broke the stare and began eating. Chelsea took a long drink of her wine and then started eating too.

After a few moments of silence, Chelsea looked up. The wine was starting to relax her and she realized the kindness he was showing her and the antagonistic tone she'd used with him.

"I'm sorry, Simon."

"John Wayne used to say, 'Never say you're sorry, it's a sign of weakness,'" Simon said but smiled in a way that conveyed to Chelsea that he wasn't chastising her.

"Do you believe that?"

"Yes and no. He said it in the context of military decisions that would result in life or death. Officers of soldiers make decisions based on the best information they have. They don't apologize for their decisions. It probably would be seen in that situation as weakness," Simon spoke almost absentmindedly.

"But for you and me, in the context of human relationships? No I don't believe it. Apologies are necessary." Simon took a drink of his wine.

"Do we have a relationship?" Chelsea ventured.

"I think you are my friend," Simon said quietly without looking up.

Chelsea thought about that for a moment and decided that it was a better answer than any other at the moment. Every relationship with a man in the past had been about one person taking advantage of the other. None would have been considered friends.

They continued to eat and the waiter returned, holding a bottle of wine.

"Can I get you some more wine?" he asked.

"Yes, I'd like another, Wade."

Chelsea nodded her agreement, "Please."

The waiter left them both eating in silence. She had been thinking about her life and the garbage that had engulfed her but she abruptly remembered one thing Simon had said. That he had made horrible decisions. She wondered what possible choices he'd made. How could this man with such insane success understand her troubles and pain?

"What decisions?"

"Hmm?" Simon asked, looking up while still eating.

"You said you are trying to live with the consequences in your life from horrible decisions. What decisions? All I see is a perfect life with money, success, a daughter, a granddaughter, a beautiful home. What poor choices have you ever made, Simon? What could you possibly know about bad consequences?"

Simon reached for his glass and took a long drink of wine. Chelsea noticed the sadness had returned to his face. The smile was gone. His eyes seemed empty.

"Let's just eat."

She realized there was something there. Something he was ashamed of, or disgusted by. Some choice he'd made was eating at him.

They finished their meal in silence, Simon no longer talking and Chelsea irritated that this man with a perfect life would somehow lecture her on choices and consequences. They skipped dessert and Simon paid the bill. They walked back to the boat quietly and as they entered the main cabin Simon immediately opened a bottle of wine and poured a glass.

"Would you like one?" he asked, holding up his glass towards her.

"No, thank you."

Chelsea sat on one end of the couch watching him as he drank half his glass. Then Simon made his way over and sat on the couch. She was aware that he didn't sit on the far end of the couch, but he didn't sit right next to her either.

"Simon. My life is filled with crap. Admittedly by choices I've made. But seriously, I want to know. What bad choices did you ever make?"

Simon turned his head slowly and looked at her. He had drunk more wine than he had in over two years. He was angry. Angry with the choices he'd made. Angry with the consequences. This woman wanted to know. She thought his life was perfect. Then he would tell her. She would understand.

❧

They had sold the business. Brian, Sai, David, and four others who had worked for more than a decade were ready to celebrate.

"Seriously guys, let's go get drinks at Sutter Bar." David had encouraged them all. David was single as were the others who all chimed in in agreement.

Simon didn't want to go. His idea of celebrating was to head home and spend the evening with Allie. In his mind he pictured her sitting on the couch waiting for him. Maybe even in lingerie.

"Nah, I'm going to head home."

"Oh come on man," David pushed. "You and Big B never come with us all." He turned to Brian, "Big B, what about you?"

"Well, I'm with Simon. I'd rather hang at home, but Kim is out of town, so I suppose I can come and have a couple drinks. Lord knows we've been working for long enough, we should celebrate, too."

Sai turned to Simon. "Yeah, we should. Come on, Simon. Hang with us tonight. You never do. And now that we're done working together, we may never get another chance."

Simon felt like a teenager with the peer pressure of kids asking him to drink. He'd never given in to it but realized this was different, and though he didn't want to, he agreed.

"Okay, let me call Allie. I'll meet you guys down there."

The guys all jetted out together, Brian locking the doors behind them. Simon made his way down to the car and called as he drove.

"Hey, Honey," Allie said as she picked up.

"Hey. The guys and I are going to Sutter Bar in Old Town Folsom. Just gonna have a few drinks. Today was the last day in the office and everyone wants to celebrate a bit. It may be the last time we are all together."

"Okay, well don't be too late. I knew you were done working today and I plan on celebrating with you tonight. I'm wearing that corset and I've got a bottle of champagne in the fridge."

"I won't," Simon promised. "I should just come home now. Your plan sounds like more fun."

"It's up to you. I'll be here waiting."

"I won't be long."

Moments later he entered the bar to the shouts of the guys he'd spent so long working with.

"Let's hear it for Simon!" David yelled above the din of bar music, voices, and general chaos. He raised his glass as did the others and cheered.

Brian approached and handed Simon a beer.

"Who's buying?" Simon asked.

"You are."

"Well, okay then." Simon joined them and drank his customary two beers. It was about as much as he preferred to ever drink, but tonight was different. They were celebrating and he had a third, then a fourth.

Two hours later he was feeling good. The buzz from the alcohol was kicking in and he was unused to it but enjoying it. He looked at his watch and his mind tugged at him. Allie was home waiting.

He had bought several rounds for everyone in the bar. Most were people he knew, but a half-dozen men and women were there benefiting from his generosity. One man, near the end of the bar, looked fully inebriated.

"One more round for everyone!" Simon shouted to the cheers of most of the patrons.

He wanted to go home now and decided the easiest way to end things was to wait a few, buy another round, then get out. After 10 minutes he set the beer he had been drinking down and called the bartender over to him.

"Hey buddy, I'm going to buy one more round for everyone but that guy at the end. I think he's had enough."

The bartender looked at the man at the end of the bar and nodded. "Yeah, he comes in a lot. I usually have to cut him off. I'll deal with it."

Simon watched as the bartender made his way to the end of the bar and spoke to the man.

Simon pulled out his phone and dialed Allie.

"Hey honey," Allie answered.

"Hey, would you mind coming and picking me up?"

"Really? I'm hardly wearing anything." Allie sounded a bit exasperated.

"Well, I've had a couple too many beers so I'm not driving. And I'd get a ride with one of these guys but they've had plenty to drink and I don't think any of them are heading home anytime soon."

"Can't you just take an Uber?"

"I'd rather see you driving in what your wearing."

"Okay, that sounds good. But when I get there, you better not have anyone with you."

Simon laughed. "I won't."

"You're at Sutter Bar?"

"Yeah."

"Okay. I'll be there in 15 maybe 20 minutes. But don't make me wait out in the car and you better be alone."

"I won't, and I will."

He hung up the phone and took a few more sips of his beer. The guys were all having a good time and Simon motioned Brian over.

"Hey B, I'm going to buy one more round then I'm going to jet."

"No problem, buddy. I'll hang with the guys and call it in an hour or so."

"Thanks."

"Simon, if you ever get another good idea, don't come tell me. I think with what we've made I'm done working forever."

"It was fun."

"I'm not sure if fun is the word. Hard, long, successful, but fun? That comes now. Kim and I already have four trips planned. We head to Hawaii next week, then after two weeks there, we will come back for a couple weeks, then we are heading to France."

"Good for you. You have earned it."

Simon watched the man at the end of the bar finish his beer and get up. He stumbled but made his way to the door and left.

Once the door shut behind him, Simon shouted. "Okay... last time. One more round for everyone."

Again, everyone cheered.

Simon turned to Brian. "I put these on our business card. I guess this is the last expense we'll ever have on that."

"I think we can afford it."

"Allie is on her way to pick me up. Can you sign for it, I'm going to get out of here."

"Sure thing," Brian said, then turned and gave Simon a big bear hug. "Man, Simon, It's been great. Thanks for everything. And I was kidding. If you ever need anything, you call me. I'll come running."

Simon grinned. "No problem. It's been fun, but it's not like we have to not see each other anymore. I'm sure Allie and Kim will want to get together. We'll hang sometime soon. Maybe we can even plan a trip somewhere, all four of us."

"Yeah, I'd like that. I know the girls would too."

"Okay, well, I'm out," Simon said. He made his way to the front door and turned to look. The guys were all engrossed in conversation. No goodbyes seemed necessary, so he turned and left.

Outside it was dark and he stood for a moment. Several sirens were blaring in the distance. There was a slight drizzle and Simon pulled out his iPhone. He and Allie had always shared the location finder and he pulled it up to see how far away she was. It took a few seconds and then the phone located her and showed her just two blocks away at the corner of Riley and Sutter Streets.

Simon waited a few moments. The sirens grew louder and he looked down the street to see if he could see Allie's car approaching. He noticed a crowd had gathered at the intersection two blocks down and traffic was backed up. Realizing she must be caught behind whatever mess was causing the traffic he stared walking towards her. Maybe he could just jump in the car and they could get out of the mess.

As he got closer the sirens grew louder and an emergency vehicle pulled up in front of him. People were crowding around and he could see there were two cars. A Chevy truck had t-boned the other car. The driver's side of the smaller car was completely smashed in and a body was laying on the ground. With sudden realization he recognized the car. It was Allie's. It was Allie laying in the street.

Two policemen were keeping people back and the paramedics had just arrived. Simon ran towards Allie but was held back by one of the officers.

"That's my wife!" Simon screamed.

"Hang on buddy, let them do their job," the officer said while physically holding Simon back.

Simon watched in desperation as the paramedics tried performing CPR and chest compressions on Allie. Everything seemed to slow down. Everything seemed to be bizarre and unreal. Allie was wearing an overcoat but it had been opened so they could work on her, revealing the corset and leggings. She had on one pink slipper; the other had been lost as she had been taken from the car.

Another officer was issuing a breathalyzer to the driver of the Chevy pickup. Simon noticed that the driver was the same man who had stumbled out of the bar only moments before.

"Damn. Damn. Damn," Simon said, still being held by the officer. "Let me go to her."

"Just hang on."

Finally, still performing chest compressions, they loaded her into an ambulance and left for the hospital. Simon followed in a squad car. He was met soon after by a doctor who informed him that Allie had died.

c∕ɔ

Simon shook himself out of the memory. His body shook violently and he took a deep shuddering breath. He looked down at the wine in his hand and wanted to throw it across the cabin. Instead he got up and took a long last drink from it then set the empty glass in the sink. Returning to the couch, he looked at Chelsea.

"We all make bad choices. Yours are no worse than mine. My choices cost the most amazing woman in the world her life."

"Simon, your choices didn't cost her. Someone else's choices did that. Someone drove who shouldn't have."

"Really? You don't see it? First choice. Letting people peer pressure me into going to a bar, when I should have just gone home. Second choice. Drinking enough so that I had to ask her to come and get me. Third choice. Not taking a ride share or a taxi. Fourth choice. Buying several rounds for everyone in the bar, including the man who was drunk and killed my wife. Fifth choice. I picked that moment to ask the bartender to cut him off."

Simon sat down on the couch and felt completely helpless. He wanted to curl up and die. He'd never told anyone of the myriad of choices he'd made that night. Guilt racked his brain and tears began to run down his face. He started to lay down on the couch. Chelsea moved over and took his shoulder and guided his head into her lap.

Simon wanted to forget everything.

"Simon, it wasn't your fault."

"Chelsea, every decision I made that night led to her death. If I had just not made ONE, she would still be alive."

He lay silently on his side, his back towards her, his head turned away from her, using her legs as a pillow. Chelsea ran her fingers through his hair.

"It wasn't your fault."

"ONE of those decisions. One of those choices," Simon repeated.

"It wasn't your fault."

"I had to tell Natalie her mother died."

"Simon, you couldn't have known."

"My granddaughter will never know her grandmother because of my choices."

They both grew quiet. Simon couldn't clear the image of Allie lying on the street for nearly an hour.

"Simon?"

"Yeah?"

"What are the positives?"

"There are none."

"No, seriously. You've pushed me to look at the positives in my life, what are yours?"

"For two years I've wondered that. Allie is gone. There aren't any positives."

They sat in silence as Chelsea thought about what to say.

"There are for me," Chelsea said quietly.

Simon sat up and moved a bit away from Chelsea.

"How do you figure?"

"Simon, I'm not saying it's an equal trade, or anything like that. But if Allie were still alive you'd have never had dinner with me, right?"

"Mm-hm." Simon agreed.

"And if you'd have never met me, I would have been thrown off that balcony. No one would have saved me. I would be dead."

Simon sat up, looked at her and forced himself to smile. "Those are positives for you."

He knew he couldn't say anything else. In his heart he knew if he had to choose he would have chosen Allie. But he also knew that even he would never want to be given such a choice. He knew that if Allie knew someone's life could be saved by her death she'd have wanted it that way. His mind raced through those crazy thoughts until he forced himself to stop thinking about it.

"I hope it's positive for you, knowing you saved me."

"It is."

The conversation about Chelsea's attack reminded Simon of the present. He stood up.

"Tomorrow's a big day. We should get some sleep."

Chapter 24

The next day Simon woke at 4:30. He looked at his phone and waited a few moments, wondering if there was any chance Chelsea was already awake. The anticipation in him was building, and he knew sleep was impossible. So he got up and made a pot of coffee. Moments later Chelsea's door opened.

"I couldn't sleep," she said

"Me either. Coffee's almost done."

"What time do we leave?"

"You sure you wouldn't be more comfortable staying here?"

"No. I'm going."

"All right then." Simon looked around. He wasn't hungry but he knew that several of the scenarios in his head could play out violently and breakfast was a better idea than not.

"Would you like some breakfast?"

"Just the coffee." Chelsea wasn't hungry either.

"Well, it's liable to be a long day. I'm going to make some eggs, you sure?"

"Yes." Chelsea carried her coffee to her berth. "I'm going to get ready to go. Should I pack my bags or will we be coming back?"

Simon thought for a moment. "Pack 'em, in case we don't come back."

While she packed and got ready to leave she felt a twinge of disappointment. The last couple of days had been more relaxing than she could ever remember. Between the sailing and the extra time with Simon, she had enjoyed it immensely.

Simon forced himself to eat four eggs, toast, and drank a large glass of orange juice. Afterwards, he did the dishes and then started packing things up on the boat. The remaining perishable food he put in a small cooler and carried it to the truck. Then he returned and did the same with Chelsea's laptop, the painting, and one of her bags. Finally he returned and helped Chelsea to the dock with her last two bags. He locked the boat and they both made their way to the truck.

By 6:30 they were leaving the Marina. The sun was rising in their faces as they drove east. Simon wanted to get to his house very early to avoid any chance that he, Natalie, or Chelsea would be seen by her attacker before they were inside the house.

The ride back to the Sierra Nevada foothills was quiet. Halfway there, Simon called Natalie to let her know they were on their way. Chelsea listened as the call was made using truck's hand free system.

"Hey, I'll be there in about an hour and a half."

"Okay, Dad."

"Listen, dress business-like. You're my assistant."

"Got it."

"Who's watching the baby?"

"Ron's working from home today. He's got her," Natalie said.

"Great. We'll head over to the house as soon as I get there."

"The appointment isn't until 1pm."

"Yeah, but I want to be there by 10. It just eliminates the possibility that he'll show up early to watch the place."

"Dad…" There was a pause. "Is everything we're doing safe?"

"I wouldn't do it if I thought otherwise. I will also have one of you ready to call the police immediately if anything should go wrong."

"One of us? Is Chelsea with you?"

"Yes."

"Want her to stay at my house with Ron and the baby?"

Simon looked over at her questioningly and Chelsea shook her head no.

"No," Simon stated.

"I still want to know what is going on."

"I'll fill you in when I get there. Love you," Simon said.

"Love you, too."

The call ended and Chelsea wondered what it felt like to have a father. He spoke to her like a father, but also like an equal. He told her he loved her almost casually like it was normal. Most men never said that to anyone. She wondered if Simon would ever say those three words to her.

They continued to drive in silence. Simon's mind worked through scenario after scenario. What if this happened? Then he would respond with that. What if that happened? Then he would do this.

Chelsea was glad she hadn't been left on the boat. To her, being alone was almost as frightening as being attacked. She'd spent most of her adult life alone, but now the thought of going back to her condo and spending even one night alone was petrifying.

Simon pulled up to Natalie's house in her affluent residential neighborhood in El Dorado Hills. The house was a beautiful wooden-sided home painted dark blue and had a covered porch fronted by a white wooden rail that wrapped around the front and one side.

Seeing it made Chelsea feel like a failure. It was like this girl who was so much younger than her already had everything anyone could want. A husband, a child, and a beautiful home. The condo that she once felt was a wonderful place of refuge now seemed small and insignificant.

Natalie exited the front door of the house and walked immediately to the truck. She opened the back door and slid in next to Chelsea's bags.

"Hey, Dad."

"Hi honey."

"Hi Chelsea." Natalie reached forward and Chelsea felt her place a warm hand on her right shoulder and give it a little squeeze. "Glad you came. I bet Dad tried to get you to stay behind on the boat, didn't he?"

"Yes."

Natalie shook her head and laughed. "Always looking out for others."

"Hey, I just thought it would be easier for her and..." Simon started the truck but stopped his sentence.

"And what?" Chelsea asked as they drove away.

"And nothing. I can handle this with Natalie."

"I still don't understand what we are doing."

"Okay, I'll explain it to you both."

∽

Three hours later a young man, driving a Lincoln Town Car, pulled up in front of Simon's 4500 square foot home. The driver was impressed, not only by the size of the house but by the location and view. The house sat on one of the highest points above El

Dorado Hills, overlooking the entire Sacramento valley, Folsom Lake, and the western horizon.

The neighborhood was private and not just gated; actual security guards sat at the front gate, checking people into the community. Moments before the young driver had pulled up and given his boss' name to the security guard, who checked his clipboard.

"Yep, got you right here. Do you know the way to the house?"

"Yes, I've got it plugged into our GPS. Thank you," The driver responded.

He glanced into the backseat and saw the man behind him who always looked both irritated and as if everything were beneath him. If the young man had described his boss in one word it would have been arrogant, but he would never have done so because the second word he would have used to describe him would have been intimidating.

The man in the backseat was irritated. He was also uncomfortable being almost forced to meet this unknown person. But $250,000 was a lot of money, and with a promise of "significantly more," it was worth stepping a bit into the unknown.

The man in the suit would have preferred to meet in public and didn't like to be asked to come alone. Whoever this benefactor was, they had at least agreed to let him bring an aide. The man speculated the secretiveness was due to several things. Rich people often didn't want the press knowing how they spent, or donated, their money. The wealthier the person, the more they kept their affairs private.

Now the man and his aide were standing at the front door and the aide rang the doorbell. A moment went by and a beautiful red-haired young woman opened the door. She was wearing a black business blazer over a white blouse that was tucked into a skirt. She held a pad-folio in her hands and greeted them warmly.

"Hello. We are so glad you could make it," the woman said and stepped back and to the side. "Won't you come in?"

As they stepped in she shook the man's hand and then, as she shook the aide's hand, she asked, "And you are?"

"Allen. Allen Heard." The aide was somewhat taken aback by the beautiful red-haired woman. "I'm just an intern."

"My name is Natalie, welcome to you both."

The man and his aide walked in. Natalie shut the front door and walked from the entryway to the side of a great room that opened up in front of them. Music was playing, not loudly, but definitely not quietly either.

"Please follow me."

She led them past the great room down a hallway and opened the first door on the right into a room that was impressive just to look at. The ceiling was at least 12 feet high and the floor was a warm stained wood. Two of the walls were covered by built-in wooden bookshelves filled with books that looked both old and well read. On one side of the room was a large desk with a high-backed leather chair sitting empty. In front of the desk were two leather chairs. On the other side of the room was a leather couch in front of which sat a wooden coffee table. The two chairs sitting in front of the desk were turned around and actually facing the coffee table, but it was easy to see that, depending on preference, they could be turned to focus on the desk.

One window brought a great deal of light into the room and on the wall behind the desk was a closed door. The man realized a person who had an office like this probably had a private bathroom. He was sure that was where the door led.

Natalie walked over to the couch and turned. "Please, if you would be so kind as to wait here, my employer will be with you in just a moment."

Then Natalie turned and looked at the aide. "Mr. Heard. If you would accompany me, my employer has already instructed me to provide a check. He did ask to just have a few minutes alone with your boss first."

The aide looked at the man for approval. It was out of the ordinary to leave anyone alone. Too many people trying to do something nefarious had made that a reality. However, knowing how much money they'd already sent, and hearing Natalie say she was going to write a check, the man nodded his approval to the aide.

"Go ahead, I'll be fine."

Natalie had done everything as Simon had instructed and it had all worked as her father had said it would. He knew there would be an aide. He knew the aide wouldn't just walk away from his boss without a reason. He knew the offer of "a check" from Natalie would give the aide and the man reason to separate them. Next, she led the aide to the far end of the house as she had been instructed, to a smaller office that had been her mother's.

"Please have a seat. You can wait here and I'll get the check," she said. "My employer will not be long. He's got a busy schedule."

Natalie was worked up and her heart was racing. With the music playing in the great room and a small radio playing in the office, the aide would never have a chance to hear what was transpiring at the other end of the house.

Simon walked into the den from the same door the man had entered and shut it behind him. The man was seated on the couch facing away from the door. Simon was expecting him to be big, but now seeing him in person, he was shocked. The man's shoulders sat a full foot above the back of the leather couch.

This was one of the moments that Simon had planned for many possibilities. He simply wasn't sure what the man would do. He might see Simon and attack him physically. He had shown his propensity towards violence and it wouldn't have surprised Simon in the least. But an all-out assault would have ruined Simon's plan. The longer things went without a physical altercation the better.

The man could simply get up and leave. That was his winning move. Simon had no way to prove anything and should the man be calm and just leave, then it would be like trading pawns. No advantage either way. But he was prepared for that too. If he started to leave, Chelsea was just beyond the door leading into his bedroom. She was watching them on video and at Simon's direction she was prepared to open the door and step into the room.

If the man was still calm enough to walk away, there would still be no advantage. However, if Simon was right, the congressman was a little bit crazy and might attack if he saw her. Simon was ready for that too, as he had now walked across the room far enough to stand between the door to the bedroom and the couch the giant of a man sat on. The door also entered behind the desk, so Chelsea was safe for the moment even if she did come in.

The man did none of these things. He simply turned his head and watched Simon with a flat stare. Simon was reminded of what a snake looked like before it attacked. Motionless and with no outward affect at all.

Simon stood in front of his desk and waited a moment longer, returning the stare.

"I'm curious. How do you like the '73 Ford?" Simon asked it out of the blue and it confused the congressman.

"What?"

"Your '73 Ford. How do you like it?"

"It's fine. How the do you know about my old Ford?"

Simon was now certain this was Chelsea's attacker. "I saw you following her. Multiple times."

The congressman was thinking, trying to decide if he needed to just leave, or if this man knew enough to ruin him. If it was the latter, what could he do but take care of him the same way he'd taken care of Chelsea? He had to stall and think.

"It was a neat little trick to get me here but it sure cost you."

"It worked, as I knew it would. Your kind are always easy to buy." Simon knew that his confidence and the statement would irritate the congressman.

"It cost you a quarter of a million dollars."

"It cost me nothing."

The senator shrugged. "What, do you think you can blackmail me?"

As many scenarios as Simon had played out in his head, blackmail was never one of them. In all of the situations he had run though in his mind, all of the if-then statements, the goal was to get him to talk. To get him say things that would prove his guilt.

"I think I can do anything I want," Simon continued, "I'm not the one with the reputation to lose."

"I've spent my life reminding people of the 'facts,'" the man said, his anger growing. "Fact number one, there is a dead call-girl. Fact number two, she fell from her balcony or was pushed. I haven't seen anything in the news yet so I'm not sure how she died. Fact number three, I was home sleeping when that happened."

Simon smirked. The man had seen her go over the edge, but had fled before Simon had hauled her up from the near fall. He didn't even know she had survived.

"Something funny?" the congressman demanded.

"You are wrong about several things, the biggest one being that Chelsea isn't dead."

"Bullshit. I saw her go over the rail."

When he said it, Simon's heart started pounding even harder. Centering breath, he told himself, be calm. Work the situation and get what you need. That was an admission, but with her still alive it was an admission of nothing. And it was still their word against his.

"I thought you were home in bed?"

"It doesn't matter. She's dead and it's my word against yours. If you claim I pushed her off that deck, I can just say I wasn't even there, or I could claim it was you. After all it was you that had been to multiple restaurants with her. You were the one stalking her and hounding her at the hospital. Who do you think they will believe? You, a nobody, or me?"

"I don't need them to believe me. She can talk for herself."

The giant stood, and even from ten feet away, Simon felt that the man was towering over him.

"This is all so very nice. But you are wasting my time. I don't know what you planned here but I think I'll be leaving."

"Just one thing." Simon walked closer to him. He wanted to provoke the congressman into saying more. He'd already said he was in the apartment and had seen her go over the rail. Simon knew if he could keep him talking his arrogance would take him down. As Simon moved closer he was also aware of the man's size. He probably outweighed Simon by 100 pounds.

"Just tell me why you killed her," Simon asked plainly.

"I thought you said she wasn't dead."

"I lied. Just tell me why."

The man looked down at Simon and smirked. "You're pathetic. You've got your phone on record or something. I'm not that stupid."

Simon reached into his pocket and pulled his cell phone out. He turned it towards the congressman and showed it to him as he powered it off. "No, I have no interest in a confession."

"Okay, it's not your phone. You're probably wearing a wire."

Simon backed away a couple of steps and took off his coat. Then he unbuttoned his shirt.

"I'd give you my word that I'm not wired, but a man like you, with absolutely zero integrity, wouldn't understand someone giving their word." Simon grinned again, deliberately trying to irritate the man. "People in your line of work are all liars and narcissists. You are no different."

"So you don't want to blackmail me and you don't want to record me. What do you want?"

"I just want you to tell me why you tried to kill her that first day she was out jogging. Then I want to finish what we started in the apartment."

The man realized Simon actually wanted to fight him, and for a moment he relished the idea of beating the smaller man. "No, I've no need to fight you, though I'd crush you like a maggot."

Simon intentionally walked inside the man's personal space. "You'd like to try, wouldn't you?"

"Go to hell." The man sneered at him.

"You know what I don't understand? As big as you are and for all your bravado, you still weren't strong enough to kill one skinny prostitute. You weren't even man enough to get that right the first time."

"But I did get it right the second time and there isn't shit you can do about it."

Simon realized that what he said could be construed as another admission, but it wasn't clear and it wasn't enough.

"So tell me why," Simon continued. "Isn't that worth $250,000?"

"Okay, you want to know why? I'll tell you. It was you. It was you and all the other lowlifes she was dating." The congressman seemed as if he were about to lose control. Simon felt like he was on the wrestling mat again and the ref was just about to blow the whistle starting the match. He was ready for anything, but the congressman continued.

"I called that stupid bitch and she actually said she was too busy for me... TWICE." His voice was raised and his eyes bulged out as if he were still in disbelief. "So I followed her. She was too busy for me and then I see she's sitting down and eating dinner with some bald skinny little fuck. A fucking nobody. Then I call her again and she says she's busy again. So I follow her again and she's sitting like a fucking little whore with you, another nobody!"

Simon wanted more, he wanted to goad the man into saying something that would be undeniable.

"A great big asshole like you? How'd you screw it up? You wait for her on a trail and can't somehow kill her? You can't even get that right?"

The man stuck his face forward and said with certainty, "I squeezed the fucking shit out of her. I saw her eyes close as I did it. I felt her die. It's a fucking miracle she came back. But it doesn't matter. I'm glad she lived because waiting in her apartment and knocking her off that balcony gave me the pleasure of teaching that little bitch a second time that you don't fuck with me. She earned every moment of the hell she got. I hope as she was falling it felt like an eternity. I hope all the way down she was thinking 'Oops I made a mistake. I guess I deserve this.'"

Simon knew that was a pretty clear confession, but wanted to get him to say it again and again. He'd watched his type weasel out of lies and wanted this to be a slam dunk.

"So first you try to kill her, then you just toss her off the balcony?"

"Like I said, she earned it. Damn right I did."

The corners of Simon's mouth raised ever so slightly in a wry smile.

"And now you'll earn every bit of hell you get," Simon said. "Before you go let me tell you how things are going to work from this point forward."

The man looked at him, stopped by Simon's certainty.

"You are going to resign tomorrow, at a press conference. You are going to tell the world that it is no longer appropriate for you to lead."

"Why the fuck would I do that?"

Simon pointed to a clock hanging on the wall. "See that clock. That's a camera in the middle. There are four other cameras in this room. You are going to resign or I will take the tape of what I just recorded and you will go to prison for the rest of your life for murder."

Senator Steve Maston felt trapped. All he could think of was to kill this little shithead, then kill his assistant, then burn the fucking place to the ground. For a moment he smiled warmly, hoping to put Simon off guard.

"No, that's not what's going to happen." As the congressman said it he took a step closer, then with a bellow charged at Simon.

Simon wasn't in the least bit surprised by the attack. Multiple days of going over the possibilities in his head had convinced Simon that if it got to this point, the congressman would lash out. Most of all, Simon was happy that Maston had chosen this route. Never in his life had Simon fought out of anger, but deep down inside, he'd always felt he'd trained those many years for a fight such as this.

As Maston came at him, Simon grabbed the man's arm and fell back at the same time. Flipping his body over, he used the man's immense size and speed against him, throwing him headfirst into the nearby wall.

Maston's head slammed into the wall and it left him dizzy. He got up slowly and came at Simon again. This time Simon attacked him. Maston felt like one minute Simon was in front of him, the next moment Simon's body was somehow up in the air and around his head. Maston lost his balance and, as he went down, all of Simon's weight came down on top of him, knocking the wind out of him.

Enraged, he tried to get up and realized that Simon had now wrapped his legs around his arm and across his chest and neck. Simon leaned back, putting pressure on Maston's arm in a perfect arm bar.

"I'm going to kill you," Maston screamed as he struggled.

"Really? Like you killed her?" And with that Simon leaned back and gave a tremendous jerk.

Both men were aware of the popping sound, then Maston screamed. Simon let go. And got up.

"Okay, once again, tomorrow you are going to have a press conference..." Simon started again. He stepped back as the giant man rolled over and used his right arm to get up. His face was white and his left arm hung uselessly.

Simon continued, "You will tell the press that you are no longer fit to lead."

Maston's rage overcame him and he lunged at Simon again, this time swinging a ponderous right-hand fist. Simon ducked under it and again seemed to almost magically fling his body up and around the bigger man's head. Off balance, they both fell to the ground and, before Maston could react, once again Simon had the man in yet another arm bar, this time his right arm.

"You aren't very good at this are you?"

Trapped again, the bigger man suddenly bit down hard on Simon's calf. Simon winced in pain but, using his anger, thrust his upper body straight back, with much more violence because of the pain. This time the man's arm didn't just pop out of its socket. Muscles tore, the shoulder dislocated, and Simon felt as though the elbow may have also broken.

Maston screamed in pain and started begging for Simon to stop.

Simon let go and got up quickly. He still didn't trust the man, but he had rendered him helpless.

"I think we are done here. Get up and get out." Simon said it quietly. The rage he had felt was gone. He had pretty much destroyed the man physically, and tomorrow he would destroy him professionally.

"I should kill you," Maston said as he rolled over and worked himself onto his knees. Both arms were hanging and the man was in obvious pain.

"Kill me?" Simon was irritated. "Would you like to see what happens next if you try? Right now you have two bad arms, want to try for a leg?"

Simon had no idea how to rip a leg out of its socket, but based on the look of fear in Maston's face, he was sure the congressman didn't know that either.

As Maston struggled to his feet, Simon reminded him, "Remember, tomorrow at noon, you need to have a press conference. If you don't, I'll make sure every news media outfit in the world has this video an hour later."

Maston could only nod. Simon moved to the door and opened it. He was pretty sure the man couldn't even open a door.

"Natalie?" Simon called. A moment later Natalie and the congressman's assistant came in. The young man looked at the congressman and immediately began asking questions. Simon quickly interrupted.

"Just a minute. The congressman attacked me, didn't you?" Simon looked at him and took a step towards him.

"Yes. I did."

Simon looked at the assistant. "You can ask him all the fun details while you drive him to the hospital."

Simon and Natalie stood in silence as the congressman and his assistant exited the front door and walked down the steps to their Lincoln Town Car.

The assistant walked around to the driver's side before Maston barked at him.

"Dammit, get over here and open the door."

Simon and Natalie waited until they were gone.

"You okay, Dad?"

"I've never been high on meth or PCP, but I wonder if the rush I'm feeling right now is similar." He laughed.

"That's not what I mean. You're bleeding," Natalie said, looking at his face.

In all the commotion and excitement, Simon hadn't realized this. He looked down and saw the blood on his shirt and felt it drip from his nose and down his face.

"I must have banged my nose in the fight. Didn't even realize it," he said as he held his nose pinched closed with two fingers.

Natalie walked back into the house and grabbed a towel from the kitchen and returned to meet Simon in the entryway.

"Here." She handed him the towel. He wiped his face and used the towel against his nose, continuing to pinch but unable to stop the bleeding.

"It's fine. Let's go get Chelsea," he said when he realized she was still hidden away in the other room.

Natalie and Simon walked back to the room next to the den and opened the door. Chelsea was sitting on the bed staring at the computer monitor with the four video feeds. There were tears in her eyes and she was visibly upset. The computer was now recording an empty room and Simon walked over and shut it down.

"You okay?" he asked gently.

Chelsea saw the blood.

"Are you?"

"I'm fine. I think I just hit my nose somewhere in there. Didn't even realize it."

"Skinny prostitute?"

"What?"

"That's what you called me."

Simon shook his head. "I'm sorry. I was trying to goad him. It's how he felt about you, not me. I used it against him."

Natalie had stepped into the bathroom and came out with a box of Kleenex and handed it to Chelsea.

"Wait a minute," Simon said. He was still almost giddy with energy after the victory and success. "After all that went on in that room, that's what you heard? Those two words?"

"No. I saw and heard it all." Chelsea stood up and hugged him. "Thank you."

Simon was doubly uncomfortable with the physical contact. Partly because it was in front of his daughter and partly because the woman was built with a body that one couldn't help but notice. Pressed up against him it impossible to ignore. He extracted himself away from her as they heard the front door slam open.

"Simon?" Brian yelled.

"In here."

Brian came into the room in a rush. "What the hell, Simon? I just watched all that on my computer at home."

"Watched it? I thought it was just going to download the backup file."

"I told you I was putting it on my cloud, but since you told me you were going to 'explain it all later,' and since you were using my cloud, I didn't think you'd mind if I watched it live."

"They say live TV is always better," Simon joked.

Brian looked at him in disbelief. "Holy crap, man. That was nuts." Then he turned to Chelsea. "I take it you are the dead girl they were talking about?"

"Yes."

"Oh. Brian, this is Chelsea. Chelsea, Brian. He's been a friend and business partner for years since college."

"It's nice to meet you," Brian said, and then in recognition added, "I seem to remember my wife and I met you once before at dinner."

Then he quickly turned to Simon. "Holy crap, what are you going to do next?"

"Well, it's not over yet..." Simon started but then was interrupted by Chelsea.

"It's not? Why?"

"Because that guy's a nut job and a politician. I have no doubt in my mind he is already trying to come up with a way to ooze his way out of this. He is like all politicians. His primary characteristic is narcissism. We have to finish this."

"How?" Chelsea asked.

"Brian, how quickly can we copy of the recording and get it sent out to the news stations?"

"You told him you weren't going to send it."

"Yeah, well, I lied. A lot of things I said in there were a lie." Simon looked at Chelsea when he said it. "Everything I said in there was to get him to confess. I wasn't worried about how he would feel about my integrity tomorrow."

"So you want to send it out now?"

"Pretty quick. I guarantee you, right now his mind is working hard to figure out a way to make up a story, or to come up with an alibi. Something."

There was a momentary pause as Brian was thinking.

"Well?" Simon asked, jarring him out of his thoughts.

"I bet I can get it done in less than an hour, depending on how much you want sent. But that also depends on how much you want to edit."

"I don't want to edit a thing. I say let's take it from the moment he walked in right up until just before he attacked me."

"Okay."

"No, let's run it right up to where I threw him the first time he attacked me. When he hit the wall."

Brian laughed. "You know someone really ought to see his arms get busted up like that. You sure you don't want just to send the entire thing?"

"We will send the entire thing to one person... Detective VanDyke. Maybe this will get his attention."

Brian pulled a small wooden chair over to the dresser and sat at the computer. "You want it sent tonight?"

"As soon as possible." Simon pulled his wallet out and opened it. "Here is VanDyke's card. Send it to the email on the card. It looks like a generic email for the police station. Maybe text him a short video clip that will get his attention and tell him to check his email for the rest of the video."

"Sounds good," Brian said, but seemed to be almost ignoring Simon. "I was going to say we need to send this to a computer with editing equipment on it first, but if I'm just taking a part of the video from one point to another I think I can do it on this one."

"Natalie, can you start looking up the main TV stations in Sacramento and get their email addresses?"

"Sure." Natalie was instantly on her phone. She left the room and came back with a pad of paper and pen. She Googled the four primary affiliates in the area, NBC, ABC, CBS, and FOX, and soon had all their email addresses written down for Brian.

Chelsea was sitting silently. As Natalie and Brian began working, she interrupted their thoughts. "Simon, I still don't understand how you knew it was him."

"I could have been wrong but I was fairly certain that the attacker knew you, which meant he was likely someone you'd seen. Twice when we were out to dinner, I saw a '73 Ford Pickup. At the time I didn't think anything of it."

Brian stopped his work on the computer and looked at Simon incredulously. "You saw a '73 Ford Pickup? That's it?"

"No, it's a little more than that. I saw the truck because I drove a '73 Ford truck growing up, on our farm. It was noticeable to me. But then after Chelsea was attacked, I remembered that it seemed to be leaving right behind her after at least three of our dinners."

They were all looking at him now and he continued.

"So when you were unconscious in the hospital I broke into your computer and got a list of names. I spent all of my free time over the next month checking each one of them out, trying to see if they owned the truck."

"And he did."

"Well, I didn't know that till tonight. He never drives it and I never got a look at his house or his garage."

"So you still haven't told me how you knew," Chelsea said.

"Okay, a few days before you left the hospital I saw a news broadcast. It was some political event of his. When he went out to get in his truck he walked around it to get in on the driver's side. The TV news folks were chasing after him, filming and yelling questions. Maston stopped before getting in the truck and answered them. He stood a full head above the cab of that truck. I didn't think anything of it at the time, other than 'that is a very big guy,' Then, when he attacked you in your condo, I realized that the man was huge. Last but not least, the person who attacked you, the doctor told me that he was a man with huge hands based on the bruises on your neck and the fact that he squeezed your neck and cut off the air, but didn't crush your windpipe."

Chelsea shuddered thinking about it.

"Maston was the only guy on the list I hadn't really ruled out the old Ford. That wasn't much evidence since any of the other guys could have been hiding a truck somewhere else. But with him I never even had a chance to look. Combine that with the fact that he was on the list. Then his massive size and again ruling out all the others as I did..."

Brian laughed. Still working away at the computer, he said, "He did what he always does. His brain works like a freaking computer. He deduced, ruled some things out, and ended up with the only logical answer left."

Simon continued, "I still wasn't sure until he saw me."

"Saw you?" Chelsea asked.

"Yeah, when I first walked into the den. He looked at me. I could tell he recognized me. The only place he could have ever seen me was in your apartment when we fought."

"You broke into my computer?" Chelsea had suspected that he may have accessed her computer, but now that she knew for sure, she felt violated as well as ashamed by the list of men's names that Simon had seen.

"That's what you just heard?" Simon smiled at her reassuringly and shook his head. "Yeah, I did. I did it to figure out who did this. I did it for you."

Chelsea still felt violated as well as embarrassed. She also felt something she never felt. She realized that this man had spent weeks trying to protect her. He had risked a physical attack trying to keep her safe. She couldn't remember a time a man had ever done anything like this for her.

She wanted to hug him again, but instead just said quietly, "Thank you."

Brian turned to Simon with his finger hovering over the keyboard. "Okay buddy, I just have to hit send."

"Is this one going to the detective?"

"Yes."

"And it's the entire video?"

"Every arm twisting second."

"Send."

Brian hit the send button. "I'm not going to be able to text that detective a video till I get to my computer and send a short clip to my phone or something."

"Never mind. I'll just call him and tell him to look for it. If I can't be persuasive enough then he will just miss out on the opportunity to be the first to know. He can always catch it on the news tonight."

"Okay... I just need to clip most of the fight off the end and... there. You want this sent to the news now?"

"Just a minute." Simon walked into the den and looked around. He dialed the detective's number and was surprised when he picked up. Simon explained what had happened. As he expected, the detective was not only skeptical but was in downright disbelief when he found out it was Maston.

"Bullshit. Is this some kind of joke?"

"No joke. The video was just sent to the email address on your card. In an hour it's going to be sent to the news stations. My guess is that the congressman is at Folsom Hospital in the emergency room. At least, that's the closest hospital. But do what you want, Detective. The way I see it, if you hurry, you can arrest a congressman. Not many cops get to do that. If you wait, someone else will get the opportunity, I'm sure."

Simon hung up and went back into the spare bedroom.

"Am I sending yet?"

"I told the detective I'd hold off for an hour. It might give him a chance to track Maston down and make an arrest."

"What about all that you said to Maston? About a press conference tomorrow and about resigning?"

"Well, at first I was thinking that was the best way to handle it. But then I realized I don't think he will. As a matter of fact, I think if he is not arrested tonight he'll either be coming after me, or he'll be given enough time to think up an alibi or some story that could somehow get him off."

"I don't know, Simon," Brian said. "It all sounded pretty open and shut. The guy admitted to trying to kill her."

"Yeah, he admitted to it all." Simon thought for a moment then added. "So why not just bury him now? Why give him one more night of freedom?"

Simon's phone rang and he answered. He listened and said, "Okay. Sounds good." Then, after another pause, he said, "No, she's okay. She's here with me... He tried, but I was able to save her... He didn't know... Yes, we'll come down." Then he hung up.

"That was VanDyke. He saw the video and is on the way to arrest Maston. He's at Mercy Hospital in the emergency room."

"It's over."

"Yeah, it looks that way." He turned to Chelsea. "VanDyke wants us to come to the station immediately."

Chapter 25

Two weeks later, things had barely started calming down. Simon was inundated with phone calls from national cable networks to local TV news stations. He had no idea how his phone number became known, but he had to have his number changed. He called to get that done, but unfortunately, someone recognized his name and passed it along. Within a couple of hours of having the new number he received a call from CNN, and like all the other times, asked that no one contact this number. So much for privacy, he thought. He hung up and called Natalie.

"Hello?"

"Hey honey, it's me."

"Oh hey, Dad, new number?"

"Yeah, but the minute I got it someone's already passed my number on to the media."

"That sucks." Natalie knew how much her dad valued his privacy and disliked the news media. "They were calling me too, but it's slowed down now. Someone must have figured out I was your daughter and got my married name, so they started calling. But I just told them 'Sorry, there must be a different Natalie Hanson.' That seemed to do the trick after about 30 different calls."

"I'm going to try a quicker approach. When you bought that burner phone, where'd you get it?"

"Oh, actually you can get them pretty much anywhere. Best Buy, Verizon, Target. What's up?"

"Since the video of me is all over the news, do you think you can maybe run and pick me up a phone?"

"Sure. I'll get you one."

"Just get the most minutes you can buy and I'll cover it."

"No problem. How's everything else going?"

"Pretty good. I called the high school coach today and I'm going to try to head down for the first day of wrestling practice and help out."

"You think you can?" For nearly two weeks news crews had been hounding around trying to get an interview with Simon, even to the point of parking outside the entrance of his gated community.

"Well, the guys at the front gate called me today to let me know that the last news van finally gave up and left yesterday, so hopefully I can."

"Well, good luck."

"Thanks."

"Hey Dad? What about Chelsea?"

"I know I don't have to tell you not to tell anyone but she's on the boat."

"Makes sense."

"Yeah. She didn't want to go back to her apartment so she took her car over there. I gave her my parking pass and the key to the boat. I think she can hide out there for the time being."

"I bet her phone is blowing up like yours, though."

"Probably not. She got a new phone and number after the first day of calls, and when I spoke to her last she didn't mention it."

"She's got to be lonely over there on that boat all by herself, Dad."

"She is, but I asked her and she said she was enjoying the time to herself."

"Well, okay, but if you don't go visit her and it lasts much longer maybe Ron and I will run over just to give her some company."

"Nat, you don't need to do that. I'll go over if she stays much longer."

"Okay. Want me to bring the new phone over tonight?"

"Nah, I'll just stop by after wrestling practice."

"Okay. Talk to ya later," Natalie said and hung up.

Simon wanted to get his life back to normal. He got dressed in sweats and headed to the high school. When he had called the coach earlier that morning and told him his plan of trying to come and practice, they had talked for a bit. Coach Lance knew the possibility of a news crew getting wind of it and he promised not to say anything to anyone.

When Simon walked up to the doors of the gym where wrestling practice was being held, there were signs on the door that read in large bold letters:

Tonight's Wrestling Practice is Closed to Everyone
Except Coaches, Students, Parents, and Invited Guests.

Simon felt his mood lift as he walked into the gym just a few minutes before the 3:30 start time. It had the familiar smell of a gym—mats, sweat, dusty, musty—and the typical high school boys clowning around. It was somehow comforting. A few were wrestling but most were still tying their wrestling shoes and getting ready for practice. Simon noticed that a few of the boys were looking at him and whispering.

The coach saw Simon and called for everyone to sit on the bleachers. Simon, the three other coaches, and all the wrestlers took a seat. The coach noticed the parents who were in attendance didn't come closer and he called for them to join in.

"I need to ask the team and everyone here for some help," Coach Lance started. "One of our coaches was involved in something that was in the news. Is there anyone here who is not aware of what happened or hasn't seen the video?"

A couple of the younger boys raised their hands. A murmur broke out with comments of, "Dude how'd you not know?" and "You gotta see it, it's on YouTube." And "Freshman!" Like that last comment explained how they could have not seen the video yet.

Coach Lance's voice rose above the noise and took control again. "Okay, so a few of you haven't. No doubt you can check it out tonight. However, most of you know Coach Simon and many of you have learned a lot from him. Many of you juniors and seniors have been wrestling with him for a number of years. Out of respect for him I'm going to ask that you all help me and help him by keeping his presence at our practice under wraps."

"If the news media gets word of him being here because we can't keep a secret, unfortunately what will happen is we will lose a great coach. It won't hurt him; it will only hurt us. So can we all do that?"

The coach's request was met with a chorus of 'yes coach,' 'yes,' and 'sure thing.'

"I'm sure you all have questions, and I do too, but I spoke to Coach Simon earlier today and he asked that we just focus on wrestling for now. He told me that one of these days in the near future he'll let us grill him with questions, like 'How do you rip a man's arms off?'"

The group of young men burst into laughter and Lance turned to Simon. "Sorry, I just couldn't help it."

Simon rolled his eyes. "It's okay."

Then Coach Lance continued, "For now, we are going to go about practice with a 'business as usual' attitude, but that is why there are signs on the doors. I would appreciate if you would pass the word along to your parents if the subject comes up. Otherwise, it's best if you say nothing at all."

Then Coach Lance turned to one of the other coaches and said, "Let's get them started."

The assistant coach, Nick, stood up and started barking orders and the boys quickly left the bleachers. Simon stood up and walked over to Lance.

"Thanks, Coach. I doubt it will work, but maybe I can get in a few days of practice."

Lance laughed. "Yeah, asking high school students to keep a secret is like asking the sun not to shine."

"I'll get some practice in today, at least."

"You do know the practice is for the boys and not you, right?" Lance joked.

Simon smiled. "Let's just say it's for both. I need the practice too."

"Man, I saw the video on the news. You don't need any practice."

Simon was embarrassed. "I spent so much time trying to figure out how to trap that guy that I never even thought about what the video would do to me. Let's just forget it and move on, okay?"

Lance laughed. "Everyone who's seen it knows you will never forget it. But I promise to move on."

Boys were now pairing off and wrestling each other, and Simon walked around offering advice and trying his best to coach them. After a bit of time he settled in, assisting three of the boys who were wrestling in the 195 pound class. Two were seniors and one was a junior. Simon had spent quite a number of days wrestling with them and coaching them in the past.

The boys traded in and out, with two wrestling each other while the third boy watched. Simon was aware that the boy, Jimmy, waiting his turn was a senior who had nearly won the state championship as a junior.

"Jimmy, what's your goal this year?"

"I'd like to win state."

"That's a great goal." Simon turned to him. "Let's you and I work together."

Simon led him away from the other two and looked at him.

"You and me. Let's have you start down."

"Okay, Coach."

They wrestled for a good few minutes and, even though Simon was nearly 10 pounds lighter, he held his own against the agile young man. Suddenly Simon found himself close to being pinned, but just as suddenly, Jimmy stopped and got up.

"You okay, Coach?"

Confused, Simon just looked back at him. "I'm fine. What's wrong?"

"Your nose. You're bleeding."

Simon reached up and touched his nose. "Weird. I never even realized I bumped it."

Twenty-five minutes and several cold compresses later, Simon was still unable to stop the bleeding.

"Sorry, Coach," Jimmy said.

"Hey, no problem." Simon kept a towel on it and it finally stopped bleeding.

"Jimmy," Simon said, "if you are serious about winning state, let's you and I start tomorrow at 3:15 instead of 3:30. We can get in a little work before practice even starts."

"Sounds good, Coach."

Unfortunately, the next day, Simon's nose started to bleed the minute they started wrestling and wouldn't stop. Then, to make matters worse, a news crew showed up and demanded to have access to practice since it was a public school.

Coach Lance didn't let them in, but he came over to talk to Simon.

"Simon, listen, you may want to head out the back door and get out of here."

"You're probably right." Simon replied, still holding a towel on his nose. "I'm not doing much good for you today anyway."

"Listen, my guess is I'll hear it from the AD or someone in the administration that I can't keep them out. So I'll let them in tomorrow and if you aren't here they'll give up. I'll give you a call in a couple of days and we'll get you back in here."

"Okay. That's probably a good idea."

Simon snuck out the back and luckily made it to his truck without being seen. From there, still holding his nose, he drove straight to his doctor's office, hoping maybe they could give him something to stop the bleeding.

When the doctor heard Simon was there, he told the nurse that he would see him immediately. The nurse invited him in from the waiting room, took his weight, blood pressure, and temperature

"The doctor will be with you in just a few minutes," the nurse said, then left him alone in the room.

Simon guessed it was one of the shortest periods of time he'd ever waited when the doctor knocked lightly then entered just moments later.

"Simon Taylor. World famous hero!" The doctor noticed the bloody towel still on Simon's nose. "I'd say what brings you here, but I think I can see."

"I got a bloody nose yesterday and it took forever to stop. But today, it's just not stopping."

"This happen before?"

"Nope. Never."

After examining Simon, the doctor ended up using a small tool and basically cauterizing the tiny vessel in his nose. It was painful, but Simon endured.

"That should take care of it."

"Thanks."

"You been feeling all right?" the doctor asked.

"I guess so. I've been more tired lately. Been sleeping a bit longer but if anything I'm sleeping better."

The doctor looked at his chart and at the data the nurse had recorded.

"Tell you what, Simon. Let's just make sure everything is okay. I'm going to have the nurse come back and we'll do a full blood work up and see if there's anything going on. Nothing to worry about, but you haven't done a full work up like this in..."

The doctor flipped back in the chart. "... I guess you've never done a full blood work up. So this is a good idea."

"Okay. Other than the bloody nose, I'm just a little more tired than usual."

"I think that's completely normal. After what you went through. Anyone who's gone through a traumatic or violent event, I would expect your body to really let down afterwards."

"You're probably right."

"So are you going to tell me about it?"

Simon knew the doctor wanted to know all the details of the story that had been circulating in the news.

"Look, there really isn't much to tell. I'm sure you've seen everything on the video. My attorney has told me under no circumstances should I be talking about any of it. So, ya know... attorneys."

"Okay. I get it." The doctor was clearly disappointed. "Regardless, it's impressive what you did and how you did it. I always thought Maston was a bit of a loose cannon."

Simon just nodded at the doctor, trying to offer no reason for him to continue the conversation. The doctor finally left and a nurse came in and took a few vials of blood.

On his way back to his house, he called Chelsea. She didn't pick up so he left a message. Moments later she called back.

"This is Simon," he answered.

"I'm sorry, I didn't know who was calling so I didn't pick up when you called."

"Yeah, I had to get a new phone. Have you been getting a lot of calls?"

"Not one."

"Good for you." Then he added, "Are you doing okay?"

"Yes. I have to drive to Sacramento day after tomorrow. I have a doctor's appointment. Hopefully they'll take this cast off."

"What time is your appointment?"

"3:30."

"Tell you what. I'll take you out for dinner after your appointment."

"Are you asking me out on a date?"

There was a pause, "I'm just asking if you'd like me to meet for dinner."

Chelsea decided not to push it. "I think it would be fun to have dinner with someone. I've been on this boat for more than two weeks and I'm getting a little stir crazy."

"Okay. Tell you what. I'll meet you at Milestone."

Chelsea thought about it for a fraction of a second. "Could we meet someplace we've never been?" It was important for her to change and going to a restaurant where she had been paid to meet him before wasn't going to help that.

"Sure. Let's go to Fat's right there in Folsom."

"Okay. What time?"

"Well, let's shoot for 5 but if your doctor's appointment runs late or anything just call me and we'll adjust."

"Simon..."

"Yes?"

"Thank you."

Not sure what to say he just said, "See you Friday."

√ɔ

Friday night arrived and Simon was seated at an outdoor table at Fat's Dim Sum Bar. The fall weather had really set in and it was cool so Simon asked the hostess if they could turn on the propane heaters that sat above the tables. A few minutes after 5, Chelsea walked up to the table, led by a hostess.

"Hey, good to see you." Simon smiled warmly and stood as he greeted her.

"You too." Chelsea knew he wouldn't move to touch her so she embraced him with a hug.

They both sat as the hostess said, "Someone will be here in a minute to take your order."

Chelsea looked around. "It's going to be cold. You sure you want to sit out here?"

"Yeah, I asked the hostess to have someone turn on the overhead heaters. It should help. I'd rather sit out here. Once it gets a bit darker, not many people will be able to see us."

Chelsea's wanted to know why. "I'm a little confused. When you paid me to have dinner with you, you didn't mind others seeing us. Now you aren't paying me and you don't want to be seen?"

Simon smiled. "No. That's not it at all. You have no idea how many people have seen that video we sent to the press. I think that was the biggest mistake we made. Everyone has been after me. The local TV news stations, national cable networks, radio people. I've had to change my number twice and for the first two weeks they camped outside the gates to my complex. I couldn't leave the house except once or twice when Ron came up and got me. Even then I had to lay on the backseat until we got past them just so I could go see my granddaughter."

Chelsea understood. "Maybe it was a mistake."

"Did my attorney talk to you?"

"Yes. He said his firm was going to represent me in anything and everything I need. Thank you again, Simon."

"I don't think you'll need them, but I think it will be good to have someone sitting next to each of us during the trial, coaching us."

Suddenly Simon noticed her arm was no longer in the cast. "Your arm. How's it feel?"

"Itchy," Chelsea said. "Itchy and gross. It was disgusting when they took the cast off."

"It doesn't look bad."

"I told the nurse I had a date and she helped me wash it really good. And then I was able to get this sweater on."

Simon seemed to notice her then. She was wearing an off-white sweater that went over her jeans. Her blonde hair was straight with a slight curl that fell across her shoulders. Her dark eyebrows were beautiful and seemed unusually large as the evening turned darker. Her red lipstick was bold, but it wasn't overdone. He realized that she really was beautiful and for the first time he acknowledged to himself that he was attracted to her.

"You look great," was all he could say.

"Thank you," Chelsea replied. For his part, Simon was once again wearing a suit as he had so many times on their previous dates.

"Do you always wear a suit when you go out to eat?"

"No, I guess I just got used to wearing them," Simon looked down at his attire. "Would you prefer something else?"

"No, I really don't care. I just got used to how you dressed for those few days on the boat."

Simon smiled and they both became lost in conversation. By the end of the meal neither had realized their new reality. Simon had spent the entire dinner without thinking of Allie. And Chelsea didn't notice that he hadn't checked out mentally.

Chelsea suddenly knew that the dinner was over and they'd soon be leaving. They both had a car in the parking lot and she wanted him to invite her to leave with him. She decided to give him a subtle hint.

She sighed, "I'm really not looking forward to driving all the way back to the boat tonight."

Simon didn't pick up on the hint at all. "You could stay at your apartment."

As soon as he said it he could see the apprehension in her face. "You know what? If you're not ready for that I totally understand."

He thought about inviting her to his house, but the thought of any woman, no matter who, staying in the home he'd build for Allie seemed impossible.

He pulled out his phone and dialed.

"Hey, Nat, could Chelsea stay in your guest room tonight?"

Chelsea looked exasperated as he continued his conversation with his daughter.

"Okay, sure. We'll be over within the hour... Okay... bye." He hung up and was met by an irritated look on Chelsea's face.

"I can just drive back tonight," she said quickly. "I don't need to inconvenience her."

"No, it's late. Let's both go over there and then tomorrow we can both drive to the boat together. I'll check the weather. Maybe we can sail."

Chelsea thought about it and figured it was better than driving all the way back, alone and in the dark, tonight.

"Okay."

Simon paid the check and they both left the restaurant together.

"Do you remember where Nat lives?" Simon asked as they approached her car.

"Not well enough."

"Okay, I'll pull around and you can follow me."

He walked across the parking lot and slid into his truck. Moments later as he was pulling out of the parking lot he looked into the rear-view mirror to make certain Chelsea was there. She was, and with another car behind her.

Halfway to Nat's house Simon was still watching the rear-view mirror. He noticed the second car was still there and decided to make sure. He made four consecutive right-hand turns, basically ending up where he'd started. The car behind Chelsea continued to follow.

Not once did he look in the direction of the car, but after the four right turns he was pretty sure the driver knew Simon was aware of his presence. Simon let out a deep breath and pulled over into a Ralph's grocery store parking lot. Chelsea followed him in as did the other vehicle. Simon watched in his rear-view mirror as the other car pulled in and stopped about 40 yards away. Chelsea pulled in front and spun her car around so that her driver's side window and his were side by side.

Simon could just make out the license plate of the other vehicle. He opened his center consul and grabbed a scrap of paper and a pen and wrote it down, then got out of his truck.

Chelsea had her window down.

"I'm going to run in here real quick. I need you to call 911. Tell the dispatcher that you have followed a very drunk driver into this parking lot. Tell them it's the Ralph's on Blue Ravine Road between Folsom and El Dorado Hills. Tell them the car is a dark blue or black Audi and this is its license plate number."

He handed her the paper.

"Simon what's going on?"

"Just trust me. I'll tell you in a minute. Make that call, okay?"

"Okay."

"Oh, and tell them you think the driver may have fallen asleep in the car."

"Don't look right at that car over there."

It was directly in front of her car and Chelsea started to look. Simon laughed.

"I said, DON'T look."

She looked at Simon sheepishly. "Okay, okay."

"Make the call."

He entered the store and bought a bottle of Jim Beam Whiskey. Like most grocery stores, there was an entrance at both ends Moments later he exited the doors on the far side, opposite the doors he had entered. Unless he seriously turned his head, the driver would not see him, and hopefully he was focused on the door Simon had entered as well as on his truck and Chelsea and her car.

It was dark out and the further he walked away from the store, the more he ended up behind the car until he was past it. Once in the driver's blind spot and on the opposite side of the grocery store he knew the driver wouldn't see him coming. As he approached the door he unscrewed the lid on the Whiskey bottle. He hoped the door was unlocked, but decided he would try knocking first.

As he stepped up to the driver's door, the man's head was still turned away. Simon set his hand with the bottle gently above the driver's window then knocked on the window with his left hand.

Startled, the man's head swung around as his body flinched. Simon grinned as their eyes met. The stranger rolled his window down.

"Can I help you?" Simon asked.

"Are you Simon Taylor?"

"I think that's a stupid question. A better question is why are you following me?"

"Look, I am not doing anything wrong. I'm just trying to track down Simon Taylor, and I'm pretty sure I have."

"Well, you seem to think you know me. Who are you?" Simon guessed he was someone from the media or, worse, a private investigator that the media had hired to find him.

"I was hired by the press to find you."

"And I suppose asking you to stop following me isn't going to be effective, is it?"

"Not likely."

"Okay, at least you're honest," Simon said and then dumped the bottle of Whiskey. It poured down over the open window and into the driver's side of the car. As it drained, he moved the bottle and shook it over the man.

"Hey, what the..." The man was startled and angry but before he could say much more, Simon tossed the open bottle past the man and into the far corner of the passenger side floorboard.

"Have a nice day."

When Simon walked back to his truck and Chelsea's car, she rolled her window down. She had seen him and the interaction with the other car.

"What was that all about?"

"Someone following us and I don't want them knowing where Nat lives, or where we are for that matter. We'll wait for the police and we'll be fine."

He climbed into his truck and rolled his window down.

"Hopefully it won't take long."

Within about 10 minutes a police car pulled into the parking lot.

Simon looked over at Chelsea and started his truck.

"Okay, time for us to go," he said and rolled up his window.

Chelsea shook her head and rolled up her window. Her car was already running and Simon waited until the squad car found the Audi and pulled in behind it. The red and blue lights started flashing and Simon put his truck into gear and they pulled away.

ဢ

Chelsea and Natalie sat across the kitchen table from each other at Natalie's house that night, each sipping a glass of wine. Chelsea was once again reminded in a million ways of how her life was a failure. The home was as beautiful inside as it was out. The kitchen was painted mostly white but had bright yellow accents that made it feel like a spring day, warm and inviting.

The kitchen table was a beautiful thick wooden thing with a live edge. And the home wasn't just exuding an expensive budget, everything had a comfortable feel to it. Chelsea imagined that some homes were furnished to look expensive but were not very functional. This home was comfortable and functional first.

Natalie's husband Ron sat in the living room facing away from them. The room was open to the kitchen and, while the TV wasn't loud, it was on with a college football game playing.

"You must have been getting pretty bored and lonely on that boat all by yourself the last few weeks," Natalie said.

"I was getting a little stir crazy, but it felt safe."

Natalie realized that, after two different attacks, any place that was safe would be a refuge.

"I'm glad Dad thought to bring you over here tonight. That would have been a long drive back."

"Yes." Chelsea was, to say the least, a bit uncomfortable. She still wasn't convinced that this girl didn't want her out of her father's life, and no relationship with a man Chelsea'd ever had included his family. It was all uncharted territory.

Sensing Chelsea's discomfort, Natalie tried to think of ways to help and decided to hit it head on.

"Chelsea, Ron and I are happy to have you stay with us. Is there anything I can do to make you feel more at home?"

Chelsea heard her but stared at her wine for a moment. Not thinking, she started to speak.

"I was planning on driving back to the boat. I'm just not comfortable going back to my condo yet, and when Simon asked me to stay until tomorrow..."

"You thought he was going to invite you to stay at his place." Natalie finished her thought for her.

"Yes." Chelsea felt guilty admitting it. She also felt like having this conversation with his daughter was bizarre.

But the next words Natalie shared with her changed all of that.

"Chelsea, I bet I can help you understand something a little better. Dad built that house for Mom, without Mom ever knowing about it. Everything in the house were things he did for her. Every room was made with her desires in mind, her wishes, her dreams. He's had a hard time even staying there since she died. I don't think he will ever invite another person to that house to spend the night, whether man or woman, guest room or his room."

Natalie was right. What she said did help Chelsea understand better.

"Up until just a few weeks ago," Natalie continued, "I was thinking Dad was going to sell the house and move, but then he told me the house is in my name now. I'm not sure what he is going to do with it, but I think he wants me and Ron to move into it and he'd like to move somewhere else."

At first, Chelsea didn't have a response. Then she finally asked the only thing she could think to say. "So will you and Ron move up there?"

Before Natalie could reply and without turning his head away from the football game, Ron barked out. "Heck yes, we'll move in. That house is awesome."

Natalie rolled her eyes. "We haven't even talked about it yet, but we probably would. I grew up in that home and it would be a great house to raise Emma in."

Then Natalie continued, "I just wanted you to understand why he didn't invite you to stay at the house."

"I guess I do now. Thank you."

354

Chapter 26

The next morning Chelsea was waiting uncomfortably in Natalie's living room for Simon to show up. It's always awkward to spend time in someone's home you don't know well, let alone spend the night. Ron and Natalie were kind and accommodating. They were also focused for the most part on Emma, their baby girl.

"Are you sure I can't get you something to eat?"

"No, really. The coffee is enough."

By 10:30, Simon hadn't arrived, and Chelsea felt like everyone had run out of things to say, the type of small talk you engage in when you are forced into a conversation with someone you barely know.

Natalie was eating a cup of yogurt and, since at least another hour had passed since she'd offered, she asked again.

"Are you sure I can't get you anything?"

"I guess I'll have a yogurt."

"Any particular kind? I have plain, blueberry, and strawberry."

"Blueberry, please."

Another 10 minutes went by and had she finished her yogurt when the phone rang. It was Simon.

"Chelsea, listen, something important has come up and I've got to work on it. It's last minute, but I'll be leaving the state for at least a couple of weeks. Please drive over and stay on the boat. It's yours to use. Ben knows my boat and even though he is elderly he can help you if there is anything you need."

"Simon, what's going on? Can't you at least come spend a day or two? Maybe we could sail out into the bay again."

"I wish I could, but I've got to deal with this immediately. When I get back I'll give you a call. I want you to know you can stay on the boat as long as you'd like."

Chelsea didn't know what to say. She wanted to know why he was leaving, but didn't want to pry. She assumed with his kind of money, business often took priority, and she knew some of his dealings were very private. She still didn't understand how to really interact with this man and felt that asking questions when he wasn't volunteering any other information was somehow wrong.

"Okay, Simon," she tried to sound positive. "Would you like me to move back to my condo?" she asked, hoping he would not ask her to.

"Only if you want to," Simon replied. "Like I said, the boat's yours to use for as long as you want."

"Simon, I don't think I'm ready to go to my condo. If you are sure it's okay, I think I will stay there."

"That's fine. And if you need anything, you can also call Natalie."

"Can't I call you?"

"Oh sure," Simon said. "You can call me anytime. But I'm not sure how available I'll be. You might not reach me."

His answer was hesitant and she somehow knew he wasn't going to be available. She wanted to ask more but didn't.

"Like I said, I'll call as soon as I can. Okay?"

"Okay."

And with that, he hung up

Natalie had overheard some of the conversation and asked, "Is Dad not coming?"

"No."

"That's weird. Did he say why?"

"No, he just said he needed to take care of some things for a couple of weeks."

Natalie looked unconcerned but confused at the same time.

"Well, I'm sure he's got something awesome going on. Usually when my dad gets secretive something good comes out of it. He built the house for mom without her ever knowing it. He built multiple businesses and sold them without the world around him ever knowing what he was up to. Even when the foundation gives money to the hospital and other charities, people rarely know what's going on until it's done."

"Well, since he isn't coming, I'm going to get going." Chelsea stood. "Thank you for the place to stay last night. You have a beautiful home."

"Are you going to stay on the boat for a while longer?"

"Yes, if that's okay."

"Chelsea, I still don't think you get me," Natalie said. "I'm so happy you are making Dad happy, I'm fine with you using his boat. Besides, it's his boat not mine."

✄

Another week had passed, and the walls seemed to be closing in around her. When she'd first seen the boat nearly two weeks ago, it had seemed huge, but now it seemed small and confined.

Chelsea was grateful the weather had been nice. Simon had told her fall in the Bay Area was usually filled with cool but sunny days, and that had indeed been the case. The first night she hadn't turned on the heat and she nearly froze. Since that night she had turned on the heat as Simon had shown her.

One positive, however, she had grown very accustomed to the tiny town of Sausalito. From the harbor she could walk to any restaurant and get to several smaller markets. The prices were higher than in the Sacramento area, but it seemed worth it. Several of the shop owners had started greeting her by name. She'd grown to enjoy the personal connection and interactions so much she began to only buy enough food for a day at a time just so she could continue walking up the dock and into the markets.

For the past week, Chelsea had simply relaxed on the boat. She got into a routine. Each morning was about getting up and having a cup of coffee. Sometimes it was just coffee until lunch; other times she would have breakfast but then skip lunch. She found one meal in the morning was enough to carry her over till dinner.

She also grew accustomed to seeing Ben, the elderly man, walking up the dock each morning, checking on a number of the boats. He became a part of her routine. He would stop by and ask if everything was okay on the boat, and she would offer him a cup of coffee.

"I'd never turn down a good cup of coffee," was always his reply. Then he would say, "James Garner, support your local sheriff."

Chelsea never understood what he was talking about and chalked it up to an old man's eccentricity. After Ben's visit she then took a long walk. The marina was expansive and just walking up and down each dock took time. She hadn't run since her time in the hospital. She knew her ribs had healed but she still resisted running. Walking was at least replacing her need to get out and about. She had found paved running paths and had walked on them, but was nervous when they strayed away from populated areas. Even walking on the paths that led into parks and through trees raised her anxiety. So she stuck with walking around the marina and through the active city blocks of Sausalito.

After her walk each day she would read. She'd started the Hornblower books and was now on the third. The afternoons in the sun were the best time for reading, but sometimes she would just sit on the deck with music playing and watch the boats come and go.

By late afternoon she'd walk up to the markets and peruse through them, buying just what she needed for dinner that night and breakfast or lunch the next day. She was greeted each day by the shopkeepers and found the experience of it all refreshing. She'd carry her small bag of food back down to the boat, cook herself dinner, eat, and then read some more.

There was a TV on board, but she hadn't turned it on. Somehow her escape from her condo, her town, and really from her life had been so refreshing that she didn't want to do anything that would take her back to her old life. And since the television had been a regular activity in the evenings when she was alone, she steered her life in a new direction.

It had been nearly two weeks into this routine when, while sitting on the deck in the sun, she made a decision. She was going to sell the condo and move. She couldn't stand the idea of moving back in and living with the anxiety for even a day. The thought bounced around in her head for several hours. She wasn't sure how to begin the process, but decided she would ask Simon when she talked to him next.

Simon had also been much on her mind. She speculated about what he was doing. The conversation with Natalie, about how he had built a home, all as a surprise for Allie, made her wonder if he was up to something like that for her. She daydreamed about him off building their dream house. She knew it was silly, like a freshman girl in high school pining after the good-looking upperclassman.

Nevertheless, she hoped whatever he was doing was something, even something small, for her. He had told her he would call her in a couple of weeks and she longed for the moment. The phone had rung only twice. Both times it was the DA back in Sacramento. Once informing her of dates for depositions and then the second time to let her know that Maston had accepted a plea deal. He would be going to prison for 10 years.

She felt like it was something that should be celebrated, but she had no one to call. She had resisted the temptation until now, but decided to try Simon. She called but it went to voicemail. After a few minutes, she decided to try Natalie. She dialed the number Simon had given her.

"Hello?" Natalie answered.

"Hello Natalie, this is Chelsea."

"Hi. What can I do for you?"

"I tried calling Simon's phone, but it went to voicemail."

"Was there something you needed?" Natalie asked.

"I just got word from the district attorney that Senator Maston pled guilty. I just wanted to see if Simon knew."

"I'm sure he knows, but I'll pass it along that you called."

"Well, if you could ask him to call me I would appreciate it."

"I'll let him know." There was a long pause and then Natalie added. "He's been busy."

"Well, okay. Thank you," Chelsea said and hung up the phone frustrated. Natalie had sounded cold. She wondered if her original expectation was coming to fruition. Maybe for all her talk Natalie was finally showing that she didn't want Chelsea around her father.

Chelsea sat on the deck of the boat thinking about everything. There was a slight breeze and it was consistently growing colder as fall was starting to give way to more winter-like weather. Earlier today a light fog had covered the Bay Area and it was definitely colder. Thankfully the wind had blown out the fog, but the sun was no longer warm enough to keep the chill off.

She got up and made her way down to the cabin below and grabbed a light black jacket. It was big enough to fit over her sweater and when she put it on it smelled like Simon. A mixture of coffee, a familiar cologne... it was definitely Simon's.

Back on the deck, she again sat pondering where he was and what he was doing. She wondered again if he was building a home for her. Chelsea made a decision. It didn't matter what Simon was doing. She would give him space. She would give him time.

The black jacket was soaking up the sun and warming her. She watched a breeze ripple across the water and then felt it as it and pushed her hair into her face. She shuddered from its cool touch. She thought about the breeze and the cold and realized that when Simon had been on board and they had sailed she had never been cold. Even with water spraying into her face and in a strong breeze, somehow being out here with him had made it all worth it.

She knew then she wanted to be with him. She admitted it to herself. She didn't know if this was what love was, but it no longer mattered to her. She wanted to sail with him. She wanted to sit across the table from him and eat dinner and share a glass of wine.

She missed all the different ways he smiled and she wanted to see them. The little smirk he gave when only the corners of his mouth turned up. The smile he made when he looked at others, her, the children in the restaurant, and when he seemed the most himself. And the big broad smile when he really opened up and laughed, like he had in the truck when she was crying and Daniel Powter's song "Bad Day" came on the radio. It was like every wrinkle and every line in his face had been created from years of smiling and suddenly all came alive.

Chelsea realized too that she would be happier being with Simon and working as a hairdresser or a waitress and having no money than having the home, the money, and all that it brought. She just wanted to be with him.

She made a decision that the next time she saw him she would tell him, and with that decision firmly in her mind she grew excited about the possibility that he could feel the same. She could no longer sit still, so she got up and headed to the market to find something for dinner.

$$\sim$$

Two more weeks passed and the weather had turned. The fog no longer burned off, and the previous day had brought rain. It was a wet drizzle that had continued throughout the night and into the morning as Chelsea drank her cup of coffee.

"Hello?"

Chelsea heard Ben's familiar voice from the dock. She made her way up the steps and opened the door.

"Ben, why don't you come on in out of the rain and have a cup of coffee."

"Well, I'd never turn down a good cup of coffee," he said quickly as he came onboard and entered the cabin. "James Garner, support your local sheriff."

He took off his wet raincoat and hung it on a hook on the back of the door.

"Here's your coffee." Chelsea handed him the cup as he sat down at the table. Then she asked, "Who is James Garner and why are we supporting the sheriff?"

Ben laughed. "*Support Your Local Sheriff* is an old movie. James Garner is the actor. And 'I'd never turn down a good cup of coffee' is my favorite line in the movie."

"Well, I'll have to check out the movie someday."

"You should. Some of the old movies are still the best."

Chelsea drank some more of her coffee and leaned against the bar.

"Ben I'm going to Sacramento sometime in the next week. I've decided to head back to my condo and meet with a realtor. It'll be a day or two at least before I get back. I just didn't want you to think I just disappeared."

"I appreciate that, Ma'am." He took another drink. "You want I should go back to looking after the boat?"

"I'm sure Simon would like you to continue doing whatever you were doing before I arrived."

"I'll do that. If you don't mind my asking, have you checked the propane tanks, the freshwater, or done any of that?"

"No. Simon never mentioned it," Chelsea replied. "He just showed me how to use everything and how to turn everything on."

"Tell you what, stop by my boat when you decide to leave, and I'll take care of it all when you're gone. Simon's had me do in the past so I'm sure he'd like that. Plus, when either of you gets back, it will be ready to sail."

Chelsea looked around at the boat and was intimidated by the unknown chores that would no doubt have to be done. "I'd love to sail it, but no chance I'm going sailing without Simon. I wouldn't know how."

"Ah, a boat like this, even as big as she is, was designed for one person to sail. You could do it. You just need some lessons from an old pro like me. I could have you sailing better than most of these jokers that have had boats sitting in the harbor all their lives. Even when they take them out, half the time the never raise the main. They burn diesel and motor around then return without ever knowing what it feels like to really have her heel over in a nice wind."

"I'd love to learn more someday. If there is ever an opportunity, I'll call you first."

"Ma'am, you ask Simon and if he's okay with it, I'll take you out first opportunity we have."

"Thank you, Ben. I will."

"Well, I've got some other boats to check this morning," Ben said and got up. He handed Chelsea his cup. "Thanks again, Ma'am."

He left and Chelsea shut the door behind him. It was raining harder and she realized that her day was going to have to change. She would still take her long walk but it was likely to be wet, and sitting on the deck in the sun for a large part of the afternoon was not an option. She had finished reading all 15 of the Hornblower sailing novels that were on board and now she wondered what other books Simon had lying about.

She decided that, with her normal routine so disrupted, she would spend the day packing up. She would haul everything up to her car tomorrow and head back to Sacramento. She still didn't intend on spending a single night in the condo, and planned to rent a hotel room until she was able to get the condo ready to sell.

A hotel would be an expense she didn't want to incur, but for years her savings account had grown. She was spending it down but there was still plenty to sustain her for months if not a year or two if she didn't spend extravagantly. A flood of thoughts came to her as she began thinking about money. What job would she pursue? Where would she live?

She put those thoughts out of her mind and began to pack her things. She made lunch and decided not to go shopping but just eat whatever perishable food remained on the boat. She hoped Simon was in Sacramento, and decided that when she got into town she would call him. If he did answer and if he was in town, she would ask him to have dinner. She thought about calling now, but put it off. She also thought about leaving that night, but realized it would mean having to spend an extra night in a hotel, and decided staying on the boat and getting an early start out of the Bay Area was a better option.

At 3pm she heard footsteps on the boat above and a knock on the door. She opened the door and saw a man in a uniform.

"Hello Miss, I'm with Charter Courier Service. I have a letter for a..." He looked down at the clipboard in his hands, "... for a Miss Chelsea Lee."

"That's me."

"Sign here please."

She signed and he handed her the envelope and left. Shutting the door, she opened the envelope and the card inside. It looked fancy, almost like a wedding invitation. She opened the card and read it. Tears started to form in her eyes. She sat down at the table and read it again.

With deepest sorrow
you are invited to the private funeral service of the late
Simon Taylor
Husband, Father, Grandfather, and Philanthropist

1pm November 2nd at Lakeridge Church
16728 El Torino Blvd., El Dorado Hills

Chelsea read it again. Tears streamed down her face. Then she saw the handwritten note at the bottom.

Chelsea, please come. My dad was a very private man and I know you didn't know he was sick. Also, there will be a small gathering at Dad's house afterwards. I know Dad would want you there as do I.

Sorry this probably came as a shock.
—Natalie

Through the tears she read it all again. Nothing made sense. Simon couldn't be dead. She had decided if she loved anyone in her life it was him. She was going to tell him. And now he had been taken away.

She felt like someone took a knife and stuck it in her. Wracked with sorrow, she wept. At first she could think of nothing. She saw only his face and that smile in her mind. For over an hour she couldn't do anything but cry. Finally, it seemed the feelings started to subside.

Then a million things crowded into her mind. He was the only man ever who had tried to protect her. The only person who had ever gone so far out of the way as to actually fight for her. She remembered watching on the computer screen as he fought with Maston. Simon had seemed so alive, and until that moment, she had no idea how capable and strong he was. She was overcome with grief and started to weep all over again.

She remembered the way he looked so at ease and at peace when they sailed. She remembered the few meals when he had interacted with her, and their walk around the lake. She could see him sleeping on the club chair in the hospital room as she had woken and realized he'd spent the night at her side.

The memories flooded through her mind again and again throughout the evening, causing her to weep repeatedly until sleep finally took her.

The next morning, she woke early and climbed out of bed. She tried to not think but just got showered and dressed. She didn't have clothes for a funeral and knew she would have to stop by the condo and get something to wear. She didn't have the energy to take her things from the boat so she just left them, locked the boat door, and made her way to the car. She knew she should tell Ben she was leaving, but realized she wouldn't be able to do so without completely breaking down. On the drive back to Sacramento, she had to pull over twice as the tears came so hard she was having a hard time seeing.

She constantly remembered Simon, and each time she thought of something else about him, the tears came again unbidden. She remembered how he looked when they were sailing, when she was worried as the boat first rose under a large swell, how she looked back at him and he looked at her with such confidence, reassuring her. She remembered how kind he was with the child in the restaurant. She thought of the walk around the lake after dinner when he put his coat around her. She remembered him sleeping in the chair next to her in the hospital. She wanted to laugh and cry at the same time as she thought of the drive to Sausalito on that night when she was attacked again and the song "Bad Day" by Daniel Powter came on the radio.

It was his little wry smile that next popped into her mind and she had to pull off at the nearest exit and park on the shoulder of the offramp until she could compose herself enough to drive again.

Finally, she made it to Sacramento and her condo. She hadn't been in the condo since the attack and she felt her skin crawl as she entered. A flood of memories came over her, mostly hanging, helpless, caught in the ornamental chain, and seeing Simon's face as he reached over the rail and hauled her up. Then the feeling of hugging him tightly. She began to cry all over again.

She was glad she had decided to sell the condo. As quickly as she could she found a black skirt and top and changed for the funeral. The place gave her the creeps. Even though for years she had felt like it was home, now it was just a reminder of her status as an escort and of Maston. She wanted to leave but knew she needed to clean herself up a bit. She'd been crying too much so she went to the bathroom to re-apply her makeup. She looked in the mirror and realized she had on waterproof mascara. Normally she would use it for a visit to a pool or beach. She'd been crying on and off all morning and the mascara had stayed on, but she touched up her face anyway, then left the condo.

She drove to the address. As she entered the church the first person she recognized was Brian. He walked over and greeted her.

"Hey, Chelsea. Glad you came."

She couldn't help herself. Not knowing what had happened was making her crazy, so she asked, "Brian, what happened?"

"Simon had cancer. No one knew. Apparently a few days after that thing with Maston he went to see a doctor and found out. It was aggressive and already well along. He got himself checked into one of the best cancer treatment centers in the world, down in Arizona, but I think it was just too far advanced."

"Why didn't anyone call?"

"I didn't know until he was gone. The only people who knew were Natalie and Ron. Simon wanted it that way."

Chelsea fought to keep the tears from coming again and Brian could see she was wrestling with it all.

"One thing Natalie told me about Simon was that he hated hospitals. He'd watched his parents die, he'd watched Allie die, he had a friend in high school he watched die... all in hospitals. I think he just couldn't stand the idea of putting others through the same thing because he was dying."

They both stood in silence as more people drifted in for the service. The only other person Chelsea recognized was Kate, the Chief of Staff from the hospital.

Brian chuckled. "You know, it's kind of funny. After that fight he had with Maston, he and I had a conversation. He mentioned that he'd been spent a lot of time at the hospital with you as he was trying to figure out who had attacked you. You know what he said?"

Chelsea shook her head no.

"He said you were the first person he visited in a hospital that didn't die. I'm sure it was a joke, but that was him."

"I wish I could have been with him."

"Honestly, after talking to Nat, I think Simon believed he would beat it. And I've known him a long time. Simon never saw even the possibility of defeat with anything."

He stopped speaking and Chelsea could see the tears building in his eyes. He swallowed hard and took a deep breath then continued, "I'm guessing he thought he would see us both again. It's no wonder he didn't call."

More guests were making their way into the church's main room. Brian's wife came over and stood next to him.

"You met once before, but I don't know if you remember. Chelsea, this is my wife, Kim. Kim, this is Chelsea."

"It's nice to meet you again... even under these circumstances," Kim said. "Brian, we should head in."

Brian turned to look at the filling pews in the sanctuary. He took a breath like it was going to be hard to go in.

"Yeah, you're right." Then he looked at Chelsea. "Chelsea, if you're alone, would you like to come sit with us?"

Chelsea was dreading everything. She didn't want to go in. She didn't want to sit alone. She just wanted everything to stop and somehow reverse time. She wanted an opportunity to tell Simon that she thought she loved him. Tears started to build again and she fought it down.

"Thank you, Brian. I'd like that."

They sat near the front, a row behind Natalie and Ron. She saw another man she realized was Simon's brother, Paul. She saw the resemblance. When he stood and spoke during the ceremony,

Chelsea started to cry. Paul's voice was so similar to Simon's that she closed her eyes and could imagine that he was there, talking about himself.

She was grateful that they'd placed boxes of tissues at the end of each pew. Kim was also crying throughout the ceremony, and Chelsea wondered for a moment if the two of them would use an entire box.

Next, Natalie got up and spoke of her father. By then most of the room was either fighting back tears or just outright crying.

Near the end of the ceremony, one of Simon's nieces got up and sang a song. Chelsea hardly listened to the words. She was just happy to have someone up front she didn't know, singing a song she didn't know. It gave her a moment of respite from the heartbreaking moments when others spoke about him, reminding her of the painful fact that he was never going to smile at her again.

Finally the ceremony ended. Chelsea felt exhausted as she made her way to the lobby. Brian and Kim were talking to Natalie as others crowded around her, waiting to personally offer their condolences. Chelsea wanted to, but then didn't. She didn't know what to say, and for the briefest moment, she thought again of how she'd met Simon. Guilt wracked her and she knew at that moment she should just go. She looked around and knew the other people were there because of a real friendship and love for Simon. Feeling out of place, she turned to leave.

"Chelsea." Brian's warm voice stopped her.

She turned and saw Brian and Kim making their way over to her.

"Natalie just told me to make sure you come over to the house. She said she needs a few minutes with you."

"Brian, I'm exhausted. I think I'm just going to head back to my place." As she said it she realized she really had nowhere to go. She couldn't go to her condo and she couldn't go back to the boat.

"No, you're not," Brian said with his big warm voice. "You're coming with us."

He was holding Kim's hand, but with his other arm he reached out and gave Chelsea a big side hug.

"You're coming with us," he repeated. "Besides, if the daughter of my best friend wants you there, I'm going to make sure you are there."

Kim looked at Chelsea. "You might was well not argue with him. When he decides someone needs to come with us he doesn't take no for an answer."

"Okay. I guess I can't fight you."

"Fight me? What do you weigh, 120 pounds? I could just pick you up and put you in the car with one arm," Brian said with a deep laugh.

"Let's not," Chelsea said. "I'll come willingly."

"Good choice."

Fifteen minutes later they were at Simon's house. Chelsea felt out of place. The home was filled with people she didn't know. Natalie, Brian, and Kim were the only people she even knew who they were. Brian introduced her to several men and women. Some were former employees who had helped Simon build the computer program. A few were close friends of Allie's and had been close to the family as a result.

A caterer had set out a spread of food, music was playing, and people were drinking wine. In one sense it was like a subdued party. Several times she heard people laugh lightly and it frustrated her but then at the same time somehow relaxed her after the emotionally exhausting ceremony.

Natalie approached her. "Chelsea, would you come with me for a minute? I've got something for you."

Chelsea followed Natalie to the study. As they entered, Natalie shut the door behind them and walked over to the desk. The room was the same as it had been after Simon and Maston's fight and again Chelsea's mind flashed back to that day. She felt her chest tighten. The man who had fought for her. Who had truly protected her. The only man ever. He was gone.

Natalie sat on the edge of the desk.

"Chelsea, please sit down for a minute."

Chelsea sat in one of the chairs facing the desk.

"I'm sorry but when Dad told me he was sick, he made me promise to not say anything to anyone. I asked him repeatedly to be able to tell you, Brian, Paul... He just insisted that he would get better and he didn't want that."

She turned to the desk and opened the laptop computer.

"Chelsea, my dad was kind of a renaissance man. Most people didn't know he liked to play guitar. Before mom died, he liked to write poetry and paint. He liked wrestling, he took judo lessons, he learned to sail. He just loved trying new things."

Chelsea felt she didn't really know the man Natalie was describing and it hurt her.

"I wish I had more time to get to know him."

"I wish we all had more time," Natalie replied, then continued. "Dad only sang for one person in his life, that I know of. He sang a song for my mother at the rehearsal on the night before their wedding."

Chelsea didn't know where the conversation was heading. Perhaps Natalie just needed to share or maybe she was trying to make Chelsea feel better, because she hadn't told her of Simon's cancer.

"Natalie, you don't need to say this to me. I don't blame you for keeping it a secret."

"Oh, no, that's not what I'm doing." she said quickly. "Like I said, he loved trying new things. While he was in the hospital and going through the chemo, he was learning a new song on his guitar. I think right at the end he knew he wasn't getting better so he had this filmed."

She turned to the computer, opened up a window, and started a video. It was Simon, in a hospital room, sitting on the edge of the bed, guitar in hand. He was wearing the typical suit that she'd become so accustomed to seeing him wear. He started playing and looked right at the camera.

"Chelsea. I've written two songs in my life. Probably not very good songs, but I wrote each one for someone who meant something to me. I hope it means something to you. Someday my hope for you, my wish, is that you'll dance somewhere wonderful."

Natalie reached over and stopped the video.

"Sorry to interrupt. But I want you to know what really happened. Dad had me film him several times as he practiced, but in the end we never had a complete video of him singing this song. So I took it and had one of his former employees, Sai, put together the different pieces that I filmed. Sai actually paid an artist to finish it and put in the accompanying music. That's why you see my dad in different clothes and he sounds a little different throughout."

She reached over and started the video again. Simon continued playing then began singing. Chelsea's tears started the moment he began.

> *From darkness at her stern do run,*
> *Set the bow into the setting sun*
> *Sail her straight to distant shore*
> *Unfurl her wings and let her soar*
>
> *Until you find a refreshing place*
> *Filled with many friendly face*
> *Settle there and be at peace*
> *The ocean storms will never cease*

Sail on and live, into the expanse,
 Your life is never a random chance
Sail on and live, into the expanse
 Make your own way, Sail on and dance.

As Natalie had said, Simon's appearance changed throughout the video. Instead of wearing a suit, he was in a hospital gown. He was thin and his hair no longer had the thick curls it once had. His skin was grey, but he was still playing the guitar and singing the song. Then his voice was slightly raspy.

Dark storms we all must overcome
 But there's the joy of sailing at a setting sun
Sail and leave behind your past
 Your life's a story for you to cast

We sailed together though it was brief
 I furled my sails and left my grief
Unfurl your sails and forget your pain
 When wind hits your sails memories will remain

Sail on and live, into the expanse,
 Your life is never about random chance
Sail on and live, into the expanse,
 Make your own way, Sail on and dance

At this point in the video, the music changed. Simon no longer sang and another man's voice continued the song along with backup singers. The single guitar Simon played gave way to the sound of a full band. The video changed to pictures of Simon. Chelsea was shocked to see that during their time sailing Simon had taken a number of pictures of her as she sat on the boat, even several short videos. She had her back to the camera most of the time, but several times he'd caught images of her as she turned and looked at him. One short clip showed Chelsea sitting on the bow as waves sprayed over her and she turned to look back at Simon with a smile. Sai had interspersed these images and short video clips with images of Simon as the song played over it.

> *Dance on distant shores with friends*
>   *Make your way to a life that mends*
> *Dance on distant shores with friends,*
>   *Sail on and live with prevailing winds*
>
> *Sail on and live, into the expanse,*
>   *Your life is never about random chance*
> *Sail on and live, into the expanse,*
>   *Make your own way, Sail on and dance*
>
> *Sail on and dance,*
> *Sail on and dance*

Crying openly, Natalie turned to Chelsea and reached for her. They hugged tightly as they sobbed. Then Natalie backed away, wiping the tears from her face.

"God, my dad was an ass to make us watch that. I'm wrecked."

Chelsea too felt wrecked.

"My dad wrote two songs in his life. He sang for only two women, my mother and you. I hope you will take this and honor his last wishes. Sail somewhere and dance." Natalie handed Chelsea an envelope as she wiped the tears from her face.

"Please open it," she said and waited.

Chelsea almost fell back into the chair. She looked at the envelope and then tore it open. It was a greeting card, much like the ones he'd given her on their first few dates. Inside was a handwritten note.

Chelsea,

Sorry we didn't have more time. I'm not really sure where things could have ended up. Please take this gift and do whatever in life you wish to do. The boat is yours. Ben is a great sailor and taught me. He can teach you. You spoke of sailing into the ocean and not turning back. Please do it. There are great harbors awaiting you in countries all over the world. Go see them. We never had a chance to dance, so dance for me.

Love,
    Simon

Chelsea broke down. She unfolded the other piece of paper that was in the envelope. Shocked, she looked at it again. It was a check written for the amount of $9,876,543.21.

She stared at it, trying to blink away the tears.

"Do you know what this is?" she asked Natalie.

"Dad thought it was funny. He originally had me write a check for ten million. Then he thought that was a stupid amount, so he changed it to this."

In her mind Chelsea could see Simon's smile as he came up with that number. The tears had stopped but now she just stared in disbelief, unable to say anything more.

"Well?" Natalie asked.

Chelsea looked up at her. "Well what?"

"He showed me what he wrote. Are you going to honor my dad's last wish and sail somewhere and dance?"

"I will."

"Just promise me you'll send a postcard."

"I promise."

Chapter 27

The middle-aged Italian man watched the sailboat as it sailed again into Porto di Sperlonga on the southwest coast of Italy. It flew an American flag and was piloted by the woman he had now seen several times before. The boat's name, *Into The Mystic,* painted on the bow and stern, seemed strange to the man. But it was an American boat and he didn't always understand the Americans who came to their marina.

One thing he did know was that the woman was beautiful and her father seemed patient, unlike many who came to his dock. As the boat motored into the marina he watched the woman at the wheel. Her dark brown ponytail slapped the side of her face in the breeze. She moved away from the wheel and the elderly gentleman took over. While the boat was still moving, she stepped to the dock and tied off the back, then the front. Then she stepped back aboard as if she had done it countless times before.

The Italian man's job was to make certain everyone followed the rules, so he made his way down the dock, this time happy he could give the beautiful woman good news. When he arrived at the boat he was disappointed. The woman was no longer in sight.

"Bongiorno," he greeted the elderly man on the boat.

"Hello again," the older man said in his American accent.

"I have your papers now. They arrived after you departed two days ago."

"We can stay now?"

"Yes, it is good."

"I'll let Chelsea know. Come aboard."

The Italian man stepped aboard and held out the documents to the older man.

The older man nodded. "Thank you for bringing those."

"Thank you for waiting. Many American insist on the day they arrive. 'I come ashore.' 'I dock here now.' 'I not have to wait.' But you wait for documents. Grazie."

On their first trip to Europe, Ben and Chelsea had stayed in the French coastal town of Arcachon. Known for its oyster industry, the town had been welcoming so they'd stayed and enjoyed the food and wine for nearly two months. Visiting the local markets regularly, they had gotten to know the owners of the boulangerie, the fromage, and the wine shops. People had assumed that Ben was her father, so he and Chelsea had agreed to keep up the façade. It was easier than explaining that he was her sailing instructor and friend.

Chelsea heard the voices on the main deck above and shouted up to Ben, "Who is it, Pops?"

After two years of sailing with him, she had in fact began to think of him as a father figure. As her sailing teacher and nearly 30 years her senior, Ben had also come to feel she was like a daughter to him.

Now she was in her berth below tidying up before heading ashore. She looked in the mirror at herself. The blonde hair had grown out and was gone. There was no way to dye her hair at sea but even if she could have, she knew now that she wouldn't have done so. Embracing the real color of her hair was in a small way embracing herself. It was a change in her mind, from her past, to her future. Ben's voice interrupted her thoughts.

"It's Giuseppe, Chelsea. The docs finally got here."

"Come on down, Giuseppe."

Giuseppe looked at her the elderly man as if to ask permission.

"Go ahead."

"Grazie," Giuseppe nodded and took the steps down and into the salon below.

He looked around. The salon was rich in different wood tones. It was a very nice boat. He had seen yachts that were worth many millions. This wasn't that, but it was nicer than most in the marina. Inside, it looked lived in and comfortable while at the same time as if everything was either new or updated.

Giuseppe had seen many boats that people lived on. Most had broken equipment and seemed in a constant state of repairs. This boat did not. It spoke of the owner's willingness to maintain their boat as well as their ability to do so financially.

One thing looked somewhat out of place. It was a fairly large framed painting of a beautiful woman in a white dress sitting with a child, surrounded by flowers in a house where the sun streamed in around them both.

The dark-haired woman came out from one of the forward berths and greeted him.

"Thank you, Giuseppe. So we are good to dock and stay now?"

"Si, yes. Here are the papers."

"Thank you." She took the papers from him and set them on the kitchen table. "I'm looking forward to fresh produce and a few other things. We'll also be getting fuel, water, and taking care of the boat while we are here."

The Italian man waited. He was impressed by her beauty and wanted to continue the conversation.

"Your father and you travel much?" he asked.

"Yes, we have. Sailing is a wonderful way to see so many places. We are looking forward to seeing much of the Italian coast over the next year."

"It is a quiet town. Sometimes too many tourists, but not this time of year."

Sperlonga was a town of less than 4,000 and like many towns that they had visited. Since the days in Sausalito, where Chelsea had gotten to know the owners of the small markets and bought her food almost daily, she now sought out these small communities. She loved that they were more intimate, and that she could walk to the different markets and interact with people and get to know them. For Ben's part, he preferred them because their ports were less traveled by large ships, safer, and generally easy to navigate. He also found the local people were nicer to work with as he was repairing or preparing the boat for their next voyage.

"Well, hopefully, we won't intrude." Then she joked, "Giuseppe, you will let us know if anyone wants the ugly Americans to leave, will you?"

He failed to understand the joke and stood taller and puffed his chest out a moment. "No one will dare. If any ask you to leave Giuseppe will speak to them."

Giuseppe was again taken by her beauty as she smiled at him warmly. "I'm only kidding. I'm sure everyone will be friendly and we will love your town."

"Miss Lee," Giuseppe ventured, using her name that was on the documents to stay in their port.

"Tonight our town has a celebrazion. A festa. There will be... uh... ballare... how do you say it?" As he said it he put one hand up as if grabbing a hand, one hand out like it was around her waist and moved back and forth.

Chelsea saw and replied, "Dancing?"

"Si, dancing. You come as my guest and see our town festa?"

"I would like that, Giuseppe. May my father come too?"

"Si. You are both welcome. It will begin in the evening in the old town square at the top. You will hear the music." Giuseppe pointed to the hill that overlooked the harbor. Sperlonga had originally been built on an outcropping of rocks several hundred feet higher than the ocean. A rocky path with stairs led from the marina up and into the town.

"We will come."

That night Chelsea and Ben sat at a table outside of La Piazzetta, eating a pizza and drinking wine. Their table was one of many sitting outside this and several other restaurants surrounding a large stone courtyard. A live band had set up and was playing on the side of the town square.

There was no beginning to the party, no announcement, no one got up and spoke. People simply gathered. Some were eating, most were drinking wine or beer. More and more of the townspeople arrived until it seemed it reached the height of the party.

At one point the band changed and began playing a tune that was clearly an older, well-known song for the locals, and when it did, the younger and middle-aged generations that were dancing in the courtyard seemed to give way. Several older couples made their way out from the tables and chairs.

Chelsea watched as one couple clearly in their advancing years shuffled out into the courtyard. The man was bent with age. His wife, with silver white hair, walked alongside him. They danced slowly as other older couples made their way out. When the music finally stopped, people applauded.

"That was beautiful," Chelsea said to Ben.

"Yeah, it's nice to see how much respect some communities have for their elders."

The music picked up again. Some of the elderly stayed and danced; some made their way back to the tables and chairs. The courtyard filled again and Giuseppe approached their table. He addressed Ben.

"Padre, posso ballare con tua figlia?"

Ben shook his head. "I'm not as educated as you, Giuseppe. English?"

"May I dance with your daughter?"

Ben looked at Chelsea, "That is up to her."

Chelsea smiled, "I think I'd like that."

For the remainder of the evening Chelsea danced. Several of the locals came and asked her to dance, including Giuseppe, whom she danced with multiple times.

Finally, tired, she sat. When asked again, she shook her head.

"No more, Giuseppe, I've worn myself out. But thank you."

"Are you ready to head for the boat?" Ben asked.

"Yes, please."

As they walked back to the boat, Chelsea commented, "I think someday I would like to find a town like this and stay."

"You mean to quit sailing?"

"Never. I'll keep sailing. But I think I'd like to find a permanent place like this town and just sail from there whenever I want."

"Why not here?"

"Let's stay for a while and see how we like it."

"I hope you do like it. I hope you find a spot that is home for you," Ben said seriously. "But when you do, I'll probably head back to the Bay Area. My boat's been sitting vacant for two years."

"I would miss you."

"You can always call if you want me to join you on a longer cruise. For now, let's just see how you like this town."

"Sounds good."

The next morning, Chelsea stopped at a local post office. She selected a postcard with a picture of the same courtyard and what looked like a similar celebration going on in the picture.

Natalie,

Last night I danced here. I hope you don't mind but I renamed the boat *Into The Mystic*. Ben told me it's a bad omen to rename boats, but Simon would have understood. I've taken her to so many wonderful places, but I would give them all up just to sail once with your father again. I have honored his wish. I hope he knows.

Chelsea

Dear Readers,

I sincerely hope you enjoyed *The Color Of Warm*. If you would like to see what comes next as Chelsea sails into Seward, Alaska in *The Complexion Of Cold*, then be sure to share on social media how much you loved this book. With your help, I can continue to write other great stories for your reading pleasure.

Post a picture on facebook, instagram, or twitter. Let others know how much you are looking forward to the next book. Hashtag your posts #thecolorofwarm and @jeffhenckel to have a chance to win a signed copy of the next book when it releases.

Follow me at:

www.jeffhenckel.com
IG: TheColorOfWarm
Facebook: Jeff Henckel
Twitter: TheJeffHenckel

Kindly,

Jeff Henckel

About the Author

Jeff Henckel resides in Eagle River, Alaska with his beautiful wife, his three children and their growing families. When not working as a Financial Advisor, Jeff loves to read, write, fish, and travel with family and friends.

Made in the USA
Middletown, DE
16 April 2022

63770860R00231